Deep Kiss
of
Winter

Deep Kiss
of
Winter

Kresley Cole
&
Gena Showalter

POCKET BOOKS
New York   London   Toronto   Sydney

Pocket Books
A Division of Simon & Schuster, Inc.
1230 Avenue of the Americas
New York, NY 10020

First Pocket Books hardcover edition October 2009

POCKET and colophon are registered trademarks of Simon & Schuster, Inc.

For information about special discounts for bulk purchases, please contact Simon & Schuster Special Sales at 1-866-506-1949 or business@simonandschuster.com.

The Simon & Schuster Speakers Bureau can bring authors to your live event. For more information or to book an event contact the Simon & Schuster Speakers Bureau at 1-866-248-3049 or visit our website at www.simonspeakers.com.

Manufactured in the United States of America

10 9 8 7 6 5 4 3 2 1

Library of Congress Cataloging-in-Publication Data

Deep kiss of winter / by Kresley Cole and Gena Showalter.
p. cm.
ISBN 978-1-4391-5966-8
ISBN 978-1-4391-6685-7 (ebook)
1. Love stories, American. 2. Occult fiction, American. 3. Christmas stories.
I. Cole, Kresley. Untouched. II. Showalter, Gena. Tempt me eternally.
PS648.L6D44 2010
813'.54—dc22
2009031082

CONTENTS

Untouchable

Kresley Cole

Dedicated to Lauren McKenna and Gena Showalter, two incredible ladies and unstoppable forces of nature, for a thousand reasons why (and not just because my fabulous editor put me in a book with my favorite author).

ACKNOWLEDGMENTS

Much love to all my fellow rabid Showalter fans, for sharing a boundless admiration and warm affection for all things Gena. To those of you about to be initiated: Yes, we have T-shirts and we meet in the bar.

And thank you to Swede, for your wintry insights and non-stop support. You didn't have to drag me over the finish line on this one, but it means a lot to me that you were ready to.

The Living Book of Lore

THE LORE

> "... and those sentient creatures that are not human shall be united in one stratum, coexisting with, yet secret from, man's."

- Most are immortal and can regenerate from injuries. The stronger breeds can only be killed by mystical fire or beheading.
- Their eyes change to a breed-specific color with intense emotion.

THE VALKYRIE

> "When a maiden warrior screams for courage as she dies in battle, Wóden and Freya heed her call. The two gods give up lightning to strike her, rescuing her to their hall, and preserving her courage forever in the form of the maiden's immortal Valkyrie daughter."

- Take sustenance from the electrical energy of the earth, sharing it in one collective power, and give it back with their emotions in the form of lightning.
- Possess preternatural strength and speed.
- Without training, most can be mesmerized by shining objects and jewels.

THE VAMPIRES

- Two warring factions, the Horde and the Forbearer Army.
- Each vampire seeks his *Bride*, his eternal wife, and walks as the living dead until he finds her.
- A Bride will render his body fully alive, giving him breath and making his heart beat, a process known as *blooding*.
- *Tracing* is teleporting, the vampires' means of travel. A vampire can only trace to destinations he's previously been or to those he can see.
- *The Fallen* are vampires who have killed by drinking a victim to death. Distinguished by their red eyes.

THE HORDE

"In the first chaos of the Lore, a brotherhood of vampires dominated by relying on their cold nature, worship of logic, and absence of mercy. They sprang from the harsh steppes of Dacia and migrated to Russia, though some say a secret enclave, the Daci, live in Dacia still."

- The Fallen comprise their ranks.

THE FORBEARERS

". . . his crown stolen, Kristoff, the rightful Horde king, stalked the battlefields of antiquity seeking the strongest, most valiant human warriors as they died, earning him the name of Gravewalker. He offered eternal life in exchange for eternal fealty to him and his growing army."

- An army of vampires consisting of turned humans, who do not drink blood directly from the flesh.
- Kristoff was raised as a human and then lived among them. He and his army know little of the Lore.

THE NOBLE FEY OF DRAISKULIA

"A warrior nobility class who ruled over all the demon serfs in their realm."

- Were *Féodals*, an ancient term for feudal overlords, which became shortened to *Fey*.
- Masters in the art of poisons.
- Males prefer to be called Drais.
- Over time, divided into numerous subsets, including fire, ice, and forest fey.

THE TURNING

"Only through death can one become an 'other.'"

- Some beings, such as the Lykae, vampires, and demons, can turn a human or even other Lore creatures into their kind through differing means, but the catalyst for change is always death, and success is not guaranteed.

THE ACCESSION

> *"And a time shall come to pass that all immortal beings in the Lore, from the Valkyrie, vampire, Lykae, and demon factions to the phantoms, shifters, fey, and sirens . . . must fight and destroy each other."*

- A kind of mystical checks-and-balances system for an ever-growing population of immortals.
- Occurs every five hundred years. Or right now . . .

"*They say I'm as fickle as winter, as shy as frost, and as indifferent as a blizzard. It's rumored my body is pure as driven snow. Nobody imagines that I might be full of fire.*"

—DANIELA THE ICE MAIDEN,
VALKYRIE AND RIGHTFUL QUEEN OF THE *ICERE*,
THE FEY OF THE FROZEN NORTH

"*Women are like bottles of liquor. They should be sampled, savored, then discarded. Matrimony is for men who can't handle their liquor.*"

—MURDOCH WROTH,
EIGHTEENTH-CENTURY WARLORD,
MODERN VAMPIRE SOLDIER

·One

"*She's . . . near.*"

At his brother's weak and broken words, Murdoch Wroth's eyes narrowed in anger toward the one who'd brought the proud Nikolai so low.

Myst the Coveted, a female immortal with a vicious heart.

And Nikolai's fated Bride.

"How can you tell?" Murdoch asked.

"Because I can *feel* her," Nikolai said.

Murdoch adjusted Nikolai's arm, which he'd slung across his shoulders to help his brother walk as they searched. The humans milling all around them merely assumed Nikolai was another drunk.

Proud Nikolai. He was exhausted from consuming too little blood, his body racked with never-ending need for a mad Valkyrie who delighted in his pain. Nikolai had lost weight, his face turning gaunt, his muscles flagging.

"Murdoch, when I find her . . . I want you to trace from here."

He shook his head. "I'll stay until you've secured her—"

"No. Don't want you to . . . see me." Nikolai's weary gaze darted away from Murdoch's. "I will lose control."

Which would shame his stalwart older brother as little else could.

Murdoch couldn't imagine how Nikolai would react when he found Myst. Five years ago, she had *blooded* Nikolai, as only a Bride could, bringing to life his dead vampire's body. She'd made him breathe, made his heart beat, and stoked his newly reawakened lust with no intention of slaking it.

That same night, another Valkyrie had shot him through with arrows and still another had mocked his desires. Myst had fled with the two, dooming Nikolai.

A blooded vampire could only take release for the first time while touching his Bride in some way. If she wasn't available, then he would remain in a state of constant sexual readiness, aching indefinitely.

Which she well knew.

"Promise me you'll leave," Nikolai grated.

At length, Murdoch said, "I will." If Myst was indeed here tonight, it would make sense that there'd be more Valkyrie out on these very streets. More of their deceiving, manipulative, violent kind. "But only to find another one," he added.

He could capture one and interrogate her about the Lore, the world of not-so-mythical beings he and his brother were now a part of.

Murdoch's knowledge of the Lore was as limited as that of any of the vampires in their warrior order of Forbearers. Their army consisted mostly of turned humans, and the Lore creatures kept their secrets well guarded from them.

"Don't underestimate the Valkyrie as I did," Nikolai rasped. "Else suffer as I have."

He suffered because fate had forced this blooding on Nikolai. *As if Nikolai needed another burden.*

The blooding process was what Murdoch detested most about being a vampire, even more than never seeing the sun again.

Though he'd once been a rake, bedding a new woman each night,

Murdoch hoped it never happened to him. To be mystically tied to a single woman sounded hellish, especially to a woman he didn't choose, and one who could spurn him, as Myst had Nikolai.

The pain had rendered his brother nearly mindless in his pursuit of her. Nikolai wanted retribution, but Murdoch suspected he also simply wanted *her*. Even after all that she'd done to him.

"Where will you take her this night?" Murdoch asked. "The mill?" They'd secured an old renovated sugar mill outside the city, staying there instead of the Forbearer castle while they'd scoured these streets.

Nikolai shook his head.

"Then back to the castle?"

When Nikolai didn't answer, Murdoch said, "You wouldn't take her to *Blachmount*?" The ancient Wroth estate—where most of their family had died in a single night of sickness and murder. "Why?"

"Because that's where my Bride belongs."

Before Murdoch could question his meaning, Nikolai went still, his eyes briefly sliding shut. Then his head swung up toward a roof-top. "It's her."

Above them, a redhead stood frozen, her lips parting in shock.

Murdoch had only briefly seen her all those years before, and now he studied the details of her Valkyrie appearance. She had delicate fey features—pointed ears and high cheekbones—but he also spied the tell-tale claws and small fangs.

At the sight of her, Nikolai stood fully, no longer needing Murdoch's aid. *"My Myst."*

Her face paled, no doubt at the sight of Nikolai, who now looked like the monster she'd sought to make him. His irises had turned completely black, his fangs descending in his mouth, dripping from thirst.

Her horrified expression almost made Murdoch pity her, but she deserved no mercy. Which was good, because Nikolai would show her none this night.

Their pursuit of half a decade was . . . *over*. At last.

Just as Nikolai tensed to trace to her, Murdoch slapped him on the back, then teleported away as he'd promised, disappearing so quickly he went unnoticed in the morass of drunken tourists. Even if they had seen him vanish, the humans would think they'd imagined it.

Murdoch materialized in a back alley several blocks away, then walked to the Quarter's main thoroughfare, Bourbon Street. As he moved among the crowds, a warm breeze tripped down the street, dissipating the swampy haze and the fumes from food vendor stands.

Warm. In February. Good hunting weather.

Yes, Nikolai would be merciless tonight, as would Murdoch. Now all he needed was to find his prey.

The hunt is on.

I'm being followed.

Daniela the Ice Maiden furtively glanced over her shoulder once more. Again she spied nothing out of the ordinary—tourists milling, witches catcalling to human males—but Danii couldn't shake the feeling that she was being stalked.

Which begged the question: what creature would be stupid enough to court a Valkyrie's wrath?

Maybe she was just spooked by Nïx's cryptic remarks tonight. Nucking Futs Nïx, her half sister and the Valkyrie soothsayer, often made off-the-wall predictions. But this one continued to replay in Danii's mind.

"Sad, sad Daniela, the broken doll who wants to be fixed. Tonight she might."

Because of Danii's pale, freezing skin—she was part Icere—she was often likened to a porcelain doll. Well, because of her icy skin and because of what would happen to her if she grew overheated. . . .

But a *broken* doll? What did that mean? And fixed—for good, for bad? *What* precisely would be fixed?

She'd told Nïx, "I can't imagine what you're talking about. I'm not broken"—*my lonely existence makes me want to tear my hair out*— "and I don't know how I could be 'fixed.'"

Perhaps by being able to finally touch another? To feel a man's skin against her own without being burned, instead of constantly fantasizing about it?

I would give anything.

Yet the only males on earth who could touch her were the Icere. Regrettably, they also happened to want her dead.

Which meant the closest she'd ever get to having sex would be reading about it in the many tomes of erotica she kept hidden in her room or by indulging in her rich fantasy life. Which also meant she was probably the world's oldest virgin. Merely awaiting confirmation from Guinness.

And people wonder why I prefer fantasy to reality.

Her ears twitched with awareness. No, she wasn't simply spooked; *something* was happening. Her senses were alert.

Hastening her pace, she carefully wound around the people on the street, negotiating the ninety-eight-point-six degree gauntlet. Even the briefest contact with another's skin would burn her. A conundrum, because she kept cool by baring *lots* of hers.

When her frosty breath fogged in the warm night air, she just stifled the urge to scream, and peeked over her shoulder once more.

This time she spotted a towering male, far behind her. He was striking, looked to be mid-thirties. But there was something unusual about him.

Was he even human? New Orleans was chock-full of Lore beings. He could be an immortal, maybe even the one trailing her.

At that moment, he wasn't looking in her direction, so she took the opportunity to duck into an alley beside a hotel. Leaping up four stories to the hotel's flat roof, she crossed to a low ledge wall overlooking the street, then crouched between two flags—one had a fleur-de-lis covered in beads, and the other said *Pardi Gras!*

Tilting her head, she studied the male below. He had longish dark brown hair, cut negligently, with a lock falling over his forehead. His face was fantasy-worthy, with a strong, masculine jaw and chin.

He wore tasteful clothes, a black button-down and jeans with a jacket that made her feel warm just looking at it. She herself was wearing the thinnest backless dress she could find.

He strode with an air of confidence. The male was gorgeous— and he knew it. How could he not, with the women gaping at him? Then she frowned. He seemed oblivious to the prancing coeds in low-cut tops angling for his attention.

His body was big, muscular in a way that hinted at immortal, but what he was exactly eluded her. Considering his size, he was probably a demon, or even a Lykae—those animals had begun prowling the Valkyries' turf as bold as they pleased.

Or could he be . . . a vampire?

She trained her gaze on his chest, watching for the rise and fall of breaths. Seconds passed. Historically, the vampires had shunned Louisiana. Yet on this night her Valkyrie coven had heard that members of both warring vampire armies, the Horde and the Forbearers, could be out in the Quarter.

What they didn't know was why.

His chest is still. Bingo. Vamp.

Since his eyes were a normal gray and clear—not crazed and red with bloodlust—that meant he was a Forbearer, one of an army who didn't drink blood straight from the flesh.

Vampires who didn't kill. At least, that was their mission statement.

The Lore was still waiting to see how that worked out for them.

Though Danii knew she needed to report back on this sighting, she couldn't take her gaze off him. What was it about this vampire? She was aware of only two Valkyrie who'd ever been with his kind. One still lived. Danii knew the danger; so why this attraction?

Yes, he was breathtakingly cocky, with his leading-man face and broad shoulders, but she'd never been so absorbed by a male. Not a real one, anyway.

Broken-doll Daniela . . . *wanted.* Him. A vampire.

When he was almost directly below her, she noticed that he seemed burdened, preoccupied even. Hardly the expression of someone who'd been stalking her.

But if he hadn't been, then who—

The unmistakable twang of bowstrings sounded behind her.

She dove for cover, and a swarm of arrows sliced the air where she'd been standing. A second volley skittered against the brick where her head had just been, ricocheting off the low ledge wall.

She recognized the creosote-like scent of the arrowheads. Poison on the tips, *fire* poison. Which could only kill ice creatures like her. *Oh, gods.*

Without looking back, she vaulted over the side of the roof. When she landed in the alley below, she tore off at a sprint.

The bows, the poisoned arrow-heads—this wasn't a Lykae threat. Not a vampire attacking.

Icere assassins were hunting her. *My mother's people.* How had they found her?

No choice but to flee, knew she couldn't remain to fight. These assassins traveled in bands, and the number of arrows indicated at least half a dozen men.

Even as she raced directly toward the mortal gauntlet, her mind rebelled. She hadn't seen another of her kind in centuries. *I thought I'd be safe from them here.*

Her only hope was to outrun them, yet she knew how fast they would be. Like her, they were born of the fey—

She dashed right in front of the vampire, nearly knocking him over.

Two·

Murdoch had just rubbed the back of his neck, then peered upward, convinced he was being watched.

He'd spied nothing, started on his way again . . . and almost ran over a small blonde in a skimpy backless dress.

With lightning speed, she darted in front of him, sparing him the briefest glance. He caught a glimpse of high cheekbones and alarmed silvery eyes before she sped across the main thoroughfare toward another alley. A pointed ear had peeked out through the wild spill of her long fair hair.

Pointed ears, silver irises, running too fast to be a human.

An immortal—possibly one of *them.*

That glimpse of her was all it took, and the chase was on. He hurriedly followed her into the alley, then traced, vanishing and materializing ever closer to her.

Though small, she was swift as she navigated through a maze of shadowy blocks, heading toward the river. He was barely gaining on her.

What kind of being could run as fast as a vampire could trace?

As he neared, he made out finer details of her appearance. Her legs were taut and shapely under her short dress. Her bared back and arms were slim. She wore silver bands above her elbows, and elaborate braids threaded her long hair.

She seemed foreign, unusual. Like women from faraway lands in olden times. *I can't wait to get a better look from the front.*

That thought threw him. Since the night he'd been turned into a vampire three hundred years ago, he'd had no interest in women, no need for them, just as he never reacted to the scent or sight of food.

Why would I give a damn about what her front looks like? He would wrest information from her. He could do little else.

His body was deadened. And he preferred it that way.

Just then, she glanced over her shoulder as she ran, and he caught sight of her elven face once again.

Those pointed ears . . . several factions in the Lore had them, at least that he knew of. Valkyrie were among them. He was becoming more and more convinced he'd found his quarry.

But she seemed to have lost sight of him altogether, focusing in another direction.

With each minute that passed, they traveled deeper into a decaying labyrinth of abandoned warehouses and stacks of railcars.

Finally she was slowing. She stumbled in a puddle, then tripped on the corner of a shipping pallet.

He stopped tracing and began running toward her. He was close enough to hear her heart drumming, her gasping breaths.

The Valkyrie his brother had encountered had known no fear of vampires. Maybe in the last five years they'd learned they had reason to flee from one. The thought made him pursue her with even more excitement. His vampire instincts rushed to the fore. The thrill of the chase overwhelmed him, and Murdoch played with her, letting her lope until she tired.

Just as he decided to end this, he turned a corner after her, running into a four-way crossing.

There was no sign of her.

Only silence.

Danii crouched on the second floor of a storm-ravaged warehouse, struggling to catch her breath and shuddering from heat.

She still couldn't believe the Icere were here. She'd thought she was safe living in such a warm climate, believing they'd never look for her this close to the equator.

Like the Icere, Danii didn't sweat. Unlike them, she could go into thermal shock if she grew overheated. But she was more accustomed to the temperature here than they were. And she knew every twist and turn of these downtown streets. As long as she didn't catch a fire arrow, she could handle the Icere.

The vampire was another matter entirely. When she'd seen him tracing after her, she'd gaped in disbelief that yet another pursuer had joined the chase.

A clear-eyed vampire, a true Forbearer.

Though hidden, she could still see him from this vantage. With a narrowed gaze, he turned in circles below, determining her direction.

Any superficial and misguided attraction she'd felt for him was drowned out by annoyance. If this male would just move on, the Icere likely wouldn't find her here.

Otherwise, he was going to get her killed.

The assassins would separate to trap her, driving her with the threat of those poisoned arrows. They wouldn't lob their notorious ice grenades at her—they'd lose valuable cold and she'd simply take the impact with a smile on her face as she soaked the chill into herself.

But those arrows . . .

Tipped with a poison that ravaged through an ice being's veins like liquid fire.

I would know. This wasn't the first time a faraway Icere king had dispatched killers after Danii, the rightful Icere queen. . . .

Instead of leaving, the vampire called out in a deep voice, "I know you're here." His words were thickly accented. Russian? Perhaps

Estonian. "You're a Valkyrie, are you not?" He stilled, listening for her. "If so, you'll want to know that my brother just captured Myst the Coveted."

Myst. Danii loved all her half sisters equally, but she *owed* Myst.

Wait . . . a Forbearer's *brother* had taken her? There was one Forbearer—an Estonian—who wanted Myst above all others: Nikolai Wroth, the Overlord. He'd done Myst wrong, but then she had definitely retaliated.

And the Overlord had brothers.

Danii had to find out what had happened to her sister. If Nikolai alone had her, then Myst probably wouldn't be in danger, since she was his Bride. But if Nikolai had surrendered her to the Forbearer king . . .

I have to know. Danii could trap the male below in a cocoon of crushing ice, then question him, but how much more cold—and time—could she stand to lose?

"Why do you cower?" Anger blazed off him. "A true Valkyrie would face me."

True Valkyrie? His taunt struck home, like a jab at an exposed nerve. She wanted nothing more than to be like her half sisters. To enjoy all the things they took for granted. *Broken doll . . .* She rose unsteadily, crossed to a gap in the wall, then stepped out.

At once, his gaze locked on her, following her down. His lips parted, revealing barely visible fangs, but he made no move to close the thirty or so feet between them.

Had she truly thought the gray of his eyes was normal? Recognition seemed to flare in them. *Recognition?* But how? She'd never seen him before—she'd definitely have remembered.

His gaze was focused . . . *predatory.* Then his irises turned black. Black in a vampire meant intense emotion. Yet his earlier fury seemed to be fading.

As they stared at each other, all other sounds—the eerie thrum of barges churning the river, the distant screech of streetcars—were drowned out.

"My brother warned me that your kind are vicious." His voice went even lower as he frowned. "I cannot see you as so."

"Where is my sister, vampire?"

"I can take you to her, Valkyrie."

I'll bet. Yes, the male before her was a Forbearer, which meant that he was clueless among the Lore.

He'd have no idea how dangerous Danii in particular could be.

THREE

A LIVING, BREATHING VALKYRIE STOOD BEFORE HIM. And she was so stunningly beautiful. . . .

Murdoch's view of her front had proved far more rewarding than he'd imagined.

He shook himself. Was she one of those who'd shot Nikolai? Had she been there to laugh at the idea of his brother's agony?

For some reason, he couldn't imagine her like that. He knew she was an enemy—one among an army of females who sought the annihilation of all vampires—and Nikolai had just warned him not to underestimate them. But this one looked even more fragile than Myst.

Though her features and lithe body were perfection, her blond locks were tangled around her pointed ears, and dust smudged her cheeks. Her face was feverishly red, and she was subtly swaying on her feet. She looked sad and miserable.

And spooked.

Chasing a female who feared him sat ill. Nikolai had sworn they were taunting, sadistic warriors. Yet this creature had hidden from him—after fleeing as if her life depended on it.

"Listen, Valkyrie, I don't want to hurt you. I just have some questions for you to answer."

She raised her hand, but lifted no weapon. Instead, she flattened her palm just below her lips as if to blow a kiss good-bye. The breath that left her mouth looked like a cloud of frost, surging forward, surrounding him.

Ice flash-froze around his boots. He couldn't move his legs. Couldn't break free. *"What the hell is this?"* Her breath continued to surround him, ice growing up past his knees, climbing to his thighs.

Then she coughed, bending over and rocking on her feet. The buildup stopped, leaving him fettered by this bizarre binding.

He strained against the ice, which seemed stronger than any he'd ever known, but he was unable to break free or trace from it. "Take—this—away."

She stalked closer. "Who has Myst now? Nikolai or the Forbearer king?"

"How do you know my brother's name?"

"Nikolai or the king?"

He spied the points of her ears twitching, and her gaze darted past him. Just as she *hissed* at something behind him, he heard movement and twisted his upper body around.

There stood half a dozen men, large Viking-looking warriors, with swords at their sides and arrows already nocked to the strings of their raised bows.

Their breaths smoked in the warm night air and their ears were pointed.

She hasn't been fleeing from me—

Arrows darkened the air around him, whizzing past his head. They'd aimed for her.

But somehow she was twisting to dodge the onslaught. Whirling around in the air, she turned to dart into another alley, her speed incomprehensible.

Then she was gone.

His hands shot down to claw his legs free, his fingers swiftly going numb. Just as the males behind him ran after her, Murdoch heard more fighting.

There are two groups. They're organized, flushing her out. Can't get this fucking ice off me.

Suddenly, her small body came flying out of the intersecting alley before him.

Thrown. She'd been *thrown.*

The force of her landing sent her skidding across the pavement. As she stabbed her claws against the bricks to right herself, a cloud of arrows followed her. The momentum took her out of his field of vision.

Then an unfamiliar scent swept him up. Though his instinct told him it was blood, his mind rebelled.

Never had it smelled so exquisite. So irresistible.

At last Murdoch broke free, tracing to intercept her. When he reappeared, his every muscle tensed in an instant.

The scent had been blood—*hers.* She was kneeling in a pool of it, her chest full of arrows. One of the males was holding her up by her hair, speaking in some foreign tongue. In his other hand, he held a glowing red blade.

She gazed up at Murdoch as crimson streams snaked from her wounds to the dirty street.

They'd done this to her?

What had you been about to do to her? His vampire nature warred with memories of the man he'd been. . . .

—*I would never have hurt her.*

—*She was* my *prey. They stole her from me. My prize.*

Just . . . *mine.*

At the thought of those men loosing their arrows at her, the idea of her pain and fear, rage erupted in him. The need to protect her, to destroy those who sought to harm her, burned within him.

Mine.

Two realizations struck him.

This strange female belonged to him alone. And these killers would die before they relinquished her.

Her gaze held Murdoch's, and she weakly extended her small hand. With tears running from her silvery eyes, she spoke, a whisper directed to him, loud above all sounds.

"Mercy."

FOUR

WILL HE HELP ME? Emotions warred on the vampire's face. Danii saw them with her vision flickering.

The poison was taking hold, leaching away her precious reserves of cold.

So hot . . . felt like she was cooking from the inside.

When she'd faced him earlier, he'd been filled with anger. Now his brows had drawn together at the sight of her injuries.

He grated, "Mercy?" Then something seemed to . . . snap. His fists clenched, and he bared his sharpened fangs. His body appeared to get even bigger. "I'm going to give you their heads, female."

Why would he? And *how?*

The vampire didn't understand how deadly these Icere were. They were expert bowmen, their fey speed unmatched in the Lore. And there were too many of them. At least eight stood between the vampire and her. They were already building ice grenades in their palms.

With an unholy roar, the vampire charged, half tracing, half sprinting. Five of the Icere rushed to intercept him, lobbing grenades with lethal speed. But he dodged each volley, and the ice the warriors had just surrendered exploded all around him in the alley.

Like some living thing, a freezing glaze crawled over the battered brick walls, skittering all the way up to the fire escapes, coating the street.

The vampire clashed with the wall of Icere, battling his way to her, slashing through the warriors with a startling brutality. When he snatched one's jugular and blood arced out like a fountain in the night, her Iceren captor began to drag her away by her hair.

The poison had weakened her, but she still fought him. Her claws sank into his arm and tore, rending skin and bone, all but severing it.

He yelled in pain and dropped her hair to take his knife in his good hand, shoving it against her neck. The blade's heat seared her skin, and a scream erupted from her chest.

In answer, a savage bellow sounded; she and her captor looked up just in time to see the vampire flying at him.

One second the knife was at her throat. In the next, the vampire had wrenched the Iceren's head free.

The others took up their bows and charged him as one, the sound of their bowstrings louder than their footfalls. The impact of the arrows slammed the vampire against a glazed wall, shattering the ice.

He roared with fury, his arms twisting back to pull the arrows free. Just as he tore all but one of them from his body, the Icere were upon him.

She could see him grappling again and again to get to her, yet they kept hold of him, preventing him from tracing.

Danii tried to crawl away from the skirmish, but the arrows jutting from her chest made movement impossible, and the poison was too strong. If she didn't get them out soon . . .

Thermal shock. A nightmare way to die. She was about to be executed, and for no reason. She didn't want her crown, only wanted to be left in peace—

Her would-be savior stumbled. From the ice coating the street? No, he seemed to be fighting some inner possession.

What's wrong with him? I can't think . . .

One Iceren punched the end of the remaining arrow until it pierced through the vampire's torso. He tore it from himself, but another's sword slashed his leg. Blood poured from his wounds.

There're too many of them.

As if he read her thoughts, the vampire caught her gaze. A last look for both of them?

"Touch their skin," she cried.

Though clearly confused by her words, he grasped one around the neck under the male's collar. The Iceren bellowed in pain.

The vampire's lips curled at the sound. Baring his wicked fangs, he laid his palm on another's face. A hand-shaped brand pressed into the Iceren's skin.

Seeming fresh to the fray, the vampire grew even stronger—and more vicious, appearing intent on making it *hurt* as he dispatched them.

Soon scattered limbs littered the alley at gruesome angles. He easily separated heads from savaged necks, yelling as if with pleasure as the blood flowed.

Yet he never bit them. She saw he truly did forbear, and still he was somehow defeating them, sustaining injuries he didn't seem to feel, wound after wound that barely slowed him.

As he faced off against the last one standing, she wondered how much of the blood covering him was his own.

But one of the Iceren the vampire had felled wasn't dead. He'd clamped his neck, stemming the rush of blood. Unseen behind the vampire, he struggled to his feet and silently collected his sword.

"Look out!"

At her warning, he twisted around. The one he'd been fighting tackled him in a wrestler's grip from behind, holding him for the one with the sword.

Oh, no, no . . . She'd be damned if she'd let this warrior vampire die.

A weapon, she needed a weapon. Her gaze fell to her chest, to the six arrows riddling it.

Was she strong enough to do this?

She gritted her teeth and fisted one of the bloody arrow shafts. Choking back a scream, she wrested it from her body.

The pain made her vision waver, her muscles going limp. *No! Fight!*

Holding the feathered end, she threw it like a knife. It skewered the swordsman's neck.

The last thing she saw was the vampire snapping his head back to smash the face of the one holding him, breaking free to snatch up a sword.

When she forced her lids open once more, he was staggering toward her, his fangs still bared, his eyes black amid the blood covering his face. He'd savaged them and now was stalking closer to her.

Yet she was unafraid. He'd told her he was going to give her their heads.

And he had.

Dropping to his knees beside her, he reached for her wrist. She shrank from him, but not quickly enough to prevent contact. When she cried out, he jerked his hand away, gaping at the burn mark he'd left on her skin.

"No . . . can't be." His tone was rough, almost snarling. "You're like them? But you're a Valkyrie!"

She blinked up at him. "Part . . . ice fey."

In that growl of a voice, he repeated, "You're *like them.*" The big male was so unsure, so confounded by her nature. "I'll burn you?"

She nodded weakly.

"Is there no way I can touch you?"

"N-Never."

"Who can tend to you, then? Do you live in New Orleans? With other Valkyrie?"

"They'll kill you." If the vampire brought her to her coven, her sisters would behead him on sight and ask questions later.

Besides, she didn't have that kind of time.

If this vampire didn't save her . . .

I'm going to shatter like ice.

FIVE

WITH EFFORT, THE FEMALE WHISPERED, "YOU . . . help me."

"How? When I'll burn you?" *Can't comprehend this. She's blooded me, this odd little creature whose skin can't be touched.*

No, she couldn't be his Bride. He couldn't be blooded. But his breaths mocked him, his thundering heart a constant reminder.

When his heart had first beat in the midst of the fight, it had sounded like an explosion, stunning him and nearly costing him his life. He'd inhaled, shuddering as air flooded his untried lungs, filling him with renewed strength.

Even now he was dizzy from his injuries, but his body still felt strong.

"I'll try to find Nikolai—Myst will be with him. She'll better know what to do."

His brother had described what happened when he'd been blooded, so Murdoch knew what to expect physically. But Nikolai had neglected to tell him that instinct, raw and bare, would take over.

"You, *please*. Arrows poison to me. No time."

Poison? No, she couldn't die like this. If she was a Valkyrie, then she was immortal.

But what did he know? He also hadn't thought a Valkyrie could be burned by his touch.

He ripped away the bottom of his shirt and wrapped his hands, then gently scooped her into his arms. Though their skin never touched, the movement jostled the arrows, making her whimper in pain.

He clenched his jaw, wanting to slaughter those fucks all over again, to punish them slowly. "Why trust *me* with this?" he snapped. Why did she want him to care for her? Why would she think him capable of it?

She tried to focus on his face, her silvery eyes going blank. "I . . . don't know why."

"You'll probably regret trusting me with your life."

In answer, she went limp, helpless in his arms.

Lord Jádian the Cold, general of the Icere, had watched the conflict impassively from his vantage in a warehouse above the street.

In his long life, he'd fought against vampires countless times, and he had the scars to prove it. But the one below had been stronger, faster. Now it crouched over Daniela the Ice Maiden. Crouched *protectively*. An unlikely ally for the female?

After tonight, there was no doubt that Daniela was Icere; it was bred into every line of her.

But she was also fierce like the Valkyrie—she'd wrenched a fire arrow from her own chest to cast at her enemy. He knew exactly how powerful that poison was, had harvested it himself from a fire demoness's horns.

Yes, Daniela was strong. As her mother Queen Svana had been.

When the vampire below disappeared with her, Jádian leapt down to collect the fire blade. It wouldn't do to lose it—the same knife had been used to take Svana the Great's head.

Jádian planned to wield it again.

He turned from the carnage, ignoring the low creatures that had already begun feeding on his fallen comrades. He walked on with the knowledge that Daniela was a threat that could no longer be ignored.

Just as Danii dimly perceived a bed beneath her, pain exploded in her chest. She woke to her own screaming, writhing in agony, bucking away from the source.

"Easy, girl," the vampire's deep voice intoned. "Have to get this dress off you."

She cracked open her lids, found herself on a mattress on the floor in some dark-paneled room. The vampire was surveying her with eyes the color of obsidian, a knife in one of his gloved hands.

He'd put gloves on? *Good vampire.* "In Kristoff's castle?"

"How did you—? No, we're not there." He finished slashing away the rest of her dress, leaving her in panties. He'd already removed her boots. "We're in a mill outside New Orleans."

He set aside the knife, seeming more uncomfortable with her nudity than she was. With a swallow, he wrapped his fist around an arrow just above her breast. He used his other hand to press her shoulder into the mattress. "We'll count to three."

She met his eyes and nodded. His gaze was frenzied, yet it comforted her. Never looking away, she gritted her teeth.

"One . . . two—"

Yank.

She choked on a scream, and lightning exploded just outside the house. His eyes darted around uneasily as he tossed the arrow to the floor.

Between panting breaths, she cried, "Remind me . . . to teach you . . . to count."

"Are you ready for another?"

Was she? How much more pain could she take?

"Think of something else, girl." He clutched another arrow. "Or tell me your name."

Another yank, another scream swallowed. Outside, lightning flashed once more, and thunder rocked the roof timbers.

He warily gazed upward before his attention settled on another arrow. As he worked the next shaft free—this one was lodged in her sternum—she clenched her fists into the sheets, fighting not to twist from him. The arrowhead grated against bone as it finally gave way.

"Your name," he demanded.

She gasped out, "Daniela."

"Daniela." He gave a tight nod. "Beautiful name for a beautiful girl."

She choked on a hysterical laugh, sending her into a wet coughing fit. Blood bubbled from her mouth when she uttered, "Beautiful . . . kidding?"

His expression darkened. "I only meant that you're lovely in form, or you would be—never mind."

"You're . . . *skeevy.*"

He gazed away, looking like he was mentally cursing himself.

After such a long life, she was going to die of poison in the care of a crazed, skeevy vampire who couldn't count.

"My name is Murdoch Wroth."

"I know." He was brother to Nikolai, which meant he was one of the Wroths, four Estonian warlords famous in their time for their ruthless defense of their country. Five years ago, the Valkyrie had learned from Myst that two of the brothers had been turned to vampires. Nikolai and . . . *Murdoch.*

"How could you know my name?"

She tried to shrug, but only grimaced.

He let it drop. "Two more to go. Who were those men who did this to you?"

"You wouldn't know them—"

Yank. Her vision began to flicker again.

"Stay with me." Had he smoothed a gloved hand over her hair? "Only one left," he said, then added in a murmur, *"Brave girl."*

For some reason, she felt a rush of pride that he saw her as brave.

She'd been weakened for so long, exiled from the very ice that made her stronger. She struggled to remain conscious, wavering in and out.

"Will more of them be coming for you?" he asked.

"They always do. Sooner or later."

"Why would they want to kill you?"

She mumbled, "I was born."

"What does that mean?"

"Can't tell you . . . 'bout the Lore."

"Because I'm a Forbearer?" This plainly infuriated him. "You think Myst won't be telling Nikolai your secrets?"

"You think . . . they'll be *talking* tonight?"

He frowned as if she was confusing him, or more like she was *throwing* him. "Last arrow."

This one was wedged under her collarbone, refusing to come out. "Almost finished, sweet." He pinned her to the mattress, twisting and pulling as she bit back a shriek. "Just hold on."

Finally, it gave way in a rush of blood. "There." He threw it aside. "Now what do I do?"

She lay stunned, panting raggedly. *Too late. . . .*

Even with the arrows removed, too much poison remained inside her. She started convulsing from the heat, couldn't stop.

"Daniela, tell me!"

In her two thousand years of living, she'd never been this hot. Ah, gods, thermal shock.

Death by shattering. Just as she'd been warned as a girl. *Porcelain doll.* The starkest fear she'd ever known welled inside her.

She weakly grabbed his shirt. "Shock. Put me in . . . ice bath."

"Shock—what do you mean?"

"'Bout to . . . die."

Six

Murdoch swooped her up so fast his wounded leg almost gave way. In a flash, he traced her to the bathroom.

Inside, he began running a cold bath. Once he'd settled her in the large tub, he traced to a gas station, returning a few moments later with stolen bags of ice.

As he ripped open the bags to dump their contents into the water, he muttered, "This feels wrong to me. Goes against everything I know."

Because she was like nothing he'd ever known.

Am I truly covering a half-naked, critically injured female with ice?

But when she was up to her neck in it, she sighed in relief. The cold wasn't bracing or painful to her—it was clearly soothing, making her drowsy.

Her shuddering lessened, and her expression calmed.

When the fear in her eyes ebbed . . . He didn't even want to think about the relief he felt to see that. "Are you still in danger from the poison?"

"Nothing else can be done." She frowned, her gaze unfocused. "You're injured."

"It's nothing," he gruffly replied.

"Take care of yourself, vampire—" Her lids fluttered, and then she was out.

Sleeping. In ice.

He couldn't reconcile this coldness in her. She was like nothing he'd ever dreamed.

But it didn't matter if he understood her. Even if she appeared more comfortable, she wasn't out of danger. Her face was still flushed angrily. If cold was good for her, then she needed more of it.

He traced to the thermostat, turning on the air-conditioning full force. Though he didn't want to leave her—not to drink from the supply of blood he kept in the kitchen, nor to bandage his own wounds—he traced for more ice, stuffing the freezer full.

That task completed, he watched over her, beginning the most anxious vigil he'd held since the night his entire family had died, one by one.

As he paced the spacious bathroom, he couldn't take his gaze off her. Though Daniela had found him *skeevy* for remarking on her looks, he could see past her injuries. She was lovely, no doubt of it.

She had long flaxen hair, spreading past her shoulders and down to cover her breasts. Her lips were softly plump, parted around her shallow breaths. *Lush lips.* He imagined pressing his own over them, then teasing her tongue with his.

With a start, he realized he was growing hard for her. He groaned. *My first erection in three hundred years.* The erection he'd been hoping to avoid. *Christ, I am truly blooded?*

By a . . . Valkyrie.

They were warlike, many rumored to be half crazed. To be tied forever to a woman like that—and one he could never touch? *A living hell.*

No, surely there had to be a way for him to touch her, to claim her. Or would this one leave him in agony as Myst had Nikolai?

He crossed to the tub, crouching beside her, his injured leg screaming in protest. Ignoring that wound, he took her hand in his gloved ones, examining it. *So delicate.* But he'd seen her fragile-looking claws slash through a male's bone this night.

He released her hand to cup icy water and pour it over her hair, smoothing blood from the strands. Then he clumsily unthreaded her braids and rinsed them.

Why this care? Because it kept his mind off his fear for her—and his apprehension about his future. So he continued to run ice over the bruises on her shoulders and arms. Gradually, the hectic red of her face diminished, leaving pale, alabaster skin. Her breaths started to smoke.

As her wounds began to close seamlessly, his own pain increased. He'd been losing blood from his many injuries, didn't know how he could still be conscious.

Before, he'd been too concerned with keeping her alive to think about much of anything else. Now he became acutely aware that her blood was all over him, marking his bed and the arrows on the floor.

The scent was like nothing he'd ever known. Thirst lashed him like a whip. His shaft shot harder. *Damn it, ignore it.*

His gaze trailed the lines of her jaw, her dainty pointed ears, her *neck.* Drinking straight from the flesh was against the laws of his order, because living blood carried the victim's memories, which in turn maddened vampires. Their enemies in the Horde, the Fallen, had all gone red-eyed with insanity.

What if he lost control and bit her? Every male in his order feared becoming one of the Fallen. Murdoch was no different, but breaking that law had never even been a consideration for him. He'd never understood the temptation.

Until now. *Am I going to make it to dawn without taking her neck?* He had to.

The damage I would do to her . . . Earlier, her wrist had all but sizzled beneath his palm. What would happen to her tender neck under his fangs and lips as he pinned her down?

Would he burn her as he licked her flesh in ecstasy?

Tearing his eyes away, he shot to his feet, tracing to the bedroom. He scooped up the arrows and stained bedding and pitched them outside. While he was there, he shed his torn jacket.

Then he traced to the refrigerator, pouring a cup of blood. Though he was depleted from his injuries, when he tried to drink, it tasted like dirt. He forced himself to swallow.

Damn it, get the cup down. Ignore this lust, blood and otherwise.

After managing barely half of the contents, he returned, gazing down at her face. She lay so still, her blond-tipped lashes a sweep against her pale cheeks.

The mere idea of hurting her sent him reeling. He needed to *protect* her.

Without opening her eyes, she whispered on a frosty breath, "Murdoch?"

"Do you need more ice?" he quickly asked. Most of it had melted, but the wounds that had marred her chest were practically healed.

She shook her head.

"Do you want to get out of the water?"

In answer, she lifted her arms to him. He frowned. *So trusting, so vulnerable.*

He gathered her against his chest, then traced her back to his bed. Still holding her, he grabbed a towel for her to lie on.

Her breasts moved against his arm as he laid her down, and his cock shot even harder. For three hundred years, Murdoch had had no interest in women's breasts.

Now he nearly growled with pleasure.

Drawing back, he saw that her eyes were open, half-lidded. Gone was the silver. They were an aquamarine almost too vivid to be real.

"When I slept, I didn't dream of them. I dreamed of you." She sounded delirious. "Vampire, are you going to stay with me?"

He'd wanted to capture a Valkyrie and get her to talk. Why not now? "Yes, I'll stay with you."

This seemed to comfort her, and her eyes slid closed again, but he knew she was still awake.

"Daniela? Who were the men who attacked you?" He recalled the blade and the male's intoned words that had sounded like a sentencing. Tonight's attack had been an assassination attempt.

"The Icere, the fey of the north."

"Why did they want to hurt you?"

She shrugged. "Wasn't the first time. I stay on the move. Just two centuries ago, he sent a troop, but I was able to get away."

"Who sent them?" She was more than two hundred years old?

"Their king, Sigmund. This time they surprised me. 'Cause I was distracted."

"What distracted you?"

She grinned but said nothing.

"Why do they want you dead? Daniela?" When she pressed her lips together, he knew she wouldn't tell him more about this subject, so he decided to move on to a new one.

Nikolai had described the other Valkyrie he'd encountered. One had had skin that *glowed*, and one had been a supernatural archer. This female was some kind of ice creature. Perhaps all the Valkyrie had overarching similarities, but they could be born of different species.

"Daniela, your sister Myst is not cold like you. Why?"

Without opening her eyes, she murmured, "We share a set of parents. But one of our mothers is different."

"One of your mothers? An adoptive mother?"

"No. Have three parents."

She's delirious. Or was she? One thing he'd learned about the Lore was that nothing made sense to him. The laws of the Lore defied the laws of nature.

"How is that possible?" When she seemed to be going back under, he gave her shoulder a gentle shake.

Her blond brows drew together. "Wóden and Freya struck my mother with lightning to bring her back to life. I was in the lightning. The three are my parents."

No, she's definitely delirious.

"Myst was born of Wóden, Freya, and a human Pict."

Picts? They'd lived centuries ago. "How old are you?"

"Two thousand or so."

"Two *thousand*."

"'m a Pisces."

"I see. Why did you want to know whether Myst was with Kristoff or Nikolai?"

She softly answered, "Myst likes Nikolai. If he's nice tonight, he's going to be plus-one with a Valkyrie."

"Nice tonight?" he repeated. Murdoch suspected his brother would be many things with Myst. *Nice* was not among the possibilities. Feeling an unaccountable flare of guilt, he traced to the kitchen, returning with a glass of water for Daniela. He lifted it to her lips, but she turned her head away.

"Don't drink."

"It's just water."

"Don't drink anything."

"I suppose you don't eat either."

"Un-unh."

If *any* of this was true. . . . He needed to talk to Nikolai—

"Murdoch?" Her eyes were open once more, and they were focused on his mouth. "You have the most kissable lips I've ever seen."

He swallowed. "And would you like to kiss me? If you could?"

"If I started . . . I don't think I'd ever stop." Her words were throaty, so damned enticing. She wasn't a warrior, she was a *temptress*.

And a lesser man could get snared if he wasn't careful.

Her lids slid closed again. She seemed to be in that delirious state where the mind didn't want to cede to oblivion.

She eased her arm over her head, those sexy bracelets clanking, and the damp locks covering her chest fell away, revealing her perfect breasts.

They were little, but high and so plump that he ached to sink his fangs into one. Instead, he dug a fang into his bottom lip. He imagined the blood seeping on his tongue was hers.

He pictured how her breasts would bounce as he fucked her.

These lustful thoughts were so unfamiliar, so futile. She would never be beneath him. He angrily palmed his erection behind his jeans, which he knew was a risk, because the worse his arousal grew, the worse it would stay—if he couldn't get her to relieve him of it.

Just this once, he would need her to break the seal. Then he could go on his way, satisfying himself with others.

In his human life, he'd had women falling all over themselves to attract his notice. Whenever he hadn't been on the battlefield, he'd been cradled between a woman's thighs, and had grown notorious for his skills in bed. But if none of the tricks he'd learned would work on Daniela, then how could he seduce her to ease him of this burden—

"Murdoch," she sleepily sighed, "my panties are wet."

A shaky exhalation of breath. "Are they, then?" Had his voice broken?

She wriggled her hips as if she wanted them off her. With a hard swallow, he reached forward and dragged the scrap of lace down, revealing silky blond curls. Another groan, another coarse swipe over his shaft.

Too much temptation. He was about to fall on her, to mount the soft body naked before him.

Three centuries he'd been denied this. His fangs were throbbing along with his cock. He wanted to bury anything he could inside her.

With a sharp shake of his head, he snatched up a sheet to toss over her. When it glided across her nipples, they budded against it. He studied the ceiling, desperate *not* to see the way her nipples strained into the material. Then he sank into the room's one chair, but just as abruptly shot to his feet to pace again. He itched to stroke her, to explore the dream woman in his bed.

Fight the arousal. Resist it—

She kicked off the sheet. He rushed to draw it back up to her neck. "Keep this here, Valkyrie."

More restless pacing. With a huff, she kicked the sheet away once more. God, could she be any lovelier?

He ran his hand over his mouth. "Damn it, Daniela. It might be a fraction warmer, but it's a world safer for you." Had he drawn up the sheet more slowly, skimming it across her nipples on purpose?

Yet again, she rid herself of the sheet, but this time she drew one knee up. He saw her sex parted and nearly went to his knees.

Never to taste her there? Fury suffused him. Never to see those blond curls damp from his mouth or wet with his seed?

Never to claim his Bride. Why the fuck had *she* blooded him then?

He traced to the bathroom, stripped, then stepped under a cold shower. He scrubbed his body with no care for his many wounds.

This blooding business was the most ridiculous rot Murdoch had ever heard of. A woman had to bring him to life, and then he was expected to be bound to that one female—not for a year or a decade. Not even for a mortal's married lifetime.

For *eternity.*

He'd had no choice in the matter, none whatsoever in the choosing of the female. What if he didn't like delicate-looking blondes? As a mortal, he'd been attracted to buxom barmaids, and milkmaids, and kitchen maids, and the occasional shepherdess—robust women with hearty carnal appetites.

For his Bride, he'd gotten Daniela, the exquisitely fine but untouchable Valkyrie.

As he ran the soap down his torso, his hand brushed his rampant cock. Unremembered pleasure shot through him like an electric current. He was as hard as he'd ever been, aching to come.

When he gripped his shaft in his fist, a strangled sound of need burst from his chest. He gave a stroke up to the crown and back. Felt so good, he had to do it again, and again.

Masturbating for the first time in centuries.

His eyes slid shut when he perceived his semen welling. In a rational part of his mind, he knew it couldn't go further without her; she had to unleash this within him.

Resentment warred with his ecstasy—if she left him like this, he would be crippled by this lust. But everything else within was greedy for the pleasure.

Uncaring, lost, he thrust hard into his fist.

SEVEN

WHEN DANII WOKE TO THE DRUM OF AN AIR CONDITIONER chugging full blast, she found herself alone—and naked.

As she blinked in the shade-darkened room, foggy memories from the night before began to surface. She remembered the vampire's savagery in the fight. She recalled him later gazing down at her in the bathtub with his brows drawn, his face pale from blood loss. How doggedly he'd kept watch over her.

But after that, *nothing*. Once the poison had begun working its way from her system, she'd blanked.

So . . . naked? She was certain he'd put her in the tub with her panties on. Now he'd seen her completely unclothed.

Had he liked what he'd seen? No, as an unblooded vampire, he'd have no interest.

A cursory survey of her body revealed a mass of twinges, but her wounds had mended for the most part, leaving only a closing tear just below her collarbone. Her temperature was still high, but would gradually drop each day.

She inspected her wrist where he'd grabbed her. The burn had healed as well.

Even after all these centuries, she was surprised by the degree of pain involved with skin to skin contact. For some reason, it was always the worst. She could skirt a car exhaust and only suffer a lingering sting.

But another's skin against hers was like fire. . . .

She gazed around the spartan room. Considering the still un-packed duffel bag and sparse furnishings—a lounge chair, a desk, and the mattress—this definitely wasn't a permanent home. Danii knew the Forbearers lived in the sinister Mount Oblak castle. So what was he doing here?

Over the drone of the air conditioner, she heard the shower going. The vampire hadn't left her? She recalled the injuries he'd sustained taking out *eight* of those Icere bastards, remembering that he'd been hurt much worse than she'd initially thought. She didn't know how he'd still been standing, much less how he'd cared for her.

If not for him, she would have died. The poison would have taken hold until even her immortality couldn't have saved her. *He* had saved her.

She grinned. No longer did she think him skeevy.

When blood had been everywhere and Danii helpless before him, Murdoch hadn't even tried to drink from her. And Valkyrie blood was supposed to be irresistible to vampires. Myst had confided to Danii that she'd given a drop to Nikolai the Overlord five years ago, and he'd been *wild* for it.

Oh, Myst . . . What should Danii do about her sister's abduction? Myst, who'd once done her a favor so great that she could never repay it.

The answer seemed obvious. Call Nïx and tell her to launch a search and a war if need be. Murdoch had a satellite phone on his desk.

But earlier, he'd said he could take Danii to her sister—because Myst would be with Nikolai. So the two of them *were* together.

Likely only the two of them. Making up for lost time.

If Danii called the coven about this, she'd unleash a shrieking battle contingent to bust down the door of the vampire's love nest.

What would her sister want her to do? The facts: Myst was a master manipulator and enchantress. No Valkyrie was better at getting men to do her bidding. She could handle Nikolai.

Another fact: At the news that Forbearer vamps had been spotted in the city, Myst had been excited, her green eyes alight. Before setting out to *hunt* them, she'd checked and rechecked her hair.

Myst, it seemed, was already half in love with Nikolai. And if Nikolai was a fraction as thoughtful and gentle as his brother . . .

I'll get more information from Murdoch before I make a move.

With that decided, Danii rose from the mattress on the floor—typical vampire, craving to sleep as low to the ground as possible—and crossed to his closet.

Contrary to popular belief, she wasn't shy, but she still rooted through his duffel bag for something to wear. She and Murdoch had serious things to discuss, their siblings' situation, for one, and she didn't want to do it naked.

Even if he would have no interest in her that way.

She grabbed a black T-shirt and dragged it on, though it swallowed her, then explored his room. As she rummaged through his things, she found his wallet. She'd known who he was, but it was still a shock to see credit cards in the name of a warlord who'd "perished" in the Great Northern War three hundred years ago.

Likewise, seeing his sword belt lying next to his satellite phone was a jolt.

Danii knew much about him and his three brothers; most of the Lore did. The Valkyrie had had a correspondent in the field to cover the war, and she'd reported back on all the Wroths' heroic—and ruthless—deeds as they'd defended Estonia against the Russians. The four had been so merciless that even the creatures of the Lore had started paying attention.

She recalled that the Wroths all differed drastically in personality. Nikolai was the self-sacrificing general, Sebastian the quiet warrior-scholar, Conrad the mysterious one.

And Murdoch? Well, he was the ladies' man, a practiced seducer.

Or he *had* been, but no longer, now that he was an unblooded vampire. What a waste. The world just didn't have enough broad-shouldered seducers with piercing gray eyes.

She sighed, predicting that this male would star in all her future fantasies. Yes, Danii had a rich and complex fantasy life. While all her sisters were preoccupied with their latest lovers or intrigues, she listened and watched. Daniela the Watcher, observing and imagining. Forever a spectator.

But not tonight. She finally had a secret. She thought . . . she thought she might be growing infatuated with the vampire, even though her kind had a bitter history with his.

Wars, deceptions, atrocities.

Aside from Myst, the only other Valkyrie who'd been with a vampire had borne him a child—then died of sorrow shortly after.

Danii could lie to herself and say that Murdoch made it easy to forget he was a vampire. Yet in truth, she was aware of that every second with him.

She simply didn't give a damn what he was. For two thousand years, the Icere had tried to destroy her, either outright with attempts to execute her or with bounty hunters insinuating themselves into her life. She'd never met an Icere male that she trusted enough to be with.

Two millennia of stark loneliness did not a discerning Valkyrie make.

The broken doll wanted to be fixed. And somehow, she knew Murdoch was part of her journey. Even the fact that he was a vampire wouldn't sway her.

What he is can't compete with the possibility of what he could be—

She heard a stifled groan from the shower. *Ah, gods, he's still hurt.* She dropped the wallet, racing for him.

Just inside the bathroom, she stopped short. There was no steam, so she could see straight into the tiled shower stall above the half wall screening it—could see cold water sluicing over his broad chest, drops trickling over the indentations of his rock-hard torso.

Her lips parted, and her claws curled with desire. Her half sister Regin liked her men young, dumb, and hung, as she put it. Danii now knew her type: vampire with an Adonis physique. And she didn't say that lightly. She knew Adonis well.

Murdoch was leaning back, staring up at the ceiling, one brawny arm flexing as he washed himself. Stubble shadowed his lean cheeks.

She could see the trail of hair descending from his navel, but not where it ended because of the half wall.

Her ears were twitching. A warning? But why? "Murdoch, are you hurt?"

His arm stilled. When he met her eyes, she saw that his irises were black, burning with some hidden emotion. His gaze dipped.

Why is he surveying my body? Stingy about his shirt? "I borrowed this. Hope you don't mind."

He didn't answer.

"Okay, then," she said absently, distracted by the broad expanse of his chest. He had a few battle wounds from the Icere and a couple of old scars—not unexpected, since he'd been a warrior as a mortal, too. But his skin was surprisingly tanned.

Gods, she wanted to sweep her palms over those sculpted planes. She gazed at him greedily, taking in details—this would make choice fantasy fodder.

Wait. Had his chest just risen with a . . . breath? No, it couldn't be.

Her ears twitched again, and even over the sound of the water, she heard his heart beating, strong and fast. Her mind could scarcely comprehend this. He'd been unblooded before, but now . . .

"Wh-what's happened?"

In a husky voice, he said, "Come see."

As she blankly moved to the edge of the stall, he pressed his hands against the walls to lean forward, his chiseled muscles bunching and taut—

His engorged shaft extended straight out from his body. She gaped at his size. He was *glorious.*

And he hadn't been *washing* himself as his strong arm flexed.

"*I* blooded you?" If so, that would mean his erection was for her, and her alone. In answer to that hardness, her sex grew moist for it. Any lingering aches from her injuries were fading, no match for her mounting desire.

"You're . . . my *Bride.*"

He sounded angered by the fact. Maybe his need was making his tone sharp? Of course, that was it. What vampire wouldn't want to be blooded?

"Do you know what's happening?" she asked.

He gave a curt nod, leaning against the back wall again, under the water. "Some. From my brother."

"When did you realize this?"

"During the fight."

Poor vampire, how long had he been like this? He already appeared on the verge of coming, his shaft visibly pulsing. His sac looked laden, as if it ached. She wanted to cup it with both hands.

"God, I can *feel* your eyes on me." His erection jerked, straining forward into the shower's spray. He tilted his hips until his shaft hit a hard jet of water, which, judging by his slack-jawed expression, felt *incredible.*

She swallowed. "D-do you know what needs to happen now?"

He choked out the words, "Been trying."

"For how long?"

He groaned, "*Hours . . .*"

If everything she'd heard about their kind was true, why hadn't he been on top of her, releasing the pressure he was feeling?

He was hurting—so she wouldn't have to. A pang squeezed her heart.

But if he hadn't been able to achieve his release by now, he was definitely going to have to touch her. She already dreaded that grueling pain.

No, there must be some way around that. Maybe he could touch her hair?

If so, then game *on*. They'd figure something out. And then she would have a memory to replace the one of the last time she'd been naked with a man. She shook herself, ruthlessly pushing that thought away.

Excitement began overwhelming her dread. A flesh-and-blood male wanted her. He knew her nature, and he still would need to be near her.

Around her sisters, Danii acted as if she couldn't care less that she was untouched. She assumed her ice queen persona, donning a cold cloak of indifference whenever they gossiped about their bed partners.

In truth, Danii was desperate for contact. At the very least, she yearned for companionship.

This god of a male was linked to her by fate.

I lived through the night, and a gorgeous, virile immortal needs me.

Sad, sad Daniela just got happy, happy.

Murdoch's body was tensed to spring for her if she chose to run.

Valkyrie hated his kind. This one would not be pleased by this development.

He racked his brain for what to say to her. Normally, he would just take her hand and drag her into the shower for a deep kiss until she'd gone weak-kneed and mindless. In the past, he'd controlled situations with women. *I lead, and they follow.*

How to get her from here to his bed? "Daniela . . . I . . . you *have* blooded me." Even to himself, he sounded accusing.

"You don't sound too thrilled about that."

"Because I'm *not*." *Damn it, where's my smoothness?* He'd never in memory said the wrong thing to women, had always been able to sense exactly what they wanted to hear.

I have no idea what this one wants to hear.

Her expression was inscrutable. At one instant she looked shy and vulnerable, at another *ravenous*. He couldn't read her, could hardly think.

Would she run? If so, what would he do?

He tried to moderate his tone. "I wouldn't have chosen to involve you in this, but I have had no control over it." Still his anger thrummed in his words.

She blinked at him. "Lines like this got you laid as a human?"

"Yes. No." He scowled.

"I'm going to give you the benefit of the doubt and assume that your brain is scrambled right about now, and I'm probably the first female you've ever encountered that you don't know what to do with. I'm familiar with your reputation, Murdoch."

"How? I don't—"

"Let's talk *after* there's no chance of you blowing this with me." When had the Valkyrie's voice grown so sultry? "So, do you want to go see if you can't work *that*"—she pointed at his erection—"out?"

His jaw slackened. "You will stay until I can spend?" *Say yes. . . . Say yes . . .*

Her gaze was lascivious, dancing over his body, all traces of the shy Valkyrie gone. "Wouldn't miss it for the world."

When she tossed him a towel and turned toward his bedroom, the legendary Murdoch Wroth dumbly followed, tripping over his own feet.

EiGHT

ANY SELF-RESPECTING VALKYRIE WOULD BE FIGURING OUT how to kill the vampire. Being a Bride was considered shameful, unless you murdered the offending leech—which was the usual protocol.

But Danii? She was exaggerating the swish of her hips as the newly blooded vampire followed her to his bed.

Playing with fire. It had a totally new meaning for Danii.

In a husky rasp from directly behind her, he said, "I thought you would run from me." His voice was just at her ear, giving her delicious shivers. He was so close she thought his erection would prod her, but he'd slung the towel around his waist.

"Uh-uh." She knelt on his bed, then curled her forefinger in invitation.

At once, he dropped to his knees before her, running his gaze over her.

Danii wasn't shy, didn't know many immortals who were. And considering how long she'd been waiting for a night like this—*fantasizing* about it—she'd be damned if she let her lack of expertise detract from the experience.

Yet even now, *he* didn't know how to proceed. "I want to seduce you . . . but I can't kiss you . . . can't stroke you."

She'd stumped a living legend. Danii was just contrary enough to be gratified by this. "There's no need to seduce me. I've already signed my name on your roster."

He frowned at that, then said, "But there must be a way for me to have you."

She shook her head sadly. She'd consulted the witches and had been told that one of them *might* be able to help once she came into her powers, which could take hundreds of years. She'd begged the Valkyrie soothsayer Nïx to foresee a way around this curse of coldness. Nïx had told her to simply accept herself and everything would work out.

That'd been eight centuries ago.

Suspicion tinged his expression. "If there was a way, would you tell me?"

She shook her head. "Wouldn't have to. You'd already be inside me."

His lips parted, displaying his white teeth and fangs. "Another Valkyrie teasing a vampire."

"No, I'm not teasing. I'm just *imagining* it."

At that, his shaft jerked between them, distending against the towel.

"Looks like it wants attention." She didn't ogle penises in person every day, not even every decade. "The towel off, please. I'd like to see it." Up close and at her leisure.

He raised his brows, but did reach for the towel. Once he bared himself, Danii's gaze descended along the trail of crisp black hair that led to the base of his erection. His thick length jutted boldly from his body, the crown swollen and taut. Perfection. "Will you stroke it in front of me, vampire?"

At her words, he made a guttural sound, and a drop of moisture beaded on the head.

She stared as he cupped his shaft in his palm, holding her breath as he slowly closed his fingers over it.

Finally he gave it a stroke. The sight made her go soft, her sex getting even wetter. Her nipples stiffened beneath his T-shirt. And he noticed.

"Show me your breasts." When she pulled off her borrowed shirt, he inhaled sharply. "So beautiful." He reached his free hand forward to touch one, but she flinched before he could. With a curse, he closed his hand and drew it back. "Too easy to forget."

"You can't forget, vampire. If we must touch, it's got to be brief. Otherwise . . ."

He dragged his gaze from her chest to her face. "Don't want to hurt you."

Tenderness bloomed anew within her, along with the strongest desire she'd ever felt. "I believe that."

"You'll touch them for me."

It wasn't a question. Powerless to deny him, she raised her hands to her breasts. As she petted them, pressing them together, his eyes grew even more excited, frenzied even.

"That's it, Daniela."

She knew her breasts were small, but right now they felt heavy, lush. When he stared at the peaks and ran his tongue over one of his fangs, she gave a little moan.

"Let me see you play with your nipples."

Danii had *lots* of experience touching herself. She brushed her thumbs over them again and again until they puckered tight.

"Daniela!" His fist moved faster. "Spread your knees." Once she did, he commanded, "Touch your sex."

Without hesitation, she slid her hand down her belly, slipping a finger to her folds.

His breaths were coming more quickly. "Are you wet?"

"Very," she murmured.

Another groan. "I wish I could taste you, lick you." His voice had grown huskier. "Show me where you'd want me to kiss you."

Getting caught up, she spread her knees even wider, then circled a finger over her clitoris. "Here."

"Slower. Rub it slower."

She lazily flicked, gasping, "Like this?"

"Ah, God, yes!" His eyes were awash in black as he stared, his fist pumping faster.

"What would you want me to do to you?" What would a master seducer like?

With his free hand, he drew the pad of his forefinger along the sensitive slit in the crown. "You'd run your tongue over me here." When more drops of moisture slicked the swollen head, he spread them around with his thumb. "Tasting me, before you sucked my shaft between your lips."

The idea that he wanted her to know his taste made her mouth water. She yearned to lick him there, then to take that broad crown into her mouth, suckling it so deep. . . .

When her tongue dabbed at her lip, he groaned, "Almost don't want to know what you're thinking."

He seemed to be going out of his head with lust, stroking himself over and over. Gaze locked on her busy fingers, he fondled his heavy testicles with his other hand. When his brawny chest heaved with exertion, sweat lovingly trailed over the rises and falls of his bulging muscles—the most erotic scene she'd ever witnessed. He switched hands as one arm grew weak.

Visibly frustrated, he reached out. "Just want to touch your hair." She held herself still for him, and he wrapped a long strand around his palm. Bringing it to his face, he inhaled deeply. "Your scent drives me mad." He made hoarse sounds of pain, but he still couldn't come.

Daniela didn't want to see him suffer. And he was in agony, stroking so fast she could barely see his hand. "You're going to hurt yourself." She knew that the more she healed, the colder she would become. Right now, his touch wouldn't be as excruciating as usual. "You have to touch me, vampire."

He shook his head. "Lie back and open your thighs. I'm *close*. If you come for me . . ."

The Valkyrie nodded, then lay back, wantonly spreading her glistening sex.

He would give *anything* to feed his cock inside it. Anything.

When she undulated her hips, he could see how ready she was. Her abandon aroused him like nothing ever had.

For hours, he'd been kept on edge. *Now to see this?* "Need inside you so bad, Valkyrie."

Her lids went heavy and she panted, those tight breasts bobbing.

"Bury myself so deep in you," he grated. "Fill you with my seed. . . . I wouldn't stop until you begged me." When he cupped and tugged his sac, she masturbated faster.

"Inside. Slip your finger inside." Once she did, he leaned down to rasp right at her ear, "*Fuck yourself with it.*" He drew back to watch. "Does that feel good?"

"Ah, yes!"

"Then another finger inside."

Her voice was so sexy as she cried, "I'm about to . . . *come.*" Lightning bombarded the mill.

"Thrust faster, harder. Don't stop till I tell you."

As she began to climax, she arched her back, crying out. Her thighs fell open in utter surrender.

Eyes riveted to her sex, he gnashed his teeth, tortured with need. He helplessly fucked his fist as her orgasm went on and on. Her head thrashed on the bed, her body writhing to the motion of her fingers.

He still hadn't told her to stop, wouldn't. He was tormented; so would she be.

"Murdoch, I can't take more!" Finally, she curled on her side, still trembling, her hands between her thighs.

When the tremors eventually relented, Danii gazed up at him. During her pleasure, she'd heard him growl in pain. Now he was in even more misery.

"Vampire, just touch me!"

"Don't want to hurt you."

"Kiss my breasts." She went up on her knees, cupping her breasts to him in offer. "Put your lips on my nipple."

"Valkyrie," he bit out in defeat. He leaned down, about to press his mouth to her flesh.

She steeled herself against the coming pain—

With a ragged groan, he pulled back, forcefully shaking his head.

No. No more of this. Her hand shot out and covered his fist around his shaft. She cried out, and he jerked from the shock of cold.

The contact was scorching, a firebrand against her, even as he grated, *"Cold . . . so cold!"*

Tears welled. "Don't stop, Murdoch!" Keeping her hand on him took every ounce of will, like holding her hand to a flame.

Burning, burning, her skin seared. *Pain, dizzying . . .*

"Going to come!" His tone was awed as he began to ejaculate. "Ah, God, finally! Daniela. . . ."

Through tears, she watched him bucking into their hands, his every muscle strained in anguish. His expression was agonized, those fangs sharp and glinting.

When his seed erupted from him, he yelled to the ceiling. His massive body in throes, he came onto the bed, pumping out his jets of semen so hard she could feel them.

Nine

THEY LAY BACK, BOTH GULPING BREATHS.

Murdoch was struggling to recover from the most pleasure he'd ever experienced—and the hardest, most powerful ejaculation he'd ever imagined.

The release had been mind-numbing, but perhaps *all* immortal sex was better. If one had stronger senses, then why wouldn't sex be heightened as well?

With one need met, another instantly screamed within him. He'd lost blood the night before and hadn't come close to replacing it. He could still smell hers all around them.

Ignore it. He turned to her. She was cradling her burned hand, her eyes still wet.

When their skin had made contact, hers had felt like ice, definitely uncomfortable to him. His skin had made her *cry*. Yet earlier, when he'd been tearing poisoned arrows from her flesh, there'd been no tears.

"Let me see it," he grated.

She reluctantly showed him her blistered palm, and he winced, guilt assailing him. He rose to get ice for her, but was so unsteady he wondered if he could even trace to the kitchen. With effort, he made it to the refrigerator, saw the containers of blood there.

So thirsty. . . . He felt a mad urge to annihilate his supply. *Just get her the ice. She's burned because of you.*

Ice. Before now, he'd never much thought about it. Yet it had been his Bride's salvation. What would have happened if he hadn't gotten her cooled last night? Would an immortal like her truly have died?

Returning with a paper towel filled with ice cubes, he handed it to her, careful not to make contact—or to glance at her neck.

She closed her hand around a couple of cubes and sighed in relief. After a few moments, she peeked up under her lashes at him. "So what happens with us now?" The shy Valkyrie was back?

"You tell me."

"This is out of the realm of my experience." As her pain faded, her expression showed hints of excitement. She looked *optimistic.* No doubt, she thought they were embarking on something. Females always had in the past. No matter how much he warned them that he would never settle down.

Embarking with Daniela—a woman he could never bed? *I'd be consigning myself to misery.*

He just needed time to *think* about all this. He rose and yanked on his jeans, grimacing as the material scraped over his abused shaft.

She must have sensed his tension, because she dropped the ice and defensively bundled the sheet to cover herself. After a few moments, she said, "You've lost a lot of blood."

"I'll be fine. Been in worse shape."

"I expect so, since you died and all."

He turned to her. "And you know how I came to be like this?" When she nodded, he said, "Tell me, then."

"King Kristoff found you dying on a battlefield. He gave you a choice of fealty to him and eternal life—or death. That's what Kristoff does, what he's always done."

Fealty or death. Murdoch remembered that night as if it were yesterday. Kristoff had found Nikolai first, in a pool of his own congealing blood. But Nikolai hadn't feared death, so he'd negotiated with Kristoff before he would accept the king's offer.

He'd demanded to be a general in the Forbearer army, refusing to take orders from anyone but Kristoff himself. And he'd wanted Murdoch and any trusted comrades with mortal wounds turned as well.

Nikolai had also demanded the span of a human's lifetime to watch over their four younger sisters, their two younger brothers, and their father.

They'd all been dead in a matter of weeks.

Murdoch ran his hands through his hair. "Tell me how you knew who I was."

"The Valkyrie heard Forbearers were going to be out in the city. When you told me your brother had captured Myst, I put it together. He's the Forbearer most likely to search for her."

Now that Murdoch had experienced for mere hours the hell that Nikolai had endured for *years*, he was furious anew with Myst. Daniela's *sister*. "Shouldn't he have searched for Myst?"

When Daniela nodded blithely, he frowned. "And shouldn't you be demanding that Nikolai free her?"

She gave him a vulnerable grin. "If Nikolai is half as sensual as you are, I wouldn't be doing her any favors to get her freed. I'm sure they've come to an *understanding* by now."

The Valkyrie was throwing him. Again. *Too much to take in.* A new Bride. A hunger like he'd never known . . .

He gazed at her neck once more. Her skin was pale, smooth, begging for his fangs.

"Besides, the more I think about it," she continued, "the more I realize you should probably be rescuing your brother from her. She's going to twist him inside out."

Murdoch shook himself. "She's *already* done that. She tormented him for five years." His anger was growing, matching his thirst and exhaustion. "I barely got through a few hours of needing to come— imagine half a decade!"

Her pleased mien faded. "He deserved nothing less."

Murdoch traced directly in front of her, staring down. In a menacing tone, he said, "Did he? To be shot up, then left crippled by his Bride?"

She rolled her eyes at him, possibly the first woman ever to do so. "Either you don't know all the facts or you're ignoring them. On the night that Myst left Nikolai, he was about to *torture* her for information in Mount Oblak's dungeon. Our sisters rescued her from that fate, and they wanted to kill Nikolai, but Myst left him alive. Your brother owes her his life."

"Watch what you say, *plika*."

"Chit? You called me a chit?"

Figured she'd know Estonian.

Her own ire clearly mounting, she said, "And what'll happen if the *plika* doesn't watch what she says? Will you hurt me, your one and only Bride?"

"You think I'm bound by this? Bound to you?" Even as he sneered the words, he had to resist that unbearable pull toward her. *Resent it.* "You think that I'll follow you around like a dog as you scorn me?" His eyes kept straying to her neck. Would she notice?

"Scorning you hadn't even been in the decision tree for me, but now that you bring it up, it makes total sense, especially considering the repercussions otherwise," she said. Yet then she frowned. "Wait a second. I see what you're doing. Trying to scare me off."

She rose, tucking the sheet around her like a towel. "Look, I'm as freaked out about this as you are. But the fact is that I . . . *liked* you, up until five minutes ago, and I wanted to see you again—even though I'd be risking ridicule at best and ostracism at worst." She took a step closer to him, that vulnerability in her expression. "I'm sure this is all overwhelming for you. One minute you're going about your business, and the next you're blooded with a Bride—"

"One I didn't *choose*." He was taking his frustration out on her, and he couldn't seem to stop. "I didn't manage monogamy as a human, though I could have wed my pick of the most ravishing women in my country. How do you think I'll fare with a female I can't touch?" Especially now that he could have others.

Her eyes narrowed, and lightning struck outside. "Monogamy? I'm not angling for a wedding!" All shades of that previous vulnerability were gone, replaced by haughtiness. "And if you don't think I can hold my own against all those eighteenth-century mortals you were out tagging, then you're a fool, Casanova." At his expression, she added, "Oh, yes, I know all about you."

He went still. "What are you talking about?"

"I was alive back then. And all the Lore heard about the ruthless warlord brothers from Estonia. The general, the scholar, the enigma, and . . . the *manwhore*."

He clenched his jaw at the thought of having his life analyzed, especially by creatures he didn't even understand. The Forbearers could garner little information on Lore beings—their lives held secret—and yet they'd been actively following his own exploits?

"A manwhore?" Was that all he'd been remembered as? "Maybe I left behind the women I'd enjoyed because I didn't want to deal with *exactly this*." Even now he wanted to end this argument by kissing her and taking her to bed, which confused him even more. "It doesn't take a genius to figure out that the hour we just shared was the best we ever will—it's all going to go downhill from there."

"You don't have the sense to realize you were blooded by one of the only Valkyrie who would accept a vampire in her bed."

"To do precisely *what* there? Freeze?"

In a flash, she drew back her blistered hand to slap him.

"Do it, ice queen. And feel the sting with me."

Lightning struck again as she lowered her hand. "You're not worth it, leech," she said, but he was scarcely listening. Below her collarbone, a small line of blood had just risen from the last remnant of her wounds.

That stark red against her alabaster skin called to him, made him imagine following the trail with his tongue, then pinning her down to suck from her breast.

Already the scent was all around him. And now to *see* it?

Don't look at it.

How the hell had Nikolai restrained himself from biting Myst all those years ago?

Murdoch's hands fisted as he struggled not to fall upon Daniela. He'd been able to resist touching her when under the most painful pressure he'd ever dreamed of.

But I'm not going to be able to deny this call. . . .

Ten

How can this be happening? They'd been doing so well. Fantasy made reality . . . somewhat.

But now the vampire's eyes had flooded black again. So he was as angry as she was?

Danii turned from him to snag the T-shirt, donning it as she dropped the sheet. When she met his gaze, he appeared even more incensed than before.

"Obviously, I need to leave," she said, while thinking, *Tell me I'm your Bride, and that I will be staying. Be an arrogant, possessive Neanderthal vampire!*

She wanted him to simply inform her that he would never let her go and she would just have to accept that, or whatever domineering misguided tripe these manly men always said. *To women that aren't me.*

This one wouldn't even look at her. "You need to go. *Now.*"

Kicking me to the curb. She didn't know how much more of this her ego could take. Leeches were detested by most Valkyrie—by most of the Lore—yet Danii had been ready to offer this one more. *He has no idea what I'd been willing to risk for him.* "I'm a bit perplexed here. Most vampires refuse to be separated from their Brides, yet you can't get rid of me fast enough."

Because he no longer needed her. Danii had helped give him his initial release, her Bride's duty done, and now he could be with other females. She was expendable.

But one day he would realize what he'd lost—a frigid, broken female he could never claim, and one with skin issues—and then he'd be sorry.

When her bottom lip trembled, she cursed herself bitterly. *Don't you cry in front of him!*

"I thought you were going."

Exasperation drowned out the urge to cry. Exactly *how* was she supposed to leave? She didn't have a car here, didn't even know where they were. "No."

"*What?*"

"Not until you tell me why you're so intent on getting rid of me."

His gaze was transfixed on her neck, his voice a snarl as he said, "I'm about to throw you to the ground. Take your blood in a frenzy."

"B-but your kind doesn't bite." Her lips parted, and she backed away with real fear. "I'm not strong yet, Murdoch. If you did that, you could kill me."

His eyes went wide, then narrowed. Yet he'd still begun striding toward her. She backed to the wall.

Can I spare enough cold to stop him? With a grimace, she started building ice in her palm, planning to trap him as she had before.

When he was just before her, he shook his head, his entire body going off balance. With a last look at her face, he snapped, "Leave here. Before I return for you."

Then he vanished.

How much time had passed since he'd left her, Murdoch didn't know.

Hours, it seemed. But only now was the ravening frenzy subsiding.

After leaving Daniela, he'd traced to his rooms at Mount Oblak, Kristoff's castle, then attacked his supply of blood like an animal.

Now crimson was everywhere. He stared at the smeared floor and counter. *My God, what would I have done to her?*

He was still astounded that he'd been able to keep from touching those luscious breasts of hers—yet he couldn't deny himself her neck?

Once he'd caught his breath, he rinsed his body in the shower, then redressed. Having managed some level of sanity, he decided to go to Blachmount.

Returning to the time-ravaged manor was always uncomfortable—almost all of Murdoch's family had died within those walls—but he needed to talk to Nikolai.

He traced to Blachmount's great room downstairs, listening for the sounds of fighting. Or otherwise. The manor was silent. Frowning, he traced to the master chambers, and was stunned by what he saw.

Nikolai and Myst were sleeping together peacefully in the bed. Nikolai had his arms wrapped possessively around the Valkyrie, and she was clutching his chest.

Contentment suffused Nikolai's face, his visage markedly changed from the strain of the last several years. He was still pale, still gaunt, but his face . . .

Just as Daniela had predicted, Nikolai and Myst had come to some kind of understanding.

I wonder if Nikolai takes it for granted that he can hold his Bride? With a start, Murdoch realized that, for the first time, he was jealous of Nikolai. Which shamed him.

He knew of no one who deserved this peace more than his brother.

Seeing them like this eased much of his animosity toward Myst. No matter what had happened in the past, at this moment she was giving Nikolai pleasure.

Murdoch shook his head, no longer surprised that his brother had taken Myst here. Nikolai always came to Blachmount when he missed their family.

With this woman, he was planning to start a new one.

Murdoch tried to imagine what it would be like to have a female belong to him alone, above all others . . . and couldn't. It wasn't meant to be for him. He'd driven his own Bride away. Only now did Murdoch recognize that he'd taken his anger toward Myst—and his frustration over the blooding—out on Daniela. Who'd done nothing to deserve his ire; indeed, just the opposite.

But it didn't matter *how* he'd driven her away. Only that he had. This way was best. He'd just end up hurting her, had almost *bitten* her.

Even after his brother's five years of torture, Nikolai hadn't succumbed to bloodlust and bitten Myst. Her neck was unmarked.

At that moment, Nikolai drew his brows together and tightened his arms around his Bride. Though he slept, Nikolai still sensed another's presence.

So Murdoch traced back to the mill. He held his breath as he materialized, not sure if he hoped Daniela would still be there or not.

Empty. He ignored his baffling disappointment. *What'd you expect?* He'd threatened her, insulted her—

He spotted a piece of paper on his desk. Tripping in his haste to reach it, he snapped the note up and read:

> *Vampire,*
> *At some time in the future, you're really going to want*
> *my number. So I thought I would give you this:*
> *867-5309.*
> *XOXO,*
> *Daniela, the Ice Queen*

The words were embellished with whimsical hearts. *I haven't blown it.* Relief sailed through him, so strong he sagged onto his mattress.

She'll see me again. He ignored the part of him that was filled with foreboding, the part still warning that she'd be safer if she didn't.

When he felt the afternoon sun's heavy reach over the earth, his lids grew heavy. Exhaustion caught up with him and, with her note clutched in his fist, he slept.

Eleven

THE CRACKED VINYL OF THE TRUCK BENCH stuck to Danii's heated thighs, disgusting her even further.

Her hands were clenched and a steady stream of lightning trailed her as she and Farmer Ted bounced along a pitted road, closing in on Val Hall, the manor that housed the New Orleans coven of Valkyrie.

Earlier, once she'd trudged *a mile* from the mill, in the heat of a Louisiana noonday sun, she'd eventually stumbled onto a desolate county highway—and an old farmer driving by in an even older truck.

After dashing in front of him in the road, begging for a ride, she'd promptly deduced that Farmer Ted was a man of *no* words, communicating solely by strategic spitting of his tobacco chew.

With one healthy splat out of his truck window, he'd agreed to drop her near home. At least, she'd translated that as an agreement. Before he could argue—that would just get untidy—she'd clambered into the cab. The one without air-conditioning that reeked of taxidermy and Levi Garrett tobacco.

If Valkyrie ate, Danii would be vomiting right now.

All because of that vampire. The only thing getting her through this ordeal was the belief that Murdoch would regret what he'd done.

And the fact that she'd left him a special number for when he returned.

The second he'd vanished, she'd rushed to the mill's garage, agreeing that she needed to leave, stat. *Rule to live by: If a vampire warns you he's coming back to attack and possibly kill you, then you listen.*

Inside, she'd found a classic Porsche, refurbished and lovely, with a new Maserati Spyder beside it. She'd been eager to steal and trash either one, already planning to return the vehicle with a UV bulb in the overhead light. But she couldn't find the keys.

She'd tried to call for help on his sat-phone, but the service was code-locked.

Rather than stay and wait like an unwitting bag of O positive, she'd scribbled her note and set out in her bloody boots, wearing damp underwear, the vamp's T-shirt, and a cloak of rage that only a two-thousand-year-old Valkyrie could pull off.

For so long, those in the Lore had noted the differences between Danii and her sisters—including Danii. But in truth, she had just as many Valkyrie traits as she had Icere.

Most notably, Danii possessed the Valkyrie's notorious pride and need for retribution. Like her sisters, if she was wronged, then gods help the subject of her wrath.

I've so been wronged. By the first vampire in history *not* to want his Bride. She didn't know if that said something about him—or about her. If anyone found out she'd been cast away by a Forbearer, she would never live it down. Her only hope was that no one ever discovered her disgraceful morning.

To add insult to injury, she'd also remembered him *interrogating* her. While she'd been filled with poison, he'd been filled with questions.

Her supposed white knight had taken advantage of her, and she couldn't recall how much she'd told him. Surely she hadn't revealed any critical secrets or weaknesses. . . .

Stop thinking about him. You have things to do. Like fleeing the city.

Since none of the assassins from last night would be reporting back, King Sigmund would soon send another Icere contingent. He wouldn't stop until he'd killed her.

Just as he'd murdered the true queen of the Iceren, Svana the Great, Danii's mother.

Danii had to get home and pack, but she grew weary merely thinking about returning to Val Hall, weak and shamed, a vampire informer. Via Farmer Ted. How could she face her sisters now?

Myst was *still* getting razzed for hooking up with Nikolai five years ago, even by other Lore factions. Having the aggressively omnisexual nymphs ridicule one's choice of lover was about as low as one could get. Mysty the Vampire Layer was the butt of many a joke.

Who was worse? Myst, who'd dabbled with a vampire, or Danii, who'd dabbled and had desperately wanted more?

Murdoch dreamed.

Sometimes he dreamed of the sun, sometimes of old battles. Now he dreamed of his father, of walking in on him wet-eyed, clutching a portrait of Murdoch's mother on the fifth anniversary of her death.

Murdoch had loved his mother, though she'd been zealously religious, and he'd grieved her loss, but his father had been left a broken shell of a man.

At first, Murdoch had pitied him. Then he'd scorned the father who had scant time for his family, who'd all but orphaned his four young daughters with his neglect.

By this time, Murdoch had been enjoying women for years, knew that they were always about when he needed one. His father could have enjoyed the same—as a wealthy aristocrat, he could easily have found a woman to replace his departed wife.

"Get another one," Murdoch had finally demanded, unable to comprehend what kind of hold the woman had over him. His father had refused to move on, obsessed with her.

A woman's death had *broken* a strong man. . . .

The dream began to change. Murdoch found himself with Daniela in a strange room made of ice walls. But he felt no chill from it, no discomfort.

He placed his palms on either side of her ethereal face—without giving her pain. When his thumbs brushed her delicate cheekbones, she smiled up at him, but her countenance was different. Everything about her had changed.

Wisping ice crystals had formed in half-moon shapes at her temples. More crystals spiked her lashes and tangled in her wild, shimmery hair. Her skin was even paler, her lips tinged with blue. Delicate cobalt-colored designs laced around her wrists and descended over her hands. In his dream, he knew they ran across her lower back as well.

Her eyes seemed to be filled with an ancient knowing, and they glowed as if banked with a blue fire.

She looked otherworldly. Like a completely alien being. *She* is *otherworldly.* . . .

"Do you want me?" she whispered on a frosty breath, leading him to a bed in the center of the room.

He'd never wanted anyone more. "I have to have you."

"Then take me, Murdoch."

He was about to give her his standard warning, that this was only for a night. He wouldn't be interested in more. But she pressed her chill lips to his, stunning him with the cold—and with the pleasure. Perfection. Delicious.

He lost track of what he'd been about to say.

As they kissed, he slipped her skimpy dress from her, then pressed her back on the bed. He tugged her panties down, left her heels on.

Sweeping his hands up her thighs, he spread her legs. Now that he could, he made a feast of her body for hours, licking her in secret places. Instead of her own fingers delving into her sex, his now thrust inside her.

He tormented her, first keeping her from coming, then forcing her to, over and over.

In his dream, he knew she'd never been with another man. He painstakingly prepared her body for his, determined to spare her pain as he claimed her virginity.

When he'd been human, he'd never been interested in virgins. Back then, much was taboo in his conservative country. Deflowering a maid one never intended to marry was virtually blasphemous.

So why was he continuing with Daniela, positioning his hips between her pale thighs? Why was he kissing her soft breasts, rubbing his face against them, sucking on those stiff nipples? Did he want to be bound to her? *One woman.* For more than even a mortal lifetime. Possibly *forever.*

These thoughts left him when the head of his cock found her wetness.

She softly cried, *"Murdoch . . ."* Lightning fractured the night, the thunder booming all around them.

With a groan, he slowly rolled his hips up, pressing the crown inside her untried body . . . *the tightness, the connection.*

When she gasped in his ear and made little whimpers of pleasure, he ran his mouth against her neck, licking her sweet skin, knowing he'd take her blood this night.

He rode her harder, faster, shocked when she met his frantic thrusts with a hidden strength. She dug her heels in to lift her hips, seating him even deeper inside her.

She told him she was about to come, and he was desperate to feel it.

Her sheath began squeezing his throbbing cock, and the power of her orgasm sent his seed climbing. The pressure would soon make him mindless. His cock ached; his fangs ached. No amount of will could prevent him from bucking his hips to lose his semen . . . or from piercing her neck.

With a yell, he sank his fangs into her tender flesh. And it was like coming home.

"Murdoch!"

He *felt* her crying out as her blood filled his mouth, coursing through every cell in his body.

Connection.

As the overwhelming urge to come inside her grew, he slammed his body between her legs. Growling against her neck, he began to ejaculate, spending so hard he knew she felt it inside her. Still sucking her blood, he flooded her womb.

Once he was spent at last, he collapsed atop her, releasing his bite. Afterward, as their hearts pounded, he couldn't seem to stop kissing her neck and murmuring praise in her ear. This new bond between them was like nothing he'd ever known.

Yet she began fading, disappearing from him.

"Murdoch, what's happening?" The fear in her eyes was like the night before—stark, filling him with dread.

"No! Daniela, don't go. . . ."

A strange voice in his mind whispered, *"How badly do you want her? What would you sacrifice?"*

He woke to his own yelling, tracing to his feet. With her number still in his hand, he snatched up the phone, staring at one, then the other as he caught his breath.

He shook his head hard. What the hell was this? Like a spell on him, making him behave in ways he normally wouldn't.

Calm yourself. Think this through. You have bloodlust for her.

He couldn't control it. He acknowledged that. Yet he kept remembering his brother's contentment. Murdoch's mind seized on the rightness of being with Daniela in his dream.

Think, just think. . . . As he debated, he stalled, tracing to the kitchen to drink blood, though he had no appetite, then showering. He took time selecting which clothes he'd wear for the night—in case he decided to meet her again.

In the end, Murdoch found it impossible not to call her. *To hell with it.*

He was strangely nervous as he picked up the phone. After all, he'd never contacted a woman for an assignation. They'd always come to him.

He'd have to smooth-talk Daniela, since he'd left it so badly today. That wouldn't be a problem. He'd been called silver-tongued by more than one lover in the past.

Eight-six-seven-five-three-oh-nine—

"Kristoff wishes to see you," a male said from behind him.

He hastily disconnected the call, then cast a scowl over his shoulder. Lukyan, a Russian Forbearer, leaned negligently against the doorframe.

Murdoch didn't trust the former Cossack. Not bothering to hide his irritation, he said, "Can't it wait?"

"It's about your brother. You're to go to Blachmount."

"*What* about him?"

Lukyan's expression was studiously blank. "He's probably about to be executed."

TWELVE

Danii had gotten into Val Hall undetected. *Now I just have to get my things and get out.*

Although a couple dozen Valkyrie lived here at any time, the manor was quiet this morning. Most were nocturnal, as was Danii usually—it was cooler that way.

Nïx, the one half sister she wanted to see, was nowhere to be found.

Upstairs, Danii passed the most shaded chamber in Val Hall, belonging to Emmaline, her beloved niece. But she knew Emma would be asleep as well. It was day, and Emma was vampire. Or half one. No one knew who her vampire father was, and that information wasn't likely forthcoming, since her Valkyrie mother had died of sorrow decades ago.

Gentle Emma was the single vampire the Valkyrie accepted. Though a blood drinker, she was so timid that she made it easy to overlook the vampirism.

Emma was the exception; Murdoch was the rule. *Just accept it. He almost bit you. . . .*

Danii reached her room, which was basically a giant freezer, and pushed open the heavy insulated door. A blast of arctic air and the comforting drone of refrigeration met her.

She lived at Val Hall year-round. But in the summer, even the meat locker—as her sisters called her room—was barely adequate for her needs.

There simply was no call for hundred-degree days.

Closing the door behind her, she gazed around the spacious area. She'd decorated it with frost, glazing the walls with it. Icicles dripped from the blades of the ceiling fan. Valances of ice capped her windows.

She couldn't say she loved it here, but she'd adapted to life with her coven. Others could tolerate hours in the snow, but would seek a hearth at the end of the day. Danii was the same way with heat, except she sought the comfort of her meat locker.

Her slushy waterbed was filled with saltwater, which lowered the freezing point to below thirty-two degrees. Above her bathtub was an ice maker, and beside it hung an Epsom salt dispenser. On occasion, she had to add salt to the water so that *she* didn't freeze it.

Her ice-proofed computer was a military-spec laptop with a magnesium chassis and a sealed keyboard.

Yes, she'd adapted. And she'd felt some security living in such a warm climate. *I thought I was safe from Sigmund here.* It should've been the last place the Icere would look.

The attack was another reason Danii was avoiding her sisters. If she told them about last night, they would insist on her staying—and them fighting. But the Icere were an enemy the Valkyrie didn't need.

And one they could never find to defeat.

When Danii had been a girl of seven, her mother Svana had journeyed to Icergard, the Icere castle, to reclaim her crown from the vicious Sigmund. Danii's memories of this time were indistinct after the passage of so many years, but she remembered her mother saying, "If I don't return to you here, you must promise me, love, never to follow me. Never, never go to Icergard." She'd made Danii vow it.

Svana had never returned. Before she'd even made it to the castle, Sigmund had assassinated her—the mother who'd refused to linger endlessly in peace with her young daughter in the godplane of Valhalla.

Once Danii had grown old enough to leave Valhalla herself, he'd dispatched killers after her to prevent her from ever challenging his reign. As if she ever would.

Over the centuries, she'd considered breaking her vow to her mother, but only to gather her sisters and strike back at Sigmund, freeing herself from his threat. Yet even if the Valkyrie could find Icergard—rumored to be hidden within the Arctic Circle beneath a dome of ice—they could never attack the castle without getting slaughtered.

Sigmund was perfectly protected from the Valkyrie, inadvertently utilizing their greatest weakness as his defense.

Diamonds. Svana had told her they dotted the walls and perimeter fences. Though Danii was immune, most Valkyrie could be mesmerized by them.

With a sigh, she rose. She needed to pack, and then she needed to find Nïx to ask the half mad soothsayer about three things:

Myst.

Exactly *what* was supposed to have been fixed the night before.

And where Danii should flee before the next wave of Icere arrived.

There were eleven other Valkyrie covens around the world that Danii could choose from.

The latitude of the Seattle coven had always intrigued her. And then there was the one in New Zealand. Fall approached down there.

Yet as ever, Danii hated to leave her own coven. Valkyrie visited others, but they always returned to their primary coven, like preferring an immediate family over an extended one.

Plus, the New Orleans Valkyrie had plagued the others with practical jokes, which might make it awkward for Danii to pop in.

She could just see herself telling the Seattle Valkyrie, "I had nothing to do with signing you up for the emu farming franchise. And I am sorry twenty of them were released in your pool house, startling your harem of cabana demons. See Nïx."

Tonight, the wily soothsayer would likely be downtown in the Vieux Carré. So Danii would be trolling Bourbon Street yet again. Her only consolation was that she wouldn't run into Murdoch.

He and his brother had only been in New Orleans to find Myst. Good riddance.

Damn it, why did never seeing him again matter to her?

Because he saved your life and surprised you repeatedly. And she'd *enjoyed* him, had liked what they'd done together. It was the first time she'd had an orgasm with someone else in the room. She grew aroused just recalling how he'd worked the seed free from his shaft. He'd been naked in bed with her, his mighty chest heaving, yelling out as he came.

And now he was free to use those sensual lips to kiss another woman, could use that magnificent body to pleasure others. She glanced at her claws. They'd straightened with aggression.

Stop thinking about him, she told herself firmly as she crossed to one of the windows, brushing away a layer of frost. As her gaze flickered over the lightning-scorched trees in the yard, a sense of melancholy fell over her. *I don't want to leave.*

In the window glass, Danii spied her reflection. She was exhausted, which meant there was a reddish tinge to her lips and under her eyes, instead of the blue that should be there. Her face was pinched.

She *looked* miserable. Tally yet another reason why the vampire hadn't wanted to have anything to do with her. Well, other than biting and possibly killing her.

She glared down at her pale, icy skin. Never to be touched. Never without pain. Danii was stuck in this body, stuck in this rut.

Most of her half sisters were fiercely independent—many were legendary warriors or love-'em-and-leave-'em jet-setters. Danii was just . . . Danii. And she could admit she'd longed for a male of her own, maybe to make a home with. A male who would always clasp her in his arms when she ran for him.

I'm the Valkyrie who most wants to be held—and I never can be. At the thought, she felt her bottom lip trembling. *I'd rather not have had a glimpse of what I've been missing.*

She dropped her head into her hands and wept, her freezing tears making her want to scream.

THIRTEEN

TONIGHT MURDOCH MIGHT BE FORCED TO KILL HIS KING.

He had sworn fealty to Kristoff and his Forbearer order, but he was loyal to Nikolai above all others.

After Lukyan left, Murdoch quickly stuffed Daniela's note in his pocket—and donned his sword. He would strike down Kristoff in a heartbeat if his brother was in danger.

When he traced to the great room in Blachmount, Kristoff intoned, "Sit, Murdoch."

Kristoff was at the head of the timeworn table, flanked by four Forbearer elders from Russia, some of the first ones he'd turned— his own countrymen.

Within their order was a tense alliance between the Russians and Estonians. Kristoff thought the realm of the Lore superseded human concerns and wars. But history was difficult for Murdoch to forget.

Russians had killed him and most of his family.

"I imagine Nikolai will be down shortly." Kristoff was analyzing him. Would he hear Murdoch's beating heart? And if he did, would he say anything about it?

The king often acted in ways that were incomprehensible to Murdoch. He'd demonstrated blistering wrath toward some subjects, and unexpected leniency to others.

Kristoff was a natural-born vampire, not a turned human, and was as shrewd as he was ruthless. As a boy, he'd had his crown stolen by his uncle, Demestriu, the current leader of the Horde. Kristoff had been smuggled out of the capital before Demestriu could assassinate him, then raised in hiding by humans.

Once Kristoff had grown old enough to seek his birthright, he'd had no army, so he'd started *making* one, siring troops of turned human warriors.

Murdoch sat down uneasily. "What are we doing here?"

"Questioning your brother," Kristoff said. "About his crime."

Striving to make his tone level, he asked, "What crime would that be?"

"One of the worst."

The worst crimes in their order were treason and drinking living blood straight from the flesh.

There'd been no treason. Though Murdoch didn't particularly care about Kristoff's cause—he'd agreed to join the king's army because he'd wanted to live—Nikolai had always fervently believed in what the Forbearers stood for.

And drinking living blood? When Murdoch had seen Nikolai earlier, he'd been content, but he'd still been pallid, still lean. His eyes had been closed, so Murdoch hadn't been able to tell if they were red.

"My liege, you know Nikolai," Murdoch said. "He's a loyal soldier." Besides, Nikolai would've told Murdoch if he'd planned anything.

"Exactly."

Murdoch fell silent at that, knowing from experience that Kristoff would say no more. As a natural-born vampire, Kristoff was unable to lie, so instead he often ignored questions and answered others cryptically.

As they waited for Nikolai, Murdoch restlessly glanced around the decaying room. So many memories haunted this place. Here Nikolai had made the fateful decision to try to turn all of their dying family.

Murdoch remembered that time as if it were yesterday.

After he and Nikolai had risen from the dead, they'd traced home and had found their sisters and father dying of plague. Sebastian and Conrad had been stabbed through by Russian marauders and barely clung to life.

All in this room . . . How the girls had wept when they'd comprehended that they were dying. How filled with rage Sebastian and Conrad had been to be turned into vampires against their will—

Nikolai suddenly materialized. He was black-eyed with fury, his fangs dripping. He must have sensed intruders, and thought them a threat to Myst.

"Wroth, I pity the being who wishes to harm your Bride," Kristoff said.

Murdoch nearly whistled out a breath at Nikolai's appearance. His face had been beaten. His clothing was filthy, his shirt tattered and marked with blood.

Nikolai seemed to be grappling for control. "I would not wish to attend you in such a condition. I'll go wash and change—"

"No, we know you are eager to get back to her for the remains of the night," Kristoff said, then added in a proud tone, "Congratulations, Wroth. You've now been blooded *and* claimed your Bride." He studied him. "Recently. Though it appears she didn't acquiesce to you."

Did Kristoff think *Myst* had fought Nikolai? What the hell had happened to his brother since earlier this day? If Nikolai had been content earlier, now he looked *determined*.

"I'd like to meet her," Kristoff said.

"She is resting."

Murdoch thought he heard her in the bath upstairs. Leisurely bathing? If they'd fought, then why was she not fleeing Nikolai?

Kristoff said, "I suppose she would be resting. In fact, we'd wonder if she weren't."

Two of the elders snickered until Nikolai shot them a quelling scowl.

Kristoff steepled his fingers. "And you drank her blood this night?"

Deny it, Nikolai.

"Did you take her flesh as you did so?"

No, steady Nikolai would never commit this crime, the one punishable by death. Should Kristoff decree it, Nikolai would be chained in an open field until the sun burned him to ash.

When Nikolai's eyes narrowed, Murdoch's hand slipped to his sword hilt. Five against him and Nikolai. Likely the brothers wouldn't make it out of Blachmount alive.

How fitting.

Nikolai's shoulders went back. "I did."

No, brother. . . . He *hadn't* restrained himself. But why were his eyes clear?

Kristoff ordered, "Take off your shirt."

Murdoch caught Nikolai's glance, tensing to fight, but Kristoff said, "Stand down, Murdoch, no one's dying tonight."

A lashing then? Nikolai removed the shirt, too proud for his own good. His gaze darted to the stairs; even now he worried for his Bride.

"Toss it on the table."

Frowning, Nikolai did. Murdoch caught the scent just as the other elders did. Kristoff had detected traces of Myst's blood, and now they all did as well. Like the others, Murdoch's hands went white on the table, but for a different reason.

Murdoch was reminded anew of Daniela's blood—and of his dream, recalling how he'd pierced the supple flesh of her neck, sucking from her. . . . "And what was it like?" he absently asked, his voice hoarse.

Nikolai didn't answer. Then Kristoff raised his brow in a wordless command.

After a hesitation, Nikolai grated, "There is no description strong enough."

Murdoch barely suppressed a groan and was surprised that no one noticed the hectic drum of his heart.

"How did she feel about your bite?" Kristoff asked.

Again Nikolai was silent.

Kristoff's stare was unflinching. "You resist answering your king on the heels of confessing to our most reviled crime?"

Nikolai resisted because he'd accepted Myst as his. As his *family*. Wroths protected their family's honor.

Answer him, Nikolai—you can't protect her if you're dead.

Nikolai must have been thinking the same thing. Though distinctly unwilling, he bit out, "She found extreme pleasure from it."

She'd *liked* being bitten?

Kristoff relaxed back in his chair, his demeanor pleased. He asked those at the table, "Do you think I should forgive Wroth his transgression? For which one of us could have resisted the temptation when she was our Bride and her exquisite blood called?" The king stared at the shredded garment marked by a Valkyrie's blood.

Murdoch masked his shock. For centuries, this had been law. Forbearing from drinking the flesh was how they'd earned their name. Was this a license to drink from one's Bride?

"Continue as you were," Kristoff told Nikolai. "But if your eyes turn red, know that we will destroy you."

Nikolai is free to drink his Bride, to take her blood at his leisure. Murdoch envied him. Again.

Nikolai was stunned as well, but recovered enough to say, "I was coming to Mount Oblak tonight to tell you that Ivo was spotted in New Orleans."

Ivo the Cruel was a leader in the Horde, and their armies had battled in the past. In fact, Mount Oblak had once been his holding.

"He's looking for someone," Nikolai said. "I suspect it could be Myst."

That made sense. She'd been Ivo's prisoner, had already been in his dungeon when the Forbearers had taken the castle.

Nikolai ran a hand over his face, his concern evident. "I need to go—"

"We'll take care of it," Murdoch interrupted sharply. "For God's sake, you stay here and . . . enjoy . . . everything." *Everything I can't.*

Kristoff returned his attention to Nikolai, eyeing him shrewdly. "Find out as much as you can from her. And you will tell us if the memories follow the blood."

After a short nod, Nikolai traced from the room.

His brother hadn't just been spared, he'd as much as had a slap on the back from Kristoff. The king was no doubt thinking of an alliance with the Valkyrie.

And I have a Valkyrie Bride. But Murdoch could never drink her anyway, was a danger to her.

If Nikolai had succumbed, knowing he was breaking the laws of their order, then Murdoch didn't stand a chance of controlling himself with Daniela. And she would find no pleasure in it, had told him she could die from it.

Kristoff stood. "Now, which of you will volunteer to accompany Murdoch to New Orleans where this coven full of Valkyrie is located?"

They all shot to their feet.

One asked, "Does this mean we can drink from our Brides? Without repercussions?"

"Only if they're immortal and can't be killed from blood loss. I believe that's why Nikolai's eyes are still clear," Kristoff said absently, his gaze focused on Murdoch. "A word," Kristoff told him, ushering him aside. "You are charged with protecting Myst the Coveted. This match between her and your brother is critical. Scour the city for Ivo until the sun drives you back."

In the past, Murdoch had searched those city streets for his brother's sake. Now he would do the same for Myst, a female he'd hated for years. "And when I find him?"

"Take him out."

"Gladly."

"Is there anything you'd like to tell me, Murdoch?"

"My liege?"

"Your heart beats," Kristoff observed. "Don't worry, the others won't notice. Turned humans rarely think to listen for it. When did this happen?"

"Last night."

"A mere five years after your brother. While I've waited millennia." Did Kristoff envy them?

Doubtless. The natural-born vampires had the same pressing drive to find their mates. They were born fully alive, growing much like mortals, until they neared the age when they froze into their immortality. Then with each day, their hearts would beat less, their breaths—and sexual need—gradually diminishing to nothing until they could become blooded.

Just like the Forbearers, the natural-born vampires knew exactly what they were missing. . . .

"Is your Bride by any chance a Valkyrie?"

When Murdoch hesitated, Kristoff's eyes flooded black with anger. "Need I remind you that I'm your king? And I've just shown mercy to your brother."

"She is a Valkyrie."

"Have you been able to learn anything about the Lore from her?"

"I'll be able to find out more in the future," he said, hedging for some reason.

"The future? She's a Valkyrie—the odds are against her wanting anything to do with you."

Murdoch's shoulders straightened. "She told me she wanted to see me again." *Before* he'd threatened to bite her. But she'd still left her number. "She even gave me her contact information." He pulled the note from his pocket, displaying it.

Kristoff raised a brow at the *X*s and *O*s, the puffy hearts. "Call her," he challenged.

Murdoch took his sat-phone from his jacket, then dialed the number. It rang several times.

"Hmm. Not waiting by the phone for your call?"

Murdoch heard a voice-answering service clicking on. Kristoff did as well and said, "Probably in the shower, then?"

"Of course."

But a woman's voice said, "If you've reached this message and you weren't trying to contact Regin the Radiant"—

Regin?

—"then I know three things about you. One of my half sisters just tooled your ass and never wants to see you again. B. You're pop-culturally illiterate not to know that this number is a song. And three, you'll never tell another male about this humiliating prank, so the number trick can be continued indefinitely. If, however, you called for *moi*, then say something to amuse me after the beep."

Murdoch's anger was boiling. Just as he was about to unleash his wrath in a message, a computerized voice said, "Mailbox is full."

That little witch . . .

"I understand you had a reputation for being popular with women," Kristoff said as he collected Nikolai's bloody shirt from the table. "You'd better recognize that a Valkyrie is not exactly your typical woman."

FOURTEEN

"*FORBEARER SCUM.*"

"*Ignorance is bliss, leech.*"

"*Go sun yourself.*"

Being met with insults was the only way Murdoch and his men could determine that they'd even approached Lore beings in their search of the Quarter.

Hours ago, Murdoch had mapped out the rest of the city for the other Forbearers, and then they'd split up, each elder with two men under him. Murdoch had taken his old friend Rurik, an Estonian who'd served under him in the war, and they'd been stuck with Lukyan, the hotheaded Russian. Kristoff could insist that the former political alliances of his soldiers had been nullified by those of the Lore, but the wily king always put a Russian with Estonians, and vice versa.

Over the course of the night, Murdoch had grown better able to recognize the Lore beings—they seemed more adroit, more suspicious, and often more drunken than the humans—but he still didn't know what they *were.*

And not one of them would offer information. The females hadn't given him enough time to charm them. The males had looked ready to fight on sight.

The closest he'd gotten was with a scantily clad female who'd painted her skin with leaf designs. She'd at least given him a few moments to state his introduction and questions, not that she'd *listened*. She'd merely been ogling him while nodding dimly and murmuring, "Uh-huh, baby boy, you keep talking, Trixie's lis'ning."

She'd kept this up until another female, dressed and painted like her, came charging between them to harangue the first one. "He's a *vampire*. You really are a ho-hum whoreslut of a nymph, aren't you?"

"No, you are!"

Then they'd lunged at each other, deep-kissing as they went tumbling to the ground.

All in all, the Forbearers had learned nothing about Ivo's whereabouts.

Now, as midnight neared, Rurik, Lukyan, and Murdoch stood on a balcony overlooking the crowd. The other two were arguing over various topics, while Murdoch was silent in thought, mired in unease over Daniela.

Of course, he knew *why* she'd played the prank on him. And he knew why it would be best if he never saw her again. So why did he feel this urgency to find her? He craved the sight of her, needed to have her scent fresh in his mind.

This eve, he'd seen pretty women, but he had no interest in them. Though he knew so little about Daniela, the blooding made him think of her constantly.

It forced him to recall her vulnerability when she'd said she wanted to see him again. It made him remember with a disturbing tenderness the way she'd lifted her arms to him so trustingly.

As a mortal, he'd had a happy-go-lucky personality. Women had trusted him with their pleasure but little else. Yet Daniela had believed in *him* to remove the arrows in time to save her life.

Tomorrow night, he could go to Blachmount and ask Myst how to contact her sister. But then, Myst might refuse to divulge that information. If all else failed, he supposed he could try to find the Valkyrie coven, despite Daniela's warning that they'd kill him on sight.

Another source of his unease? He couldn't stop mulling over how the Wroth brothers had gone down in Lore history for their deeds, or misdeeds. After the continuous battles and hardships they'd all suffered, Nikolai had been remembered as the self-sacrificing general, and Murdoch had been classed as the manwhore?

He also suspected that this bothered him solely because that was how Daniela saw him—

"What say you, Murdoch?" Rurik asked.

"What? I didn't hear you."

"We were speaking of Brides and Valkyries."

Murdoch almost coughed. "Were you, then?"

Rurik's scarred face creased into a frown. *He can tell something is going on with me—has known me for centuries.* Rurik had been one of five dying war compatriots who'd accepted that fateful deal Nikolai had brokered with Kristoff.

But cunning Kristoff knew that these men were loyal to Nikolai and Murdoch, and always would be. Demonstrating his shrewdness yet again, Kristoff had dispatched the other four—Kalev, Demyan, Markov, and Aleksander—in separate directions on the continent to search for the Daci, a rumored hidden enclave of natural-born vampires.

Rurik alone remained, and only because of his weakness: an uncontrollable temper when in conflict. Not the best trait for a potential ambassador.

"I heard at Mount Oblak that Nikolai's Bride was fine beyond words," Lukyan said. He was a bold and skilled fighter—as a Don Cossack, Lukyan had been bred for war—but Murdoch didn't trust him. There was something off about him, even beyond the fact that he'd died on the other side of the same battlefield Murdoch had perished on. "You saw her. Is she that beautiful, then?"

"She is." But not more so than Daniela.

"I haven't really *looked* at a woman in so long." Rurik's gaze fell to the street below. In his human life, he'd been a simple farmer, a gentle giant, until he'd gone into battle; then he would go berserk. He didn't wield a sword—he carried a war hammer.

Rurik's father had often liked to say that the men in their family were descended from berserkers. After Rurik had been turned into a vampire and learned this new world existed, he'd had to wonder, *literally descended from berserkers?*

"Wouldn't matter if you'd looked at women, you'd only see half of them," Lukyan said with a smirk.

Rurik had the war wounds to show for his rages. He walked with a marked limp and was missing an eye under his rakish patch. Ignoring the Cossack's comment, he said, "Have females been showing this much skin the whole time?"

Murdoch understood his comrade's puzzlement. He himself had been disinterested in women to the point of oblivion. Until the Valkyrie.

"Christ, look at that one," Rurik said in an awed tone. Murdoch remembered that even before he'd lost his eye, Rurik had been unlucky with women. He wondered if Rurik remembered that.

With a leer, Lukyan said, "Maybe she's the one who'll tempt me back to life."

Pinpricks skittered along the back of Murdoch's neck as he turned to the object of their attention.

Daniela. Just there.

The gnawing ache he'd been experiencing redoubled at the sight of her.

She was strolling the street below them, her white-blond hair swaying about her shoulders with each of her graceful steps. She wore a wrap of black silk around her hips, with a thin swath of the material climbing up over one breast, around her neck, and down over the other.

Could she have revealed more of her perfect flesh? Her back and arms were bare, as was a good bit of her chest and flat belly. The only jewelry adorning her were those exotic armbands. A satchel was slung over her shoulder.

Damn her, she was noticeably braless. And now he stood spell-bound by how her high breasts bobbed as she nimbly wound through the crowd.

She seemed oblivious to the men she left ruined in her wake. They froze, gaping after her as if they loved her and would do anything for her.

When one male spoke to her and she smiled up at him, Murdoch's fangs sharpened. The blooding at work again?

He shook himself, disconcerted by the violent drives racking him. *Get control.*

"She's got to be an immortal." Rurik's voice was rough with appreciation, and Murdoch had to check an impulse to hurt his old friend. "Do you think her blood would be like that of Nikolai's female?"

It would be, God help me, it would be. . . .

Lukyan said, "Bedding an immortal. Can you imagine how much experience that one has?"

Can't rip out his throat. Murdoch wanted to bare his fangs at them, to growl that she was his. But it would only make Lukyan more determined to meet her.

What if Daniela blooded one of these vampires? Was that even possible? He had to get them away from her.

"Back to work," he ordered them. "I'm starting at the head of the street. You two come from the other end. We'll cover more ground."

Once they'd reluctantly traced away, with lingering looks that al-most got them killed, Murdoch descended to the street, then strode toward her.

What the hell was she doing out here alone? There could be more of the Icere out in this city. To risk her safety like this . . .

Without warning, a memory arose. "I don't understand why men get so jealous over possessions, or over their women," he'd once told his father.

His father had seemed deeply disappointed when he'd answered, "Son, that's because you've never cared about anything enough to fight for it—or to fear losing it."

Fifteen

"OH, NO, NO. THIS ISN'T HAPPENING," Danii muttered as she jogged backward three steps, then whirled around in the opposite direction from the vampire intently approaching her.

It's him! Earlier when she'd reached the Quarter, she'd asked around for Nïx, but instead had found out that Forbearers, led by a very big and handsome vamp, were going door to door, canvassing the streets for someone.

She'd joked to herself that maybe it was Murdoch out seeking her—laugh, laugh—to abjectly apologize. Had she been not far off the mark?

Or maybe he still wanted to throw her down and drink her.

"Wait, Daniela!"

When he traced in front of her, she halted with her palm raised to her lips. "Come any closer, and I'll fill your lungs with ice."

"I don't want to hurt you."

"No? You were going to bite me earlier."

He didn't deny it, just gave a curt nod.

"So what's different now?"

"I've replenished the blood I've lost. And I'm not surrounded by the scent of yours."

"Sounds like you're trying to make *your* loss of control *my* fault."

"No, it was solely mine."

"If not to bite me, then what do you want?"

He didn't seem to know how to answer that. At length, he said, "Just to talk to you."

"Is that why you and your henchmen were looking for me?" Predictably, he'd need to see his Bride.

He ran his palm over the back of his neck. "We . . . weren't . . ."

"You're *not* looking for me." *How embarrassing.* "Then who?"

"We seek Ivo the Cruel."

A Horde baddie. "Good luck with that," she said between gritted teeth, turning to leave.

He followed her. "You know of him?"

"Of course I do. I'm not the one batting for Team Oblivious like you are." She snapped her fingers and made a face of realization. "Oh, but wait, you're no longer quite so clueless since you *grilled me last night*." Again he didn't deny it. "Did you tell all the Forbearers about what I said when I was delirious?"

"I've told no one," he said, his handsome face darkening into a scowl. "What in the hell are you doing out here alone?"

"I'm looking for someone myself."

"Who?" When she didn't answer, he said, "You should be where it's safe. There could be more Icere."

Like he cared. She picked up her pace, refusing to spare him a glance—and failing. He seemed to be puzzling over what to say to her.

Finally he decided on: "You gave me the wrong number."

He called? Her immediate high promptly nosedived. Of course, he'd only called for help with Ivo. "You have a lot of nerve bringing that up."

"Why would you do that?"

"For—fun." *To get your hopes up and then have them dashed. Like mine continue to be.*

She reminded herself that any "hopes" she might have had about him were firmly in the tense that was past. "And for the record, I wasn't seeking to wed you, vampire"—*I might* have been right after we came together—"and I wasn't even looking for an exclusive relationship." Unless he'd been interested in one. With that, she stormed off.

He was right behind her. "Where are you going? Why won't you give me two seconds of your time?"

I don't think my battered ego can take it. Like her body, it hadn't quite recovered.

"You've easily forgotten that I saved your life last night!"

She rounded on him. "Which wouldn't have needed saving if you would've just shut up and moved on!"

He didn't even seem to be listening—instead his gaze raked over her, from her chest to her uncovered navel. "What are you wearing?" he grated. "For someone whose skin is in danger of being burnt, you show enough of it."

Too late, he was acting like a domineering vampire with a Bride he considered worth having. "Because otherwise I'd burn up!" She wished she could criticize his clothing, but he looked irritatingly GQ in his tailored slacks and expensive shirt. His black cashmere jacket fit his broad shoulders to perfection.

Normally, she'd have been ecstatic to be seen with such a man.

"Then why do you live in this warm city?" he asked.

"Because this is where my coven is. For now."

"For now? Is it moving?"

She narrowed her eyes up at him. "Don't you have someone to be searching for? I'm sure you need to catch up with all the other little Forbearers."

He cocked a brow at that. "We've split up. You could help me."

"Oh, that's rich. The last time I 'helped' you, I got nothing but a burned hand and a death threat."

He closed in on her, forcing her to back up until she met a shop window. Looming over her, his voice a husky rasp, he said, "Is that all you got out of it, *kallim*?"

Kallim meant "darling." *Woo-hoo, a step up from "chit."* "Does this usually work on women?" Somehow she managed to be cold and unaffected. Or to look it. She hoped. "The threatening and then the full-court press?"

He exhaled. "I regret how today ended."

"Just as you predicted, it all went downhill from that one good hour." Where she'd made contact with the window, ice crystals fanned out on the glass, outlining her bare shoulder and upper arm with frost.

He noticed and said, "I'm glad you're, uh, cooling." Then he bit his lip, looking like he was inwardly kicking himself.

"I see why you were so popular with the ladies, Murdoch Suavé. With lines like that, how could you not be?"

"Murdoch Suavé?" With a shake of his head, he said, "We're looking for Ivo because he might be a danger to Myst."

Ivo could be. If the creep was in town, he'd probably be looking for his former captive.

"I've been ordered to protect her," Murdoch added.

"Protect Myst? This is a considerable change from"—she imitated his low, accented voice—"Myst is Nikolai's enemy! We hate Myst! She's *mean*."

His lips quirked, which seemed to surprise him, then he resumed his scowl. "They have come to an . . . understanding."

"Told you. So what do you need my help for?"

"My men and I can't get any leads. I've tried to question beings from the Lore—"

"But no one will speak to any of you. The rookies keep striking out?"

His glower deepened at her comment. "Finding Ivo is critical to me, Daniela. My brother would be destroyed if anything happened to Myst. The blooding is making him fall for her."

"That's not what the blooding does, you oaf!"

His expression indicated that he'd never in his life been called an oaf.

"The blooding doesn't *make* you fall for your Bride. All it does is indicate who you'd be most likely to have a successful relationship with—biologically and emotionally. That doesn't mean you're *capable* of a relationship," she said with a pointed glance at him. "Look, if Nikolai's falling, then it's just love. Real simple."

"I don't believe that. Then have you ever seen a fated pairing that didn't work out?"

"Oh, it happens." *To my mother for one.* Svana and Sigmund had been fated mates, and a much-celebrated love match. She'd taken him as her husband and prince consort. Then he'd stolen her crown and murdered her. Danii shook herself. "Now, if you don't mind, I have things to do."

"You wouldn't help me to help your sister?"

Danii stilled. *I owe Myst.* Unbidden, a memory washed over her.

Centuries ago, Danii had been captured by a sadistic Roman senator. He'd kept her among his slaves, bringing her out of her sweltering prison cell just to *play* with her, burning her naked skin with his touch.

She'd remained a virgin only because he'd intended to offer her to the Emperor, due to visit that season. Before he'd arrived, Myst had seduced her way past the senator's legions of guards, then killed him.

"I want to help her," Danii finally said. "But I won't work with you."

"Why not? You can't go about alone on these streets. The Icere could return."

"I've got a couple of days before they can get this far south. Besides, who's more dangerous to me? Them? Or the vampire who was about to attack me just hours ago?"

"Damn it, I told you why—"

"Have you ever bitten anyone before?"

"You know I haven't. My eyes are clear."

She shrugged. Actually, the Forbearers had it wrong. Vampires only turned red-eyed when they *killed* as they drank.

"We've pledged to our order that we would never take blood from the flesh."

"What would happen if you did?"

His brows drew together. "We . . . well, after tonight, it's *complicated*. But I vow to you I won't bite you. Just help me."

Danii hesitated. She was a skilled fighter, as were most Valkyrie, but because she risked overheating, she could seldom go into a protracted conflict here in southern Louisiana. And her special talents—conjuring blizzards as battle offense and frostbiting enemy armies—had been relegated to the past.

Since the coven had moved here seven decades ago, she'd felt . . . *underutilized*. Finally she would have a chance to assist her sisters in a meaningful way.

And she could do damage control. If he hadn't told anyone about what she'd divulged last night, then she could extract a vow from him never to do so!

Yet she feared there was nothing so noble ultimately steering her decision.

Sad, sad Daniela . . . so lonely and lame that she still yearned to be around the vampire.

No! Remember Farmer Ted, Danii!

In the end, it wasn't what Murdoch said that convinced her, but what he did. When three trashed frat boys leered at her as they passed, Murdoch's fists clenched.

He did feel *something* for her. Perhaps he did truly like her, but was afraid to settle down after so many centuries alone. Maybe he had bachelor's panic.

Maybe it's him, not me. "I'll help you, on three conditions."

"Let's hear them."

"You protect me if we encounter any more Icere—"

"Of course. I will protect you from any threat."

"Hold on there, I don't need your help with anyone but them. Second condition: you'll answer any questions I ask you. And third, you'll vow never to tell another about anything you learn tonight— or learned this morning. Or anything about me."

Seeing he was about to balk, she said, "I'm risking a lot by being seen with you. I could search on my own. And I would, if I thought you wouldn't follow me."

"Daniela, that's not—"

She turned to walk on.

He grated, *"Agreed."*

She faced him once more. "And if you even peek at my neck, I *will* go cryo on you."

Sixteen

Yet another female cajoled to do my bidding, Murdoch thought as they started out. He hadn't lost his skills.

"Where do we go first?" he asked, trying to tone down the smugness in his voice. *I control situations with women.* Just as it had always been. Which sometimes made for boring fare since he was never surprised, but that was unavoidable.

"We're off to a bar, a few blocks east on Bourbon. I know a demon. If we don't have any luck, then we can stop by a store that caters to Loreans."

"Very well." Now that he'd received the promise of her help, Daniela had become a means to an end. He would be staunchly focused on what he needed to do.

But, God, her hair smelled so damned good, giving him a shot of her scent each time her braids played about her bare shoulders. . . .

As they meandered through the crowd, humans kept looking at her, some more intently than others. He felt his fangs sharpening.

Did that fuck just ogle her br—

"You're going to have to cut that out, vampire."

His head whipped forward. "Cut what out?"

"Baring your fangs anytime a mortal checks me out." Now *she* sounded smug.

"I was *not* baring my fangs." He might have been baring his fangs. "Daniela, you'll find that I'm far from a jealous person."

"Uh-huh."

"Maybe I'm just concerned that you'll get burned. Since you're displaying so much skin." *That I can't touch.* He had to stifle the impulse to drape his jacket over her to protect her from injury—and lecherous gazes. "You're not nervous about making contact?" He thought *he* was more anxious about it than she was.

"I've threaded through the ninety-eight-point-six degree gauntlet many a time. Have you forgotten how fast I am?"

He hadn't. Still, for the next several minutes, if he spotted any passersby more intoxicated than others, he ran interference for her. When he almost grabbed her elbow once to steer her out of the way, she warned, "Ah-ah."

He ground his teeth in frustration, then said, "I'll return directly." He traced back to Mount Oblak, snagged a pair of thick gloves, then traced back so fast that she'd hardly had time to react to his disappearance.

When he held up his gloves, she said, "That's just weird."

"It's convenient." He drew them on.

"You would still have to be extremely careful with me, and I'd need to know how thick those were—"

He placed his palm flat on the small of her back, his hand nearly spanning it. "They're as thick as the ones from last night. I didn't burn you then."

She stiffened, but after a few moments, she allowed it, continuing along the street.

Even with such an innocuous touch, he found himself hardening for her, his second erection in centuries. Though his glove and her dress separated their skin, he could still feel her moving beneath his hand, her shapely hips swishing.

For many minutes as they walked, she was silent, seeming deep in thought. Had he made a mistake by tracing, reminding her what he was?

She'd wanted to be able to question him, but hadn't. So he said, "I went back to the alley where we fought last night. What happened to the bodies?"

She frowned. "They were probably eaten. By low creatures."

"By dogs? By rats?"

She gave him a cryptic smile. "Nothing so *generic*."

"And you won't specify what kinds of creatures? Come on, this is ridiculous," he said. "Do you think Myst won't tell Nikolai everything? So many beings in the Lore can't all keep such secrets."

"Humans think we're myths. Enough said."

A dead end. He let that drop. Yes, he'd succeeded in getting her to help him tonight, but he'd begun to suspect that this situation might not be precisely under his control.

Finally, she glanced up at him. "You said you were ordered to protect Myst. By whom?"

"By King Kristoff himself." *But I'd do it anyway.* Murdoch recalled the expression on Nikolai's face when he'd been grilled by Kristoff about Myst. Loyal, steadfast Nikolai had disobeyed his king, and looked as if he'd do it again for that woman. If she were killed, Nikolai would be as doomed as their father had been.

"Forced to protect her. That must grate."

"Grate? I was angry with her . . ." At Daniela's raised brows, he admitted, "I was furious for what she did to Nikolai. It's hard to see someone you care about and respect in misery, and Nikolai suffered as you can't understand. If anyone deserves happiness, it's him."

"Why?"

"He carries the weight of the world on his shoulders, guilt as you wouldn't believe."

"For what?" she asked, but he hesitated to answer. "Already breaking the terms of our deal?"

Murdoch scowled. "Nikolai believes he failed his country."

"There's got to be more than that."

"There . . . is." He exhaled. "Does the Lore know what happened to other members of my family?" When she shook her head, he said, "Nikolai tried to save their lives with his 'tainted' blood. He feels guilt for both succeeding and failing at that."

"How did he succeed *and* fail?"

"Daniela, this is a difficult subject."

"You have no idea what a good listener I am."

He looked down at her eyes. So vividly blue. As they'd been in his dream. He found himself recounting how he and Nikolai had returned home to watch over their family but had found them all dying, and in unimaginable pain. He told her how they'd fed blood to his brothers and sisters, his father.

Though Murdoch had never revealed to another living soul the details, the words fell from his lips as if she'd drawn them from him. "Most were out of their heads, but my brother Sebastian was awake, aware. He even figured out what we'd become and demanded that they be allowed to die in peace." At the memory, Murdoch ran his hand over his forehead. "Sebastian was particularly close to the girls, a kind of substitute father, and he hated Nikolai and me for trying to turn them. Even more so when only he and Conrad rose from the dead."

"What happened once they woke?" Daniela asked, her tone softer.

"Sebastian tried to kill Nikolai. And Conrad . . . when he comprehended what had been done to him, he went mad, bellowing as if in unbearable pain, and ran into the night. We haven't seen either of them in three centuries."

"Do you believe your brothers are still alive?"

"I have to," he answered, then waited for her to ask another question. Again, she remained silent, contemplative, so he said, "I was thinking about your enemies. If a king wants to kill you simply because you were born, then your very life is a threat. Which means that you're an heir. A royal one."

She shrugged. "You got me."

"What title do you possess?"

"I thought you knew. You called me an ice queen earlier today."

"A . . . queen." And if her delirious ramblings were to be believed, then she was also the daughter of gods.

"Yes, of the Icere," she said. "From a long line of Winter Queens."

"But Sigmund usurped your throne?"

She stiffened beneath his palm again. "You *did* get me to talk last night."

"Why don't you rebel and get your kingdom back? Gather the Icere to follow you?"

"It's not that simple. Sigmund is very powerful."

"There are none here to help you against him?" When she shook her head, he said, "I have a hard time believing that every last one of the Icere is united against you."

"New Orleans isn't exactly a coldbed of Icere."

"You're here."

He thought he heard her mutter, *"Not for long."*

"Is Sigmund any relation to you?"

"Not by blood," she said. "He was my mother's prince consort. I wasn't born until after his men had mortally wounded her."

"Do you know how crazy that sounds?"

"Welcome to the Lore. Little makes sense. Rules are fluid. Just when you think you've got it all figured out, you hear about a vampire unaffected by the sun, a mute Siren, or a chaste nymph."

"So there's no one here like you?" he asked.

"Are you trying to plan a coup for me, or attempting to find out if I have a boyfriend?"

He grated, "Do you?"

"Why would you care?"

"I'm curious. You don't strike me as the disloyal type, and you were just in my bed. Eagerly."

"Hey, now." She peered around and made a dampening motion

with her hands. "Not so loud, vampire. Let's not expedite the death of Danii's respect in the Lore."

"Earlier, you weren't too concerned about this, not when you were telling me that you wanted to see me again," he said, then added for good measure, "And that I have kissable lips."

"I said that before I concluded the risk-benefit ratio was one hundred percent risk and none-point-none percent benefit." She cast him a glare. "And I *really* wouldn't keep reminding me of all you learned last night and this morning."

"None-point-none?"

"Exactly. Unless threatening to drain me was your way of asking for more."

He wanted to tell her that the threat had been groundless, that he'd never hurt her like that. But the way he'd been feeling at that critical moment . . . ? It'd be a lie.

"Look at your vexed expression! Don't worry, Casanova, I didn't exactly take your behavior as an invitation. You made it very clear how you felt."

"I just didn't want to be blooded."

"Most vampires long for it to happen to them," she pointed out.

"Why? For the strength?"

"Sure. But also because immortality is lonely." Another display of that shocking vulnerability in a warrioress.

"Daniela, who were you searching for earlier?"

"You wouldn't know her."

Not a man. *Relief?* "And you're not going to tell me more about her." When she shook her head, he asked, "What happens in a couple of days when the Icere return? Will you and your sisters attack them?"

"No."

"Are you just going to wait until they take another shot at you? I thought the Valkyrie considered themselves the top of the Lore food chain. Have you never launched an assault, or sent assassins back to kill him?"

"There's something about their castle that repels my kind." At his questioning look, she said, "I won't reveal more. Besides, we can't find the Icere kingdom." She obviously hated to say *king*dom. "No one can, not even through scrying. You know, considering you washed your hands of me, you're awfully concerned about the Icere."

"Yes, because no matter what happened afterward with us, twenty-four hours ago I was plucking their arrows out of your body."

When her hand flittered about her chest at the painful reminder, he gentled his tone. "What would have happened if you hadn't gotten cooled?"

She cast him a begrudging expression as if she supposed she owed him the answer to this. "Thermal shock. At some point, the rapid temperature change would basically make me shatter."

"*Shatter.*" His voice sounded astonished even to himself. "How's that possible?"

"If glass is heated evenly, it just gets hot. But when it's heated unevenly, it cracks. Well, I don't heat evenly."

"All Icere are susceptible to this?"

"No. Like them, I have freezing skin. But because I'm part Valkyrie, my blood is a fraction warmer than theirs."

He slowed. "If you're at risk like that, why would you ever be out here alone?"

SEVENTEEN

BECAUSE I DON'T FIT IN WITH MY HALF SISTERS. Because, in lieu of true companionship, I'd rather be alone, so I can get lost in my fantasy world, dreaming about sex and snow. Maybe even sex in the snow. . . .

"The arrows are what made me so heated," she finally said, relieved that they'd almost reached their destination. "Take away the poison, and I would have survived. I can usually handle myself just fine."

"Usually? Have you gone into shock before?"

"No. Last night was the closest I've been."

"Then how do you know what will happen?"

"I was warned." *Danii, your face is red!* Svana had cried again and again. *You've been playing with your sisters too long. You know what your godparents said about getting too hot. . . .*

"Warned? By your parents?"

"Murdoch, I appreciate your candor about your family." An understatement. His tale had moved her in unexpected ways. "But I won't share it about mine." When he opened his mouth to ask more, she said, "Besides, we're here." With a negligent wave of her hand, she indicated their first stop, Jean Lafitte's.

Though on Bourbon, the tavern was situated at the opposite end from all the hustle and bustle, so it was more like a normal bar without the artificially inflated Bourbon Street buoyancy.

One of the Valkyrie's allies, a storm demon named Deshazior, hung out here whenever he was in town. Fitting, since he was a former pirate. Of course, he'd been hanging out in this building since the infamous Lafitte brothers had run a smithy in it.

Pausing outside the closest set of double doors, Danii told Murdoch, "You should wait here."

"Why?"

"Because my contact and his crew will want to kill you, and also, I might have to flirt with him."

The garrulous Deshazior had a known weakness for Valkyrie—and a lot of Valkyrie had known weaknesses for him.

Desh had even propositioned Danii, solemnly telling her in his briny accent, "I'd risk freezin' off my bollocks to claim yer maidenhead."

"You think I'll be jealous?" Murdoch's tone was disbelieving. "I believe I can handle it."

So arrogant, so dismissive. *Ego takes another hit. Round four, ding ding.*

With that, he guided her inside. As they entered, cigarette smoke wafted around them. Nick Cave's "People Ain't No Good" crooned from the jukebox. Drunk, glum mortals stared into their drinks.

Murdoch muttered, "This is a human bar. I thought you mentioned a *demon*."

"I know where Loreans loiter, okay?"

She swiftly spotted Desh. He was hard to miss, since he stood seven feet tall. And since he sported large, forward-pointing horns. "See that big guy with the horns—"

"He goes out like that?" Murdoch snapped under his breath. "With them uncovered for everyone to see?"

"Yes, whenever he likes. Humans think Deshazior and his crew are in costume. The demons draw straws to see who gets to wear that." She pointed out a sulky-looking demon wearing a neon pink T-shirt that read: *"Big Easy Movie Casting! We arrive in costume!"*

Humans asked them about prosthetics in cosplay, autographs, and movie release dates—not about their blatant protrusions.

Desh turned then, spotting her. "Ah, if it ain't the fair Lady Daniela," he called. He caught sight of Murdoch behind her and immediately tensed. "With a blightin' vampire. Ye'll be tellin' me why me and my boys won't be eviscerating the leech."

Murdoch watched as Daniela's friendly demeanor turned cold in a flash. "Because I'll turn your blood to slush if you do," she said, raising her palm to her lips.

She was so small compared to the hulking demon, but Deshazior held up his hands in surrender.

"Now, now, beauty. No need to be freezin' an ole demon like me. It hurts." When she dropped her hand, he added in a mutter, "Ladies goin' with vampires? City's gone to hell whilst I've been away."

"I'm not *going with* him. We're in an unlikely alliance on a dangerous mission to help Lorekind. An alliance with an expy date of . . . oh, dawn."

"This one's lookin' at ye like yer together," the demon said. "All possessive-like."

That noticeable?

"And how am I looking at him?" Daniela asked in an innocent tone.

"Like ye'd be well rid o' him," Deshazior said with a chuckle. "So what can I do for ye, luv?"

"Have you seen Nïx?"

Who was that? And why was Daniela seeking her?

One of the demons with Deshazior said, "Nïx is out tonight?" He anxiously smoothed a palm over each of his horns and straightened his collar.

"I guess that answers that question," Daniela said with a sigh. "I'm also looking for Ivo the Cruel."

A flicker arose in Deshazior's eyes as he said, "Aside from the one loomin' over ye just now, I haven't seen any vamps."

He's lying.

"That's a shame." Daniela pouted, traipsing closer to him. "I thought I could count on you for information." She reached up and ran the back of one claw along his right horn. At once, Deshazior's muscles tensed. The other demons gasped and groaned.

Murdoch didn't see why her behavior would elicit a response like that, but their eyes were spellbound by her stroking claw.

Deshazior had begun quaking. "Givin' me fits, Valkyrie!"

"A word alone," Daniela purred. "Outside."

With a defeated exhalation, the demon followed them out, mumbling about teasing Valkyries and "horn jobs."

Once the three were out on the street, Deshazior glowered at Murdoch. Then, after an uneasy glance back at his crew inside, he muttered to Danii, "Ivo's here in the city. I don't know where, but watch yerself. He's got some on his side that even I wouldn't tangle with."

"How do you mean?" Murdoch said.

Deshazior ignored him. "And if ye've need of a partnership to save Lorekind, I'm yer demon." He thumped his colossal chest. "No need to sully yerself with the likes of him."

Murdoch eased his lips back from his fangs.

"I appreciate the offer," Daniela said. "But I can make it a night. Will you leave word at the coven if you spot them?"

"Aye—" Suddenly the demon began disappearing, as if he were involuntarily tracing. "Damn it! A swimbo calls."

"What the hell is a swimbo?" Murdoch asked; they *both* ignored him.

The demon gazed down at Daniela as he began to fade. "Remember, ice maiden," he murmured intently, "my other offer still stands as well."

The vampire was in front of Desh in an instant. "Whatever you offered, she's not interested." But the demon was already gone.

Murdoch turned to her. "What was that?"

"I told you I might have to flirt to get some information. Now will you admit you're jealous, vampire?"

He surprised her by answering, "Yes." Just when she felt a flare of pleasure, he doused it by adding, "Though I'll be damned if I know why."

"You truly just said that?" She glared at the sky, imploring it for patience before facing him again. "Maybe because I'm cute and intelligent and I was in your bed last night, and because—oh, I don't know—I'm your Bride."

"What was the demon's offer?"

"That's between me and him."

"Is he your type, then? Really? You like behorned demons who growl *yar!* after every bloody sentence? I thought you'd be more discerning."

"And I thought you were supposed to be seductive and charming. You're just insulting, gruff, and brooding."

"With *you*." He took a step closer, frustration in his expression.

"What's that supposed to mean?"

"I don't know. I've never been jealous before. And I've never been clumsy with words around women." At that moment, a pair of name-tagged conventioneers ogled her, earning a killing look from Murdoch. When they hurried on, he said, "This is *not* my typical behavior." He exhaled. "And I can't control it."

He looked defeated, like he couldn't reason out this situation and might just stop trying. "Valkyrie, I've never been more at odds with myself in my entire existence."

She almost felt sorry for him, and gentled her tone. "Maybe I'm getting under your skin."

He muttered, "Like a thorn."

Danii was just contrary enough to be pleased by this. "Every thorn has its rose, vampire."

Eighteen

With that, the Valkyrie sauntered back up Bourbon, drawing slack-jawed stares from more men than he could bare his fangs at.

Murdoch followed, dimly aware that this might be the longest conversation he'd ever had with a woman.

The steady stream of them in his mortal life meant that he'd never had to spend a lot of time *talking* to any single female. In fact, he'd long felt as if he spoke two languages: one he used with men and the other with women.

The former was direct, used to convey information. The latter was laden with innuendo and flirtation, and consisted of little more than compliments.

With Daniela, he seemed to have forgotten the woman language. Maybe he was just out of practice. Didn't matter anyway, since she was having none of it, probably didn't even speak it.

When he caught up with her, he said, "Now we go to the store?"

She nodded. "It's back up Bourbon for a few wild and woolly blocks, then west a couple more."

Up ahead, the crowd had burgeoned as the night wore on. Each bar they passed had begun blaring its own style of music. "Then we have some time to kill. You might as well tell me what a swimbo is. And who's Nïx?"

"Might I?" she said, and that was *all* she said.

He took another tack. "Deshazior called you 'ice maiden.'"

"That's one of my names. Along with 'ice queen.' Which you like calling me when you're being unpleasant."

"You aren't . . . are you a virgin?"

She gazed away. "Why do you sound so dismayed by this?"

Because you were a virgin in my dream. "Because you've lived a long time. Surely in all those years, you've found one of your own species to be with."

"*Species*, Murdoch Suavé? Really?"

He could have phrased that better. But he was a shade shocked that he could be walking next to a two-thousand-year-old virgin. "Answer me. Has no man ever claimed you?"

"Only another within my own kind can touch me without hurting me. And yet they've been trying to kill me since I first left Valhalla," she said. "You put it together."

God, she's never known a man.

Whatever she saw in his expression made her glare. "Don't you dare pity me, Murdoch."

"Have you sought help for this . . . coldness?" he asked, squiring her well away from a performing fire breather.

"You make it sound like a condition! But, yes, for your information, I've gone to the House of Witches, to wizards, and even to the patron goddess of impossible things. So far, the best I've been offered were incomplete spells—like a hex that would prevent me from feeling pain, even though my skin would still burn, or vice versa."

"And the goddess?"

"She gave me a pair of bowling shoes."

"Bowling shoes?"

Suddenly plastic beads rained down on them, tossed by topless—

male and female—tourists on a balcony to their left. Without missing a beat, Daniela cast the strands to another group on a balcony directly to their right. "Yes, bowling couture. Don't ask me why."

"There's got to be a way, some other power in the Lore—"

"I've been to all the reliable, vetted mystical sources I know of. Unreliable sources would extract too high a penalty."

"What does that mean?"

"I could go to a Lore bazaar where magics are peddled, but would probably end up worse than I am."

"Worse off?"

"Magic dispensed by the wrong hands begs for cosmic justice, and it's usually in the form of a paradox. So if I hired some random practitioner for this, I might become touchable—by, for instance, growing scales. And then no one would *want* to touch me."

"I see." Fables held the same. Like the dying man who journeyed to a mystic for a cure, but perished in a freak accident on the way home.

"This is just something I have to live with," she finished with a shrug, as if she'd long since accepted this reality, but he sensed that nothing could be further from the truth. "I'm the one virgin you won't be adding to your collection."

"I've never had one before." But he longed to now. *To claim Daniela . . . to show her what sex can be like.*

To see that vulnerability in her eyes just as he entered her.

This plainly surprised her. "Am I supposed to believe that?"

"In my time, taking a virgin meant one risked a sword-point wedding." *Beget no bastards, deflower no maids.* As long as he'd followed those two simple rules, he'd always gotten to do as he pleased.

"I thought guys like you were forever on the hunt for the next rascally cherry to subdue."

"Women always think men bed virgins because of the conquest."

"You're saying that has nothing to do with it?"

"No. The conquest is definitely a part. But I believe the truth runs deeper: Men like virgins because women always remember their first lover. Men want to be remembered sexually."

"So if you didn't enjoy any virgins, did you not want to be remembered?"

He closed in on her, backing her up against the wall of a closed bistro. Resting his hand beside her head, he murmured, "I had no such fears or desires. I always knew I'd be remembered—not as the first, but as the *best.*"

In a clear attempt to disguise how curious she was, Daniela said, "And how does one get to be the best? I mean, aside from the obvious answer of *practice.*"

In his mortal life, he'd been considerate in bed. He'd made sure he brought great pleasure to every woman he'd been with. This wasn't out of selflessness. Quite the opposite. At an early age, he'd learned that the more word got around that he was a skilled lover, the more women dallied with him.

He'd had an agenda going into each encounter. He'd been painstaking, his actions measured—and he'd never, never lost control.

Now he inched closer to the Valkyrie. "I was generous with my attentions. And I was always in complete control of myself, able to go as long as I needed to go . . ."

"In order to be generous," she finished for him in a breathy voice. "You must have been devoted to women."

"I was." To *women*, yes, though never to one. "But that's not *all*. I—" He stopped.

"What? What were you going to say?"

"I don't want you to think . . ." He trailed off, running his fingers through his dark hair. "Damn it, I fought just as hard as my brothers in the war."

"Murdoch, sometimes history isn't kind—"

"I don't want *you* to believe that I shirked my duties. I dug in just as doggedly to protect our people. And I always came through when it counted. The only difference between me and my brothers is what we did in the downtime between conflicts. Sebastian spent his time reading, Conrad disappeared for reasons unknown, Nikolai paced his tent with the weight of the world on his shoulders. I was carefree...."

"And you enjoyed women," she said. "Why do you care what I think about you?"

Why? He had no good answer for that. *Because the blooding tells me to.* Everything he'd been thinking and feeling tonight was dictated by it.

That had to be what was happening to him. Or else he was a masochist about to get attached to a woman he could never touch.

Nineteen

"I'LL TELL YOU WHY IF YOU REVEAL THE DEMON'S OFFER TO YOU," Murdoch said.

"No, thanks, vampire, I gave you a surplus of information last night," Danii said tersely, still annoyed that he'd interrogated her.

"You did tell me much," he said. "But I believe little of it."

"Is that right?"

"You said you didn't eat."

She raised her brows.

"*Can* you?"

She shrugged. Valkyries *could*, but since they took nourishment from the electrical energy of the earth, they didn't need to. Besides, refraining from eating was a sort of inherent birth control. Her kind had no courses and were infertile unless they "ate of the earth."

"You told me you were two thousand years old," he said, keeping his gloved hand on her lower back—and keeping pedestrians *away*. Since he'd learned about the threat of thermal shock, he seemed to be continually checking on how warm she'd become, monitoring her to see if her breaths were smoking.

His attention was flattering, softening some of her anger. "Two thousand is roughly my age."

"And two of your *three* parents are gods?"

She gave him a pointedly blank expression, which she could tell irritated him.

"Then why would they let you get hurt?"

"Because they're asleep."

"Gods . . . sleep?"

"To conserve power. They derive strength from worshippers. And when was the last time you passed a temple dedicated to Freya?"

He deftly drew her out of the way when a full go-cup dropped from a balcony above, then said, "The one thing I believed without question? You told me that if you started kissing me"—his shoulders went back, cocky grin in place—"you didn't think you'd be able to stop."

Could he be any more handsome? Though her attraction to the vampire was wrong on so many levels, it remained as fierce as ever.

All night, Danii had been drawn to him. Not surprisingly. Every time she regarded those broad shoulders and steely gray eyes, she recalled their time in his bed. Whenever that lock of hair fell over his forehead, she'd just stopped herself from sighing.

Though she was an ice queen, acting coldly uninterested with him was becoming more difficult. And coldly uninterested was her shtick!

When he'd said he'd been the best lover . . . ? Gods help her, she'd *believed* him.

But she'd also been anxious about him possibly biting her. She didn't think she'd ever forget the look in his eyes this morning. "We'll never find out about the kissing, will we?"

His brows drew together, as if she'd uttered something monumental. "No. We won't, then. Ever." They walked on in awkward silence until she directed him off Bourbon.

"What's this store like?" he asked.

"It's owned by a purported voodoo priestess named Loa." Her very name meant *voodoo spirit.*

"Loa is a *female* shop owner?"

When Danii nodded, he perked up. And considering what Loa looked like, Danii mused that this might be a bad idea.

But Nïx often dropped by there, and even if Loa knew nothing—doubtful—any of her patrons might have information.

"Does she have powers?" he asked.

Just as they reached the shop, Danii drawled, "You have no idea."

On the door hung a sign with the universal symbol of the Lore, recognized by all Lorekind—except for the Forbearers. Beside it was a sticker with the word *Vampires* overlaid with a cross bar. Beneath that were the lines, *"No shirt, no soul, no service. We use UV protection."*

Murdoch frowned. "UV protection? Is that a joke?"

She shook her head. "It's candlelit inside, but along the ceiling are UV lights that can be turned on with a panic button—a fail-safe vampire security system." The Valkyries had wanted a similar setup for Val Hall, but their shrieks would just have shattered the bulbs.

As unabashed as ever, Murdoch shrugged and opened the door for Danii.

"Are you sure you want to go in?"

"You said the owner of this place is a woman? Well, I have a way with women. No panic buttons will be pushed tonight."

She rolled her eyes, then entered, with him closely following.

The front of the shop was a typical tacky tourist haunt, with preserved gator heads and fake gris-gris bags made in China.

But, like many of the Loreans in the Big Easy, Danii knew there was a back room. Inside those walls was everything from demon-size condoms and non-acetone horn polish to intoxispell hangover relief and ghoul blood remover.

As expected, candles lit the darkened shop, the bulbs above unused. For now. A lazy, old-fashioned fan buzzed softly, making the candle flames dance.

"Does that UV really work?" he asked with a glance at the ceiling.

"Oh, yeah. I was going to swap out the overhead light in your Porsche with one before I left town."

"Left New Orleans? Where are you going?"

Loa sauntered out from the back room, saving Danii from answering. As usual, the sight of Loa made Danii scowl. Gifted with flawless café-au-lait skin and a brick-house body, she spoke with a lilting island accent that men found sexy as hell.

Would Murdoch?

Tonight she was wearing an impeccably fitted red silk dress that highlighted her every abundant curve.

Murdoch gave Loa an appreciative glance, but so far he hadn't looked like a slavering cartoon wolf in a zoot suit.

Loa was an enigma. She'd come here—to a town filled with immortals at the most tumultuous time in the Lore—as if she wanted to be first in line for the unrest and war of the Accession.

When Loa had taken over the shop for her grandmother, Loa Senior, a voodoo high priestess, she'd assumed her new role almost *too* well.

Danii recalled telling her at her first open house, "There's something puzzling about this island vibe you've got going. Loa Senior told me her granddaughter was raised in a ritzy suburb outside Parsippany and graduated from Notre Dame. So how'd you get the Caribbean accent?"

Loa had narrowed her bright amber eyes and answered, "Loa Senior tells tales to impress a Valkyrie." Then she'd added under her breath, "Don't try to stuff me into one of your little mental boxes. I won't fit—any more than you would."

"Well, Valkyrie," she said now, making the word sound like *Vakree*. "Slumming with vampires, I see. If your sisters found out . . ."

"They won't. Because you won't tell them if you want to stay in business."

"What are you thinking, bringing a vampire into my shop? Can you not read the signs?"

Loa's attitude rankled. Her red, curve-hugging dress rankled.

"Probably not as well as you can, since I don't have a fancy college degree from Notre Dame."

Between gritted teeth, Loa said, "Damn you, I did not go to Notre Dame."

"Go Fighting Irish, rah-rah."

"I'm Murdoch Wroth, of the Forbearer order," the vampire interjected smoothly, extending his hand. Loa offered her own out of habit, then clearly thought better of it, but he'd already leaned down and kissed the back of it. "And you must be the *incomparable* Loa."

Could his deep voice be any sexier? It reminded Danii of how he'd sounded in bed this morning.

Loa gazed up at the vampire, looking a bit thunderstruck. "Murdoch Wroth? Aren't you one of the legendary Wroth brothers?"

"One and the same." He cast Danii a superior grin.

"If I recall, you were the wayward, bed-hopping one."

Danii thought a muscle ticked in his jaw, but he was all polished composure as he said, "Only when around women as lovely as you."

Loa actually tittered. "Well, I *suppose* if your eyes are clear, I could make an exception to my no-vampire rule."

"Thank you. It's a pleasure to meet such a beautiful proprietress."

I'm going to be sick. Except I don't eat.

"And I can hear that you've been blooded," Loa said. "Surely not by the ice maiden?"

"Yes, by her," he answered in a noncommittal tone.

Loa smiled. She should. Vampires simply didn't flirt like this once they'd been blooded. At least, not with anyone but their Brides.

"What a rogue this one is, ice maiden. You'll never tame him, child."

"Don't want to."

"So you won't mind if I put you two in Loa's betting book? The notorious rake blooded by the ice queen—but how long can her frozen clutches keep him from straying?"

Knowing Loa would do it regardless, Danii affected an uncon-cerned demeanor. "Knock yourself out." *Cold as a block of ice.*

"I suspect we'll soon be calling you the Forbearer's forsaken one—"

"Can we just get to what we came here for?" Danii interrupted sharply, her cold façade cracking.

"Ah, yes," Murdoch said. "Loa, have you heard any information about Ivo the Cruel?"

Loa turned to Danii. "Why ask me?"

"Ivo's in the city."

Her lips parted, her amber eyes excited, glowing in the candle-light. "Vampires overrunning us, Lykae hunting these very streets.... It's the Accession. Finally!"

"And you sound like you're *looking forward* to it?" Danii de-manded. "What? Do you want to have an Accession sale or some-thing?"

"Some people benefit. People like me."

"Alumni, rah?"

"Ladies." Murdoch seemed to find Danii's surly behavior amus-ing. If she were surly, it was only because the air was hot in here. Danii always got irritable when hot.

"This makes sense," Loa said. "I'd heard Lothaire is here, and he often travels with Ivo."

At the mention of Lothaire, Danii stifled a shudder. Ivo was an evil, sociopathic fiend, but he was at least manageable.

Lothaire, the Enemy of Old, was incomprehensible. No one knew what he wanted, and no one could predict what he'd do next.

"You know where they might be?" Danii asked.

"They're definitely staying in the area."

"How do you know?"

"Because Lothaire has been seen night after night," Loa replied. "There are kobolds camping in the sewers by the river. Ask some of them."

"I'll do that. Have you seen Nïx?"

"Aye, she came round and bought . . . She made a purchase. But I don't know where she went. Now, back to you, Murdoch." Loa leaned over the counter onto her elbows, displaying more cleavage than Danii could manage with a thousand water bras.

When he raised his brows in admiration, Danii stormed from the shop. "Going to make a call outside." She refused to watch any more of this. After Lafitte's, she'd gotten her hopes up about the vampire, again, only to have them dashed now. *Do I need to see a neon sign flashing* THIS GUY'S A PLAYER?

"*Directly* outside, Daniela," he ordered, surprising her that he'd even been aware she was leaving—and making her bristle at his commanding tone.

On the street, fog from the river was stealing over the Quarter, wrapping it in haze. She took a deep breath of low-tide air to calm herself and debated ringing up Nïx. Usually calls were reserved for emergencies, because you never knew when a Valkyrie might need silence for stalking something.

Deciding this was an emergency, Danii pulled her sat-phone from her satchel, then dialed Nïx's number.

And heard Nïx's Crazy Frog ring tone going off in the next alley over.

TWENTY

"I AM ASTONISHED SHE'S EVEN TALKING TO YOU," Loa said after Daniela had walked out, her tone turning decidedly neutral.

Murdoch narrowed his eyes. She'd been flirting for the Valkyrie's benefit? "Why give Daniela such a hard time?"

"Ooh, the vampire doesn't like Loa toying with his Bride."

"Answer me."

"Because she wants to be treated like other Valkyrie, and that's how I treat them," the priestess said. "Want some advice?" When he grudgingly nodded, she said, "Watch for her claws curling, vampire. In a Valkyrie, that means she needs a male to sink them into."

Daniela, with her claws sunk in my back as I took her—

"Oh, and here. These are on sale," Loa said as she bent down behind the counter. "For the ice maiden." She tossed him a pair of gloves. "Tell her I said to handle you with care. . . ."

When Murdoch left Loa's, he wore a victorious grin. He'd purchased the gloves and had garnered a secret about the Valkyrie that could be very helpful to him.

But by the time Murdoch emerged to the now foggy street, Daniela was gone.

He started back toward the main thoroughfare. After several moments, he spied Lukyan at a distance, still intently prowling the streets for Ivo. The Cossack always seemed to be devoid of fear, almost as if he had a death wish. Vigilant Rurik traced on the roofs above him.

Yet there was no sign of Daniela.

Danii rushed to the sound, peering down the stygian alley. Finally, she spotted the soothsayer, talking to some figure in the shadows.

"Nïx!" By the time Danii reached her, the figure had hastened away. "Who were you talking to?"

"Hmmm?" Nïx's raven-black hair was wild, her golden eyes vacant as usual—she often saw the future more clearly than the present—but she also looked frazzled and tired. Though she wore an immaculate white dress, her hands were filthy.

"And why are you so dirty?" Danii asked her.

"*I'm* dirty? You're the one getting busy with a leech. You naughty, freaky minx."

"Answer the question," Danii gritted out. "Who was that?"

"Who was who?"

Typical Nïx—she could be playing innocent, or she truly could have forgotten who she'd just been talking to seconds before. "What are you doing here?"

She blinked at Danii. "Laying low like po-po?" At Danii's glare, Nïx's mien turned playful. "Trolling for some strange! No? Composing a tweet?"

"Nïx, are you following me?"

"Do I need to be?"

Danii inhaled for patience. "I was looking for you. I need to tell you about—"

"Myst. Don't concern yourself. She's taken care of. As for your next question, you should go somewhere that is not here." She gazed around as if they might be overheard, then loudly whispered, "There are dempires about."

"*Dempires?*" Danii had never, in her long life, heard the term.

"And Lykae all around as well." Nïx jerked her chin in the direction of the main drag.

Danii glanced over and spotted three Lykae walking by, twins and one more. All of them were striking examples of heart throbbing maleness, but then, Lykae often were.

Now they stopped, turned toward Danii and Nïx, and sniffed the air. All three tensed with awareness of other Loreans. A standoff. Danii drew ice into her palm.

Then Nïx wiggled her dirty fingers, beckoning them. Looking scarily crazed with her wild hair and unsettling eyes, she cooed, "Come, puppies. Come meet Destiny." Out of the corner of her mouth, Nïx stage-whispered, "Destiny is my fist's name."

When the trio spoke in Gaelic, and carried on, Nïx chuckled.

"What? What'd they say?"

"That we weren't worth the bother. That you're the frigid one and I'm crazy. Seems they've got our numbers!"

The frigid one. Lowly Lykae thought of her like that? *My ego's on life support. Prognosis grim.*

"We're eventually going to be allies with them, you know," Nïx said dimly. "In-laws, even."

Danii snorted. The Valkyrie considered the Lykae little better than animals. "You're joking, right?"

"Would I joke about something like this?"

"Emphatically, yes. Now tell me, why did you predict I'd get fixed last night?"

"I said you *might.* Look at the upside: you got to enjoy a male who wasn't an Icere bounty hunter and who didn't have designs to murder you. At least, not until he got peckish."

"Would Murdoch have hurt me? *Will* he?"

Nïx tilted her head in the direction of Loa's shop. "I used to be able to read him as easily as his brothers, like open books. But now

I get little on him. I just see that you've got him confounded, not knowing up from down anymore. At three hundred years old, he'd thought he was quit of uncertainty like this."

"Wait, you said *brothers*? Does more than one live?"

"You'd better get back to the vampire, he's about to spot—"

"Daniela!" Murdoch's voice boomed down the alley.

Danii glanced over her shoulder at him, then back, but Nïx had already vanished. *Damn it.* She swiftly hit redial on her phone, yet all was silence.

When Murdoch reached her, Danii saw genuine concern on his face. "Why did you leave?"

She hiked her shoulders. "I thought you'd be longer in there."

"Now who's jealous?"

"Hardly."

"I just wanted to prove that I'm not gruff and brooding," he said. "Or that I only am with you. And besides, I was just flirting to get information." When she still glared, he said, "Admit it, you were jealous."

"No, I'm *embarrassed*. Because everyone would expect you to be possessive and intent only on me. They're going to see this as a failing in *me*."

"You said the blooding didn't make one want his Bride."

"No, not if the Bride or mate or whatever was objectionable. But am I really that objectionable?"

His brows drew together. "You truly can't understand any hesitation on my part?"

He was making her feel like more of a freak than anyone had in two thousand years.

But that was a lie. There'd been the Roman. . . .

"Vampire, I think you're afraid to settle down—with anyone. You were single for years and celibate for three hundred more. And now you have bachelor's panic."

"I don't even know what you're talking about."

"BP? It's when a man irrationally fears a woman he especially likes. He gets *ascared* of said woman's toothbrush breaching the perimeter of his man cave, et cetera."

"Panic? I don't panic," he sneered the word. "Daniela, you can't be touched."

The frigid one. Enough of this. "No, you can't! Your heart's colder than mine. *You* are the untouchable one."

She turned from him, wanting away from this vampire with his unflinching honesty. Because it . . . hurt. *The life I have inside my head . . .*

Murdoch followed her. "Just because I'm not ready to blindly accept a Bride I hardly know—for eternity—makes me coldhearted? I'd say it makes me rational."

"Oh, so maybe it's not me, it's you? Make up your mind!"

"Even if you were all things perfect for me, I would resent this situation. The Forbearers have learned to fear bloodlust because it makes vampires crazed and out of control. But so does the blooding! Yet we're supposed to welcome it?" He hastened in front of her, blocking her way. "It's making me behave in ways I normally wouldn't. Would you wish this for yourself? To have your personality completely rewritten?"

"If I had your personality? Ab-so-lutely. Because here's the thing—you're not special anymore. You're not unique in the Lore. You're a leech who used to have it easy getting laid. And now, you're just *predictable.*"

He advanced on her until she backed up against the wall of a building. "Just a manwhore, huh?" They were in each other's faces, her breaths smoking between them.

"That really bothers you?" They were fighting—she needed to stop glancing at his lips.

"Shouldn't it?"

When his gaze dropped to her breasts, transfixed as she panted, she demanded, "*What?* What do you want from me?"

He faced her with his eyes narrowed, turning that fierce obsidian color. "The same thing I wanted this morning." His voice grew husky. "To stop fighting with you and start kissing you."

She swayed on her feet. He'd wanted that? "But you can't."

He shook his head. "I can't smooth my fingers over the inside of your wrist." With his gloved hand, he lifted her hair. "I can't run my lips over your neck . . . or suckle your breasts. And it's driving me mad."

He eased his body even closer to hers, resting his forearms against the wall on either side of her head. His mouth was right at her ear as he asked, "Am I too close? Does this hurt you?"

She felt his erection press against her belly and choked back a moan. "No, no. . . . But how do I know you won't bite me?"

"I won't. I swear it."

Just when she perceived his hips drawing back, and she knew he was about to thrust against her body, her ears twitched.

She shoved him away. "We've got company."

Daniela had spotted something. "Grab that one!" she cried, pointing in the direction of a garbage heap down the alley.

Murdoch spied a gray-haired gnomelike being with a miniature cane and traced forward like a shot. But the creature was fast, scurrying from him. It took several minutes of cat-and-mouse before Murdoch caught it by the collar, lifting it up.

The little thing had red cheeks and a kindly appearance, but looked terrified.

"That's it!" Daniela called from a distance, hastening to catch up. "Now smack it around!"

He glanced back at her. "*Smack* it?"

Once she reached them, she jerked her chin at the gnome. When Murdoch turned back, it was twisting around to take a bite of his arm. Murdoch gave it a shake, and for the briefest instant, he thought he saw a reptilian-like visage flicker over its face. "Christ! What is this?"

"Can't tell him, Lady Daniela?" it said. "He's a Forbearer leech. But you might tell all if you became a vampire's whore, like the Coveted One? How far you Valkyrie fall!"

Daniela strode forward and slapped it, stifling a wince at the contact.

The creature growled, then locked its eyes on Murdoch. "What are you doing with a cold bitch like this one?" it asked, becoming the first being to question why *Murdoch* was with *her.*

Now Murdoch cuffed it.

"Where is Ivo the Cruel, kobold?" Daniela asked.

Kobold? As Loa had spoken of.

"Why should I tell you?"

She lowered her voice, looking sinister when she said, "Because if you don't, I'm going to freeze you solid, then chip away your flesh with your own little cane."

The kobold swallowed. "I-I might have seen Ivo and Lothaire about earlier."

"Where are they staying?"

When it hesitated, Murdoch gave it another violent shake.

"Outside the parish! In the bayou. Near Val Hall."

"Near Val Hall?" Daniela repeated in amazement. "Have they no fear?"

"They're *different,*" the kobold said. "You can't fight them." The same thing Deshazior had told them.

"How do you know this?" she asked.

"Heard it from a rat demon who heard it from one of the crocodilae shifters. That's all I know—vow it to the Lore!"

"Toss him," Daniela said. "Hard."

Murdoch flung the kobold back into the garbage heap, and it skulked away with a gurgling hiss.

"Okay, vampire, you have plenty to go on now," she said, still catching her breath from her earlier sprint. "Dawn's only a couple of hours away, so I think this is where we . . ." She trailed off when she saw him frowning at her. "What?"

"Are you hot?"

"No, I'll manage," she said, but her skin was reddened, her face pinched.

He swallowed. "Daniela, your breaths aren't smoking."

TWENTY-ONE

THE VAMPIRE STARED DOWN AT HER WITH ALARMED EYES.

"I'll be fine," she assured him, but she was still hot from the night before and had exerted herself too much keeping up with Murdoch's chase. "It's . . . nothing." *If she could get back to the meat locker quickly enough. How many blocks is it to my car—*

He grabbed her hand. "What are you doing?" she demanded.

"You'll see."

Suddenly she was in a cold, dark room. *He traced me?* She'd never been traced when she was fully cognizant, and it made her dizzy, as if she'd just stepped off a pitching ship. She warily darted her eyes around them.

The heat and sounds of New Orleans were gone. She and the vampire now stood in what looked like an old-fashioned drawing room with sheet-draped furniture. Extensive marble floors conducted the chill until it seeped right into her bones. *Delicious.* "Where have you taken me?"

"A hunting lodge in Siberia."

"Siberia?" The very word connoted cold and made her toes curl with pleasure. "Why?"

"You were getting hot."

"It happens, you know. You didn't have to trace me out of Louisiana." She started toward one of the soaring windows, taking in details as she crossed the spacious interior.

She could tell that Murdoch wasn't actively living here, but the lodge was clean and in good repair. It was also *opulent*, with gilt walls and moldings inlaid with gems. Elaborate wood carvings adorned the doorways and the great hearth.

This place was a time capsule, like a tsar's hideaway preserved from hundreds of years ago. At the window, she gazed out, then inhaled sharply at the night scene.

"If you'd rather go . . ." he said from behind her.

Snow. Everywhere. Danii adored monochromatic landscapes, and here white fluff blanketed the grounds—as it *should*. "Is this property yours?"

"Yes, it's one of my war spoils."

Then this was a kindness, bringing her here. Maybe he'd been right before—maybe when it really counted, he came through. "There are so many trees," she said. Copses around the lodge led to the dense forest beyond. They were all coated with ice, their branches ponderous with it.

"Larch trees," he said. "One of the few kinds that will grow here."

In front of the manor, a lake lay frozen and glazed, reflecting the blue aurora borealis above. *Stunning*. Without tearing her gaze away, she asked, "You've kept this since the war?"

"Surprisingly, there's not a large market for Siberian hunting lodges. I know, I scarcely understand it myself."

Her lips curled.

"My brothers and I divided anything we won. Nikolai needed no residence, because he would have Blachmount, the family manor. This property lay in the middle of nowhere, with lands all the way to the Arctic Ocean, yet the lodge was incongruously lavish. I wanted it," he ended with a shrug.

"Why is it so lavish?"

"It belonged to a baron. He owned a nearby diamond mine."

"Do you ever stay here?"

"Sometimes I come here to hunt in the winter," he said. "Lots of game, since we're at the edge of continuous permafrost. It stays frozen almost year-round, only thaws for a month or two in the summer."

She could tell he was already feeling the cold, though as an immortal, he could withstand some seriously harsh elements. The temperature here was getting to her as well, *invigorating* her, even as she felt herself relaxing from the stresses of the night.

Here there was no threat from the Icere. Or the vampire. For hours, she'd been both attracted to him yet fearful at the same time, but no longer.

He wouldn't be able to bite her here. She'd be too powerful.

"I haven't seen snow in decades." Were those sideways icicles? Her heart sang—that meant some formidable storms blew here. "I can have ice, but never snow."

"You could visit cold climes."

"I'd almost rather not," she said. "Since it would be too hard to return."

"But now you *can't* return. You were leaving New Orleans tonight for good, weren't you?"

"My suitcases are in my car," she admitted, her mind working. Murdoch had taken her to the vastness of Siberia, which spanned a third of the northern hemisphere. She couldn't find a better place to disappear. Tracing vampires couldn't be followed. There'd be no travel arrangements for Icere assassins to unearth. No airports where she might run into Sigmund's spies.

And more, something about this place called to her. Breathing deeply of the crisp air, she said, "It's so lovely here." With the natural cold permeating every cell in her body, she felt better than she had in memory. She grew more confident, brazen even. At that moment, she decided that he didn't appreciate his Siberian paradise as much as he should. She would do a far better job of treasuring it.

Danii would be *staying*.

Now she just had to convince him. Should she prove unmoving and intractable as a glacier? Or should she dazzle him like a rare frost flower?

When she faced him, the look in his eyes made her decision easy. His gray irises were flickering with black, his mien showing hints of that possessiveness she'd detected earlier this eve.

I'll show him frigid. . . . "You know, vampire, nothing feels quite so decadent as snow against my bare skin," she murmured, slipping off her satchel. "And ice can be a wicked pleasure. If I'm . . . naked."

As she began unlacing her dress, he swallowed audibly. She could see his shaft thickening in his slacks. "You're getting hard. But then, you don't need me for that anymore."

He drew closer to her. "Maybe I want you for it. I'm hard—*for you.*"

"Maybe you should have thought about that before you treated me so badly."

Again, he denied nothing, just gave a sharp nod.

"But perhaps there's a way you can make it up to me."

"Let's hear it."

She tilted her head. "Murdoch, do you spook easily?"

"I haven't been known to. . . ." He trailed off when she turned to the door, heading outside into the night, stripping as she went.

TWENTY-TWO

ALL THOUGHTS OF *I LEAD AND WOMEN FOLLOW* vanished when he tripped outside after her.

As her delighted laughter sounded in the distance, he realized he couldn't remember the last time he'd felt this much excitement.

Christ, when she'd begun removing her skimpy dress . . . exhilaration had spiked in him, not to mention arousal.

He was so very rarely surprised by women. Now he had no idea what she'd do next.

Soon he came upon her little boots, kicked off in the snow, and he gave a low groan. *Will she strip completely?* Each second, his shaft was getting hotter, even as the temperature dropped.

A dozen feet farther on, he saw her discarded dress. He scooped it up, bringing it to his face to inhale her cool scent. His heart—which had begun beating for her alone—was thundering.

When he reached her, she was lying back in a snowdrift, stretching with her arms above her head—in nothing more than a wisp of black silk panties. Her perfect breasts were uncovered, her nipples so stiff they looked like they ached.

His fingers went limp and he dropped her dress, hissing, "*Almighty.*"

She laughed anew at his reaction. Not surprisingly, she had a musical laugh.

His jaw clenched. *Where's my control now?* Seconds before, he'd found himself thinking, *I'd follow her anywhere.* "No compunction about being stripped in front of me?"

"Never. Besides, you've seen every inch of me." She seemed drunk from the snow, shoveling her fingers through it, bringing handfuls up to her lips to kiss.

He turned away from her, disconcerted by how much she affected him, by how her laughter seemed to make something twist in his chest. Determined not to even glance at her until he regained some equilibrium, he sat back against a frost-coated tree trunk.

"You're angry with me, vampire?" She was walking on her knees toward him.

Don't look at her. His hands were fists by his sides. "Not angry." *Bloody confused, exasperated.* "No, I'm—" He broke off when she was kneeling inches before him. In a strangled voice, he said, "What the hell is happening to you?"

Here in the cold, her appearance had begun to change. She was *transforming.*

Her hair had become laced with ice and lighter in color, so blond it was almost white. Shining tendrils were frozen in long streams, descending to cover her breasts or spreading out from her head as though whipped in the wind.

Her lashes were tipped with ice crystals, and more crystals formed semicircles around her eyes. Her lips were pale, bluish even, and were parted, but no smoke came from her breaths. Because they were freezing as well.

Delicate cobalt blue tracings swirled around her wrists in wispy patterns. Her eyes were bright beneath the aurora, a fiery blue matching that in the sky. They burned with an *ancient knowledge.*

Everything about this moment with her should feel foreign. But it . . . didn't. *I've dreamed of this.* Would she think him mad if he told her he'd seen her like this in a vision?

He'd been hard for her before, but now he was throbbing. These changes attracted him fiercely. He feared he could go off right in his pants. *No, I never lose control.*

Keep telling yourself that, Murdoch.

"You like?" she murmured.

"What is this?"

"This is how I'm supposed to look. And how I'm supposed to feel."

The cold clearly aroused her. His greedy gaze took in her shallow breaths, her trembling lithe body. Her little claws had turned blue and were curling sharply.

I know what that means now. At the thought of her sinking those claws into his back as he plunged inside her, he had to stifle a groan.

Behind her, lightning speared through the aurora. "The lightning is *yours.*" He was surprised his voice was steady. Her gaze was mesmerizing.

She nodded. "Valkyrie give it off with emotion."

"I dreamed of you like this, Daniela." *Connection.*

When she cast him a doubting expression, he said, "Don't believe me? Those lines of blue trace along your lower back as well."

Her eyes widened. "What else did you dream?"

"I took your virginity," he blurted out.

She shivered. "And how did I react?"

"You wanted me to. You wanted . . . me." *You let me take your neck.* His eyes fixed on her supple flesh, and his fangs ached for her. He raked his tongue along one of them for a shot of blood, pretended it was hers.

"Come closer, vampire."

In a flash, he was up on his knees before her.

Without removing his coat, she began unbuttoning the shirt underneath, spreading the edges. "Will you be too cold?"

"I can take it."

Once his chest was bared, she drew closer until her lips were less than an inch away from him. She eased down his torso like this, her breaths like little bites of frost, as if she were running an ice cube along his skin. He shivered—but not from cold.

As she made her way back up, she said, "Murdoch?"

"Uh?" was all he could manage.

She leaned up to whisper right at his ear, "You're going to let me stay in this place." When she nipped his earlobe with her teeth, his cock jerked in his pants, his sac tightening.

Wait, what had she just said?

She moved to his other ear. "Would you like to do that?" she breathed, making him shudder with want. "I'm going to install my-self—a female—in one of your properties. And I'm going to deco-rate it as I see fit."

Can't . . . form . . . words.

"You want me to, don't you?" She slowly gazed up, looking at him from under a lock of shining, icy hair. She nibbled her plump lip, and he was finished, defeated. He watched, bewildered, as his gloved fingertips traced the crystals at her temple.

"Yes." *I can't believe I'm saying this.* "You can stay." He'd always wanted to discard females—not move them into his home.

He was dimly aware that the seducer was being seduced. The player had just gotten played.

Yet he was still in the game. "You'll stay here. But first we need to seal this deal, Valkyrie. And I know just how."

"Oh?"

He took out the gloves Loa had given him. "Put these on."

TWENTY-THREE

HE BOUGHT ME GLOVES? "What did you have in mind?" Danii asked as she gamely drew them on. For the first time in ages, she felt powerful. The ability to bring this massive warrior to his knees was heady.

"You'll see." His voice was rough with need, his expression one of single-minded intent.

With each second, she grew more aroused for him. Yet then the wind came up, and the snow-covered limbs raked the drafts. They soughed like music, like secrets. The sounds, the scents, teased her. Something within the dark depths of that cold beckoned. . . .

"Daniela?"

Murdoch competed with the pull. She faced him once more, gazing up into eyes grown black with desire.

Anticipation. Danii felt it, was getting caught up in it.

When he took a lock of her hair and used a curl to stroke her nipple, she gave a cry and arched her back. The cold amplified every whisper of touch—she needed more. "Put your hands on me, vampire."

He groaned, covering both of her breasts with his gloved palms, molding them, cupping as she panted. With a master's skill, he tormented the tips, puckering one, then the other. Once he'd made them throb, he placed a hand flat against her chest, pressing her back.

As she stretched out in the snow, he curled his fingers in her panties, dragging them from her. Yet then he merely gazed over her naked body for long moments, his shaft bulging.

She reached forward, stroking his erection through his pants as his head fell back. Eager to use her gloves, she murmured, "Take it out, Murdoch."

"It will freeze," he said, facing her.

"If it did, then I could suckle you at my leisure."

He groaned. "Would you?"

"For hours. But for now, I'll be sure to rub you really fast, keep it warm with friction."

With a hard shake of his head, he set her hand away. "I want to see you come first. When you're like this. Want to see your face," he said, moving to kneel between her legs. "Daniela, put your arms over your head. Part your thighs for me."

Following his commands, she eased her arms back, then spread her legs.

"That's it," he rasped, his gaze riveted to her sex. He might as well have been petting her there, because her body responded.

When he licked his lips, looking desperate to taste her, her hips rolled. *What would his kiss be like?* Would he be gentle with her? Or ravenous . . . ?

"Wider," he grated, and she let her knees fall open. With a harsh groan, he lowered his head to run his face alongside her thigh, never touching her. But she could feel his breath, making her tremble.

Over and over his breaths trailed up and down her thighs as his gloved hands fondled her breasts. She was shameless, undulating for his mouth, nearly ready to endure the burn just for a brief touch of his tongue.

"I want to kiss you so much." His mouth was an inch from her sex, his fogging breaths tickling her clitoris. "Spread you before me and lick you till you scream for me."

"Murdoch," she moaned. "I can't take much more of this."

"Do you want me to make you come?" he asked, leaning up.

"Yes!"

"You told me the ice feels wicked against your skin." He reached to his side and plucked a long, thick icicle from a twig. "Were you hinting to me?"

His eyes were dark and fierce. Hers went wide. Ah, gods, did he plan to touch her with that?

She held her breath . . . until he grazed the smooth end over her cheek, making her shiver.

"It doesn't melt against your skin," he murmured, seeming fascinated as he traced it lower to her parted lips.

With her gaze holding his, her tongue darted out to lick the tip just before she sucked the phallus-shaped ice between her lips.

A strangled sound broke from his chest. *Heady power.*

When she relinquished it with a last darting lick, he skimmed it down her chest to the beginning swell of her breasts. They were heaving with excitement, her nipples begging for attention.

With the ice, he circled one taut peak, then the other, until her back was arching up to meet each frozen caress. *So sensual, so perfect.* "Yes, Murdoch . . . clever vampire." Now he was using his mind, delighting her by taking her here, pleasuring her body with the ice.

She swallowed when he trailed it along her torso, past her navel. He repeatedly teased it just above her curls, making her undulate for it, sometimes holding it just out of reach to play with her. "Do you want this?"

"Yes!"

"How badly?" He smoothed the edge of the ice down until it was just against her aching clitoris.

"Please, please . . ." When he began lazily rolling it over the bud, she gasped, then moaned low.

"My female likes this." His smoldering gaze was rapt on his ministrations.

"Ah, gods, yes!" Again and again, he worked it back and forth, sending her closer each time. Between ragged breaths, she said, "More, Murdoch."

He skimmed her slick opening, making her cry out with bliss. Lightning streaked across the sky.

Their gazes met; his held a question. "Yes, do it! Inside me . . ."

Then . . . he slipped it into her wetness. She arched her back, moaning with abandon. *Cold. Exquisite.*

Emboldened by her response, he began languidly thrusting the phallus inside her sheath.

Her gloved hands dug into the snow, her head thrashing. She'd never been brought to come by another.

I'm about to be.

He'd meant to tease her. To send her out of her mind with pleasure.

But now *his* mind was in turmoil, his shaft rampant in his pants, about to erupt.

"Don't stop . . ." When she rolled up her hips to drive the ice deeper, his own hips bucked uncontrollably in response.

Sex. Want sex. Want to plunge hard into her. He needed to replace the ice with his cock so badly he thought he'd go mad.

"*Murdoch,*" she moaned. "I'm coming!" As she climaxed, her body writhed in a wanton display—and he felt the beginning tremors in his shaft.

Her cries made him frenzied. Now, for the first time, this encounter wouldn't be about building his reputation so he could secure pleasure for himself.

This was going to be rough and unplanned and dirty. Because he was about to spill in his pants.

As soon as she pushed his hand away, spent, he said, "You're going to make me come, Bride." He tore open his zipper, took his cock in hand, and almost went off. He had to squeeze down tight on the head to stop his seed. "Do you want to?"

She breathed, "Oh, yes."

"Then stroke it." He didn't recognize his own snarling voice.

As he held on to the head, she cupped the shaft in her fingers, running her fist up and back.

"Ah, God, again!"

On her second stroke, he widened his knees, thrusting up to her grip. His balls drew tight, readying, swelling. *"That's it. . . ."*

On the third stroke, he removed his hand.

At once, he began ejaculating in her fist, the crown of his cock steaming with hot seed. *So fucking good . . . feels . . .* A brutal groan broke from his chest as he watched her milking him steadily, pumping his semen out into the snow, again and again.

Once she'd wrung him dry, he collapsed onto his back, hurriedly tucking his rapidly cooling shaft back in his pants.

Unable to help himself, he turned on his side to stare at her. Daniela the Ice Maiden had so much fire . . .

A man could get burned.

If I'm not wary, I'm going to become dangerously obsessed with a woman.

He'd bragged to her that sexually he'd been able to last as long as he pleased—because he always had been. Yet within hours of his boast, he'd almost come in his pants. He'd told her that he never lost control—she'd made him *totally fucking lose control.*

She was smiling, glancing up from under her icy lashes. "You should probably go get my things before dawn breaks in New Orleans. I left two suitcases in my car. It's a red X6, parked near the corner of Dauphine and St. Philip." She had that optimistic air about her again, her eyes glittering like the crystals on her face.

Her expression reminded him of the hopeful one she'd evinced their first morning together. He stiffened, reacting to it as poorly as he had then.

She noticed his sudden tension. "Murdoch, we had an agreement."

How did she turn this around on me? He felt like scratching his head in bafflement. *I control situations with women.* "And how are you to stay here?"

"You know I don't eat. I don't need or want heat. This is ideal for my needs," she said, her tone growing absent. She seemed distracted, her gaze fixed on the drifts in the distance.

"Fine, suit yourself." He stood, buttoning his shirt. "Though I don't know when you think I'll be able to return."

She blinked up at him. He thought he spied a brief flash of hurt in her eyes, but it vanished so swiftly he decided he imagined it— especially when she said, "Vampire, after you fetch my stuff, I'm not asking you to return at all."

With a scowl, he traced back to the Quarter and found her car just where she'd said it'd be. He traced inside to grab her bags.

Back out on the street, holding two suitcases, he thought to himself: *My God, what have I done?*

TWENTY-FOUR

WHILE HE WENT TO COLLECT HER THINGS, Danii slipped on her dress, then explored her new hideout.

Murdoch had modernized the lodge to a degree. There was running water, lighting, plumbing, and a fairly new generator. She found bedding and towels.

In every spacious room, the timeless sculptures, decorations, and brickwork had proved impervious to cold. Which meant this place was perfect for her. She was a nester. Her star sign decreed nesting, and she was helpless to resist.

The first thing it needed was . . . ice.

When he returned with her bags, Murdoch gruffly showed her to a guest room, acting like he'd made a huge concession by letting her stay. But he also appeared a bit wild-eyed as he glanced from her to the suitcases and back. She supposed BP would be worse in him since he'd been single for so long.

"Do you have something in your bags to write my number on?" he asked her.

"Yes, but you can just tell me. I'll remember."

As soon as he uttered the last of the digits, he hastily said, "But keep in mind that I'll be *extremely* busy following our leads and hunting Ivo."

She gave him her best ice queen impression. "Of course, I understand." But did she? If she were honest, she would acknowledge that deep down, she'd hoped to convince him to stay here with her.

Which regrettably hadn't panned out. But no matter what, she still had this prime place of safety to hide out for a time—and that's what really counted. If he didn't want to experience more of the exquisite pleasure they'd just shared, then it was his loss.

Which means it's mine as well—

"Good bye, then," he said, tracing away before she could say anything else.

Once she was alone, she gave a casual shrug as if she wasn't hurt. But fooling him was easier than fooling herself. Ignoring the pang in her heart, she proceeded to decorate, figuring it would be many days before she saw him again. . . .

Hours later, she lay on the stripped bed in the master room, eschewing the smaller chamber he'd stuck her in. A delightfully chill wind blew, rushing in through the outer doors and windows—which she'd opened to the freezing night.

She was fatigued from her labors, but pleased with her progress. Icicles embellished all the woodwork and doorways, and ice sheets covered each of the walls.

Yet then she frowned. The glazed walls looked faceless, the flawless ice seeming barren to her.

Those unbroken sheets bothered her, like an off smell or a discordant sound would. And the irritation was sharp, as strong as the pull she'd been feeling to this place.

She rose and crossed to the bedroom window, looking at the dark woods surrounding the lodge, then back inside at the walls. Out, then in. *Wrong.*

Unable to stand it any longer, she fashioned a spear of ice, galvanizing it with layer after layer, honing it.

Once finished, she took her makeshift chisel to the wall, stabbing the glaze. Then again. And again, until peculiar markings began to take shape.

Murdoch would *not* return to Siberia. *I've made it seven days, I can make it seven more.*

He'd finished chasing his leads for the night, and dawn was approaching—Lukyan and Rurik had already returned to Mount Oblak.

But it would be dark in Siberia.

Lulls in action were dangerous for Murdoch. They made the temptation to return to Daniela harder to resist.

No, he *refused*. Because of the blooding, he was just supposed to succumb? To tolerate this total loss of power? Welcome a complete personality rewrite?

He was determined not to go to her like some lovesick lad, especially since she obviously couldn't have cared less when he'd been about to leave that last night. And she hadn't called him once.

Part of him resented how easily she'd manipulated him. Another part resented her encroachment. But that didn't mean he had bachelor's panic, as she'd accused—which, he'd noted, handily placed all the blame on him for this, while ignoring the difficulties she presented as a Bride.

In any case, if a woman's toothbrush was this age's symbol of female encroachment, try two stuffed suitcases.

So for the last week, he'd kept himself occupied, endeavoring not to think of her at all. With Lukyan and Rurik, he'd been following the leads she'd helped generate, closing in on Ivo with each one. He'd tried repeatedly to see Nikolai, but his brother was usually . . . engaged with Myst.

During this time, Murdoch went to bed exhausted every day, hoping that he wouldn't dream of Daniela. But he always did. And each time, that strange voice asked: *What would you sacrifice? What would you do for her?*

He glanced at the lightening sky once more, feeling nearly powerless not to return to her, to check on how she was settling in, to see if he'd imagined the blue of her eyes or her crisp, clean scent.

In his homeland, the fall came with a pounding rain, scouring the countryside. Then one morning the rain would be gone, and they would wake to a white landscape. The air would be briskly clean, carrying the slight tang of the nearby northern seas.

Daniela smelled like those rare mornings. The ones he had never forgotten.

Wait—maybe she hadn't been able to recall his number. What if she'd wanted to contact him but couldn't? He should go just to check on her. Yes, to make sure she had everything she needed. He traced back to the lodge.

Murdoch's jaw went slack at the scene that greeted him.

The windows were all open and ice was . . . everywhere. She'd spun it all over the manor like a spider spins a web.

He'd been raised on the Baltic in the seventeen hundreds. Keeping a home warm had been paramount. Yet now ice arched in the doorways, rounding out the square doorjambs. Icicles dangled from the ceiling and descended from the windows like curtains. The walls were covered in a white glaze, and she'd carved primitive-looking symbols into the ice.

She had no right. Bachelors panicked over a toothbrush? Try having an otherworldly *female* leave a permanent ice storm in one's *hunting lodge.*

Who *wouldn't* panic?

And she was nowhere to be found. As he stalked from one empty room to the next, the level of disappointment he felt both staggered and perplexed him.

When he reached his bedroom, he saw that she'd been sleeping there—she'd stripped the bed of all its blankets. Why would she stay here and not in the room where he'd initially put her bags?

She's been sleeping in my bed? That knowledge did something to him, touching some dark, primal drive within him. The thought of keeping his female protected within his property, in a stronghold won by his sword . . . *aroused* him.

Sleeping in my *bed.*

He gave himself a shake, then turned to one of her unpacked suitcases, finding a couple of erotic novels with titles that had him raising his brows and a collection of lingerie he'd be imagining on her for years to come. He picked up one of her silk nightgowns, inhaling her scent.

Not surprising, he grew hard as rock. But his fangs also sharpened. Why was she the only one who tempted him to drink from the flesh? He'd never been tempted before her and hadn't had the slightest urge all week until now.

Setting the gown away, he opened the second bag. It was filled with containers of *salt*. What could she need so much of it for?

He crossed to the dresser. Atop it sat her sat-phone, which he checked in case she'd been unable to contact him. Not a chance—fully charged, the ringer muted, the screen displaying numerous missed calls. He scrolled through her contacts, finding his number saved as VAMP PHONE. She'd could've called, but hadn't.

Tethered to the phone was a rugged-looking laptop, apparently ice-proof. At times, the world of the Lore proved boggling for him; the idea of internet capability in this lodge ranked right up there with the notion of an otherworldly ice being inhabiting it.

Once he entered the bathroom, he discovered what she used the salt for. A container was opened beside the old fashioned bathing tub. Daniela needed salt so she wouldn't *freeze her bathwater.* He dimly thought, *No wonder she smells like the sea.*

This was too bizarre to be believed. . . .

The north wind gusted through the window, blowing snow inside. Without thought, he rushed forward to close the window, but it was frozen open.

He stared out into the harsh, wintry night. She was out there, somewhere, the little Bride he could never touch. Everything about her, about this situation, was unfathomable to him.

And all the ice was a blatant reminder that he could never drink her. *You have blood lust for her. Leave this place.*

His chest felt like it had a band tightening around it. He traced away, out of breath and mystified by the female living in his manor.

I'll be damned if I ever return.

Twenty-Five

Murdoch glanced at his watch yet again.

The night was waning, and still he waited on Rurik and Lukyan. They were to meet here in the Quarter to investigate a new lead, and it wasn't like Rurik to be late.

Lulls in action were *still* dangerous for Murdoch—even after his ill-fated trip to the lodge a week ago. Yet he was determined to fight the unnatural pull toward Daniela. Yes, he'd experienced mind-blowing pleasure with her. But that just brought into relief how much he missed sex. The driving need, sweaty bodies writhing, hips pumping. And kissing. God, he missed kissing.

No, there was no future with her. Monogamy was not his way. He'd seen it destroy better men than he was.

And she iced my goddamned lodge.

After leaving Rurik another message, Murdoch leaned against a light post. He caught the eye of an attractive brunette in a low-cut top. She cast him a lascivious smile, but all he could think was that she wasn't a fraction as comely as Daniela. He turned away.

In fact, over the last two weeks, he'd compared all women to Daniela, and without exception, they were all lacking.

But at least they could potentially be touched.

When his gaze wandered back over the female, she stared at him with undisguised interest. No, he hadn't wanted to be blooded, but now that he was, he might as well enjoy it.

He knew from experience that he could have that woman with little more than a crook of his finger. Old habits rose to the fore, even as he told himself he didn't have time for this. He needed to give his undivided focus to finding Ivo.

But without Rurik and Lukyan, Murdoch could do nothing but wait, and he needed to slip the leash Daniela had put on him.

If he could blunt this need, he'd be more focused, more effective. A tall brunette seemed just the thing. . . .

"May I wear it, mama?" Danii asked. Svana had just taken her crown out of safekeeping for her upcoming trip. As ever, Danii was fascinated with it.

"Just for a bit, dearling," Svana told her as she placed the band of ice and diamonds atop her braided hair. Jewels dropped down over her forehead. "There. My little winter princess."

"I want to show the other Valkyrie."

"But they would be spellbound."

"I'm not."

"No, daughter." Svana smiled as she adjusted the crown, but it was too large. "Because our kind comes from a land of diamonds and ice."

"Is that where you're going now?"

Her beautiful face had grown grave. "Yes."

"When will you come back?"

Svana knelt before her. "Daniela, I might not make it back."

"Then why do you have to go there?" Danii asked, beginning to cry. "Just stay with me."

"I must reclaim my throne. I'm a queen from a long line of queens. And one day you will be, too."

"*How will I find you?*"

"*If I don't return to you here, you must promise me, my love, never to follow me. Never, never go to Icergard. Not until you're shown the way. . . .*"

Danii shot up in bed, awake in an instant. *My gods.* She'd just recollected more of that fateful day when her mother had left her. *Not until I'm shown the way?*

Who exactly would be directing Danii to Icergard? And why was she only just remembering this?

The dream had been so realistic, she could almost feel the weight of that crown on her head. Svana had worn it when she'd gone to meet her destiny, even knowing she'd likely die. How brave she'd been.

Danii rose, feeling a pleasant jolt as her bare feet met the freezing marble, then crossed to the open window. The north wind blew with a proud gust as if embracing her. She closed her eyes, swaying with it.

The vampire—who had yet to return—had talked of dreams. Now she'd been awash in reverie each night. Was it the cold or this particular place that drew forth her memories and dreams?

She loved it here. The frigid winds affected her like adrenaline, each flake of snow a balm on her soul. For two weeks, she'd indulged in ice hunts, followed whispers, explored the countryside. And she'd continued to carve arcane symbols into any ice face she'd come across.

The markings were simple in form, like the inscriptions on ancient rune stones from northern lands. She didn't think she'd ever seen these designs before, and had no idea how she knew them.

Eventually, she'd begun creating her own ice tablets to carve on, some as large as a table, later placing them in different parts of the forest and snowdrifts, settling them just so. She didn't know why she did this, just felt compelled to.

With each day here she was growing stronger, thinking more about this puzzling new pastime—and less about the vampire. *Yes.*

Some minutes less than others. At first, she'd wondered if her carving was merely a desperate bid for distraction, like a Valkyrie/ Icere equivalent of downing a gallon of Häagen-Dazs.

But she'd concluded it must be more, because the compulsion intensified—even as her desire for him should've begun dwindling. . . .

Murdoch kissed three different women that night.

Mere minutes after spotting that first brunette, he'd found himself with her in an alley behind a bar, taking her lips with his own.

And still he'd thought of Daniela. Ultimately, he'd broken away with a muttered curse. "Sorry, sweet. Have to go."

She'd clung to him, begging him not to stop. What should have excited him had wilted any arousal he might have managed by imagining it was Daniela he kissed.

The second woman had been passable, but there'd been no distinct intelligence shining in her eyes. So different from his Bride. He admired Daniela's tricky mind, liked the way he could rarely read her expressions.

The third smelled of cloying perfume and whatever she'd dined on earlier. Such a contrast to Daniela's clean scent. . . .

Now as he thought back, he realized that not one of the three had tempted him to take her neck. Another reason he needed to stay away from Daniela. *Easier said than done.* He felt as if he was waging a losing battle, and in his life, he'd bloody had enough of those.

He'd died in one.

Why fight this? It would *have* to be easier to resist drinking her than to go without seeing her face again—which was proving impossible. . . .

He pictured his Bride sleeping in his bed, as if she were awaiting him. If he were going to settle down, why not with the most exquisite, intelligent female he'd ever known? Even if she was an ice being. He recalled the supernatural scene that had greeted him at the lodge and came to a determination.

It'd never be dull with her.

Could the reason he'd never committed to a woman be that he'd been waiting for her all his life? He glanced at the sky. Dawn was only a couple of hours away. Too late to do much here. But it would be dark in Siberia.

Why not try this out? *If I'm ever tempted to drink from her, I'll trace away.* At least then he'd know.

With that conclusion, he almost wished he hadn't pursued those other women. He thought he might be feeling . . . *guilt.* Him.

He spied a flower street vendor on the next corner over. Murdoch knew women—they loved flowers. He snatched up a bouquet of roses, tossed a twenty to the half-asleep vendor, then traced to Daniela.

Again, she wasn't inside. When he heard the front door creaking open, he traced downstairs with the bouquet behind his back. "Daniela?"

Her lips were even bluer than before, her skin pale as milk. She had twigs in her icy hair.

God, she's lovely beyond words. He cast about for a compliment and came up empty. *What's new?*

She gazed at him, not with the excitement he'd anticipated, but with measured curiosity.

"Where were you?" he asked.

"Just got back from a walk."

She was barefoot in a halter top and shorts. He wondered if he'd ever get used to seeing so much of her perfect body exposed to the elements. "I hadn't heard from you. Wanted to make sure you're settling in."

She shrugged, turning toward the stairs.

He followed her up. "I am just stopping by. To check on you."

"You kind of said that already. And as you can see, I'm doing great."

"You've been busy here," he said when they reached his room.

Since he'd been here last, she'd added to those carved designs in the glazes that coated the walls. More snow had accumulated. "Busy *decorating*."

Again, he felt that sense of encroachment. But when he didn't feel the accompanying resentment, he figured he'd become inured to it. "Those symbols you carve—what do they mean?"

"I'm not sure." Her eyes darted around the room. "Just stuff I made up."

For some reason, at that moment, both of their gazes fell on the bed. His voice was rough when he said, "Why are you sleeping in here?"

"My room faced south. In here, the north wind blows right in."

Sleeping in my bed. He grew aroused at the idea once more. He might not be able to claim her, but there were other benefits. Reminded of that, he offered her the flowers.

Her gaze flicked over them. "A bouquet? Like in the days of old?"

"I thought that bringing flowers to a woman one desires was a timeless gesture."

"The timing was fine." She canted her head to the side. Had her ears twitched? "But your supposition about the woman was off."

Is she studying my face? Could she tell he'd kissed other women? "What do you mean?"

In answer, she wiggled her fingers, motioning for the flowers. The moment he handed them to her, they began to wither. As he stared, they blackened and died.

He ran his gloved hand over the back of his neck. "Glad I didn't get you a kitten."

She tossed them into the unused fireplace. "You have to understand that I'm not like the women you knew. This world is not like you thought. Everything has changed for you. And you can't apply your human expectations to it."

"Then tell me about this world. Teach me."

"Would you like me to give you a lesson right now?"

"Yes. Absolutely."

"Valkyrie have a superhuman sense of smell. Not as strong as Lykae or demons. Maybe not even as strong as vampires. But enough so I can smell the women you've been with."

Ah, Christ.

TWENTY-SIX

DANII SMELLED WOMEN'S PERFUMES. *Plural.* She could tell he'd been close enough to them to pick up their scents, but she couldn't detect exactly what he'd been doing with them.

At her words, he'd gone still, his eyes narrowing. Now he shrugged, and any hint of guilt she might have imagined was gone, replaced by nonchalance. "I kissed . . . a couple of women."

Her claws straightened with jealousy.

"Just wanted to see what it'd be like. After so long."

Lightning flashed outside. His cavalier manner infuriated her. "Did you do more?"

"Daniela, you're making an issue out of something trivial. The women were humans, and I *only* kissed them."

"Trivial? Did you just happen to know these mortals? Or were they tramps you picked up while you were supposed to be searching for Ivo?"

At his expression, she grew queasy. *Bingo.* She could just see him lustily making out with skanks in some alley in the Quarter.

I've always ridiculed tourists who did that.

There were so few secrets within the Lore. Gossipers abounded. Everyone would know Murdoch had spurned Danii to be with other women. And it was bad enough for a Bride to be forsaken by a leech, but it was entirely humiliating to be passed over for mortals.

"We never made a commitment to each other," he finally said. When lightning flashed again, he scrubbed his palm over his mouth. "You simply *informed* me that you'd be staying here. And I haven't kissed a woman in three hundred goddamned years."

"Then why didn't you do more with them?"

He exhaled wearily. "They left me cold—"

"Cold?" she cried, a hysterical note to her voice. "I'm so glad I made you swear not to tell anyone anything about me, not that they won't all know now. I hope you put money against us in Loa's betting book."

"We aren't wed." His own ire spiked. "I made you no promises. You have no call to be angry with me."

"I'm angry because you've finally seen what's been just before you all along. But you've seen it too late."

"Too late? Again, I only kissed them. I came *here* tonight, to be with you, even though I had those women begging me for more."

Begging him? Was he that good a kisser? She shook herself— she'd never know. "And yet you chose to come here and be with me, a female who *can't* give you more. I find that difficult to believe!"

"Believe it, ice queen. You've broken me—I want no other!"

"And that makes you *broken*?" She gave a cry. "Gods, I am so sick of you!"

"Sick of me? When I admit that I chose you above others? Your timing is ridiculous."

"Because I don't buy this! If you think you're broken, then you're going to want to get fixed. Not to wallow in your brokenness. Trust me, I know this!" *Sad, sad Daniela . . .*

"So now you've got me all figured out, when you've known me for a couple of weeks? Ah, that's right, I'm merely a manwhore and nothing more."

"I've only known you a short while, but I know men. I've witnessed the entire spans of their lives. You're not a man who won't deign to commit. You're a coward who's *afraid* to."

"Coward?" Though he sneered the word, Danii saw a flicker of some emotion in his eyes. She'd hit a nerve.

"A *selfish* coward! You expect me to just be waiting here, standing by for whenever you decide you want more from me?"

"You *are* just waiting here, Valkyrie."

At that, she began building ice in her palm, and he eyed it with contempt. "Leave here, vampire. And don't come back!"

"This is my house!"

"Does this look like *your* house any longer?" A gust of flurries blew in the window to punctuate her words.

"Fine. Have it! Consider it a gift for a couple of pleasurable nights."

With a bitter curse, Murdoch traced from the lodge. He returned to his meeting place in case Rurik showed—

And found himself surrounded by beings.

They looked like demons, but they had red eyes like fallen vampires. They were immense and carried medieval weapons, cudgels and maces.

Behind them stood Ivo, his bald head gleaming. Just five years ago, they'd met on a battlefield. *Finally, I've found this prick.*

"We seek the halfling," Ivo said. "If you have information about her, we might spare your life."

Halfling? "I wouldn't tell you anything, even if I knew what you were talking about."

In a bored tone, Ivo commanded, "Then kill him."

Murdoch drew his sword in a flash, swung it at the closest demon. The male laughed as he easily dodged the blow.

The speed was inconceivable. *You can't fight these beings.* Just as he'd been told.

Before Murdoch could retreat, they were upon him, preventing him from tracing. A cudgel caught him across the face, tearing and crushing at the same time. Blood sprayed.

A blow to his leg bludgeoned his femur, sending him to his knees. Another shattered his arm.

The strength . . . *monstrous*. A studded mace hit him directly in the chest, embedding in his sternum. *Can't breathe, can't . . .*

Against his will, his blood-drenched eyes closed. Realization dawned. *I'm about to die*. And all he could think about was how he wanted to see Daniela just one last time.

Ivo ordered, "Take his head—"

A roar sounded. Murdoch struggled just to crack open his lids. Rurik and Lukyan, here? *They must've been trailing Ivo earlier.*

As the two charged into the fight, Murdoch tried to warn them, but couldn't speak. *Jaw not working?*

Rurik went fully berserk, wildly swinging his battle hammer. Lukyan wielded his two swords, looking as if he hungered for death—and planned to take with him as many as possible.

But when Rurik received a hit that felled even his giant frame, Lukyan muttered, "Fuck this." Then he traced away.

TWENTY-SEVEN

I'M GOING TO MISS IT HERE. But Danii knew she couldn't stay.

She'd be relinquishing the vampire's gift for two nights of pleasure.

How could she even be surprised that he'd remained away? After all, he was probably busy mugging with mortals in back alleys. Which left Danii to be the Forbearer's forsaken one.

She reminded herself yet again that she'd dodged a bullet with Murdoch. This could have been much worse. Anything between them could never have worked out. If she threw all in with him and then got jilted, people would ask, "What was she thinking, to make a grab at a rake like that? With no warm bed to offer him?"

She sighed. Damn it, she'd liked him—and she'd liked it *here*.

The pressure to carve had continued to grow within her, as if she were nearing some goal and gaining momentum. It was satisfying to her, and brought into stark relief exactly how little in her life had contented her before.

Her mother had told Danii that she descended from the line of the Winter Queens, but Danii had never felt a connection to that ancestry. She felt more Valkyrie than ice fey. Of course, she didn't fit in with the Valkyrie either. *Sad, sad Daniela.*

Were these symbols the very first tie to her heritage? Why was she only now seeing them?

Didn't matter. Her time here had ended.

If she remained, she'd get too attached to the lodge. The longer she stayed, the longer she'd want to. And she could just see Murdoch bringing another woman here in a few years and finding Danii still inside, putzing around in her nightgown, muttering, "Oh, hai. Don't mind me."

Danii had determined and finally accepted that Murdoch equaled misery. Unfortunately, she'd concluded this *after* she'd begun falling for him.

Time to leave.

Now I just need to find a ride.

"You should see the other guy," Murdoch grated from his bed.

Nikolai had already been pale when he traced into the room at Mount Oblak. Seeing Murdoch like this made even more blood drain from his face.

He knew how bad he looked. A metal brace was screwed into his leg to stabilize his crushed femur. One arm was immobilized in a cast, and bandages swathed more of his body than not. His face was lacerated from the corner of his mouth to his ear, held together only by stitches. All in all, he was lucky to be alive.

No. Not *lucky.*

Murdoch and Rurik lived only because Lukyan had returned directly with a full battle contingent. It turned out that Lukyan didn't like to merely fight—he liked *to win.*

Nikolai finally found his voice. "What has happened to you?"

"I was about to ask you the same. My God, Nikolai, you look worse than I do." His brother was always so stoical, always sure of his actions.

So what the hell was going on?

Nikolai's eyes grew dark before he glanced away. "We'll talk of my problems later. Who did this to you?"

Murdoch let the subject go for now. "Ivo has demons. Demons turned vampires. They are strong—you can't imagine it. He is looking for someone, but I don't think it's your Bride. They mentioned something about a 'halfling.'"

"How many?"

"There were three demonic vampires in his party, other vampires as well. We took down two of the demons, but one remains." Murdoch glanced behind him. "Where's your Bride?"

Nikolai hesitated. "She's at Blachmount. We're . . . I'm . . ." He ran his hand over his haggard face, then said in a rush, "Ever since I tasted Myst's blood, I've been dreaming her memories. . . ."

It was all Murdoch could do to mask his shock as Nikolai continued talking, the words spilling out. So the memories *had* followed the blood. Why weren't his eyes red? Would Nikolai confess this to Kristoff?

Through these dreams, Nikolai had learned that in the past Myst had been a calculating femme fatale who'd used and discarded lovers without mercy. She'd been bent on tricking Nikolai, acting as if she wanted more with him, when she'd actually had ulterior motives.

Before Murdoch could even formulate a response to this, Nikolai delivered yet another bombshell. He'd come into possession of an enchanted chain—that *controlled* Myst. By owning the chain, Nikolai could make her do whatever he pleased.

This was their *understanding*? Some kind of enthrallment?

Long moments of silence passed before Murdoch said incredulously, "You took away the free will of a creature who has had it for upward of two thousand years. A good wager says she's going to want it back." Nikolai had dealt with war, plague, and famine all in one decade. He'd lost most of his family. And yet he'd always acted honorably. Until now.

It figured that it'd take a woman to break him.

"No, you don't understand," Nikolai said. "She's callous. Incapable of love. It eats at me, her deception, because it's the only thing that makes sense." More to himself, he muttered, "Why else would she want me?"

Murdoch weakly grabbed his brother's wrist. "All these years, I've seen you continually choose the best, most rational course, even if it's the most difficult. I've been proud to follow your leadership because you've acted with courage and always—always—with rationality," he grated, stopping for a ragged breath. "I never thought I would have to inform you that your reason and judgment have failed you, Nikolai. If she's as bad as you say, then you have to . . . I don't know, just help her change, but you can't *order* this. Get back to her. Explain your fears to her."

"I don't think I can. You saw her, Murdoch. Why would she so quickly acquiesce?"

"Why don't you just ask her?"

His brother's expression said it all. He didn't want her to know how desperately he needed her.

"And about the other men," Murdoch said. "This isn't the seventeen hundreds anymore. This isn't even the same plane. She's an immortal, not an eighteen-year-old blushing bride straight from a convent. She can't change these things, so if you want her, you have to adjust."

If her skin can't be touched, you have to adjust. . . .

Nikolai ran a hand over his face and snapped, "When did you get so bloody understanding?"

Since I met Daniela. Since I nearly died. Murdoch shrugged, then stifled a wince at the pain in his chest. "I had someone explain a few rules of the Lore to me and learned that we can't apply our human expectations to the beings within it." *Some men's Brides are untouchable.*

"Who told you this?"

I can't tell you. I took a vow.

Nikolai didn't press for an answer. "Will you be all right?" he asked.

"That's the thing about being immortal. It'll always look worse than it is."

Nikolai attempted a grin—and failed.

"Good luck, brother," Murdoch said. As soon as Nikolai left, he lay back, weak from hiding how much pain he was in, and still astounded by what he'd just seen. *First my father, then Nikolai, now . . . me.* Was it Murdoch's inescapable fate to become obsessed with one woman?

After witnessing his brother like this, he came to a conclusion. Murdoch was *already* ruined without Daniela regardless.

I'll be broken if I lose her in the future—or if I lose her now.

Now that this realization had struck him, Murdoch was oddly resigned to it. *It's too late for me.*

"I'm besotted with her." He gave a laugh, then grimaced as his wounds punished him for it. At least now he knew.

For the first time in weeks, he felt optimistic about his future. All he had to do was convince her to forgive him. Though he'd proved he was in no way silver-tongued with her, he would somehow figure out a way to persuade her. He always came through when it really counted.

He craved seeing Daniela again and was eager to get this sorted out between them, but he was still too weak, and he didn't want her to see him like this.

Kristoff had put him on two weeks' leave, so Murdoch could wait another day or two.

After all, he knew exactly where she'd be.

Twenty-Eight

Danii's ear twitched a split second before she heard the masculine demand: "Where the hell are you going?"

So the vampire's returned. "Away," she said as she zipped up her second suitcase.

"You were just going to disappear without a word?"

"I'll bet you've *never* done that to a woman. Besides, I didn't figure you'd even notice I was gone. Thought you'd be busy trolling for humans."

"I haven't looked at another woman since—"

"Anyway, I wrote you a note on the dresser," Danii interrupted, uninterested in whatever he'd come to say.

He snatched up the paper where she'd written: *Murdoch, it's been real. Daniela.*

"How were you going to leave?"

"I have ways." *Ways* being the one Sno-Cat operator in Russia who would journey to this place, the one due to arrive in an hour.

Murdoch crumpled the note in his fist. "How would I have been able to find you?"

She paused in her packing, briefly glancing up at him. "I guess you *wouldn't*."

Then she frowned. Though he always dressed well, tonight he seemed to have taken great care with his clothes. He wore an expensive sweater and luxe overcoat. His boots had been polished.

She sported a miniskirt and a camisole. With no shoes. "Why are you all dressed up?" she asked irritably.

"This night is important to me." He was moving stiffly, and stood at an odd angle to her, keeping half of his face in shadow. "I need to tell you something."

And I need to see why you're not showing me the other side of your face. She moved to get a better look at him. *Stitches?* His face had been cut up, and yet he'd still tried to shave. What was so important? "Murdoch, what happened to you?"

"I almost got killed by a few half-demon, half-vampire beings."

"There's no such thing." She waved his words away. "It's one of the rare 'myths' in the Lore that's actually false."

"They had horns and fangs and were stronger than any vampires I've ever fought. They also had *red* eyes."

All Fallen vampires had red eyes, but very few species of demons did. There'd been rumors of Ivo plotting something major. Had he conceived of a way to turn demons into vampires?

"Remember when Deshazior and the kobold said they were different and unfightable?" Murdoch said. "Well, they are."

She had to contact Nïx about this. *Wait . . .* Her sister had mentioned *dempires* the last time they'd spoken. *Demon vampires.* Nïx already knew.

Murdoch began pacing, stabbing his fingers through his hair, his energy seeming to take up the entire room. But he was limping. And she thought she heard a barely perceptible squeak. A leg brace? Whatever he'd tangled with had inflicted some serious damage.

"Daniela, I think I know why I'm like this around you. Why I'm always at a loss for words and gruff. It's *you.*"

"Blaming much? *This* behavior used to impress the ladies? Really?" She turned back to her packing.

"That's what I'm trying to explain. I wasn't like this. I was smooth, compliments falling easily from my lips."

"Murdoch Suavé?" She knew he hated it when she called him that. "Then what's different now?"

"Now I fear that . . . I think that this . . . matters. You matter. To *me*." He ran his hand over his forehead. "I feel a lot of pressure not to fuck this up with you."

"What do you want from me?"

"I don't know. A chance? To see where this leads."

She felt a spark of excitement at the idea, but mentally snuffed it. *Murdoch equals misery.* When would she finally accept that?

"Stay here, Daniela. With me."

She narrowed her eyes. "With you? Like living together?" Had his nod been the tiniest bit hesitant? "What's changed?"

"You said that I was afraid, and I think you were not . . . wrong."

She didn't reply, just raised her brows.

"I didn't see it before, didn't understand my reluctance. But when I was ambushed and believed I was going to die"—he stopped, meeting her gaze—"all I could think of was you."

Oh. She felt herself softening. *I've been thinking about you, too. No matter how hard I try not to.* If she hadn't had her carving, she'd have gone mad.

"And then a few days ago, I saw my brother. He's a wreck over Myst. I thought that I'd never seen a man so twisted inside over a woman. But I have. Our father was that way for our mother."

Murdoch resumed pacing. "He was obsessed with her. When she died, he never again laughed, never moved on. He used to sit in their room and stare at her portrait for hours. I think I feared something like that happening to me, if I sought more with you. But then I realized I'm more afraid of missing this with you."

A breath escaped her as she edged closer to him. *I want him. I want reality over fantasy.* "Murdoch, did you practice that speech?"

"Continually for the last two days."

No, remember Farmer Ted! Remember Loa's betting book! "Since we've been seeing each other, you've threatened me, frightened me, and put me in a position where I was forced to walk out into the heat of noonday to hitchhike in a hell vehicle that reeked of tobacco. When you went out trolling in the Quarter, you . . . hurt me," she said. "So you think long and hard about this. I saw your frustration when you wanted to bite me. I saw your hunger as you stared at my neck. And I've seen you clench your fists when you want to touch me."

Closing in on her, he asked in a husky voice, "And did you see nothing else, *kallim?*"

She swallowed, unable to look away from his intense gray eyes, already flickering black with emotion. "You can never touch my skin, never drink from me. I'm colder than I've ever been. The pain would be much worse for me, and for you as well."

"I understand."

"Murdoch, there's no magic that's going to change our situation, no way to circumvent it—not now, and potentially not ever. Do you think you can be satisfied with that?"

"Satisfied? Completely? No. But I think we can be happier together than apart."

If he had waxed rhapsodic about their chances, she probably would've run screaming. Instead, he'd been honest. And she agreed—she wouldn't be satisfied completely either.

"I'll give this a few months," she eventually said. "On two conditions."

"What are they?"

"Just as before, you can never tell anyone about me. Not until I'm ready."

"Why?"

Because I give this a one-in-fifty shot of working out. "Because I don't want to be the butt of jokes or the betrayed one on the betting books. And I don't want to be known as the Forbearer's forsaken one."

"You expect me to forsake you."

"Any reason why I shouldn't?"

"I'm not my history. At least, that's not all I am. Anymore." He frowned, as if he couldn't believe what he was saying.

"You've told me that you can't do monogamy."

"I'm going to. Do it. Now. But you must as well." When she gave him a "no kidding" expression, he gritted his teeth. Again, clearly not pleased with what he'd said.

"I won't be dissuaded from this condition. You must keep us a secret."

"My brothers will hear my heart beating. They'll know."

"Do you agree or not?"

Finally, he said, "I agree. And what's the second?"

"You have to vow never to bite me."

"I vow it."

Don't get too excited, Daniela!

He placed his gloved hands on the sides of her face, gazing down at her. "Now, does this mean you've signed back up on my roster?"

Too late. "Did you practice that line as well?"

That lock of hair tumbled over his forehead. "Repeatedly."

Twenty-nine

"COME ON IN!" Danii called to the vampire pacing on shore. "The water's great."

Under the moonlight, Murdoch looked as if he were actually considering joining her as she swam amidst the ice floes. He was also probably regretting that he'd agreed to trace her to the northern limits of his property, which extended all the way to the Arctic Ocean.

Seconds after she'd seen the water, she'd been skinny-dipping in it.

Poor vampire, pacing at the very edge of the sea, wanting to follow her, his gorgeous face tense. Her heart tugged at the sight, just as it'd been doing daily for these last several weeks, ever since the night she and Murdoch had started living together.

After they'd paid off the irate Sno-Cat operator, of course.

"Maybe the water's a jot brisk," she teased. These closing months of winter had been particularly harsh, an idyll of blizzards and negative degrees for her—and of course virtually twenty-four hours of darkness for him.

Without complaint, he endured the cold to be with her. She slept during the brief murky daylight to spend more time with him. And when they hadn't been talking, learning more about each other, they'd been indulging in bouts of sensual—albeit inventive—bliss.

She'd never been happier.

"Out, Daniela," he called, still pacing. "You've been in long enough."

"If you don't come join me, a merman might get frisky with me!"

He stopped and canted his head, wondering if she was kidding, growing increasingly agitated.

"Oh, very well. I'll come in." She wanted to walk some of the way back to the lodge anyway, and needed to budget time for snowball fights—she might let him win one tonight. She loved playing in the snow with him. When he had all his cold-weather gear on, they could roll around without having their skin touch.

As she swam in, she called, "Trace and get me a towel?"

Obviously reluctant to leave her for even seconds, he disappeared, returning moments later with one. He met her at the shore, wrapping her in it. As he rubbed her dry, her eyes closed with pleasure, reminded anew of their earlier encounter. For hours, she'd teased him with ice cubes, running them all over his body, everywhere she wished she could lick him.

"You were kidding about the merman, right?" he said. "You'd never told me they existed."

"I haven't gotten to merfolk yet." Yes, Danii had relented, finally divulging the secrets of the Lore, once she'd sworn him to secrecy. She owed him her life and couldn't stand the thought of him out there engaging opponents that would try to kill him just for being a vampire—enemies with powers and weaknesses he wouldn't understand. "I've only covered the first two hundred or so beings, and there are more than can be catalogued. And that's just on this plane."

She'd outlined many of the larger factions, from the demon kingdoms called demonarchies to the history of the noble fey. "They were feudal lords called *Féodals*," she'd explained. "That's where they get the name. They hailed from the plane of Draiskulia, but once they came here, they became divided into different factions. Like the Icere." And she'd related humorous trivia: "Some demons, like Desh, can be involuntarily summoned by previous bed partners. They call those summoners *swimbos*—a play on She Who Must Be Obeyed. . . ."

"Merfolk," he repeated now, handing Danii her clothes. At times he seemed overwhelmed by all the Lorean histories and details. Admittedly, it was a lot to take in.

He'd probably learned the most via laptop, by following the web results and commentary on the Talisman's Hie, a sort of immortal *Amazing Race*, sponsored by Riora, the flighty Goddess of Impossibility. Entrants from all factions crossed the globe, competing for mystical prizes.

Through the results, he'd discovered that his brother Sebastian was indeed alive and well—because he was competing in it. "My brother's alive?" he'd said that day, shooting to his feet. Just before he'd swung Danii up in his arms, he'd abruptly dropped his outstretched hands, drawing back self-consciously. "Can you believe it? I have to let Nikolai . . ." He'd trailed off. "Why did you just go pale? Daniela, is Sebastian in danger?"

Regrettably, Sebastian was competing against Danii's half sister, Kaderin the Coldhearted, a vicious vampire assassin. "The rules state that the competitors can't kill each other until the final round," she'd said, not wanting to extinguish his hopes, but Kaderin had never lost a Hie. And this time they played for Thrane's Key, which unlocked a door *to the past.* Since Kaderin felt responsible for the deaths of two of her full-blood sisters, she'd be a ruthless menace in order to win that key.

When Murdoch had asked Danii if she could find out anything about this—like exactly why Sebastian would enter—she'd left a message with Nïx. Yet though Nïx was the most powerful oracle in the Lore, she was also forgetful, capricious, and notoriously bad at returning calls. . . .

Danii finished tugging her skirt up her thighs, then she glanced up—to find Murdoch's fierce gaze rapt on her body.

He took her shoulders in his gloved hands, staring down at her with his obsidian eyes reflecting moonlight. The breeze blew that unruly lock over his forehead. "You couldn't be lovelier," he rasped, the mere sound of his husky voice making her body go soft for him.

Her gaze dipped to his lips. The moment was ripe for a kiss. "Vampire, I would give anything to taste you right now." *Anything.* Though this time together had been almost perfect, frustration simmered just below the surface. With each day, she wondered how much longer they could go without real touching.

His hands tightened on her shoulders. "As would I."

She was fantasizing about wicked sex even more than she had *before* she'd met Murdoch. Danii envisioned suckling his thick length for hours. She imagined how it would feel plunging inside her. *What would it be like to have his scent all over me?*

Would his kiss make her breathless and weak-kneed, her toes and her claws curling?

As his gaze flicked from her eyes to her mouth, he grated, "Almost don't want to know what you're thinking right now." He broke away, turning from her with clenched fists—instead of claiming the kiss that should have been his due.

Yet another reminder that the broken doll was in no way fixed.

"We need to get back," he said. "I should check in at Mount Oblak."

"But you just went there two nights ago," she reminded him. "You said you weren't going to be needed there as much." Now that there was no impending threat from the Horde.

In the past months, the vampire world had been rocked to its core. The Horde king Demestriu had been slain by Emmaline, Danii's lovable niece. Emma had discovered that he was her father, and then she'd somehow managed to defeat him in a fight to the death. Ivo, too, had been assassinated for seeking to wed Emma, the 'halfling.' Apparently Lachlain MacRieve, her new Lykae protector, had taken exception to that, because he'd released his savage inner werewolf, slaughtering Ivo and the remaining *dempire* as well.

"Is there some new threat?" Danii asked. "Or has Lothaire returned?" Rumor held that the Enemy of Old hadn't even remained on this plane.

"No, nothing like that, just the usual aggressing bands," Murdoch said. Without Demestriu to lead the Horde, their numbers had been divided into smaller, weaker factions, but they could still prove deadly. "It can't hurt to check in. I'm sure you want to carve, anyway." Had his tone been a shade brusque?

Maybe she was carving too much, but getting each symbol perfect felt so crucial. Sometimes she worked till her fingers bled. If Murdoch was there, he'd take her hands in his big gloved ones and ice her wounds.

The first time he'd found her like this, he'd demanded, "Daniela, why do this to yourself?"

How to explain the compulsion? *The Call of the Wild* meets *Holiday on Ice*? "I feel antsy and full until I carve. It's like an instinct, or maybe some kind of genetic memory, passed down by blood. Kind of like how you might get my memories if you ever drank from me."

Always, Danii pondered the mystery of who would lead her back to Icergard, a puzzle as yet unsolved. Could her carvings be some kind of clue?

Reminded of that, she said, "Yes, maybe I could work a little." Though she felt selfish on occasion, investigating her memories, this was her time. There was no one to keep secrets for or from, no one to *observe*, except her own determined expression in a mirrored glaze of ice.

The world was passing her by. One month, then another. . . .

"Very well." He took her shoulders once more to trace her back to the lodge. Before he left again, he said, "I might see Nikolai tonight. Have you thought about my request?" Murdoch had announced a couple of weeks ago, "Myst has consented to marry my brother. I want us to visit them." When Danii had hesitated, he'd said, "Just think about it."

He continued pressuring her to go public with their relationship. Though she was tempted, always something made her reluctant to take the leap. Now she told him simply, "It's not time yet."

"When will it be time?"

"You agreed to my condition. I'll tell you when I'm ready."

He gave her a tight nod. "I'll return when I can," he said, brushing a kiss over her hair, but the tension between them was thick.

Danii sighed when he left. Murdoch had once admitted to her that he'd never cared about anything very much. And that, other than defending his country, he'd committed to nothing. She couldn't shake the feeling that he hadn't committed to them.

Though she wanted to trust him, he had been a player. *Once a rogue, always a rogue, right?* Especially since she was unable to fulfill not just one, but two of his most basic needs.

Sometimes, even though he knew how badly his bite would hurt, he still stared at her neck. Each time she got an unpleasant feverish tremor, like she supposed others might have chills. . . .

Yes, the world was passing her by—but the pressures were escalating. Each denial made them hunger for each other even more.

They knew pleasure, but were never completely sated, and the frustration built and built, like a volcano that vented steam but would inevitably erupt.

THIRTY

JÁDIAN THE COLD CLIMBED THE STAIRS past the guards he'd killed, stealing toward King Sigmund's tower chamber.

Though he found it distasteful to dispatch his own kind, Jádian had done it without mercy. He had to act quickly. The Valkyrie's time was nigh.

"Any word on where that little bitch is?" the king demanded as Jádian entered, not even glancing away from his glazed window. "I thought you were closing in on the Valkyrie."

"Yes, I know precisely where she will be." Eventually she would come to him. Each month, she neared, without even knowing it.

Sigmund whirled around. "Then why does she yet live?" he bellowed, slamming his staff into the floor, sending up shards of ice.

Jádian slowly unsheathed the fire blade that had slain Sigmund's queen, relishing the fear dawning in the king's eyes. Jádian had been awaiting this sight since Sigmund had stolen a throne that didn't belong to him, and plunged the Icere into a needless war with the fire demonarchy.

The war in which Jádian's own pregnant wife, Karilina, had perished. "Daniela lives, because it's your death that comes next."

Like a shot, Jádian lunged for him, forcing a hand over Sigmund's mouth as he sank the blade into his heart—Jádian needed him quiet to savor the hiss of burning skin and the futile flailing of the king.

Blood sprayed, wetting Jádian's hair and face. When he yanked the knife free, Sigmund lived still, even as Jádian began slicing through the skin and bone of his neck.

By the time he had Sigmund's head, Jádian was covered in gore, but his heart was calm.

He turned to the south. Now, *now* was the Valkyrie's time.

If Daniela keeps up this carving, her hands will bleed.

Did she not think about what the sight and scent of her blood did to him each time?

As Murdoch watched her, he wondered yet again what could force her to work like this. Her elven face was tense with focus, her blue-tinged lips pressed together.

Over the previous winter, she'd seemed to be rediscovering herself, exploring those elemental instincts she could scarcely explain to him—or to herself. Yet then had come the summer. What had started as a dark and cold paradise for them turned sunny and mild. Their contentment had melted away as surely as her ice.

For those months, there'd been continual sniping between them. Any accidental contact could set either of them off. But she'd refused to leave the lodge for a colder clime, as if those genetic memories of hers had ended in a cliffhanger and she wouldn't leave the book behind.

Now, fall was upon them at last. *But we still aren't like we used to be. . . .*

Despite the strain between Murdoch and his Bride, things had begun to look up for the Wroth family.

Nikolai had wedded Myst, once she'd forgiven him for using that enchanted chain against her. Nikolai had ultimately realized that he'd misunderstood Myst's memories, discovering that she'd been more Fury than femme fatale, using her wiles to seduce evildoers to their downfall. Then he'd had some apologizing to do.

Sebastian had somehow won both the Talisman's Hie *and* Kaderin, the deadly little assassin who'd actually been dispatched to execute him.

Though his brothers' Brides were half sisters, they were as different as day and night. One was a bold redhead, legendary for her beauty. The other was a golden-skinned killer with a predilection for stringing up vampire fangs as trophies.

Mine is an ethereal ice queen. Exquisite and always just out of reach. . . .

Murdoch and Nikolai had at last reconciled with Sebastian. Naturally, now that the three brothers were speaking again, their conversations turned to Conrad—how to locate him, where he'd last been seen. They'd all begun searching and had unearthed some leads, though they chose not to believe the rumors that Conrad was a Fallen, red-eyed assassin who drank all his victims.

They were close to finding him. Murdoch could *feel* it. Yes, things were finally looking up for the brothers.

But between him and Daniela . . . Even though they found ways to pleasure each other, Murdoch was continually tormented by how soft her skin looked. He'd never been one for open displays of affection, had never felt any sort of romantic attachment before. Now he found himself checking impulse after impulse to simply stroke her cheek or run his palm down her arm.

And to kiss her—Christ, he wanted that so much.

She felt the yearning, too. He often found her dreamily gazing at his lips while running her fingertips over her own.

Sometimes he unreasonably felt as if fate was punishing him with her for all his previous sins. Never to hold her; always to suffer this need—and to bear the knowledge that it would forever go unslaked.

If "faint heart never won fair lady," then the opposite should hold true. Murdoch had meant it when he'd said he would do anything to have her—anything but risk her safety. He needed gates to storm, an enemy to fight and defeat. Instead, he could do nothing but covet what was already his. . . .

At that moment she nicked her forefinger. Rich blood beaded, and he clenched his jaw at the scent. *Never to drink her, though I dream of it more and more.*

On occasion, she'd caught him staring at the alabaster skin of her neck, but she still stayed with him. Which meant she trusted him not to hurt her.

His gaze fixed on the small welling of crimson. With each day, he wondered how much he trusted himself.

"Nïx, is that really you?" Danii cried. When her phone had rung, she'd expected Murdoch or even Myst again.

"In the telephonic flesh," the soothsayer replied.

"I've called you repeatedly!"

"Then I must've not wanted to talk to you."

Danii pursed her lips. "What are you doing?"

"Just *chillin'* since you gave us the *cold shoulder*—huzzah! Somebody stop me! How's the vamp? Too hot to handle? Because I could do this all day!"

"Ha-ha." Today Nïx was playful. Which unfortunately meant she'd probably be forgetful as well. "And I'm not giving you the cold shoulder. You knew why I had to go."

"Did I? Guess I forgot. Mental note: stop telling people that Danii's gone missing. Cease hinting feral koi to blame."

Danii sighed. Nïx could be incredibly useful. And incredibly frustrating. "What's that noise in the background?"

"Your room. No one can figure out how to turn off the freezer."

Danii swallowed. "Why would you want to turn it off?" *All my ice!*

"Because Soloflex and litter-box storage wait for no one?"

"You're acting like I'm never coming back."

"Are you?" Nïx asked.

"You tell me, soothsayer," Danii said, but her words were breaking up. Nïx's call waiting kept clicking.

"Who keeps calling you?"

"Not the same person. All different. Everyone wants a piece of Nïxie," she said, a hint of weariness in her tone. "Lemme block them. There. Speaking of calls, Myst said she's tried to contact you several times."

Danii hadn't picked up. "Look, I know what she'll say to me—that I can't possibly keep Murdoch from straying and we'll never work out in the long run." *Pressure building . . . time passing.*

Instead of arguing that point and reassuring her, Nïx only made a noncommittal sound.

"How is Myst, anyway?" Danii asked.

"Even more insufferably ravishing, with the glow of a female who's well loved," Nïx answered. "Married life suits her."

I want to be well loved. Would kill to be. Instead, Danii lived in an increasingly untenable situation, blinders firmly on as she strove to build a life with him. *Like building a house of tinder atop a powder keg.*

And Murdoch had never mentioned marriage.

"Don't forget fierce Kaderin!" Nïx added. "Sebastian's turned her into an amorous Kiddy Kad. So, Kaderin and Myst are both freaky, naughty minxes who get it on with vampires. Just like you, Danii! They both wear their bites proudly, bragging to everyone how orgasmic it feels."

"Orgasmic?" Great, yet another thing to fantasize about with Murdoch. "They, uh, like it?"

"I know, *right*! The coven considers them bite bores. But Sebastian did use Thrane's key to whisk Kad's two sisters back to the future, and he saved Kad's life. Plus, Nikolai tried to sacrifice his life for Myst's. Not that she'd needed him to. So some Valkyries have stopped overtly plotting to massacre the two brothers. Though Murdoch and Conrad are still fair game," she concluded brightly.

"Conrad? I knew he was alive!" Danii said in a rush. "Are the rumors true—is he fallen? Will they ever find him?"

"He lives. Dunno if he's fallen. And yes, eventually the brothers will locate him. I've been helping Nikolai, you know."

And *only* Nikolai. Nïx refused to meet with Murdoch or Sebastian. "I know you have. Murdoch keeps me up to date about everything."

"Indeed? Did he tell you that the Goddess of Impossibility gifted Sebastian with another turn of Thrane's Key? So he could go back in time and bring his own sisters and family forward? Obviously Riora grew quite enamored of the studly scholar."

Murdoch hadn't told her that. *But why?* This was huge! Instead of answering Nïx, Danii demanded, "Why are you meddling in this? You don't even really like vampires."

"How can you say that?" Nïx asked in a scandalized tone. "I have *never* in my life meddled."

Danii gave a harsh laugh. "You even got the House of Witches to sell Nikolai, a vampire, mystical goods." If Conrad was indeed fallen, the brothers planned to capture him to keep him from killing again. Nikolai's first purchase had been unbreakable manacles that prevented the wearer from tracing.

"*Gold* got those mercenaries to sell to him," Nïx countered. "I merely brokered the deal. Would you rather I not help? Hmm. You seem irritable. Usually when I speak to shacked-up Valks, they sound cheerier."

"Bet they can make skin-to-skin contact with their co-shackers."

"Is that the only reason for trouble in paradise? Tell, Nixie, tell. You know I'll just forget."

"I think he's . . . avoiding me. He spends night after night away, following leads about Conrad. That's where he is tonight."

"Do you think he would avoid you if you two could touch?"

"No, I don't. This situation has to be tormenting for him." *Because it is for me.*

"I was thinking about Mariketa the Awaited," Nïx said. "She's finally begun to come into her powers. In another fifty years, she might be able to help you."

"Truly?" Mariketa was supposed to be the most powerful witch ever born to the House of Witches. "I've been waiting for this since she was a girl!" No one in the Lore had known how long they'd be *awaiting* Mariketa to attain her full strength, which could've taken anywhere from years to millennia.

"Mariketa's taking deposits, escrowed of course. You could sign up on her waiting list."

Danii *could*, and until the time came, maybe another less-powerful witch could put her and Murdoch to sleep, hibernating like Wóden and Freya. When Danii and Murdoch woke, they'd be able to be together.

Yet she almost didn't want to tell Murdoch about this idea. Fifty years would still sound like an age to him. Besides, it was in no way certain.

"I don't suppose you know of any way that might predate the fifty-year wait?" Danii was aware of other immortal competitions with outrageous prizes, as well as those extensive Lore bazaars where magics were peddled. Both tended to be held around the Accession.

Could there finally be a magic out there that would allow her and Murdoch to touch? Without exacting a devastating—and potentially scaly—penalty?

"I'll have to see into the future on that and get back to you," Nïx said. "But for now, let's *gossip!*"

For half an hour, Nïx filled her in on Lorean current events, such as the marriage between Emma and Lachlain MacRieve, her werewolf protector. "Told you so about Lykae inlaws," Nïx chirped.

And she related how Kaderin had set about acclimating her medieval sisters to this time: "Video games can be deeply enlightening to the uninitiated."

"What about Regin?" Danii asked. "Surely, she's drummed up some kind of trouble." Regin the Radiant was the coven's resident prankster, hopelessly immature and proud of it. Her "superhero identity" was The Fellatrix, and she was prone to snicker and say things like "The song 'Come On Eileen' doesn't have a comma after *on.* . . ."

"She's been skirting nuclear meltdown since her b.f.f. Lucia went scarce without her."

Surprisingly, brash Regin and level-headed Lucia the Huntress were inseparable best friends. Her past shrouded in mystery, Lucia was an archer who'd been cursed to feel indescribable pain if she missed a shot. At least, that was one of her curses. "Why would Lucia do that?"

"She's gone on walkabout, with her own Lykae admirer hot on her heels. . . ."

While she and Nïx gabbed, Danii endeavored to explain her obsessive carving and the arcane symbols, but the soothsayer revealed nothing, saying only, "Your ways are not like our earth ways."

"Oh!" Nïx suddenly exclaimed. "I almost forgot, I'm sending you a pressy."

"When?" Danii liked gifts! As did every Valkyrie. "How will you know where to send it?"

"As if I don't know exactly where you are! Now, I must go. I have mayhem down at five o'clock and *Survivor* at eight."

"Will you tell everyone that I said hi, and not to steal the clothes I left behind?"

"The second of those requests has already been rendered moot. Literally a free-for-all."

"Nïx!"

"One last thing, do you remember those pesky dempires?"

"Do I ever," Danii said. Murdoch had barely survived his encounter with them. "Want to say you told me so about them as well?"

"No, no, I just wanted you to know that they're mewling creampuffs compared to Conrad Wroth. And when I said that his brothers would eventually locate him? Eventually is *tonight. Ciao!*" Click.

Thirty-one

Murdoch and Nikolai entered Erol's—a ramshackle bayou tavern that catered solely to Loreans—with Sebastian due to meet them any minute.

A contact had told Nikolai that Conrad was within this bar on this very night, and had been returning here repeatedly.

As if to draw his brothers out.

In the past, Conrad had wanted to kill Murdoch and Nikolai, had hated them for turning him, even more than Sebastian had. Did Conrad still want to? They'd soon see.

Murdoch scanned the interior of the dimly-lit tavern—

He's . . . here. "In the back," he muttered to Nikolai. Conrad sat at a table in the shadows, clasping his head as if it pounded. *Our brother. Just here. After so long.*

"He's wearing sunglasses?" Nikolai muttered back.

To hide his red eyes? *Christ, don't let it be.*

Conrad must've sensed them. He lowered his hand and raised his head to face them. At once, he drew his lips back, baring his fangs menacingly.

A standoff. Patrons noticed the sudden tension and fell silent. One look at Conrad and they exited in a hurry. The place emptied, right down to the bartender.

Quiet reigned. Murdoch said nothing, dumbstruck to see his brother after all this time, to find him alive. Nikolai was speechless as well.

Sebastian entered then, his countenance grave. He crossed to his brothers, standing with them in a united front.

Murdoch gave Sebastian a quick nod, gratified once again that he'd allied with them. *The first time in centuries the four of us have been in the same room.*

Conrad drew down his sunglasses, revealing eyes as red as blood. Murdoch's lips parted, and Sebastian muttered a curse. Nikolai winced, but he squared his shoulders, and the three strode forward—

With uncanny speed, Conrad lunged from his seat. In one astonishing move, he vaulted over the table at them and struck Sebastian with a skull-cracking blow, sending him hurtling into a wall.

Before Murdoch and Nikolai could react, Conrad snatched them by their throats, one in each hand as they fought to free themselves.

"Three hundred years of this," Conrad hissed, his red eyes blazing with hate.

Then all hell broke loose.

Pace forward . . . and back. Sit. Carve on tablet for huffish moments. Rise and repeat—

The phone rang. Danii dove for it, answering in a rush, "Murdoch, is that you?"

"We have Conrad," he said, his voice rough. "He's . . . Fallen."

"Oh, Murdoch, I'm so sorry." Danii's heart hurt for him. She knew how much Murdoch cared for his brother, how devastating this was to him.

"He was an assassin, but he drank all of his hundreds, or even thousands, of victims. He took all their memories—and their strength."

"Is he crazed?" she asked, though she knew the answer.

"He nearly totaled Nikolai's car. From *the inside.* We barely captured him, and only because the Lykae Bowen MacRieve showed up and helped take him down. By swinging a bar rail into Conrad's face."

"Are you safe? Were you hurt?"

"Let's just say we're all glad to be immortal," he muttered, then added, "We've got Conrad locked up on a property outside of town, a place called Elancourt."

"I know of it." Elancourt wasn't far from Val Hall and had always struck Danii as creepy. Surely the decrepit gothic manor there wasn't even livable. "Why would you put him there?"

"Nïx advised Nikolai to."

What does she have up her sleeve with this?

"It's going to take a lot of work for the three of us to make it comfortable for Conrad."

More time away. *Avoiding me.*

"But it's hidden," he reminded her, which was important considering what they were doing. One of the primary rules of the Forbearer order was to kill Fallen vampires—without mercy.

To harbor one would be considered treason, punishable by death.

"What's the plan now?" she asked.

"We'll keep him here, try to rehabilitate him with a potion from the witches. Basically do everything in our power to save him. If we can keep him from killing, this might work."

The common wisdom was that the Fallen couldn't be brought back. They couldn't be rehabbed. "What if he's beyond saving?" she asked quietly, wishing she could spare him the inevitable failure.

"We might have other options," Murdoch said cryptically.

Reminded of what Nïx had revealed, Danii asked, "Like using Thrane's Key? Why didn't you tell me Sebastian had it?"

"I take it Nïx finally called you." He exhaled. "Danii, it wasn't my secret to tell. I keep Sebastian's, just as I keep yours."

"Will you use the Key?"

"We plan to in time," he said. "But it was meant to retrieve *all* our family. If we bring Conrad back from the past with them, his present self would fade. We'd wipe out three hundred years of his life. At the very least, we want to get him well enough to make the decision. We won't make this one for him. Not like last time."

"I see," she murmured, disappointed that he hadn't confided something so major—even as she knew that Murdoch couldn't exactly ask Sebastian to let Danii in on the secret. Because Sebastian didn't know about her.

In a distracted tone, he said, "Look, when we finish up with Conrad, you and I should visit Riora. Maybe we could get her to help us—we're in an impossible situation, right?"

He doesn't even realize how hurtful that is to me.

And he also didn't realize that Riora was the flighty goddess who'd given Danii the bowling shoes. . . .

Thirty-two

"LEAVE ME!" Conrad bellowed, straining against his bonds so hard the manacles cut into his wrists.

Murdoch was baffled by this sudden change in his brother after two weeks of gradual—some would say plodding—improvement. He hesitated, contemplating whether he should try again to reach him, or to leave.

When blood began dripping down Conrad's wrists, Murdoch stood. "Things are heating up overseas," he finally said, "and none of us will be back until late tomorrow." Kristoff had warned that a league of Horde vampires might attack Mount Oblak soon. "Do you want to drink before I go?"

"Get out of my sight!"

"Conrad, calm yourself," Murdoch said, to little effect. Damn it, he'd thought they'd been making such progress with him. They'd gotten him to drink from a cup without spitting blood in their faces and even to shower. Lately, he'd had long spells of lucidity where he'd engaged the brothers in conversation.

But Conrad was still hallucinating, seeing scenes from all those memories he'd harvested, and more recently—an invisible "ghost woman," who he believed lived in Elancourt with him.

Then today had come this inexplicable setback. All Murdoch had done was try to talk to him about finding his own Bride, about all the benefits inherent in that—because the brothers had discovered that Conrad . . . had never been with a woman.

And they'd at last determined why he'd gone mad from the turning. Unbeknownst to the entire family, Conrad had been a vampire hunter for more than half his mortal life, had even secretly joined a *monastic* order sworn to wipe out the species. He'd given up everything—his freedom, his future, women—for this cause.

Then Murdoch and Nikolai had turned him into his starkest nightmare. No wonder he still struggled.

When Conrad began rocking on the bed in a snarling fury, Murdoch murmured, "I'm leaving," then traced downstairs. Christ, this was a piss day. Had he actually once lamented that life was too boring? Now it seemed a thousand demands were converging on him.

He couldn't reach Conrad.

Kristoff prepared for war. The three Wroth brothers were to be ready and on call, yet Murdoch couldn't shake the feeling that their king had become suspicious of what they'd been doing in their downtime.

And Daniela . . . Murdoch knew he'd been neglecting her. First he'd had to find Conrad, then capture him. Now Murdoch was investigating his brother's past for anything that might help him recover. Remarkably, Murdoch had yet to learn of a single instance when Conrad had slain an innocent.

But how many times had Murdoch told Daniela he'd be back at the lodge by a certain time, but then Conrad attempted an escape or went into a rage? Murdoch would call to explain, and oftentimes she wouldn't even answer. Would she tonight? He dialed her number. "Pick up, Danii," he muttered. No answer. He tried her again.

Murdoch was growing so weary of his double life. *Can't talk about my Bride, can't bloody touch her.* Even as part of him yearned to be near her, another part of him was growing to hate the temptation that was never satisfied. Having his lips a breath away from her flesh and being denied a taste . . . He didn't know how much longer he could hold on.

Where the hell is she?

He could simply trace to the lodge, but she might be out, anywhere within that vast forest. Besides, he'd planned to follow leads this eve.

Yet if he were honest, he'd admit he was reluctant to return to their freezing home. Earlier when he'd left, the first Siberian blizzard of the season had just begun raging, delighting her, and dismaying him. Tonight there would be no warm hearth, no warm wife to gather close to him. No warm body to lose himself in. . . .

No answer. His fist shot out, slamming into the crumbling plaster wall.

Long hours passed before Murdoch returned to Daniela, and he arrived even later than he'd intended to. Surprisingly, she wasn't at work on her ice tablet—it sat idle against the wall. Nor was she outside.

He found her in bed, dressed in a wispy black gown with her hair loose. The ice crystals around her eyes glinted in the room's dimmed light. *She's so beautiful.*

"It's late," she quietly said.

"I tried to call you earlier, but you didn't answer. I had some things to look into."

"Murdoch, if I didn't know better, I'd swear you were looking for excuses to be away from me."

"You know how important this is to us," he hedged. "And we're running out of time. I'm asking for you to be understanding about this, and for your patience with me."

But she was still upset, lightning streaking outside. Luckily, he'd had the foresight a few nights ago to buy a get-out-of-jail-free card, an emerald comb he'd kept in his pocket for just such a time as this. "Just to show you that I've been thinking about you, I got you a surprise."

"A gift for me?" Her eyes instantly grew bright. "I love gifts!"

Grinning, he made a mental note always to have one of these on hand and dug into his coat pocket. *Empty.* "It's . . . not here?"

She cast him a sad, crestfallen look that seemed to rip into his chest. "That's fine. You didn't need to get me anything."

A piss day. "Damn it! It was an emerald comb. I just bought it the other night for your hair." He checked all his pockets, then tore through his things. Nothing.

He must have evinced his disappointment, because she sighed, and her tone softened. "We'll find it later, Murdoch. But for now, you look exhausted. Why don't you come to bed?" She patted the spot beside her, glancing up at him from under her icy lashes.

Undone. Just like that, he grew hard for her. "You don't have to ask me twice."

Ignoring the cold, he stripped off his clothes—everything but his gloves—as she pulled off her gown. Once he joined her in bed, he snagged a blanket. She nibbled her lip, her eyes excited, knowing what he wanted to do.

"Lie back."

As she reclined, he drew the blanket over her, covering up to her breasts. Barrier in place, he eased above her, settling between her legs. He rested his upper body on his elbows, leaving his gloved palms free to fondle her luscious little breasts.

With his face buried in the flaxen hair spread over her pillow, he rocked his shaft against her, shuddering with pleasure.

This was his favorite position with her. At least like this, he could imagine he was actually inside her. And it made him recall his recurring dream of drinking her. The more tense their situation became, the more he dreamed of it. Now as he moved over her, he dragged his tongue across one of his sharpening fangs for a shot of blood, pretending it was hers, pretending he was truly taking her.

When he rolled his hips again, she wriggled her own, putting his shaft in just the right spot. "There, *kallim?*" he grated with another thrust.

"Ah, *yes*," she moaned, letting him know he'd rubbed directly over her clitoris.

Squeezing her breasts, he ground against her there, making her cry, "More!" He gave her more, harder and harder. As her moans grew louder, she writhed wildly, meeting him.

"Come for me," he rasped desperately, about to spill on her.

She arched her back, her body tensing beneath him as she neared her peak.

Suddenly he felt his ankle brush hers, skin to freezing skin. *The blanket rode up?* His eyes went wide, just as she cried out in agony.

"Murdoch, no!" She shoved him off her, scrambling away.

There she sat on one side of the bed, quivering with pain, while he moved to the other, sitting with his head in his hands. "Christ, I didn't mean to hurt you."

"W-we have to be more careful."

"Damn it! I need to touch you, or I'll go mad!"

She whispered, "Do you think this is any easier for me?"

He raised his head, staring at the wall as he said, "I want to make this better, I want to fix this for us. And I can't. There's nothing I can do."

He heard her pull on her gown before she walked on her knees toward him. "Murdoch, there might be a way. I didn't want to say anything because it's so uncertain, but there's a witch who is coming into her powers. The strongest one. In a mere fifty years, she could find the answer for us."

"A *mere* fifty years? Half a century of this?"

"We could get one of them to cast a spell and make us sleep, or—"

"Sleep? You mean hibernate?" He shot to his feet, yanking on his pants as he whirled around to face her. "Like goddamn animals? You expect me to lose five decades of my life?" he demanded, his frustration goading him. "Maybe this wasn't meant to be." As soon as the word left his lips, he regretted them.

But when she blinked at him as if he'd spoken blasphemy, his temper flared hotter. *As if she's never thought that.*

"Not meant to be?"

"What? You've never considered bailing on me?"

"No. I haven't."

"When we are together, all we do is fight. It just wasn't this hard . . ." He trailed off.

She stood as well, moving to face him. "What? What were you going to say?"

"Nothing."

"It just wasn't this hard with other women?" When he didn't deny it, her lips parted. "I am so sick of you talking about your past conquests!"

"I can't do this anymore!" He kicked her latest ice tablet, shattering it.

She stood motionless, her eyes growing silver with hurt and confusion. A tear spilled, then another, each one a knife to his heart.

He wanted to comfort her, to take her in his arms and ease that confusion. Then he remembered he *couldn't.*

"If you don't think fighting for us is worth the trouble," she murmured, "then I'm not going to bother either." She strode from the room, down the stairs, then out into the night.

He gave a vile curse, fighting the impulse to go after her. He was still angry, still exhausted. They would only fight more.

So he dressed, then traced to Mount Oblak, seeking one of his brothers or Rurik. He needed to talk with someone, to unburden himself. But never to speak about Daniela. No, never about her. What would he say anyway? *"Just looking at her wrecks me. I'm tempted every second by something that's dazzling and perfect—and always just out of reach."*

Though his brothers weren't there, he found Rurik, Lukyan, and a few others gambling in the castle's common area.

"Murdoch, join us!" Rurik called. "Have a drink."

Lukyan gave a snide laugh. "He won't."

Clearly nothing had changed between Murdoch and him since the demon attack. Worse, Lukyan was right—Murdoch had been just about to decline. When had he become so domesticated? So *predictably* domesticated.

Why not stay here? He resented another night of not having her, resented the strife between them that had no end in sight. A stiff whiskey seemed just the thing.

He took off his gloves and settled in front of the great hearth fire, rebelliously basking in its warmth.

Numb the ache. One shot down.

Blunt the need. Then another.

Thirty-three

DANII MARCHED STRAIGHT OUT INTO THE BLIZZARD. All around her, snowdrifts crested and furrowed, illustrating the path of the gusts.

With her gown whipping about her thighs, she sniffled, running her forearm over her teary eyes. She hadn't expected things to be easy between her and Murdoch, but she'd thought the prize was worth the fight.

Maybe he was right. *Maybe I should bail.* She'd never considered it before. Not until he'd all but dared her to. Another swipe over her eyes.

Murdoch equals misery. They would just keep hurting each other. Where was the limit? *When do you give up on someone you love?*

Ah, gods, she did love him. With all her heart.

Though the Valkyrie didn't have "fated mates" per se, they believed that one would know her partner when she realized she would always run to get into his arms.

If he came back now, I'd run right to him.

Which meant there'd be no bailing for Danii, not yet—

Her ears twitched. Even over the wind, she heard something

moving behind her. Danii sensed she was being followed, but for some reason she didn't believe it was Murdoch.

Then who the devil would be out here?

When a footstep crunched in the snow, she whirled around, spied a male in the icy shadows. His breaths didn't smoke. He had pointed ears.

An Iceren. No, not again! Her eyes darted, scanning for the rest of the assassins in the blustery night. She'd been unwary; now she would pay for it.

And all she could think of was how she'd left things with Murdoch.

Yet the male raised his palms. "My name is Jádian the Cold." His voice was deep-toned, raspy.

"How did you find me?"

"Actually, you found us. The cryomancy symbols you've been carving were about to unlock a portal. We learned you were nearing and merely awaited."

Cryomancy? Portal symbols? "Now you've come to kill me?"

"Not in the least. I mean you no harm."

She gave a bitter laugh. "Where's the rest of your battalion to back you up?"

"I've come alone."

"Your mistake. Since the last batch you bastards sent didn't fare so well."

"They were sent by Sigmund—before I assassinated him."

"He was . . . killed? By you?"

This Jádian nodded. "I was a general in his army and led a coup against him."

"Wh-why?"

"Because our people want their true queen back."

Had he just said *our* people? True queen? *Stay standing.* "Why now?"

"First I had to find you. Then I had to determine whether you were strong enough to rule. To make sure you were worthy to be Svana's heir. You are."

"This could be a trick, a way to take me prisoner."

He frowned. "Nïx didn't tell you about me?"

Was this Icere male the "pressy" coming her way? The one Nïx had mentioned directly after Danii had tried to explain the symbols and carving? "Uh, not in so many words."

"She told me she would."

He and Nïx had been *talking*?

"But then, your sister also said you'd be more accurate with your cryomancy."

"What does that mean?" Danii demanded.

"You're one symbol off from creating a portal into our realm. But yours would have opened two hundred miles south of Icergard, amid the White Death—a frozen wasteland that even you would have difficulty crossing."

"Then how did you find me?"

"One of your symbols was shattered tonight. It sounded like a cannon blast through the castle, and was a beacon for me."

When Murdoch kicked my tablet. . . .

"I opened my own portal directly to you here." He pointed in the distance, to an oval of diffused air that rebuffed the driving snow.

She shook her head irritably. "My shoddy cryomancy notwithstanding, this doesn't make sense. Why would they want me? My mother was reviled for attempting to kill Sigmund."

"Not reviled, *revered*. But the Icere were too fearful of Sigmund to rebel. Especially once Queen Svana was gone and they knew of no one to replace her. They have a holiday in Svana's name now."

"Oh." Such a queenly answer. But to be fair, this was *staggering*. "Wait. They knew of no one to replace her?"

"It was forbidden to speak your name. After a few centuries, new generations didn't even know it." He stepped closer to her, now mere feet away. "But they do now. And they await you."

"Jádian, there have been too many years of suspicion and running. If our positions were reversed, you wouldn't just blindly accept my word," she said. Yet even as she spoke, she realized she *did* believe him.

Danii knew men. And this one was telling the truth. Her previously twitching ears were still.

"You should contact Nïx if you have doubts," he said. "Until then . . ." He pulled something from his vest.

"Oh, gods," Danii breathed. *My mother's crown.* With shaking hands, she accepted the piece from him, staring down at it through watering eyes.

And as she held the crown, cold and right in her hands, fresh memories of the day her mother left finally surfaced.

"Never, never go to Icergard. Not until you're shown the way."

"Who will show me, mama?" Danii cried. "When?"

"When the time is right, you'll show yourself."

"How? How will I know?"

"You already know the way, my darling. You just haven't remembered it yet. . . ."

Danii exhaled a stunned breath. She'd been making *her own way* to Icergard, because the time was right. All of this was . . . real. Danii felt it, down to her bones, as pure as a chill. All those years of fearing the Icere soldiers and spies were over.

She could have a normal life. No more assassination attempts! She could be with her own kind. This was the solution to all her problems.

So why was she suddenly so depressed?

Because her first thought was that she couldn't wait to tell Murdoch. And because this new life didn't have a surly vampire in it.

"Jádian, this is a lot to take in."

He drew nearer. "You only need accept what's yours." The corners of his lips curled, disconcerting her. "What's been yours for so long."

Is he flirting with me? Brain overload. *I can't believe I'm in my nightgown. . . .*

Jádian was kind of *sexy*. He stood as tall as Murdoch and had intense blue eyes, the color of glacial ice. Berserker ravels tangled in his thick blond hair. His sleeveless shirt displayed muscular arms and the cobalt tracings of the Icere. But whereas her markings were delicate, his were wide and bold, designed to attract females like her.

And still, for Danii, the vampire won hands down. "Um, let me think about it," she said. "You can just make another portal here, right? Let's meet at the same time tomorrow night."

She turned to go—and felt fingers close around her bare arm. She stiffened. A split second later, comprehension hit her and she gasped.

No pain. She turned back.

Again that sensual curling of his lips. "Maybe I need to explain the other benefits of coming back with me."

Jádian was *very* sexy. "You're, uh, really devoted to your people. You'll resort to flirting to get me to return."

"There's no hardship."

"I'm not . . . yours or anything?" Could she be a vampire's Bride *and* a noble fey's lady?

"I'm not a big believer in fated mates." Had a shadow of some emotion flickered in his blue eyes? "But I could kiss you to better tell."

"K-kiss me?" She'd never been kissed. Her curiosity prodded her. Her head spun. What about Murdoch? Gods, she loved that vampire.

But he doesn't even want to fight for me.

Jádian took the matter out of her hands. "I think my queen would like a kiss," he murmured, leaning down to her.

Danii tensed when his lips touched hers. She couldn't help the defensive reaction. Yet again there was no pain. Instead she felt the firmness of his lips, the delicious brush of his tongue.

So this is kissing. If only she could do this with Murdoch, she'd never stop. . . .

THIRTY-FOUR

"MURDOCH USED TO SAY THAT WOMEN ARE LIKE BOTTLES of liquor—sample them, savor them, then discard them," Rurik drunkenly declared, his eye patch crooked.

More vampires had joined in the gaming, and they all laughed. Yet Rurik's words sounded hollow to Murdoch, hollow like the ache in his chest. *What a slavering jackass I used to be.*

He remembered other men slapping him on the back over his conquests. They'd been so envious of his success with women. He no longer shared their definition of success.

Rurik quieted his tone, skewering Murdoch with a look. "I wonder if he still feels the same way."

He's aware that my heart's beating. At length, Murdoch answered, "Until you meet the one woman who's meant to be yours. Then you hold on and never let go."

How well was he holding on to Daniela? *I'm driving her away.*

She'd been so vulnerable when she suggested they sleep through five decades. And he'd been so busy raging over the unfairness of their situation that never once had it registered what *she* had just offered to do for them—sacrifice fifty years of her own life.

He hadn't thanked her for her offer. He'd ridiculed her for it.

I've been such a fool. What the fuck was fifty years if they were together? *She's my life now.*

Clarity. His brother Nikolai had told him that love would feel different from anything he'd ever known. Murdoch concluded he was right.

I'm in love with her.

He pushed away the bottle. *Go to her . . . apologize.* He'd left her crying. He'd been such an ass, like the old selfish Murdoch who'd boasted about women being as expendable as liquor.

With that thought, the truth sank in. *I'm not worth her tears.*

But he *could* be.

He stood unsteadily, donning his coat and the obligatory gloves, then traced to the lodge. When he didn't find her inside, he started out into the still-raging blizzard, following her fading tracks.

Finally, he caught sight of movement among the thick drifts. Just as he was about to trace to her, he spotted something that defied belief. He stared in drunken shock, squinting through the flurries.

There was another male, one who looked to be of her kind, with Nordic coloring and pointed ears. He was easily as tall as Murdoch.

And Daniela was up on her toes . . . kissing him.

Can't be real. I'm drunk. Can't see through the blizzard. Somehow she was withstanding the male's touch, receiving his kiss. The bastard grasped her bare upper arms—with his ungloved hands. Murdoch gnashed his teeth. *Skin to skin.*

A jealous rage ripped through him. All the frustration he'd grappled with for months roared to life. His fangs went sharp with aggression, his heart pumping with wrath. Just when he realized he loved her, she would betray him?

The words from his dreams echoed in his mind: *How badly do you want her? What would you sacrifice?*

Anything, he'd do anything. . . .

Didn't she know that she belonged to him? *After tonight, she will.*

* * *

This is nice, Danii thought. *But it's not as I imagined it.*

There was no loss of control or breathless wonder. No weakening of her knees. No *lust.*

Because it wasn't Murdoch.

Just as she began to pull back from Jádian, her ears twitched. Something was wrong—

Jádian went flying away from her into a tree. She blinked, struggling to get her bearings. Murdoch? *He's back!*

And he was seething, staring at Jádian with deadly intent, his eyes flooding black.

"No, Murdoch!" she cried. "This is Lord Jádian. He's come to offer me my crown! He's killed Sigmund. Murdoch, are you hearing me?"

Nothing.

"Are you drunk?"

Finally he spoke. To *Jádian.* "You dare touch my woman?" He launched himself at the Iceren, who eagerly met him. They clashed in the snow and howling winds, throwing punches.

Jádian was fast, skilled, and in his element, but against Murdoch's tracing and palpable fury he was no match. Until Jádian raised ice in his palm. . . .

Oh, gods, Murdoch. "Stop! Both of you, stop fighting now!"

Jádian immediately dropped his hands. *Following the order?* He gritted his teeth just before Murdoch roared and swung his fist, connecting with Jádian's temple like an anvil hit. Jádian staggered.

She rushed between them. "Jádian! Are you all right?" Never taking his eyes from Murdoch, he nodded. "Stay here, please." To Murdoch, she said, "Vampire, come inside with me. *Now!*"

She couldn't believe she was talking like this to the drunk, infuriated vampire who'd just caught his Bride kissing a strange male. Yet when she strode toward the lodge, Murdoch did follow her, though he seemed to be getting more and more enraged with each step.

Once they were inside, she said, "This is not as bad as it looked."

"He *kissed* you," Murdoch grated, his eyes wild. "He took what doesn't belong to him."

"What are you talking about?"

"Your first kiss—it was mine to give you one day. But you let him."

"I just wanted to see what it'd be like," she said, repeating his words from all those months ago. "It's *trivial*, especially compared to what has happened tonight. Jádian has come to take me back to Icergard, to my people. They want to offer me my throne."

"And *Jádian*"—he sneered the name—"had to kiss you to extend the fucking invitation?"

"You have a lot of nerve to blame me for kissing another, since you did it to me."

"*Before* we'd become committed."

"Committed?" she cried. "You don't even know the meaning of the word! You leave me here, avoiding me, and when you do return, you're distant and preoccupied."

"You let him touch you!"

"I did, and it was nice. *More* than nice!" she added the lie. "But maybe you're too drunk to notice that I was pulling away from him—because of you. I chose you, over a male I can touch! And now I see that I chose poorly. Luckily, I can rectify the situation." She held up her crown, clenched in her fist. "I'm going to Icergard with him."

Something in Murdoch seemed to snap. "No, Daniela, you're not." He stalked closer to her. "You're going to stay with me—because you are *mine*." Finally he was behaving like the domineering vampire. "My woman to possess, to kiss, to drink." As he stared down at her, his irises were black as night and just as fathomless.

Wait . . . to drink? "No, no. Don't, Murdoch!" But she was caught, mesmerized by the desire in his eyes. "Ah, gods . . ." When his gaze dropped to her neck, she knew he was going to do it.

So why am I not fighting him?

His gloved hands clamped her shoulders, squeezing them as he held her in place. His parted lips covered her neck, seeking. . . .

Just as she cried out, he groaned and bit down. She flailed, but he held her tight. Pain seared her skin, his fangs like two brands shoved into her neck, his tongue like a flame.

THIRTY-FIVE

MURDOCH FELL UPON HER, PRESSING HER INTO THE WALL as he sank his fangs deeper into the sweet flesh of her neck. The cold pained him, so badly he nearly released her, but soon blood wet his mouth. The taste . . . He growled against her, the pleasure was so intense.

Finally, she's in my arms. At last, I can hold her, taste her.

Couldn't believe he was doing this, needed to pull away. *I'm taking too much.*

He could *feel* her cries against him. When she screamed, he somehow released her, stumbling back. "Oh, God, Daniela!" He stared in horror at her ravaged neck, her tender skin burned.

As she backed away from him, her silver eyes welled with tears. "How could you, Murdoch?" Her pupils were huge with shock. "You *vowed* to me."

Between heaving breaths, he rasped, "Daniela, I don't know what happened."

"You lost control. And you'll do it again."

He wanted to deny it. *Christ help me, I can't.* His expression must have betrayed his thoughts.

Her tears spilled, her face paler from blood loss. "Now you're the second man who's touched me against my will." Her words were growing weaker, indistinct.

He grated in confusion, "The second?"

"I'm leaving, and I never want to see your face again as long as I live."

Jádian rushed into the lodge then, his watchful gaze taking in the scene. "You *bit* her?" He looked at Murdoch like he was scum, like he was a monster. "I will slaughter you for harming my queen."

"N-no," Daniela said through her tears, tugging on his arm. "I just want to go."

Go, with that male, away from Murdoch. Forever. "Don't you leave me!" he bellowed.

In answer, she put the back of her hand against her mouth and sobbed. Unsteady, crying freely, Daniela turned to the door without a glance back. When Murdoch charged after her, Jádian stood in his way. Murdoch tensed, about to attack him once more—

Daniela's legs gave way, her body crumpling. In a flash, Jádian swung around and caught her up against him. "Queen Daniela?" Then his eyes narrowed. "Blood loss."

"Give her to me," Murdoch grated with outstretched hands, "or I'll kill you so slowly."

"So you can drain more of her?" Jádian shifted Daniela into one arm; with his other, he hurled a handful of ice at Murdoch.

The hit connected with his chest like a freight train, sending Murdoch crashing into a wall. His skin began to freeze, trapping him in place.

He thrashed to break free, but the ice was too strong. "Don't you dare take her! She can't see that this is a trick—"

With Daniela still in his arms, Jádian loomed over Murdoch. "There is no trick. I've eliminated any threat against her. Her sister even told me how to find her, because she wants Daniela to be with her own kind."

"Then where the fuck were you for the last two thousand years?"

Jádian didn't answer the question, just said, "I will leave you alive, but only because that was her will."

"Give her time to wake, so I can talk to her—"

"You believe you can convince her to stay with you? You attacked her. Look at her neck. *Remember* this sight. This is what you are to her—pain."

"No . . . no . . ."

"I'm taking her to where she can be content, vampire. Where she will be safe."

"Like her mother?"

"Her mother didn't have *me* to protect her." With a wave of the male's hand, the ice began to build up over Murdoch's torso, crushing him. Higher and higher, climbing up over his chin.

Powerless to do more than watch them leave, Murdoch had time for a last breath—and used it to bellow her name. But they were already gone.

Ice swallowed him, cutting off his air. Soon blackness followed. And in that time, he dreamed Daniela's memories, taken from her blood.

Unable to wake, his clenched fists frozen, Murdoch watched as a Roman senator took her from a cage so he could run his fingertips over her delicate skin, fascinated by how it burned.

Murdoch *felt* her pain, her revulsion.

How long she'd been trapped in that hell, he couldn't determine. But he experienced her relief when Myst—the female Murdoch had hated for so long—and two other sisters had come for her. Myst had saved her life and murdered the Roman.

Why had Daniela never told Murdoch about any of this? About being a captive? Rage consumed him for the long-dead Roman who'd tortured her.

And yet Murdoch had hurt her just as badly, if not worse. After all, she'd trusted him.

Daniela thinks of me as she does that monster.

And she should. *The look in her eyes when I released her neck. . . .*

When the ice had melted enough to be broken and he regained consciousness, his driving need to go after her was extinguished.

Who the hell was he to take her away from her fate? From her own kind?

Her whole life had been made better, fixed. Part of him still wanted to believe that she'd been tricked, that she would need him to save her . . . but the disgust shown by Jádian had been real. And he could easily have killed Murdoch.

As much as it enraged him to recall how Jádian had kissed Daniela, Murdoch knew they looked right together.

She's gone.

For hours, he mindlessly roamed the too-quiet lodge, cursing bitterly, ignoring his brothers' calls. Even as Daniela's blood still thrummed in his veins, his chest felt empty, aching for her.

I've lost her. The look in her eyes . . .

Murdoch punched the wall. The pain briefly diverted his attention from the hollowness in his chest.

So this is love.

He'd lost the one woman he'd ever loved. No, not *lost.* He'd driven her away with his selfishness and neglect. With his broken vows and attack.

Now that he could think about the night with a clearer head, he remembered that she *had* been pulling away from Jádian. *Because of me.*

Murdoch had never understood Conrad's madness. Now he did. There were some things the mind was not made to handle, differing in each person.

I'm not made to live without Daniela.

The phone rang yet again. There'd been talk of an upcoming battle. Maybe that was exactly what Murdoch needed. To fight. To be a vampire. To kill and destroy and not think about how Daniela would be happier away from him.

He answered the phone.

"We go to war," Nikolai said.

Perfect.

Thirty-six

So this is Icergard, Danii thought as Jádian gave her the grand tour of the castle the next day. *I'm definitely getting a Fortress of Solitude vibe.*

When she'd awakened, sharp-eared Icere maids had smiled shyly as they laid out a gown of the softest silk Danii had ever imagined, along with Svana's crown.

A fire had burned in a hearth of ice—a blue fire that emanated *cold.*

Which was just *cool.*

Last night, it had been late here when Jádian had sneaked her into her new royal chambers. He'd thought it "politically unwise" for the Icere to see their new queen's face wet from tears, her body lifeless, with her neck bearing the unmistakable mark of a vampire.

"As in most factions of the Lore, vampires are feared and hated here," he'd explained.

Without wonder. She still couldn't believe that Murdoch had bitten her. "What did you do to him?" she'd asked.

"I left him in ice. I would have killed him, but you ordered me not to fight."

"And you follow my orders?"

"You're my queen," he'd said simply. "One who'll be crowned in three days, if that's acceptable to you."

"It is. But what are the Icere going to think of me?"

"They're going to love you as they did your mother. . . ."

Now, as he showed her around, she tried to concentrate on what he was saying, but her mind was troubled over the events of the night. Murdoch's bite had been the worst pain she'd ever experienced, and yet she'd felt some kind of connection to him.

He'd taken her blood, lots of it. Would he dream her memories? At the idea, embarrassment suffused her. Would he know how lonely she'd been?

Gradually, her neck had healed, but she was still uneasy, fretful. Guilt weighed on her. She didn't believe she'd brought on the attack—or that she'd deserved it in any way. But she still felt complicity, because she hadn't repelled him.

She could have frozen Murdoch, could have blasted him with the fury of that blizzard. Instead, a fatalism had swept over her, as if she'd been *waiting forever* for his bite.

Myst had taken pleasure from it, as had Kaderin. It'd been a nightmare for Daniela—

"Do you regret coming here?" Jádian asked, rousing her from her thoughts. He was gazing straight ahead, his face impassive, but she could sense his tension.

"No, not at all."

"You are quiet."

"Uh, I'm just amazed by what I'm seeing." In truth, Castle Icergard was an engineering marvel. Built beneath an invisible dome of ice, the structure was bricked with baguette-cut diamonds—each half a foot long. The prisms at the ends of the diamonds glinted unrelentingly, like a Valkyrie's worst nightmare. *Good thing I'm immune.* "It's remarkable," she added.

"It's . . . home," Jádian said simply.

Inside the castle, elaborate designs were carved into all the walls, with smaller diamonds embedded throughout. Thin sheets of polished and etched ice comprised the windows. Chandeliers of ice hung from the great-hall ceiling, their lights that cold blue fire, shimmering like the aurora borealis dancing in the night sky.

The more Danii saw, the more she loved it here. *Ice, ice, and would you like some ice with that ice?* Here, plants grew from it. The people held it sacred, just as other cultures worshipped the sun or the earth as life-giving.

Earlier, any of the Icere they'd come upon had been reserved, but as word got around that Danii was personable, more approached her.

A female even asked her to bless her baby girl. Danii swallowed nervously as she gathered the babe in her arms. She'd never in her life held one.

The mother said, "Welcome home, Queen Daniela."

As Danii traced the backs of her fingers over the baby's soft cheek, tears welled.

This is where I belong. Where she'd always belonged.

I am home.

The cell door slammed behind Murdoch, Nikolai, and Sebastian.

"We're screwed," Sebastian muttered.

Murdoch did not disagree.

When the three had shown up at Mount Oblak ready to go to war, the king's guards had instead forced them into a barred suite.

These chambers were used for political prisoners. Here were facilities, a shower. Yet no one could trace inside or out, and the walls and door were mystically reinforced.

Luckily, the three brothers hadn't been taken to the dungeons below, filled with Ivo's old torture devices. But then, Kristoff had made it clear he had no intention of torturing them.

Or freeing them—until they gave up Conrad. Which they would never do.

How long would the king keep them here? Weeks? Or more? At the thought of a protracted imprisonment, Murdoch swore under his breath. Though he had decided not to go after Daniela, his resolve hadn't lasted long. No matter what, he was deeply ashamed of hurting her, and wouldn't rest until he'd apologized to her.

Now he paced, barely listening to his brothers.

"We knew this might happen," Nikolai said. "A one-in-a-thousand chance."

"How did Kristoff find out?" Sebastian snapped.

"He has ways."

"Ways? As in Lukyan or some other Russian," Sebastian said. "When I find out who informed on us—"

"You'll do what?" Nikolai demanded. "We're the ones at fault here. *We* broke the law."

"But how can Kristoff expect us to give up our own brother?" Sebastian shook his head. "Conrad would be powerless against his men, unable to defend himself, unable to escape."

"We might as well swing the swords ourselves," Nikolai agreed. "But if we think Myst and Kaderin are going to just sit around and accept our capture, we're deluded."

"Kristoff must know they'll wage an attack," Sebastian said. "As soon as they find out what happened, they'll likely plot to take this castle and execute him."

When a chill night breeze sieved through the barred window, Murdoch crossed to it. He sucked in air, feeling hot, claustrophobic.

"Murdoch?" Nikolai said. "Are you even listening to us . . . ?"

How could I have bitten Daniela? When he loved her. And what was fifty years? He could wait an eternity. But he couldn't get to her to tell her this. Frustration strangled him like a noose.

In Murdoch's absence, would Lord Jádian continue kissing her? His fists clenched. *Kissing my Daniela.* When he punched the wall, he broke every bone in his hand, the protected stone mocking even his immortal strength.

Murdoch turned in time to see Nikolai and Sebastian share a glance. They had to know that he'd been blooded—even Conrad had heard Murdoch's heart beating—but they'd said nothing over the last several months. Probably because of all the secrets they'd been keeping, as well.

"What the hell is going on with you?" Sebastian said.

Murdoch knew he must be shocking them. For so long he'd been carefree. "Don't want to be here," he muttered. The need to talk to his brothers pressed on him, but he volunteered nothing, keeping at least one vow to Daniela.

Only now did he understand why she'd been so secretive about them. *I wouldn't have bet on a future with me either. Definitely wouldn't have advertised it.*

When dawn came, his brothers slept, but Murdoch dreaded dreaming about her, stealing more of her memories. Hour after hour, he paced, feeling a madness creeping over him. The bars were keeping him from her. Silently, he strained against them. *Want to be with her.* He couldn't budge them.

Eventually, exhaustion ruled and he passed out, unwillingly slipping into dreams. This time, he saw the reflection of a young girl—he knew it was Daniela—gazing back at him from a mirror. A striking woman with the same unusual coloring as Daniela was behind her, fitting a crown atop her head. Her mother? They spoke to each other in a language that sounded similar to Icelandic, but he understood it. . . .

"You already know the way," the mother said. *"You just haven't remembered it yet."*

Then came a more recent memory: Daniela staring at her ice carvings, wondering, *Are these clues how to get to Icergard . . . ?*

Murdoch woke in a rush, shooting up from his cot in the middle of the day. "It's so bloody hot in here!" He yanked off his jacket in irritation.

When Nikolai rose to stoke the fire, Murdoch grated, "No, no fire! Put it out." He imagined frost. Blood served cold. For once, he craved being back amid the ice at the lodge.

Sebastian was awake as well and frowned at him. "It's actually cool."

"How can you say that?" he snapped, unable to contain his aggravation. Then he stilled. Were his breaths . . . smoking? He traced to the suite's bathroom, gazing in the mirror. His breaths didn't fog the glass. As Daniela's didn't. Blue tinged his lips and under his eyes.

My God. The reason he'd felt so hot—her blood was running through his veins.

Nikolai had told him that Myst's blood made him even stronger. Sebastian had said the same about drinking Kaderin's.

Why couldn't Daniela's make Murdoch more like her? He gave a shout of laughter. *I've found a way to touch her!*

Then his heart sank. *Just when I've lost her.* He was trapped by his own king, by his loyalty to his brother. . . .

Another day dragged by, then two. As their imprisonment wore on, Murdoch began returning to his normal temperature, which maddened him even more. He couldn't lose this coldness—otherwise he'd have to hurt her again.

If he was ever freed from this bloody cell. And if she'd ever let him drink her.

"Nikolai! Where are you?"

Murdoch shot awake, his gaze darting. He could have sworn he'd heard Conrad—in Oblak—yelling for Nikolai. But all was quiet, his brothers still sleeping. He must've dreamed it. Strange, he usually dreamed of nothing but Daniela.

With a weary exhalation, he rose. *More than two weeks gone.* The brothers and their king were locked in a stalemate. Would they stay here indefinitely?

As he did every night, Murdoch tried and failed to drink enough to sustain his weight. Then he prowled from one wall to the next, deciphering more scenes from Daniela's life that he'd witnessed in sleep.

Her memories were becoming clearer to him. When he dreamed, he felt how lonely she'd been, how she'd tried not to nurse hope over Murdoch. *Once a rogue, always a rogue.*

He'd done so little to set her mind at ease, had done nothing to make sure she understood her loneliness was over. *I never told her I'm in love with her.* Instead, he'd voiced his doubts.

During one miserable day, he'd seen her memory of that night with Jádian and had learned her thoughts as she'd kissed the Iceren.

She'd been thinking about Murdoch. Danii had chosen *him* over a male who could touch her, a nobleman of her own kind who could kiss her. She hadn't been thinking about bailing on Murdoch at all. At least not before he'd hurt her, *attacked* her.

This situation was intolerable. To be kept from Daniela now? Murdoch wanted her so much, he'd once actually considered betraying his brother—

"Nikolai!" The word boomed down the castle corridor, echoing.

Nikolai and Sebastian shot awake.

Dear God. "Was that . . . ?"

"Conrad," Nikolai said. "He's *here.*"

Maybe I'm not home.

Danii sat upon her throne, among her own kind in a paradise of ice, and she was . . . bored.

Days ago, she'd been crowned with much fanfare. The Icere had prepared banquets, carved sculptures in her honor, and played music. Plus, they'd declared a snow day at the castle—literally, it had fallen from the ceilings.

And since the festivities?

Jádian was a constant bodyguard, always nearby, always solemn. Most of the fey she'd met could be described as "serious." She'd figured this was an aftereffect of having an evil dictator ruling them for so long—but had learned this was just their nature.

Here, there were no practical jokes, no sisters bent on thieving her clothing. No gorgeous vampires to tackle into the snow.

Time seemed to be moving as slowly as the glaciers surrounding them. She wondered if it was possible to expire from boredom. *The study begins . . . now.*

To make matters worse, she missed Murdoch like an ache. Every day, she dwelled on what she could have done differently. *Perhaps I shouldn't have kissed another man? Just a thought.*

But that indiscretion hadn't mattered. She and Murdoch had already been finished. Danii had thought they would be together forever, but he hadn't agreed, hadn't believed that they were worth the fight—

With a sudden flush of guilt, she recognized that maybe she hadn't *truly* committed either. Hadn't she herself given them a one-in-fifty shot? She'd been betting against them from the beginning, might as well have gone and signed Loa's book. . . .

Across the throne room, Jádian turned to her with his brows raised. Since she'd arrived, she hadn't seen him smile once. There'd been no more flirting from him. She'd concluded that he *was* devoted to his people, had probably only kissed her to sway her to come to Icergard.

His name of Jádian the Cold was well earned. Thinking back over his fight with Murdoch, she recalled that Jádian's pulse had never gotten elevated. He'd been indignant, ready to die for his queen. But he hadn't been ready to lose his temper for her.

Aside from being unemotional, he had a reputation for cold-blooded ruthlessness. Her ladies-in-waiting had told her how he'd blamed the death of his wife on Sigmund, conspiring relentlessly for years, only waiting for Daniela to be located before striking.

They'd also spoken of sordid rumors that Jádian had once kept a seductive fire demoness as his prisoner hidden in the dungeon. . . .

He crossed to Danii then. "You are unhappy here." It wasn't a question, but he did sound disbelieving.

"I . . . it's been a big change."

"You'll grow accustomed." He was no-nonsense and logical to the point that most Valkyrie would deem him a buzz kill. But he was beloved by the orderly people here.

"Jádian, I was recalling our kiss."

He stiffened, as if he thought she'd want to resume some dalliance with him. "What of it?"

"You weren't thinking about me."

"And you were imagining that I was a vampire," he said with the tiniest hint of irritation, adding, "my queen."

Busted. It was too true. Though Jádian was as sigh-worthy a male as she had ever seen, she still longed to run her fingers through dark hair. She yearned to gaze up at gray eyes that turned black with lust. "Was it just a play to get me to return with you?"

He shrugged. "You needed to be here."

So their kiss hadn't even been real. Now her curiosity redoubled. What would a *real* one be like—

"And you need to accept that this is where you belong," he said.

Yes, no longer was she living in the sweltering heat of Louisiana, surrounded by people she couldn't touch. No longer was she in a relationship that was doomed by her very nature.

Here, the broken doll was all fixed. *And I'm miserable.*

Thirty-seven

"*Nikolai!*"

Stoic Nikolai looked flabbergasted. Then he shot to his feet, tracing to the cell door. "Conrad?" he called back.

"He's come *here*?" Sebastian bit out. "How did he get free from those manacles?"

Murdoch cursed under his breath. "Kristoff will take his head."

"If his guards don't," Nikolai said.

Conrad appeared outside their cell. Through the bars, they stared in bewilderment. Conrad had blood and mud splattered across his beaten face and matted in his hair. His red eyes glowed with menace. Gaping wounds covered him.

"What in the hell are you doing here?" Nikolai demanded. "And whose blood is that?"

Conrad studied the cell bars. "I don't have time for questions."

"You have to leave!" Murdoch said. "They'll execute you if they capture you."

He gave a rough laugh, clamping hold of the bars. "Defy them to do either." Gritting his teeth, he strained against them.

"Those are as protected as your chains were," Sebastian said. "The wood, the metal, and the stone surrounding them are all reinforced. You can't possibly—"

Conrad wrenched them wide, breaking the metal.

"My God," Nikolai murmured.

Conrad had gotten *stronger*?

"Need your help to find my Bride!" In a frenzy, Conrad yanked the wreckage free. "I'm not mad . . . but I need you to trace me to every cemetery in New Orleans. Do you know where they are?"

Nikolai gaped. "Your . . . Bride?"

"His heart beats," Murdoch said.

"Do you know where they are or not?" Conrad bellowed.

Nikolai nodded slowly. "I know all the cemeteries. Myst and I hunt ghouls there."

"Will you do this?"

"Conrad, just calm—"

"Fuck calm, Nikolai!"

"So this is Conrad Wroth," Kristoff said from behind him, surrounded by his personal guards.

Without turning, Conrad sneered, "The bloody *Russian*. What do you want?"

Kristoff seemed amused by this. "I'd known the Wroths were genetically incapable of fawning to a king, but a modicum of respect . . ." His demeanor was self-satisfied, almost like he'd planned this all along.

Conrad faced the natural-born vampire.

"You've taken out my entire castle guard," Kristoff said in a casual tone. "Something a Horde battalion couldn't do. My informants didn't tell me you were *this* strong." His pale eyes were expressionless, yet Murdoch knew he was calculating. "But then, you've been blooded."

"I don't have time for this!" Conrad snapped. "I'll kill you just to keep you from speaking."

The guards tensed, hands at their sword hilts.

"Kill me? You wouldn't know your Bride if not for me, if not for your brothers. You'd have been dead three hundred years ago."

"I've put that together!"

To Nikolai, Kristoff said, "He took out the guards without killing a single one—almost as if he was making a point. You were right. Conrad isn't lost." He cast Conrad a quizzical glance. "He's . . . quite a few things, but he's not irredeemable. And I can concede when I have made a mistake. Though you should have come to me instead of willfully breaking our laws."

Nikolai exhaled. "I couldn't take the risk that you would say no. He's my brother," he said simply.

Kristoff turned back to Conrad. "Swear fealty to me, and all of you leave today as allies. Otherwise we fight."

Conrad gritted his teeth, eyes darting, but eventually he grated, "I'll vow . . . that I'll never engage you or your army."

After an appraising look, Kristoff said, "It will do. For now." To the other three brothers, he added, "Take a week off. And do get your Brides to cease plotting my downfall."

When the king and his men disappeared, Nikolai said, "Conrad, you must tell me what's happened for me to help you. Who is your Bride?"

Conrad hastily said, "Néomi, this beautiful little dancer. Love her. So much it pains me. Have to find her."

We're free. I can go to Daniela at last, Murdoch thought, barely hearing what Conrad told them, something about cemeteries and resurrections—needing to listen for his Bride's heartbeats?

Sebastian said, "The ghost thing again," just as Murdoch muttered, "Con's thoroughly lost it."

Conrad snapped his fangs at them, his red eyes glowing. "This happened!"

"I don't know what outcome I'm hoping for," Sebastian began. "Either Conrad's irretrievably mad, or his Bride is a spirit from beyond whose corpse is lost. This seems like a lose-lose."

"He always did things differently," Murdoch said absently,

scarcely believing the fact that Conrad had gotten loose—and been blooded—and that Murdoch and his other brothers were freed. All was right with Kristoff.

I can possibly win Daniela. And keep her. But first he had to find her. Murdoch dared a slap on Conrad's back, saying, "I would like to stay, but I have an emergency that's weeks overdue. Good luck, Con." With that, he traced from the castle.

He could think of only one person who'd know how to reach Daniela.

In the past, he'd gone by Val Hall to see where she had lived for the last seventy years—it was a haunting place protected by flying, spectral wraiths.

Now Murdoch returned there, ready to do battle with them in order to see Nïx the Ever-Knowing. The soothsayer had been helping everyone else.

Why not me?

Thirty-Eight

"Because you bit her," Nïx told him before he'd spoken a word.

While he'd been wasting precious time determining how to evade the cloud of wraiths and storm Val Hall, they'd suddenly parted for Nïx as she'd casually strolled from the manor.

"That's why I won't tell you where it is," she continued. She was chewing gum and wore a pink T-shirt that read: *Jedi Kitty*.

Taken aback, he said, "Nïx, I'm Murdoch Wroth. You've been working with my brother Nikolai, and I need—"

"I know who you are. And what you've done to poor Daniela. You've driven her straight into the arms of that hot-on-a-stick Jádian."

No, Daniela wasn't lost yet. She *couldn't* be. "Tell me how to get to her."

"Why should I?" the soothsayer asked in a mulish tone. "I like her with Jádian. He doesn't, oh, burn her cold skin as he drains her blood."

Murdoch flushed.

"Maybe you should do the selfless thing and let her go," Nïx said. "What if she can be happier there?"

"Maybe I should give her all the information she doesn't have yet, information she'll need to make this decision."

"What doesn't she know?"

"That I'm in love with her, and I'm willing to do whatever it takes to be with her." His father's words arose in his mind: *Son, you've never cared about anything enough to fight for it—or to fear losing it.* Though this might have been true then, now Murdoch was making up for three centuries of not caring.

"I never told her these things." Murdoch closed in on Nïx. "Valkyrie, I won't rest until I get the chance to."

She cast him an appraising glance, squinting as if he were a book she was trying to read in dim light.

He ran his palm over his face. "Look, I know you helped the Lykae Bowen several times. You've even assisted Nikolai. But you won't help me? Why, damn it?"

She blinked up at him. "Because I play favorites?"

He scowled. "Tell me anything. Anything at all."

"Anything? Okay—a lot of people have some serious money on the fact that you're a cad."

"No longer," he bit out. "Can't you see the future and know that I'm going to be good to her?"

She narrowed her eyes. After long moments, she said, "Huh. You remain eternally faithful to her. I did *not* see that one coming."

Irritation flared. Like he needed her to tell him that.

She shrugged. "I still won't help you find her. Even if I was moved to *deus ex* your *machina*, I refuse to portend for every Tom, Murdoch, and Harry. It cheapens the experience, and before long I'll have a reputation as a sooth-whore." She fogged her claws, then buffed them on her T-shirt. "Besides, you already know how to reach Daniela."

"How? Tell me!" From the memories?

The moment began to feel surreal, as if all of his life had been leading up to this. The world seemed to spin. He pictured Daniela carving tirelessly; he strained his memory to see precisely what she'd wrought—

"Fine, I will divulge one thing. . . ." Nïx said. "Danii's going to make Jádian her king. If she hasn't already."

Ah, Christ, no.

With that prediction, Nïx traipsed back past the wraiths—*handing them a lock of hair?*—leaving him with a knot of dread in his chest. What if Daniela had married Jádian?

Murdoch's fangs sharpened. *Then she'll become a widow.*

He traced back to Siberia to gear up at the lodge, dragging a backpack from a closet. When he turned around, Nikolai and Myst appeared in the room.

"So this is where you've been hiding out," Nikolai said. Then he frowned. "The last place I would've looked for you. Literally, the last of your properties we've tried over the months. Siberia, Murdoch? There's only one way it could make sense to live here."

Murdoch punched clothes and cold-weather gear into the pack. "I don't have time for this."

"Make time," Myst said. "We know you're with Danii."

"I'm *not* with her. That's the goddamned problem."

Whatever Myst saw in his expression made hers soften. "What are you planning?" she asked more gently. "To go to Icergard?"

"Yes."

"To bring her back?"

He said nothing, just continued to pack.

Her eyes went wide. "To live there? You won't survive it. The Icere lands make Siberia feel balmy."

Nikolai added, "It's dark now, but what will you do in the summer? At that latitude, it will be light twenty-four hours a day."

"I'll stay inside. In a coffin, if I have to."

"And Kristoff?" Nikolai asked. "You swore your fealty. And now that we're finally working on an alliance with the Valkyrie, you plan to desert the army? He'll be forced to kill you for that, especially on the heels of our last transgression."

"I know this! God, I know."

"You won't be able to see your family any longer." Nikolai moved in front of him. "Speaking of which, I know you're too preoccupied to ask, but Conrad is fine. I just left him. He was telling the truth about his Bride, Néomi. She's a comely little dancer who—if you can imagine this—adores him and calms him."

Murdoch slowed. "I am glad for that."

"How are you even going to get to this Icergard?" Nikolai said. "It's late fall in the Arctic. The temps could already be forty below. Damn it, Murdoch, *think* about that. If you spit, it will freeze before it hits the ground."

"No planes can fly there," Myst said. "Not even Lore planes."

He fastened up his pack. "I'll get as far north as I can, then trace the rest of the way."

"You can only trace as far as you can see," Nikolai said. "You better hope the visibility is good."

"We'll call Kaderin," Myst offered. "She'll be able to help with the logistics. She knows how to get to places better than anyone."

Murdoch shook his head. "I don't have time. And I think I know a way."

Daniela had been missing one cryomancy symbol, the one Murdoch had shattered. He would use her memories to recreate it.

Because he'd dreamed her meeting with Jádian and had heard their conversation, Murdoch was aware that her last symbol wasn't correct. He knew if he copied Daniela's work, the portal would open two hundred miles south of Icergard.

He also knew that Jádian doubted even Daniela could survive that cold wasteland—*the White Death.*

Murdoch shook his head hard, resolve like steel inside him. So he would have to trace a couple hundred miles north—quickly.

How bad can it be?

Murdoch had never comprehended what cold was.

An arctic blizzard raged around him, howling so loudly it pained his ears.

The visibility was maybe two feet, which meant he could trace no farther than that at a time. His muscles were weakening, flagging more with each brutal minute. He'd been forced to ditch his gear miles back.

Hour after hour dragged by. . . . *I've gotten turned around somehow.* His compass didn't work. There was no way to see the stars in this never-ending storm. *So confused.*

If he stopped, he would freeze here. But it wouldn't kill him. He'd live on, frozen and trapped, until someone dragged him to a warm place to thaw.

Yet even that horrific fate wasn't enough to keep him moving.

No, it wasn't until he thought about never seeing Daniela again that he gritted his teeth and pushed on. Envisioning her elven face kept him going—

Were there lights ahead in the distance? *Imagining it?* Struggling to make out the hazy sight, he pulled aside his face guard, taking off a frozen layer of skin with it. He staggered, feeling like acid had just doused his face.

Ignore the pain. How far was it to those lights? He teleported forward, but got no closer, forced back by some kind of invisible barrier. He tried once more. Nothing. He fought to get there, grappling to reach the lights, to reach *her*.

Toiling . . . over and over.

Ultimately, his strength ebbed to nothing, and he collapsed to his knees in the snow. A vicious gust roared over him, laying him out.

With his last ounce of will, he stretched a hand forward.

"Daniela . . ."

Thirty-nine

DANII SAT ON HER THRONE, THINKING ABOUT WITCHES—and abdication.

I could meet with Mariketa the Awaited, bring her a bucketful of softball-size diamonds, and ask her to put me on her list.

Even if Murdoch wasn't keen on waiting fifty years, reserving a spot couldn't hurt.

And Danii could return to Val Hall, now that she could live in New Orleans safe from assassins. She'd add some serious tonnage to her A/C and really get some cold cranking.

Maybe she could be happy there. It would be even harder staying in Louisiana so fresh from the cold. But fall had arrived there, at least.

Was she an idiot even to contemplate relinquishing her throne—and her new life, tucked away amid the freezing security of Icergard? Could she truly leave behind an ice world where she lived among her own kind, to seek a vampire she could never touch?

Over and over, Danii recalled the look in his eyes when he'd yelled for her to come back that night.

Yes. She would try once more to convince him that they could—

"My queen," one of her ladies-in-waiting said as she hastened into the throne room. "Come quickly. There's a *stranger* in Icergard. He crossed the White Death. . . ."

When Murdoch woke, he lay in a bed in a bizarre room of ice. Though it was lighter and quieter here out of the wind, the temperature wasn't warmer.

He was wearing new pants and a coat of sorts that kept him from freezing. Someone had cleaned him and bandaged his frostbitten hands. He must be within Icergard. Which meant *she* was near. *Have to get to her.* He labored to rise—

Jádian strode into the room. "So, it is you. Why have you come to our realm?" His expression betrayed no surprise, no emotion whatsoever.

This is the bastard who knows what it's like to kiss Daniela.

And I can't kill him. Yet.

Murdoch managed a sitting position. "I seek Daniela." His words were hoarse, his body still exhausted.

Jádian crossed his arms over his chest. "Why would I ever let one such as you near her?"

"I just need to speak to her. And then, if she still doesn't want to see me, I'll never bother her again." *What a lie*—

Daniela entered. And Murdoch sucked in a breath.

She was more stunning than he'd ever seen her, her body bedecked in diamonds. Her hair was wild beneath a band of ice and jewels—the crown from Daniela's memories, her mother's.

To see her again. These mere days had felt like eternity.

She looked dazed to find him here. Surely she had to know he'd come for her.

He couldn't read her expression. Was she not pleased at all to see him? Then his heart sank as comprehension took hold. *I'm too late.*

Oh, gods, Murdoch was *here.* He was wild-eyed, with his lips and hands frostbitten and his face abraded.

He'd crossed the White Death? *To come for me.*

Jádian was eerily calm. "I say we throw him back out and let the cold take him."

Pointedly ignoring that, she said, "Murdoch, how did you get here?"

"I followed your memories. But the portal was . . . off."

"My memories," she repeated softly. He *had* taken them from her blood. "Why have you come?"

"Can I talk to you? Alone. Please, Daniela, just a few minutes of your time."

"My queen, this is ridiculous," Jádian said. "Remember what he did to you last time?"

Murdoch cast him a killing look, then turned back to her. "I have an idea—there's a way we might be together."

"What? How?"

"When I drank from you before—"

"Why bring that up to me?" Her hand flittered to her neck at the reminder.

"Because now I know why it was so irresistible to me."

Jádian said, "Because you're a parasite."

"Jádian!"

"He plans to bite you again."

"Of course he doesn't. Murdoch, tell him."

"Daniela, speak with me alone." Somehow he managed to make it to his feet. "I swear I won't do anything to you that you don't agree to."

His words piqued her curiosity. He hadn't promised not to hurt her, not to bite her, yet she felt no threat from him. "Very well," she said, turning to Jádian with raised brows. After a hesitation, he turned for the door, stonily silent.

As soon as they were alone, Murdoch demanded, "Are you marrying him?"

"What? No!"

"Nïx told me you were."

"She must be confused then, or you misheard her. Now, tell me. What were you talking about?"

"Daniela, before I took your neck, I'd dreamed of doing it. More and more as we grew apart. Every night. Now I believe it's the way for us to be together."

"I don't understand."

"With your blood in my veins, everything felt warm to me. My brothers were chilled, but I couldn't stand to be near the fire. Your blood made me *cold*."

"That can't be right. I can't turn you into an Iceren."

"No, but I can pick up characteristics of your kind," Murdoch said.

"Do you have the skin markings, then? Are you unaffected by the sun?"

He shook his head. "There was a blue tinge under my eyes, but not the body markings. When I tested my skin in the sun, I still burned, even when I was immune to the cold."

"Immune? Then why are you freezing right now? How did you get frostbitten?"

He ran his bandaged hand over the back of his neck. "The effect only lasted a couple of days."

"So for this to work, I'd have to repeat that pain?"

"One last time. After that, as long as I drank every day or two, I'd never hurt you again. We could be together." His voice went lower, and his eyes flickered black. "In all ways."

Her mind was whirring. Yet then she recalled what had happened after the last bite. "But I-I went unconscious."

Looking shamefaced, he said, "I took too much. I wouldn't this time. I know I don't deserve your trust, but I'm asking for it anyway."

"Why should I do this?"

"Because I'm in love with you," he said—without a hint of hesitation.

Her lips parted and the world seemed to shift under her feet.

After what he'd done to reach her, she had to believe he did. But to hear him say the words, with his eyes so intense and dark. . . .

Maybe the vampire *did* always come through in the end.

"And I think you love me, too." Hope tinged his words.

She turned away, breaking his searching gaze. "Maybe that doesn't matter," she said over her shoulder. "Maybe we're only fated to make each other miserable. You forget we'd fought before all this happened. You'd given up on us."

"No, just before I returned that night, I realized that fifty years was nothing if we could be together. I'd come back to tell you that. But then I saw you kissing Jádian . . ."

She faced him once more. "I'm sorry for that."

"It doesn't matter now," he said, but she could tell that she'd hurt him. "When I was in jail—"

"Jail?"

"That's why I wasn't here sooner—Kristoff imprisoned us at Mount Oblak for harboring Conrad. It's all worked out now, but we spent weeks inside. And while I was there, I determined that I would do anything to be with you. Desert my order. Live here in the cold in twenty-four hours of daylight."

"Murdoch, that's not the point. You're talking about biting me again, about more pain. And not just mine. I'm colder than I've ever been. It would hurt you too," she said, then added, "If this did work, you might be vulnerable to thermal shock, like me."

"I don't give a damn about that!" He crossed to her until they were toe to toe. "Please, Danii, I know I'm asking for a lot more than I deserve, but if you can endure this one last time . . . Just give me your trust."

Hadn't she said she'd give anything to know his taste? To touch her lips to his?

Before, even amidst the agony of his bite, she'd felt a connection to him.

I will trust him. Fantasy finally made reality. And reality sometimes took sacrifice.

Daniela bowed her head, then gazed up at him from under her lashes.
And again, he was undone.

"I do trust you." She pulled her hair to the side, baring the pale
column of her neck to him, inviting him.

"You won't regret this." But even as his fangs sharpened for her
flesh, he hesitated. "I dread hurting you. When I think about how I
took you last time . . ."

"I'm afraid I'll try to break away," she admitted. "Or that you
will—from the cold."

Each would want to recoil. They'd have to force each other to
hold on. "Hang on to me, *kallim,* because I'll be holding you tight.
We do this now, and then we have forever."

She inhaled a steadying breath. "I'm ready."

What would you do for her . . . ? The scent of the supple skin he
was about to taste proved too much temptation. He couldn't resist.
He laid his bandaged palms on her hips and drew her closer.

Her hands rose to clasp his shoulders. "Do it," she whispered.

In a flash, he sank his fangs into her. This time he groaned—in
pain. She was even icier than before.

Stabbing cold shot through him. The urge to release her screamed
in him, but he held on, squeezing her hips. He felt her little blue
claws digging into him as well.

Yet with each of his draws, the pain lessened. At the remembered
sense of connection, his eyes slid closed in bliss.

Mine. Forever. Thoughts were a jumbled knot. *Slow . . . slow . . .
Don't take too much this time. This is a gift. . . .*

FORTY

By the time Murdoch released her, they were both out of breath. And Danii was crying.

"Christ, I tried not to take too much—"

"Y-you didn't." But it had still been excruciating.

He winced at her neck. "You're burned."

"It'll regenerate quickly with the cold. Did you even drink enough?" she asked, struggling to disguise how much pain she'd felt. "Do you think this will work?"

"The effect takes time."

"You're already better." With her blood accelerating his regeneration, he began healing almost at once, his battered lips and face soon returning to normal. He unwrapped the bandages from his hands as they mended and flexed his fingers.

But his breaths still fogged.

Minutes passed, then half an hour. She sank onto the bed, and he paced. Another hour had trudged by in anxious silence before he said, "Daniela, why didn't you tell me about the Roman?"

"You saw that?" At Murdoch's nod, she said, "He's in my past."

"You think of me as you do him."

She shook her head. "No, Murdoch. I was angry when I said that. Bewildered."

"But it's true that I took what didn't belong to me."

"We both felt the pull. I could have stopped you. And I've wondered again and again why I didn't. Now I think it was instinct telling both of us the way to be together. If . . ."

"If this works? It will." He ran his hand over his forehead. "Damn it, if you were brave and strong enough to withstand this—twice—it's got to work."

"Will you still want me if it doesn't?" she asked quietly.

Reaching for her, he cupped her waist between his hands to tug her to her feet, then gazed down at her with fierce eyes. "Look at me, Daniela. I'm in love with you," he grated. "I want you always, no matter what!"

"Murdoch, I . . . y-your breaths aren't visible." Was there the slightest blue tint under his eyes?

He frowned. "The temperature doesn't feel as cold in here. It's becoming *comfortable*."

"Could this truly be working?" Her hand trembled wildly as she reached up to his face.

"Careful," he warned. "Maybe wait a little longer."

"I can't. I have to know." When she caressed his cheek, his eyes went heavy-lidded.

No pain. With a strangled cry, she sagged against him.

"Daniela, are you hurt?"

"I just can't believe this." Tears gathered and fell. She could be with him—Murdoch, the vampire she loved. After two millennia, her constant yearning would end at last.

"Please don't cry." With an audible swallow, he tentatively laid his palms against her face, brushing his thumbs over her tears. *No pain.*

For so long she'd felt lacking, and the answer had been within her, within them, all along. "I'm crying because I'm happy." She unbuttoned his jacket, pulling it off him to display the chest she'd imagined stroking. Then she placed her hands on him, finding his skin was the perfect temperature.

No pain. His muscles went rigid, tensing to her fingertips. She gave one exploring sweep, then another, until she was rubbing her palms all over him in delight. *Only pleasure.*

He was still caressing her cheeks. "You're so soft, Daniela. Softer than I ever imagined—and I imagined constantly." He tipped her face up. "I've got to kiss you."

"I'm yours to kiss. I'm yours."

His voice a husky rasp, he said, "You're about to be." He cast her a slow, possessive grin, flashing his fangs—no longer would she look at them with fear. They'd been the means to her and Murdoch's deliverance.

Then he leaned down. "Close your eyes."

She did. After the space of a heartbeat, she felt the lightest brush of his firm lips to hers. The barest contact sent tingles through her. Drawing her closer, pressing her body against him, he slanted his mouth over hers.

His kiss grew unyielding, intent, even as he gently coaxed her lips open so he could stroke a sensuous lick against her tongue. When she moaned, meeting him, lapping softly, he wrapped his arms tightly around her, as if he couldn't get close enough, as if he feared she'd get away.

She clutched his shoulders in turn. Their tongues tangled. Their breaths mingled and grew hectic.

Now *this* was a kiss—deep, frantic. What she'd long imagined. *Hearts thudding, bodies shaking.* She whimpered against his mouth as her knees went weak. But he held her steady and safe against his chest as he continued to plunder her mouth.

Too soon, he broke away, leaving her dazed and panting.

"I need to claim you." He pulled her hair to the side and skimmed his lips across the now healed skin where he'd bitten her.

She shivered violently, her nipples hardening in a rush.

"I never want to be apart from you again," he murmured. "Now I'll be able to stay with you here."

Oh, Murdoch, no. Should she lie to him, act as if that could possibly happen?

When he drew back to meet her eyes, she forced herself to smile, though she knew the Icere would never accept him. Vampires were despised here.

She should just enjoy this miracle. *Worry about what to do later.*

"What? Something's wrong."

"Uh-huh." Her hands dipped to his pants, untying the waist. "You're not naked enough," she said, working them past his protruding erection. When he stood unclothed before her, she gripped his gorgeous length.

He hissed in a breath; she gasped. She could perceive his shaft throbbing in her palm, could feel the texture of his smooth skin stretched taut over the veined ridges.

Against her sensitive fingers, it grew. . . .

So incredibly hard. Could she even take him? *We'll know soon enough.*

While she explored, he slipped the thin straps of her gown from her shoulders. Gathering the material in his fists, he skimmed it down her body. He paused just before he revealed her chest as if he wanted to prolong this moment.

At last, the silk inched past her erect nipples. He stared at her breasts as if he'd never seen them.

"Murdoch, please . . ."

Without warning, he gathered her in his arms, moving them to the bed so he could place her in his lap. Once he had her settled over his erection, he lifted a finger to circle her nipples—one, then the other, his gaze transfixed as the tips swelled to his touch. With a desperate groan, he pressed his lips against one breast, palming the other.

When she felt his tongue snake out over her nipple, her head lolled.

Again and again, he flicked the puckered bud. "Do you want me to suckle you?"

"Yes, oh, yes. . . ." She ran her fingers through his thick hair, cupping him to her.

He drew one of her nipples between his lips, sucking, licking, giving a harsh groan that vibrated into her breast.

"Oh, gods!" Lightning exploded outside. He knew what the lightning meant and drew even harder. Once her nipple was stiff and wet, he moved to the other, delivering the same attention. Then he gazed at them as if in awe.

"Vampire, no more teasing!"

Looking slightly dazed, he grinned. "My fire and ice Bride. Never shy about what she wants."

She shook her head. "Especially not when I've wanted it this long."

FORTY-ONE

THOUGH THEY'D BEEN TOGETHER FOR MONTHS, Murdoch was anxious with Daniela, determined to make this perfect for her.

Since she'd waited more than twenty lifetimes for it.

And he'd noticed that she hadn't replied when he said he wanted to stay with her here. Maybe she still needed convincing? He was up to the task.

"If you knew how good you taste." He nuzzled her ear, dimly marveling that her body didn't feel cold—because his was as well. "I can't wait to taste all of you."

She inhaled sharply, shivering against him.

His hand trailed from her breast down to her spread thighs, quaking in anticipation of feeling her flesh for the first time. Reaching under her dress, he tugged her silk panties to her knees. Then returned his hand . . .

His palm met damp curls. "*Almighty,*" he rasped, as he cupped her slick sex. Gently, he slipped his forefinger between her folds and into her tight sheath, making her jerk in his arms. "Easy, baby," he murmured. "I've got you."

"Oh, gods, Murdoch!" Her curling claws bit into his shoulders, which only stoked his arousal, already nearing a fever pitch.

"So perfect. You feel so good." Needing to taste the wetness he was stroking, he withdrew his finger. Her lids went heavy as she watched him suck it between his lips, then shudder from how sweet she was.

"I need *more*." His voice broke low on the word.

Laying her back on the bed, he removed her panties and dress completely. When she was naked to his gaze, he stared at her, wanting to remember her like this forever.

She was a fantasy made flesh, her body arrayed with diamonds, her shining hair fanning out around her head. Her silver eyes glittered like the stones adorning her. *Mine.*

And I can touch every inch of her.

She was panting, her breasts quivering, the peaks pouting. He knelt before her on the bed and nipped each tip with his teeth, giving them each a short, hard suck. "Spread those pretty thighs for me."

As she did, he drew back to watch, exhaling a shaky breath. It took all the discipline he'd ever garnered to keep from falling upon her like an animal.

Her flesh was lush with arousal, misted wet. At the sight, his cock surged harder, hanging down between his legs like a steel rod. The crown dragged against the sheet as he bent down to her sex, inch by inch.

Whatever she saw in his expression made her murmur, "*Oh.* Murdoch. P-please go slow. At first."

"Trying to. Never wanted anything so bad in my life." With the first brush of his lips against her thigh, she tensed in reaction, as if she'd been burned. "Daniela?"

"No, no, keep going." She threaded her fingers though his hair, surrendering to his kiss.

"Do you want more?"

"Yes, more," she bit out, her voice throaty.

Good. *Because I crave this—must have it.* She whimpered when he used his thumbs to part her damp flesh. Then, at last, he pressed his mouth to her.

The first flick of his tongue against her made her moan. When she quivered for him, his cock jerked in answer, the head brushing the sheet.

How he'd dreamed of this. But nothing could have prepared him for her maddening taste, the softness of her folds yielding to his mouth, the tight bud of her clitoris swelling under his tongue.

The act was beyond imagining and felt as if something right and natural was shifting into place. He was meant to bring her pleasure like this.

He spread her wide, fingering her as he licked and sucked, until she was wantonly rolling to his tongue. *No inhibitions.*

Her response had him rocking his shaft up and back, wetting the sheet with his precum. *I'm going to spend before I'm even inside her.*

But his eyes closed in bliss when she whispered, "Please, don't stop. . . ."

"*Never,*" he growled, setting upon her once more. Laying his hand over her flat belly, he pinned her in place, holding her fixed to his mouth as he suckled her clitoris between his lips.

"*Murdoch!*" At once, she began coming in a wet rush, her head thrashing.

Never releasing her, he watched as her back arched like a bow, her stiff nipples pointing to the ceiling. He groaned against her even as he sucked.

He wrung every last ounce of pleasure from her, and was still unwilling to give up this prize. Stifling growls, he licked her clean until she had to grip his face and draw him away.

When he finally rose up on his knees, he hissed a curse at how luscious she looked—her pleasured sex slick from her orgasm, her eyes glinting with passion, her hair wild.

"You'll make me lose my mind, Daniela." *My control as well . . . About to take her virginity like a rutting beast.*

"Would that be so bad?" she purred.

Have to be gentle with her. He'd had sex before, but now he wanted to make love to his woman. Was she ready for him? "How do you feel right now?" His voice was unrecognizable. *I can do this. I can hold on. Just a little longer.*

"Aching. Empty. Hungry."

He swallowed, and his voice broke low as he uttered, "H-hungry?"

Forty-two

When Danii licked her lips and pressed him back on the bed, his expression wavered between excited—and agonized.

And the seducer might even be nervous.

Kneeling between his legs, her palms flat against his chest, she kissed down his torso, nuzzling the trail of crisp hair below his navel. "Remember when I said I'd do this at my leisure? For *hours*?" When she took him in hand, he bucked as if helpless not to.

"Hours? This might be over before it starts." His accent was thicker than she'd ever heard it. He was watching her as she gave her first seeking lick. "Daniela! Ah—"

Another lick silenced him. A third made him growl. Soon she was raining wet flicks over the slit, tasting him, just as he'd described all those nights ago. He was delicious, with a salty tang.

"Umm, I love your taste," she murmured in a delighted tone.

He cupped her head with shaking hands. "You want me to lose my mind for you? We're on our way."

"But Murdoch, I need more of this." Unable to stop herself, she continued her wet kiss, closing her lips over him. And while her mouth slid down his length, her fingers explored, hefting his sac, which seemed to madden him more.

"*Ah, that's it, Danii. . . .*"

Sucking hard, she darted her tongue all around until she'd built up a cold, freezing friction.

He groaned, "You're doing it so good, *kallim*." Digging his heels into the bed, he let his knees fall open. "I'm close. Pull back."

She ran her cheek along his damp shaft. "Let me make you come," she said before she took him back between her lips.

He seemed to be struggling to keep his hips still. Hoarse groans erupted from his chest.

"Daniela, going to come in your mouth . . . if you don't stop." The big hands palming her head couldn't seem to decide if they wanted to draw her away or press her down.

"No!" He tried to pull back, but her claws were sunk in his ass, so he couldn't move without hurting her. "*Ah, baby, I can't hold on.*"

She could feel his shaft thickening, straining as he began to ejaculate against her tongue.

She's done it—made me lose my fucking mind.

"Daniela!" he roared as he came into her hungry mouth.

His eyes rolled back in his head when she sucked him as if she were starved for him. As if she'd waited two thousand years just to swallow him down, over and over. . . .

Once she'd drained him dry, they both lay back on the bed, gasping, as they had that first night together. Only now could he reach over and hold her hand.

Recalling every wicked instant of what they'd just done had him rebounding in a rush. When he raised himself over her, Daniela's gaze dipped and her lips curled. "My man has talents."

But as he used his knees to spread her thighs, she tilted her head at him. "Murdoch, are you nervous?"

"I want this to be worth the wait."

"It already has been. Anything else is a bonus."

"I haven't done this for a while." He frowned. "Actually, I've never done this." When she quirked a brow, he said, "Claimed my virgin female for all time."

"Oh." She gave him that soft look from under her lashes, the one that made his heart twist in his chest.

"When I make you mine tonight, I'm never letting you go."

She gazed up at him with that exquisite elven face, mesmerizing him. "I never want you to."

He took himself in hand, positioning his cock at her slick entrance. The crown met her wetness, beckoning him inside. He wanted his shaft covered in it, wanted to stir himself in it.

As the head nudged inside, he stared down at her eyes. "*Ma armastan sind.*"

Her eyes glinted at the words, and she whispered, "I love you, too."

Mounting her untried body, he inched inside, stretching her sheath. "Don't want to hurt you," he grated, fighting to go slow.

"It's not . . . too bad. Just keep going." She was clutching him to her, her curling claws holding him as if she'd never let go.

"You're so tight. Like a fist squeezing me." Once he'd seated his cock deep, he forced himself to go still, letting her grow accustomed. With untold will, he waited until she began undulating under him.

Only then did he draw his hips back, giving her a measured thrust. The pleasure was so intense that his vision wavered.

"Murdoch, yes!"

Another withdrawal, another pump of his hips that made her moan low. Once he began a rhythm, rocking between her thighs, he kissed her again, delving his tongue in time with his body.

The friction made it warmer, but it was still cold, and cold felt so damn *good*.

"Daniela, tell me that you're mine."

"I am *yours*. . . ."

Already, he didn't know how much longer he could last with her nipples rubbing against his chest. The drenched clench of her sex called for his seed, demanding. . . .

"I'll never get enough of you, *never,*" Murdoch rasped with his brows drawn.

His expression made Danii's heart squeeze, even as his determined thrusts were sending her closer to orgasm. His scent drove her wild; his strength captivated her.

As his body worked hers, magnificent taut cords of muscle stood in relief. The latent power of a male vampire. She desired that power, savored the way he toiled under her claws.

His arms bulged as he held himself up to alternately buck his hips hard, then languidly stir them. *Gods, the man knows how to move.*

Cupping her ass with his fingers splayed, he lifted her, wrenching her along his shaft.

"Murdoch!" she cried, already on the verge again.

He worked her up and down, harder and harder until her teeth clattered with each landing.

She wrapped her legs tight around his waist, which seemed to spur him. He went wild, possessively pinning her arms over her head, so that even more of their bodies could touch.

Surging over her, he rode her sheath in a frenzy. His face was an agonized mask, his body straining for her. "Come, *kallim.* Let me feel you."

At that moment, she wanted to give him anything he desired. She needed to surrender to him. Surrender everything to him.

"Take my blood," she managed to whisper.

"What?"

"Drink me."

"Ah, Daniela, you don't have to ask me twice. . . ." He licked her neck, then sank his fangs into her.

As he pierced her, Danii's eyes went wide, and she gave a shocked cry—she'd begun to come immediately. He must have felt her, because he gave a frenzied growl.

"Murdoch! Ah, yes!" As her orgasm ripped through her, his shaft thickened even more, swelling until he could barely move inside her.

Then he went motionless, snarling against her. Just when she felt the first lash of his semen, his hips began plunging like a piston, taking him to the very end.

As he drew her blood, he flooded her with seed. She felt every pumping jet, prolonging her own ecstasy.

With a final groan, he released his fangs, collapsing atop her, his breaths cooling against her new mark. With seeming great effort, he rolled off her, but only to enfold her in his arms.

She lay on his chest, skin to skin. He clutched her to him, pressing a kiss into her hair.

"That was worth my wait, vampire."

"I'm glad, Valkyrie. Because I'd have counted down eternity for that."

FORTY-THREE

"If I could kiss you, I don't think I'd ever stop," Daniela had told him all those months ago. Now they could and she didn't stop—for hours, they lazily kissed and touched.

So this is utter contentment. Murdoch had never known it before.

For the first time, he experienced the luxury of her smooth legs entwined with his. At last, he could trace all the cobalt markings on her skin that had always tantalized him. They'd discovered that the tips of her ears were ticklish—she'd been unaware. He reveled in her taste, her responsiveness, wanting to go to his knees in thanks for the Bride he'd been given.

He'd been trailing kisses along her delicate collarbone when she sighed, "Now I understand why my sisters enjoyed being bitten so much."

"You liked my bite, little Bride? You'll be able to endure it every other day?"

"I'll *demand* it every other hour. And I'll make sure you're properly exerted, so you'll be thirsty all the time."

Just getting better and better. "That won't be a problem."

"But Murdoch," she began, her tone uneasy, "about your living here. . . ."

He pulled back to meet her gaze, dread drumming in his chest.

"They'll never accept you," she said. "Not after what happened to my mother. They'll reason that if Sigmund could turn against his own queen, then a vampire surely could . . . and they were punished by Sigmund, every day."

"Daniela, you told me you were *mine*. I warned you I'd never let you go. But I won't ask you to give up your crown."

She grew still. "You won't?"

"No, but just as before, we'll have to find a way to be together, because you can't ask me to give you up either."

She seemed pleased by his answer. Had she expected him to demand she relinquish her throne? The old, selfish Murdoch would have. He would have believed it was her honor to be with him. Now he knew it was the other way around.

"Explain to me exactly what Nïx told you," Daniela said.

He scowled. "Still planning on marrying Jádian?"

"Murdoch!" She play-punched his arm, then seemed to get briefly distracted by the feel of his skin. "Now tell me."

So he did . . .

When he'd finished, she said, "You know, I didn't need a sooth-sayer to convince me that you'd be true."

He gave a decisive nod. "My thoughts exactly."

"And I have an idea," she said. "A way we could be together—and do only as we please."

"No, no," Murdoch grated. "Not a chance. I can't let you do this for me. Daniela, I saw your memories. Your mother wanted this for you."

Danii shook her head firmly. "I think she'd want me to be happy. And this is the only way. Murdoch, if you saw my memories, did you not feel how long I've waited to be happy? A lonely life of service will *not* be forthcoming from me."

"I did feel it. But don't you even want to think about—"

"I have been thinking about this," she said, meeting his gaze. "And it's what I choose."

After long moments, he said, "I'm with you, Daniela. Whatever you want, I'll support you."

"Then let's get some clothes on, because what I want is to get this settled as soon as possible."

Once they'd dressed, she called for Jádian. When he arrived, she wasted no time. "I'm abdicating, and I want you to take over the throne. I'd like you to be king of the Icere."

Instead of jumping at the chance, Jádian almost seemed put out and kept glancing at the door.

Danii said, "You don't appear too happy about this."

"I had . . . other plans, once you got established here," Jádian replied. "But I'll do my duty, if this is your will."

Jádian the Buzz Kill, all duty, no fun. "Yes, it is. But I have a few conditions. I want to visit whenever I like, come around for holidays and such, once I get the cryomancy down. And the Icere must always ally with the Valkyrie."

"Agreed. But I have some conditions as well," Jádian said. "If I die with no heir, you'll resume the throne. And you'll take with you your mother's crown."

"But it belongs here—it belongs to your future queen."

"I'll never take a *wife* to wear it."

Still waters run deep with the Iceren? "Then I can agree to that."

Jádian nodded to them, then strode to the door. As he left, she thought she heard him mutter a curse, demonstrating the most emotion she'd ever observed.

When they were alone, Murdoch pulled her back into his lap. "I think Jádian was a shade shocked at your offer."

"Well, Nïx did say that I would make him my king—so I did." Danii smiled brightly. "Now it seems I'm a woman of leisure."

Murdoch nipped the tip of her ticklish ear, making her laugh. "Good. Then you can take a day to marry me."

EPILOGUE

Christmas Eve
Blachmount Manor

THE WROTH FAMILY—FOUR COUPLES BROUGHT TOGETHER by the Accession, and in some cases by Nïx—had gathered to celebrate Murdoch and Daniela's marriage, the holidays, and the renovation of Blachmount.

Myst and Nikolai had completely restored the manor, and now it was lavishly decorated for the festivities.

While the brothers drank whiskey, the females gathered around an enormous table laden with food and drinks. But Myst and Néomi were the only ones with plates. *Myst eating?* There went the Valkyrie's inherent birth control.

Danii raised her brows, but Myst only shrugged. "What can I say? Nikolai's big on family. And I felt sorry for my poor biological clock, having to tick for millennia."

Kaderin received a questioning glance as well, but she held up her hands. "Don't look at me. I've got shite to do and no pity for clocks. . . ."

When they convened by the fire to exchange gifts, naturally Danii and Murdoch took the chilly settee farthest away from the heat.

Murdoch gazed around again, still seeming stunned by the changes. "It looks just like home used to."

Nikolai took Myst's hand in his. "She wanted to keep it as close as possible to what I remembered," he said, looking like he was about to explode, he was so proud and satisfied.

All of the brothers gave that impression. Even Conrad, with his flame-red eyes. He was doing so well, seeming more of an eccentric than the madman Danii had expected, but he did appear to occasionally get lost in memory. Whenever he did, his new wife, Néomi, was there, gently tugging him back to the present.

Danii had liked Néomi immediately, though she was a bit puzzled about how the ballet dancer had gone from ghost to human to the more powerful phantom. Now Néomi was telekinetic, with the ability to become incorporeal and vanish at will.

Néomi wasn't spilling the details—even though she was visibly tipsy, speaking in a mix of her native French and English. *"Merry Noelle!"*

The atmosphere was cozy and domestic, and Danii relaxed, enjoying herself, savoring the time spent with her sisters and siblings-in-law. Murdoch drew Danii even closer into the chill of his arms until she all but sat on his lap. He rubbed his big, cold palm up and down her arm. With his other hand, he held hers.

Constant contact. Over the last few weeks, he'd barely kept his hands off her. She soaked up his affection as she would frost.

After Jádian's reluctant coronation, Danii and Murdoch had been married in a simple Lore ceremony. He'd been Catholic, and she was a pagan. Simple was best.

Since then, Danii hadn't had time for fantasies anymore. Her husband had proved deliciously insatiable. Each sunset, he would ease into her, waking her that way, drawing just enough blood to keep him cold. Though she always wanted him to drink more.

He'd taken the icy changes in himself in stride. And if she'd expected his brothers to be disappointed with this development, she would've been wrong. They'd easily accepted Murdoch's decision.

With much fanfare, the family began exchanging gifts. Murdoch had bought her an extravagant case to hold Svana's crown—and an emerald comb to replace the one that Néomi had admitted to stealing right out of his pocket at Elancourt.

Danii gifted him with her own creation: an intricately carved ring of ice for his forefinger, to wear as a type of cold monitor, until he got accustomed to his transformation. They didn't know if he could overheat, and she never wanted to find out.

Yet every present was upstaged by Sebastian and Kaderin's gift to the family. Thrane's Key.

At the sight of it, Danii stifled a shiver. She'd heard that the key didn't always do as one hoped, and it didn't always go back to the exact time one wished.

But Murdoch had such hopes of being reunited with his family. He'd told her his father would be so proud to see that Murdoch had given his heart completely.

She shook away her apprehension. This family was so formidable, fate should yield to it.

"We go back at the beginning of the new year?" Sebastian asked, wrapping his arm around Kaderin's shoulders. Danii curbed a smile when fierce Kaderin melted against him, half-lidded with happiness, all but purring. Danii made a mental note to razz her about that later.

"Yes, it's time," Nikolai said. "We've all gotten settled."

Conrad's red eyes grew blank, his fists balling as he went awash in a memory. But Néomi tenderly cupped the side of his face, tugging him back into the conversation.

"*Néomi?*" he rasped in confusion.

She smiled lovingly, with infinite patience. "*Écoute-le, mon coeur.*"

He gave her a nod, his red gaze filled with what could only be described as adoration.

"Are you ready to go back for your sisters?" Néomi asked him.

Conrad faced the others with a decisive nod. "I'm ready."

"Are we all agreed about this?" Nikolai asked. "I am most concerned about how the girls will do. They were so young, and they'll be thrust into not only a completely different world of beings, but a completely different time."

Kaderin said, "My sisters are managing well—aside from the occasional slain toaster—and they were premedieval."

Myst said, "And look at how fabulous the girls' aunts will be with them. I can instruct them in high fashion, and Néomi can teach them to dance."

"*Bien sûr.*" Néomi nodded. "And I can go invisible and follow them to school, watching over them."

Kaderin said, "I can teach them how to fight."

"What can I teach them?" Daniela asked quietly.

Myst answered, "How to get exactly what they want when the odds are stacked against them. Oh, and how to reform rakes."

"*Rake.* Singular," Murdoch grated with a possessive squeeze of her knee, making them laugh.

The talk turned to reminiscing, and though Danii wanted to learn more about Murdoch's family, the fire was blazing.

The instant she even perceived being uncomfortable, Murdoch seized her hand, leading her to the balcony. He told the others, "We're going out for some cold air."

Outside, she said, "Thank you. It was getting warm."

He took her into his arms to give her some of his coolness, pressing her face into his chest. "For me, too, love."

"Doesn't it bother you?" she asked him. "Not to be able to sit with them around the fire?"

She gazed back at the scene, the family laughing around a hearth, holiday decorations glittering in the firelight. A Hallmark card. Except that a phantom, Valkyries, and vampires populated the portrait.

"Sitting around the fire, versus making love to my wife as soon as we can possibly ditch?" Cradling her face in his palms, he kissed her forehead, her lashes, the tip of her nose, and a corner of her lips. "Danii, I've never been more satisfied with my life, didn't know I could be."

Between his light kisses, she felt snow beginning to fall. She raised her face in delight, laughing softly.

When her gaze met his once more, his eyes had darkened to black. "I can't get enough of you, Valkyrie."

Her hands slipped up his chest to meet at his nape. "Then kiss me, vampire." *And don't ever stop. . . .*

TEMPT ME ETERNALLY

Gena Showalter

To Kresley Cole and Lauren McKenna—a true dream team. Kresley, I met you years ago, drooled all over you (which is an ongoing problem), now send you way too many pictures of myself, and won't let you get off the phone until I've talked so much your ears are practically bleeding. You're welcome, my sweet! And of course, no dedication would be complete without saying thank you to the incomparable Jill Monroe, a very difficult person to be interviewed by.

ACKNOWLEDGMENTS

Yes, Kresley Cole is in the dedication, but she also needs to be in the acknowledgments. That's how fabulous she is. Little girls are made of sugar and spice, but Kresley is made of glitter and rainbows. I heart you.

·ONE

They were coming.

Warriors unlike any other. Monsters of unimaginable power. Otherworlders. Fierce creatures with the ability to look inside your soul, glimpse your greatest fear, and present it to you with an unrepentant smile.

Should've stayed home, Aleaha Love thought. *'Cause we're gonna get spanked. Hard. And not in a good way.* Instead, she'd answered her cell and her captain's call to action, and now found herself crouched in the middle of a gnarled forest, staring into a snow-laden clearing, moonlight shooting bright amber rays in every direction as flakes wafted in the breeze like fairy dust.

Though she wore white from head to toe, had a pyre-gun stretched forward, and was burrowed in a drift as cover, she felt exposed. Vulnerable. And yeah, damn cold.

What in the hell did I get myself into?

"Everyone in position?" a voice whispered from her headset.

A whisper, yeah, but it startled her. She managed to cut off a yelp, but couldn't stop tremors from sweeping through her. *Steady.*

She'd never hear the end of it if she accidentally fired her weapon before the fight had even begun.

"Premature weapon ejaculation," they'd say with a chuckle, and she wouldn't be able to deny it.

One by one, twenty teammates uttered their assent. They had wicked cool nicknames like Hawk Eye and Ghost. Her turn, she said, "Lollipop, in place."

As in, so tasty you could lick her. She rolled her eyes. "Dress her up and watch her play bad alien, delicious cop," the boyz had laughed before giving her the stupid moniker her first day on the job. "Naughty lawbreakers will want to taste her, not outrun her."

That had been, what? Five weeks ago, she realized with a jolt. Oh, how life had changed since then. From hiding in the shadows, afraid of what she was, to working cases with New Chicago's elite team of smart-asses, content with her somewhat pampered existence. A pampered existence she didn't deserve and hadn't earned, but whatever. No guilt for her. Really.

"Need someone to snuggle against, Lolli?" a quiet, amused male voice asked. Devyn, supposedly a king of some sort and a self-proclaimed collector of women. He wasn't really a member of Alien Investigation and Removal but was a special contractor, as well as the man who'd once wired her gun to blow bubbles rather than fire at target practice.

Word on the street, he was more powerful than God and deadlier than the devil, though no one would tell her outright what he could do. He was an otherworlder, that much she knew. That, and most of AIR's flunkies kept their distance from him. They feared him, which only heightened Aleaha's need to keep her own secrets.

She, too, was different.

She didn't know whether she was human or alien. Or both. She didn't know whether there were others like her or not. She didn't know who her parents were or why they'd abandoned her on the dirty streets of the Southern District—a.k.a Whore's Corner—of New Chicago, and she didn't care. Not anymore. All she knew was that she could assume anyone's identity with only a touch. That person's face became hers; their height became hers; their body became hers.

For years, she'd lived in fear of being found out, of being hunted and tortured for her unnatural ability, afraid that everyone who looked at her saw the truth and knew she wasn't who she claimed to be. But she couldn't drop the mask. As herself, she was wanted for theft, assault against a police officer, and more theft. And then maybe kinda sorta murder. Not that she was culpable. He'd deserved it.

She'd rather lose a limb than spend any more time in jail.

Her fear of discovery was waning, though, and she was settling comfortably into her newest life as Macy Briggs. *Maybe one day I'll even be worthy of it.* Again, not that she felt guilty. *Really.*

But with Christmas only a few weeks away . . . ugh. Worst. Holiday. Ever. Her "friends" would bake Macy's favorite foods, not Aleaha's. They would give her gifts meant for Macy, and reminisce fondly about good ole days she knew nothing about, and she would have to smile through every minute of it. And yeah, okay. Fine. *Then* she would feel guilty.

"What, ignoring me?" Devyn said with another of those snarky laughs. "Wasn't like I was going to ask to feel you up or anything. I mean, I was just gonna surprise you with my handsiness."

God, she was on the job, yet she'd lost track of her thoughts. Mortifying. "Can you take nothing seriously?"

"Hello, have you met me? I take making out very seriously."

All the men on the line snorted in their attempts to muffle their laughter. They might be wary of him, but they couldn't help but enjoy his perverted sense of humor.

"Fuck you, Chuckles," she said, trying not to reveal *her* amusement. Irreverent bastard.

"Excellent. We're on the same page, because that's exactly what I'm trying to do to you."

Give herself to Devyn? Not in this lifetime, and not because he wasn't attractive. If anything, he was *too* attractive. Hell, he was total screw-like-an-animal perfection. Tall, with dark hair, wide amber eyes, and skin that glittered like a jewel; there was no one else like him. There *was* a recipe for his smile, though: wicked desire dipped in acid, wrapped in steel and sprinkled with candy. The recipe for his laughter? Well, that was wicked desire tossed in the gutter, wrung out in a whorehouse, and slathered with scented body lotion. Women threw themselves at him constantly, and he ate it up like they were his own personal smorgasbord.

They probably were. Thank God she wasn't in the market for a boyfriend. Or, rather, a lover, since that's all someone as fickle as Devyn could ever amount to. Macy—the real Macy—had been dating a piece of scum Aleaha was still trying to lose and she didn't have the time or patience to throw anyone else into the mix.

"Temper, temper," Jaxon Tremain chided. He was one of two agents who hung out with the sexy otherworlder, and the resident smoother. There was something unnaturally calming about his presence, as if he could slink inside a person's psyche and wash away her fears. "Would you kiss me with that mouth?"

Not "would you kiss your mom with that mouth," but "would you kiss *me*." "Funny," she said dryly.

She could hear the others chortling and snorting with more surprised amusement. Someone said, "Soliciting kisses from women, Jaxon? Mishka will kill you for that."

"If by *kill* you mean *seduce,* then yeah," Jaxon replied. "You're right."

Mishka was Jaxon's wife and a hired killer who possessed a robotic arm. Aleaha had only seen her once, but that had been enough to scare ten years off her life. Never had she seen eyes so cold or heard a voice so uncaring. Of course, the moment Mishka spied Jaxon, her entire demeanor had changed. So had Jaxon's, for that matter. Usually he was as conservative as a priest. One glance at Mishka, though, and he'd morphed into gutter man.

Aleaha had marveled at the change in him, a change she was witnessing once again. Empathetic as he was, perhaps he was veering onto the perverted track now to get her mind off the bloody massacre sure to begin. Apparently, though, she didn't need help today. She couldn't concentrate worth a damn. What was wrong with her?

"Well," Devyn said, drawing the spotlight back to him. As always. "Be a good lollipop and answer the man. Will you kiss him or not?"

"I could give you a list of all the things I'll never do to you with my mouth," she muttered. "How 'bout that?"

Devyn laughed, and, yep. It was wicked desire. "She reminds me of Mia when she talks like that. Tell us, Lolli, is that list for everyone or just Jaxon?"

"All right, team," Mia Snow herself interjected before Aleaha could reply. "Save it. You know I only want you to stun these men. Do not burn them. I repeat, do not burn them. An open wound will bleed and that will spread their infection. And believe me, I will kill every single one of you myself if that happens."

There was a moment of frightening silence. Infection. What a delightful reminder. Not only were the warriors coming here vicious, there was a possibility that they were bringing the plague with them.

"Good," Mia continued. "I've got your attention. Solar flare approaching in ten." She was inside a van about a mile away, watching the action on a night-vision monitor with a handful of backup agents. "Nine."

Aleaha tensed. A few months ago, a big case had busted wide open and AIR had learned that otherworlders were traveling to Earth through interworld wormholes that initiated with solar flares. Then, a few weeks after that, another case had come to light. Members of a race of aliens known as the Schön had descended, their bodies carriers of a virus that passed to humans through their blood and ejaculate. This virus turned men and women into cannibals. Their queen—or living host of this sickness—was on her way here, due to arrive in the near future.

Tonight, ten members of her horde were supposed to utilize one of those wormholes. Their purpose: to smooth the way for her. Which meant, destroying AIR.

"Six."

Shit. The countdown. Despite the frigid temperatures, sweat beaded on Aleaha's brow, dripping from the brim of the white cap she wore. *Stay calm. You have to stay calm.*

"Five."

Though her résumé claimed she'd worked as a cop for more than two years, this was actually *Aleaha*'s first mission.

What seemed forever ago but had only been a few months, she'd stumbled upon the body of a woman who'd been raped and killed in a back alley—a woman she'd recognized as Miss New Chicago's Finest in Uniform calendar girl, Macy Briggs.

She'd almost walked away. The higher the public profile, the more scrutiny she received. But . . .

Already tired of the adult-toy-store clerk identity she'd previously stolen, Aleaha had seized the chance to better herself, hiding the body and shifting so that she was an exact match to Macy's appearance, thereby claiming the woman's life as her own.

Only later had she learned that Macy had applied to AIR and been accepted. To back out would have looked suspicious and changing identities yet again hadn't appealed. So she'd done it. She'd attended that first day, then the next. And the next. They'd watched her suspiciously, as if they knew the truth, but they had never accused her and she'd realized she was probably paranoid. Soon they'd even relaxed, accepting her as one of their own. Now, here she was, done with trials and on mission one.

"—must have been off, so I'll try this again," Mia said, cutting into her thoughts. "Ten. Nine."

Shit. She'd missed the end of the first countdown? She was practically begging to be killed tonight.

"Seven. Six."

Oh, God. What if she did, in fact, die out here? What if she lost everything she'd worked so hard to gain? Her gun hand shook. *You have to stay calm, damn it.*

With bouts of extreme emotion, she shifted from one identity to another without any control.

"Four. Remember, guns set to stun and only stun."

Her pyre-gun was already dialed to the proper setting, so she curled her index finger around the trigger and swallowed the hard lump in her throat. *Breathe in, breathe out. You do know how to fire a weapon, at least.* A skill she'd learned from her only true friend, Bride McKells. A vampire, and her champion. They'd been separated more than a decade ago, chased apart by cops who'd caught them breaking into homes for food, and Aleaha hadn't been able to find her since. She'd never stop looking, though.

"One."

All the air in Aleaha's lungs escaped on a sudden rush, hot and blistering, burning her throat and mouth. She tensed, waiting. Waiting. And then it happened. Overhead, the gloomy darkness gave way to sparkling orange-pink flickers. The wind picked up, swirling leaves and beating limbs against each other. Snow danced in every direction.

Then . . . nothing. It was almost disappointing. Almost.

The flickers died, leaving only the haze of stars. The wind quieted, leaving only the rasp of human breathing. Gradually, she relaxed. Maybe the Schön had decided to stay home. Maybe there'd be a party tonight rather than a war, and she wouldn't have to worry about—

"Commander?" someone asked.

"Hold," Mia replied. "Hold steady. We'll stay here all night if we have to."

Easy for her to say. She was nestled inside that warm van.

Several minutes ticked by in silence. Shudders of cold began rocking through Aleaha, causing her teeth to chatter. This sucked. Much longer, and her gloved fingers would be frozen to her gun. If that happened, growing a penis would be easier than shooting. 'Cause, yeah, she could even become a man. And had, on several occasions. Hadn't been as fun as she'd assumed. Penises were weird. They were also—

One second the circular clearing was empty, the next it was bursting with hulking, black-clad warriors. And there were far more than the expected ten.

"What the hell?" someone barked.

Aleaha jolted in surprise, sizing the visitors up in one panicked flash: living weapons. They were tall, well-muscled and radiated absolute power and authority. In the traitorous moonlight and snow, she could see that their features were humanoid—if you didn't count their glowing, golden eyes, like twin suns crashing through daybreak.

"Fuck!" another of her teammates shouted. "They aren't Schön, they're Rakans! What do we do?"

Rakans? The peace-lovers? Couldn't be. There was no damn way these ready-for-combat warriors would be waving a white flag.

"Do not kill," Mia commanded. "I repeat, do not kill them. Continue with stun. I want to know why they're here. Now go, go, go."

Just as she was about to squeeze her gun's trigger, a honey-scented breeze wafted through the air, taunting, beckoning her to lassitude and . . . How odd. Her nipples were beading, but not from the cold. Moisture was dampening her panties, her skin tightening over her bones, and drugging heat pouring into her veins.

Surely not. Surely the scent was *not* arousing her. Yet . . .

Why shoot them when she could kiss them? Kiss them . . . yes . . . Naughty images saturated her mind. Images of naked, writhing bodies—one of them golden. Seeking, hungry mouths—one of them golden. Wandering, teasing hands—again, a pair was golden. Satisfaction was only a heartbeat away, the anticipation of pleasure a consuming ache. All she had to do was drop her weapon, stand, and strip.

Strip? Seriously? What the hell was wrong with her? Was she the only one feeling this way? Like her, no one else had moved.

"Beautiful," an agent said.

"Want," another moaned.

Apparently not.

The warriors remained unmoving, silent, as if they were disoriented and needed to sober.

"Why are you just lying there, lusting after them? Did you not hear me? I said stun them, damn it," the commander growled.

Forcing her mind to blank, one of the toughest things Aleaha had ever done, she hammered at the trigger with her index finger. Other agents followed suit, and multiple blue stun-beams erupted in the night, blending with hers and charting a direct course to the aliens.

Hit. Hit. Hit.

As the beams made contact, the Rakans were rendered immobile, aware of their surroundings but now unable to move. But most remained untouched, their comrades having acted as their shields.

As though realizing what was happening, those men quickly gained their bearings and charged forward, successfully dodging the next round of rays.

Aleaha blinked in shock. Never in all her twenty-six years had she seen anyone move so swiftly. They moved so swiftly, in fact, that they left some kind of ethereal, ghostly outline of themselves behind. Their spirits? Those outlines then had to play catch-up with the tangible bodies, which created a dizzying blur of movement, light, and shadow.

"I'm down! I'm down!" someone cried. "Had the shit knocked out of me."

"I can't fucking freeze them," Devyn said. Odd. He had refused to bring a gun to this fight, the cocky bastard, so he wouldn't have been able to freeze them anyway.

After that, absolute chaos erupted. There were screams of pain, frantic footfalls, and humans collapsing. Aleaha pinched off a few more rounds. And, goddamn it, she missed every time.

She never missed. People who lived on the streets often depended on their aim for survival. She'd taught herself to hit whatever she aimed at—no matter what she was doing or what was going on around her. This was unacceptable.

Calm. Focus. She concentrated on the blurs as best she could, narrowing her eyes until she saw—

Squeeze.

This time, she hit a target dead-center. No, she realized a baffled moment later. She'd hit his spirit, that ghostly animation or whatever it was. Damn it! Unaffected, his body continued moving, darting from one place to another, felling one agent after another. And then, before her horrified gaze, the Rakans scattered in precise, measured increments. They weren't running away, but were encircling the entire AIR team and lethally closing in.

Caged, she thought. *We're being caged.* Despite the direness of their circumstances, the agents continued to fight, and Aleaha was utterly proud of them. Blue stun-beams glowed throughout the enclosure, lighting up the snowy night with majestic fury.

"Shit," someone said. "What the hell should we do? I can't see them anymore. I can't fucking see them!"

An agent ran over her, mowing right over her legs. No longer quite so proud, she popped to her feet, abandoning her cover in favor of protecting her limbs. Her knees knocked, but she managed to remain upright.

"Keep firing," Devyn commanded one and all. "Stay together, and for God's sake, stay calm."

He sounded so close that she turned her head—and found him standing right beside her.

"You okay, Lolli? You staying calm like I said?"

If her emotions wouldn't listen to her, perhaps they'd listen to him and calm. "Yeah." At the moment, she wasn't capable of saying more. Okay, so no. Her emotions wouldn't be listening to him, either. Fear still held her in a tight clasp, growing as another agent fell just in front of her. Much more, and she might lose her hold on Macy's image.

Jaxon sidled up to her other side, firing two guns at once, each pointed in a different direction. His green eyes were eerie in the darkness. Eerie but calming. Just being near him was like finding shelter in the midst of a raging storm. Finally, blessedly.

"Aim just ahead of the bodies," he instructed. "Or rather, ahead of the lights. It's the best way to lock on them."

Grunts, groans and screams filled her ears, louder by the second, distracting her. She pivoted and fired, pivoted and fired, trying to direct her beams in front of the blurs, just as Jaxon had said.

To her consternation, she only managed to nail one of the warriors. How many were out there, damn it? They seemed to be multiplying like flies.

"Help me!" an agent sobbed. "Please, help me."

Automatically, her gaze searched the night, the frenzied crowd. Before she found the beseeching male, one of the Rakans bypassed Aleaha's protective wall of testosterone and slammed into her, shoving her to the ground. She landed flat on her back, suddenly breathless and experiencing a moment of terror and anger, helplessness and courage.

As she raised her weapon to defend herself, she could feel her face and body beginning to change, the bones adjusting to accommodate a new form. No. No, no, no. When she changed involuntarily, she never knew who she would end up looking like.

The alien with glowing golden eyes leaned down, not to strike her but to . . . kiss her? She struggled against him, and, yep, he opened his mouth to fit it over hers.

"Woman," he said, voice slightly slurred. "Mine." Just before contact, an azure shower of sparks exploded around him, framing his large body and freezing him in place. Panting, instantly comforted, Aleaha crawled backward, forcing her image to conform once again to Macy's.

Jaxon held out a hand to help her up, and Aleaha prayed he hadn't seen her mini-transformation.

"Thanks," she rasped, somehow finding her balance. She ripped off her headset and tossed it on the ground. No more distractions.

"These guys are Rakan," he said. "Don't worry if you were dripped on."

Until that moment, she'd forgotten about possible contamination. Shit. Rakan or Schön, she was going to be more careful. The few times she'd been sick, she'd unknowingly transformed into an ailing identity. Each experience had taught her that it's more fun to be stabbed than ill.

"On my signal," Jaxon told her, shooting around her, "I want you to run and lock yourself in one of the vans."

The vans, hidden as they were, would offer a reprieve from danger, injury and death.

"No," she said, surprising herself. She'd stay and she'd fight, even though the prospect terrified her. How could she live with herself if these men died and she'd done nothing to help? "I'm staying."

"Don't argue," Devyn snapped. "Women are always prettier when they agree."

Pig. "I need to stay." She wouldn't defile everything Macy had built with her own cowardice. "I *have* to sta— Ohmygod!" One of the aliens had just stepped into an agent. *Stepped into.* Like a demon intent on possession, the otherworlder's body had entered the human's, fusing them until only the human was visible.

There was a tormented scream. The agent spasmed, shaking and quaking as he raised his own gun to his temple and fired. Brain tissue sprayed, obscene against the snow, and Aleaha gaped in horror.

"Fuck," snarled Dallas Gutierrez, Mia's second in command, as he joined them. "They're motherfucking soul jumpers."

Soul jumpers. She didn't know what that meant exactly, and she didn't want to find out. Her hands shook as she increased the speed of her shots.

"I've controlled the energy of a Rakan before," Devyn said, his voice strained. "But I can't grasp on to a single energy molecule to control these guys."

"Unlike Eden, they weren't raised on Earth. Maybe that's the problem. But it doesn't matter. Surely they'll tire soon," Jaxon replied. "That kind of speed has to drain them."

Aleaha lost the thread of the conversation. Energy molecule? Eden? All she knew was that a few more minutes passed and the aliens *didn't* slow. Their unparalleled swiftness only seemed to increase, so much so that she had trouble fixing another target in her sights.

"Shit." Devyn slid a knife from his boot. "You were wrong, my friend, and we're out of time. They're coming for us next." He slapped the hilt of the knife into Aleaha's free hand, the silver tip gleaming in the moonlight. "Be ready, Lolli. Go for the jugular."

She gulped. The blade weighed less than her gun, but somehow felt all the more menacing. "O-okay."

Jaxon turned those eerie green eyes on her. "There's still time to run."

Sixteen Rakans remained standing and they continued to close their circle, hopping over fallen agents. There might as well have been a thousand. Not long before she, Devyn, Dallas, and Jaxon—who held the center of that circle—would be reached. But Jaxon was right. There was still time to escape. Not much, but enough.

"No." Determined, she shook her head. "I'm staying. We can win this." If not, if AIR fell, she'd fall, too. *For Macy.* Aleaha owed the woman that much.

She kept firing with one hand while gripping the hilt of the serrated knife with the other, trying to prepare herself for what she might have to do. She'd never used a knife on anyone but herself, and the thought of slicing into someone else's flesh . . . *You can do it.* A cornered animal did anything necessary to ensure survival.

Another agent placed a gun to his own temple and fired.

Yeah, she could do it.

"For all that's holy, Lolli," Devyn snapped. His hard tone of voice made her blink. Especially since he'd used it twice in one night and that was twice more than ever before. Where was his dry sense of humor? Where were his dirty jokes? "The knife was supposed to scare you, not empower you. Hit the vans so we don't have to worry about you!"

"Stop worrying and do your job!"

"Go." This from Dallas. "Run."

"No!" Even as she spoke, strong fingers of compulsion and agreement stabbed their way into her mind. *Do what he says. Don't argue with him. Run.*

Aleaha was almost into the woods, sidestepping the Rakans as Dallas distracted them, before she realized what she was doing. She stopped short and frowned. What . . . why?

The answer hit her with the force of pyre-fire. Mind control.

Which agent was responsible? Devyn, Jaxon or Dallas? Didn't matter, she supposed, because they were all bastards. Somehow, someway, one of them had controlled her with a thought.

Scowling, she whipped around. Trees stretched on both sides, so close she had only to reach out to hug their trunks. Their twisted, snow-heavy limbs shuttered her line of vision, so she brushed them aside.

The sight she next drank in would haunt her for years to come.

Most of the agents were lying on the ground, some writhing and groaning sounds of impending death. Others were motionless in the blood splattered snow. Dallas, Devyn, and Jaxon were slashes of white in that violent nighttime canvas, the tallest of the Rakans stalking the outer edge of the circle. Other Rakans took turns taunting them with punches and kicks, each expertly evading the pyre-fire launched at them.

What can I do? What the hell can I do? "Stop," she called, hoping the distraction would give her friends some kind of opening to . . . what? Take off? Attack? "Stop!"

The stalking alien obeyed, stopping in a ray of moonlight, his gaze quickly finding her. Jolting her.

Aleaha trembled in shock, another honey-scented breeze suddenly enveloping her. Arousing her. *Kiss*, she thought again. The man was utterly and absolutely breathtaking. A hedonistic god fallen straight to Earth. Sensual, exotic, with kohl-rimmed eyes of gold, a strong nose, a square chin, and chiseled . . . everything.

He put Devyn to shame.

What little of his skin was visible glowed like liquid rays of sunlight poured over hot steel. His hair hung to his jawline, the same golden shade as his skin. He was mesmerizing, unimaginable power and dark savagery blanketing his expression. And God, he was a predator, the knowledge banked in every line of his big body. Yet he was also a being so beautiful, he lured with only a look. Probably snared women before they could snap out of his spell.

"Female," he said, his voice as mesmerizing as his face. How did he know English? In fact, how had the other, the one who'd tried to molest her?

"Oh, no, you don't," Dallas said, breaking through the circle and punching him in the jaw.

The Rakan's head whipped to the side. Quickly finding Aleaha's gaze again, he reached out, grabbed Dallas by the neck, and tossed him against a nearby tree. "Mine."

The force he used—amazing. The speed and agility—dumbfounding. Dallas slumped to the ground, unconscious. Jaxon roared, a wild sound, and attacked. The beast reached out yet again. This time, he slammed a ghostly hand inside the agent's chest cavity and twisted.

Jaxon crumpled and like Dallas, he didn't get up. Devyn watched it all, a hard smile on his face. A smile that promised death. But he didn't strike. No, he held up his hands in surrender.

Aleaha could barely believe her eyes. That wasn't like him. He'd rather be stabbed than lose a fight. Dear God. The situation must be grimmer than even she had realized.

Instinctively, she backed up, halting only when she considered a new possibility. Maybe, hopefully, he had a plan. Maybe he was pretending to surrender while giving Mia and crew time to get here. Yes, of course. But why hadn't help already arrived? They were supposed to swoop in if something like this happened, and close as they were, they should have been here by now.

The tall golden alien strode toward her, shoving his own men aside. With every step, he appeared more indomitable. Deadly. Her heart drummed erratically in her chest as he came closer . . . closer.

Do something! He was almost upon her. "Stop," she shouted again. *Good going. I'm sure he'll obey.* "Stay where you are." If Mia needed more time, it was up to Aleaha to stall this man.

Surprisingly, he stilled at the sound of her voice. Except for his eyes. Those trekked over her, hot and blistering, as if she were his property, already naked and begging for his touch. Goose bumps broke out over her skin; her mouth dried.

"One more step, and I'll shoot." Trembling, she raised her gun until she had a direct shot at his groin. Men tended to agree to anything when their dicks were threatened. "Let's talk about this. Maybe we can work something out. Why are you here? What do you want?" *Come on, Mia.*

Slowly he grinned, silently promising that he'd do whatever he wanted, whenever he wanted. Clearly there would be no chatting. Bastard. She squeezed the trigger. Just like the others had done, he darted away from the azure beam as if it were nothing more than a pesky insect.

A second later, he was in front of her, appearing in the blink of an eye and towering over her. She gasped in surprise as heat radiated off him and enveloped her. Heat and that honey smell. Her nipples beaded again, reaching for him, and her stomach fluttered. The need for him to strip her, to slide inside of her, was potent, heady, part of her wanting to drop to her knees and beg him for it.

Who are you? she wondered, dazed. In fact, the urges were so unlike her, common sense easily fought its way to the surface. *Kill him. Now. End this!* Mia had told them not to kill, yes, but Mia wasn't here. At this rate, Aleaha would be dead before backup arrived.

"I told you I'd shoot you, and I never lie." Of course, that was a lie. Her entire life was a lie. This, however, she would do. "I mean it! Back away or I start firing."

He remained in place. "Shooting has not been favorable for you so far, has it?"

"There's a first time for everything."

"I agree. Like the first time I disarm you."

Before she could act, he knocked the gun from her hand. It clattered to the ground, out of reach, and he purred silkily, all kinds of erotic in the undertones. "What do you plan to shoot me with, my female?"

Two·

INSTANT, SEARING AROUSAL. That's what Breean Nu, now leader of the Rakan army, had experienced when he first heard the woman's raspy voice drift through his fight-craze. When his gaze had landed on her, bathed in moonlight as she'd been, that arousal had only intensified and, foolishly, he'd lost sight of everything but her. Understandable, considering his past.

He'd seen, and he'd wanted. Desperately.

He'd whisked himself to her with every intention of claiming her as his own, for every warlord deserved a prize after a victory. He was a warlord, he had won, so *she* would be his prize. Even now, *especially* now, blood roared through him, hot, hungry. And not for more fighting. For every inch of her.

"Mine," he said again. The females of Raka had been decimated by plague after aliens began sneaking onto their planet several years ago. Those females had then begun to eat the men. Eat, as in meals. Having never encountered disease before, the Rakans had been at a loss, not knowing what to do or how to help. And then it had been too late. So many had died, hardly anyone had been left.

Trembling, his prize jerked her wrist from his hold and backed away from him. One step, two. Oh, there would be none of that. Too much did he enjoy being near her.

"Stop," he said, as she'd said to him a moment ago.

She raised her chin, stubborn, and kept moving. "Don't think so."

A refusal? From a war prize? He'd never owned one before, only knew that other soldiers on other planets often kept them as slaves. And slaves were to do as they were told. He would just have to instruct her.

Although, to be honest, Breean had never thought to find himself in this type of situation. He'd been a simple fisherman and Raka, as peaceful as the planet had been, had never had to utilize its royal army. Most citizens had obeyed the king without question, and otherworlders had never been allowed to enter their land. Until the Schön came in secret. Until the Schön destroyed them, infecting the women who then took out the soldiers and everyone else.

At the time, Breean had been living on the seas that cover most of Raka, the sole provider for his mother and sisters. He'd returned one day to find them dying, and thousands of others already dead, for once the females had lost their food supply, they'd turned on each other. So he'd gathered what uninfected survivors he could and they'd started fighting back, driving the Schön away.

The experience had changed them. They were not the innocent, naive men they'd once been. They were harder, meaner, utterly unforgiving. And that's the way they had to stay.

"I told you to stop, female." There was no room for compromise in his tone. "You will obey. I am your master."

"How cute. The big boy thinks he's in charge." She whipped out another pyre-gun from the holster at her side. He'd never actually seen one until tonight, but he'd seen pictures and knew what to expect from them. In the other hand, she held a knife. With knives, he was already intimately acquainted. "Now back off."

War prize or not, she should have responded to his scent by now. "Come to me," he said, just to see what she'd do. "Touch me." Since building his own army, he was used to having his every command obeyed.

She shook her head, continuing her slow backward journey. Her eyes were large, luminous, and crystalline, swirling with flecks of silver and cerulean. Underneath her cap, her hair was pale. Her nose was dainty, her cheeks rounded. But something about her was . . . wrong. The more he studied her, the more it seemed as if *another* face lurked underneath the first. A face with wider-set *green* eyes. A more aristocratic nose. Slimmer cheeks. *Dark* hair.

All together, that packaging was not as pretty. And yet it was more erotic, more sensual. The lips were more lush, redder, and made for sucking. The hair was silkier, and he could easily imagine the dark strands fisted in his hand while he pumped in and out of that delectable body.

She wasn't the reason for such strong, instantaneous fantasies, though. Any female would have triggered the same response. It had just been so long since he'd known pleasure, so damned long. He missed sex more than he would have missed an arm.

"Why are you looking at me like that?" she snarled. She glanced behind her as if searching for someone else. Her shoulders slouched in confusion when she spied no one. When she faced him, she must have realized he'd inched closer because she yelped. "Get back!"

Breean didn't know what to make of this woman. Not the dual faces, and certainly not the fact that she seemed to be immune to him in every way. Granted, he hadn't been around a woman in two years, but surely he was still capable of seducing one. And what had happened to his determination to force a slave to his will?

Drop the weapons and touch me, little human. Or was she alien? He frowned, not liking that he didn't know. Actually, there was a lot he didn't know and the answers were far more important than his hunger. "How did AIR know we were coming?" He'd visited several times in secret, hadn't talked to anyone, and had remained in the shadows. Still. They could have seen him, he supposed. But why not attack before now?

"They were good people," she said angrily, ignoring him, once again backing away. "You shouldn't have hurt them."

"*We* are good people." He stepped toward her just as slowly. "Those agents should not have tried to hurt *us*."

She swallowed. "Our guns were set on stun, not kill. You and yours, however, killed, so excuse me for not agreeing that you are good. And how many times do I have to say this? Don't you dare come any closer!"

"The warrior who killed those agents will be punished, believe me." In a movement so quick no eye could see it, Breean swooped in and slapped the second gun out of her hand. "Now, there will be no more shooting from you."

Shock settled over her lovely dual-features. He didn't give her time to threaten him with the knife. He simply snatched the blade out of her hand, studied its serrated tip in the moonlight, and sheathed it at his back. Could be useful.

Her mouth hung open in furious disbelief, revealing perfect white teeth that were a little sharper than those he'd seen from the other humans he'd encountered. Her kiss would have bite.

His cock twitched in reaction to the thought, and he frowned again. Biting was no longer allowed among his people. A rule he'd instigated and a rule he would keep. Always. Anything that drew blood, the liquid poison that could very well carry thousands upon thousands of diseases, was now forbidden. Disobeying meant death.

He watched as she tossed another glance over her shoulder.

"Are there more agents out there?" he asked.

"Of course not."

Which meant, yes, there were. With a tilt of his chin, he motioned for several of his soldiers to scour the area. Instantly they headed into the trees. Though they were dressed in black and clashed against the snowy backdrop, they moved liked midnight apparitions, barely noticeable.

"What is your name, female?"

Silent, she slid her gaze to the gun that lay several feet away on the ground. His remaining men stood in a semicircle around it, he noticed, arms crossed over their chests, waiting for his next order. The living agents sprawled behind them, already cuffed and gathered in an unconscious heap.

"I won't let you win," she said, ignoring him. Again.

"But I already have. Your brethren are defeated. You are the last one standing."

"That just means it's up to me to kick your ass."

"I'll let you do many things to my ass, female, but kicking it isn't one of them." He leaned into her, eating up the rest of the distance, in her face before she could blink. The fragrance of newly fallen snow and dark, mystic nights drifted from her, and he inhaled deeply, savoring. "I'll let you massage it. Caress it. Grip it while I pound inside of you."

Her cheeks colored prettily, and she growled, "What about rip it to shreds?"

If she was half as passionate in bed as she was now in the face of danger, she would burn him alive. And, oh, he wanted to be burned. "If you ask nicely, yes," he said honestly. "As long as you draw no blood."

"Fuck you."

"I hope so," he replied as his men returned, shaking their heads. No one was out there, and there was no sign of anyone having been there. He relaxed.

His female was still choking out a breath. "Never," she finally managed.

"Never is a long time. Perhaps we should negotiate."

No reply. Instead, a look of intense concentration claimed her features. Her eyes narrowed, the blue somehow darkening, becoming . . . golden? Impossible. Yet as he watched, her body seemed to grow taller and more muscled, her clothing ripping to accommodate the new bulk. Within moments she was his exact height, her features realigned to match his.

He was gazing at his own face, he realized, mouth falling open in shock. The green-eyed temptress was still underneath, still barely visible, but that didn't dampen the shock of seeing *himself* in place of the sweet-faced blond.

"How did you do that? *What* did you do?"

She peered down at her hands. No—*his* hands. Turning them over, studying them. Big, golden, calloused. Reeling, he considered the rest of her. She no longer had breasts but was solid from head to toe. She even had a bulge between her—his—legs. A nice sized one, if he did say so himself.

"Will I be able to move like you, do you think?" she asked, more of herself than of him.

His voice. She did not merely look like him, she now spoke with his voice. How was any of this possible?

Breean reached out to touch that familiar visage. What would he feel? Warmth? Cold? Surely this was an illusion. But just as his hand was about to make contact, the . . . whatever she was disappeared and his hand swiped only air.

He blinked. Confusion, anger, and more of that shock pounded through him. He glanced left, then right, but saw only the sway of trees and the swirl of snowflakes.

Brow furrowed, he wheeled and confronted his men. "Where did she—I—go?" More to the point, *how* had she gone? If she had always been able to move as swiftly as him, why had she not done so before now? If she hadn't, and this was as new a development as her appearance . . . damn. She might posses *all* of his strengths now. "Did you see her?"

Expressions as baffled as his must be, they searched the clearing for some sign of her.

From the corner of his eye, Breean caught a blur of movement, a flash of white and gold. That blur paused directly in front of the first pyre-gun he'd liberated from the woman. A second later, her— damn it, *his*—image solidified. She wobbled on her feet as though dizzy, weariness glinting over her still-masculine features. A frown pulled at her brow while she rubbed her temple with one hand and snatched up the weapon with the other.

He pounded toward her, intent. Sensing him, she looked up. Their gazes locked, gold against gold—and, thankfully, that hint of ethereal green. Sweat beaded her forehead, and she was panting. With fright? Fatigue? Or with the thrill of the chase?

A moment later, she grinned. Thrill of the chase, definitely, for that grin did not belong to a frightened female but to a taunting agent. Surprisingly, that aroused him all the more, this new challenge of her.

He didn't whisk to her, but stopped, continuing to watch her, curious about what this human—alien—would do next. What race could assume another's appearance, as well as another's abilities?

She threw an I'm-the-boss look at his men and barked, "Stay where you are. This is between the woman and me."

They had been inching toward her with determined expressions, but now they froze in place.

"Which one is which?" one of the men asked, glancing between the two of them.

"Look at the clothing," someone said. "Hers is a different material and ripped."

"But what if even that is a trick?"

"Stay where you are," Breean told them, parroting the female. "I will handle her."

"*I* will handle her and the prisoners," she said as if she truly were him. That intense glaze of concentration fell over her, and once more she disappeared.

His eyes narrowed as he searched the field, trying to zero in on a blur . . . seeing nothing . . . nothing . . . there! She materialized in front of the sleeping agents and crouched.

Her back was to him, and she seemed to shrink before his eyes. Her short golden hair lengthened and paled, appearing exactly as before. One of her hands shot out, slapping a human across the face. Pause. Another slap. Pause. She leaned to the side, muttered something, and slapped a second agent.

Who was she hitting? Slight as her body now was, it still managed to block Breean's gaze. He was afraid to move, however. Afraid she'd change personas or leap into motion again. Afraid he'd lose her.

A second later, she shoved to her feet and faced him. Leveling two guns, she edged to the center of the clearing, her left shoulder toward him, her right shoulder toward his men.

When had she picked up the second gun?

"Why won't they wake up?" she demanded angrily.

As he soaked in her blue eyes and womanly form, relief was like a living entity inside him. Much as he liked himself, he didn't want to seduce himself. Well, not anymore. There'd been enough of that over the past two years to last a lifetime. "They are merely sleeping."

"You had better wake them up. Or, to answer your earlier question, I'll shoot you with *this*."

Fierce, passionate, and now protective. His admiration spiked, and yes, so did his desire, damn his hot-blooded nature. And damn his abstinence. Yet he couldn't deny that he was glad the first woman he'd stumbled upon was this one. Even though he could not control her, she was delectable. To have her the way he wanted her, he would have to calm her, something else he had no experience with.

"Be easy," he said. Surely that would work.

"Don't just stand there," she snapped. "Wake them."

Or not. "Your commands will continue to go unheeded." *That is not how you calm a female, I don't think.* It was just, Rakan females had striven to do all they could to satisfy those around them—before the disease, that is. They'd rarely argued and had never disobeyed. They'd accepted and they'd agreed, as though the need to please had been ingrained in them at birth.

This woman obviously bowed to no one. That should have angered him, or at the very least deterred him. Yet he could suddenly imagine being tied up, *dominated*, helpless to this female's pleasure as she ground herself on his cock.

Interesting, but not something he could allow. There was just too much risk. To give up control was to invite bloodshed.

He stood there, unsure how to proceed. How *did* you calm a female you could not bend to your will, if silken commands failed? His men shifted uncomfortably, as if, like him, they were trying to decide what to do. They meant well, but he didn't want one of them to take her down or touch her in any way.

"Hold," he told them.

The woman's hand shook—what was her name? He found that he wanted to know as intently as he wanted to know what species she was. Which also happened to be as intently as he wanted to lick her until she came, starting with her breasts and working his way down.

"Didn't I tell you once before to get that look off your face?" she said breathlessly, then fired both guns simultaneously.

He easily leapt out of the way, the blue stun-beam sailing past him. As fast as he could move, the gun's rays were slow motion to him. But one of his men, Eton, did not see the approaching beam and was nailed, instantly freezing in place. The other warriors glanced to Breean, clearly angry that another of their brethren was immobilized and would have to be carried. They wanted to act.

"No," he said. "Mine." To her, he added, "What look?"

"Like you're going to eat me. I don't like it."

"The look will disappear, I'm sure, after I *have* eaten you." The good kind of eating, too. Not the kind his people had enjoyed, there at the end. He shuddered. "Do not worry, though. I promise not to use my teeth."

Scowling, she fired again, but once more he easily dodged. "Will you just be still already?" Her gaze circled the clearing and she pushed out a frustrated breath. "Come on," she muttered, though he didn't think she realized she'd said anything aloud.

There'd been no sign of anyone out there, but she obviously expected someone to show up and didn't like that they hadn't yet. Better they came here to fight amid nature than to fight amongst the innocents living in the city. He, too, would wait for them. Silver lining: another fight might help dull his arousal.

"What is your name, female?" he repeated, remaining on alert.

"Why did you come here?" she demanded, pretending yet again that he had not spoken. "What do you want from us?"

There had to be a way around her reluctance to share. "Why should I answer your questions when you refuse to answer mine?" Excellent. Soliciting her sense of fair play.

A heavy pause. A grind of her teeth. "My name is . . . Macy."

Macy. It was a lovely name, as stunning as the woman herself— whichever face she happened to don (even his)—but it didn't fit her. Still, it was worthy of shouting while pumping inside of her. Over and over again. "I am Breean, and I'm here to make a new home for myself and my men." He'd been searching forever, it seemed, but he'd finally found the perfect place to relocate.

They'd spent the last several months coming and going, preparing. Earth had everything they needed: water, technology beyond their comprehension, medical supplies, and warm female bodies. More than that, the people here knew how to survive. If plague struck, they most likely had a cure. If not, they could create one.

Never again did he want to watch those he loved die of debilitating sickness, helpless as a craving for living flesh bloomed inside them. Never again did he want to feel powerless as others died and he remained strong.

"Earth might play host to all manner of alien races, but its people are in no way welcoming," she said, and she sounded bitter about it.

Did she have firsthand knowledge of that lack of welcome? "Humans will have no choice but to accept us."

"Oh, really? Just like that?"

"Just like that." He hoped. "And now, this standoff is becoming tiresome, Macy." Waiting, he decided, could be done in a more pleasurable way. He approached her, his yearning intensifying—soon, he would be touching her—the scent of honey drifting from him with increasing potency.

Her nose crinkled as though she smelled something distasteful, but her nipples were already pearled for him, pretty and perfect against her clothing. "What *is* that smell?"

"Arousal," he said, seeing no reason to deny it. He hadn't smelled the lust-craze, which was far more pungent than his fight-craze, in so long he'd despaired of ever smelling it again. Right now, he reveled in it. "Do not try to pretend it displeases you." Not while he could see the rosy flush of her cheeks.

Macy's lush mouth floundered open and closed, and her hands shook. "Arousal makes a man burn, yes? Well, I'll show you something else that burns." Using her thumb, she changed the setting of the pyre-gun and fired at him. Just as before, he grinned and side-stepped the beam—a yellow beam this time, which meant she was through trying to stun him and now wanted to fry him.

Swiftly he closed the distance, stopping mere inches from the barrel. "I believe I mentioned that I'm growing tired of this."

She almost fell backward with the force of her gasp. "And I grow tired of telling you to stay back!" Another shot.

This time, close as he was, he wasn't quite fast enough to dodge. The yellow-gold flame singed his upper arm. "That *hurt*."

"Really? I thought you liked to burn."

The scent of honey should have dissipated as that small patch of skin blistered and sizzled. It didn't. In fact, it only seemed to increase. That he desired her enough to emit the telltale perfume despite being injured was baffling. Even with his two-year abstinence, which blew his "I'm just desperate" theory.

How was she drawing more desire from him than any other female ever had?

She wasn't (naturally) golden, as he would have preferred. She wasn't biddable, as he was used to. Being perplexed by her, even enchanted, he understood. She was a novelty. But this much desire? Just then Breean suspected he would have wanted her even if he were sated.

Quite simply, she tempted him on every level.

In theory—he was full of those today—he could have disarmed her, and had her on the ground, penetrated, before she even realized what was happening, the lust-scent making her want it despite everything around her. While some part of him would have enjoyed that, because God knew, he *was* a man, the rest of him knew that her willing, wholehearted participation would be a thousand times sweeter. The hardest battles, he'd come to learn, elicited the most gratifying victories.

"You're surrounded, Macy. Drop the weapons and admit defeat. No one is going to hurt you."

"I'll admit defeat when I'm dead. How's that?"

"I'm afraid I cannot grant your request. Your death would disrupt my plans for you."

Her cheeks drained of color, and she lost some of her bravado. "W-what plans?"

Rather than answer her, he tilted his head to the side and regarded her intently, drinking in her sparkling blue eyes with that hint of green and remembering the way she'd moved only a few minutes before. "What planet do you hail from?"

Undiluted panic flooded her expression. Breath rasped from her, so loud in the ensuing silence that the sound of it scratched at his ears.

"I'm from here." She fired. "I'm from Earth."

He ducked. The ocher stream glided straight through the top outline of his essence, which had been left behind by his swiftness. "Liar."

"I am!"

"You say that after everything I've witnessed?"

"Yes." Fire.

Duck. Finally he cut through the rest of her personal space, nothing between them but a whisper. He might not want to force her, but he *would* have to subdue her before she ran or injured him further. "A human could not change faces and bodies as you do."

"What I am doesn't matter." Just as before, she backed away. Her bottom lip quivered, and tears suddenly glinted in her eyes, crystalline pools of pain, sorrow, and intensified fear. "Now, let the agents go and leave this planet! Please."

Were those tears real or fake? Either way, he actually experienced a desire to wrap his arms around her and . . . comfort her? Comfort a woman shooting at him? Strangely enough, yes. Desire truly did screw with a man's common sense.

There had to be a way to stop those tears, disarm her, *and* get that sweet body under him as quickly as possible, all without using physical brawn. He'd mentioned negotiating earlier. She hadn't seemed interested, but then, they hadn't been discussing her friends.

"Do you wish to bargain for the lives of your fellow agents?"

She stilled, though she didn't lower the weapons. The tears dried, at least. "B-bargain? What is it you want from me? What do I have that you could want?"

"I thought I had made that clear. I want *you*."

For several drags of time, she did nothing. Gave no reaction to his words. No matter her response, he had no plans to kill the agents. They were to be tickets allowing his men to freely roam Earth. He would trade a life for a life. An agent for a Rakan. And if AIR proved dishonorable, attacking after agreeing to such a trade, well, they alone would be responsible for the war that erupted. All he desired was peace for his men. Peace and a new, disease-free life.

Macy couldn't know that, and he didn't mind letting her think she was the cause of his benevolence. If mercy was what she found attractive, merciful he would seem to be.

Too eager, though, he would not be. That would lessen his power. His years negotiating fair prices for his fish had taught him that. "My offer will end in three seconds," he said. "One. Two."

"Three. My answer is no. I'll free them myself."

That intense look of concentration descended over her features again. He tensed, knowing what was coming this time. As her appearance changed from woman to Breean, from humanoid to Rakan, he kicked into hyperdrive. But she quickly gained her bearings and raced to the far edge of the clearing before he could catch her.

Their eyes met in a moment of charged electricity. In challenge. Then, she disappeared again. He was standing in the exact spot she'd vacated a split second later. As his spirit caught up to his body, he looked for her. Spotted her just ahead. Cursed and leapt forward. She might actually be better at this than he was.

She was rushing around the group of agents, trying to uncuff and wake them, and when that didn't work, drag them away. He was there in the next instant, right beside her and gripping her arm, doing his best to contain her without bruising her. Gasping, she jerked from his hold and disappeared.

When he next spotted her, she was darting through the trees, racing away. "Take the prisoners to the dungeon," he flung over his shoulder to his men, then gave chase. He still didn't understand how the AIR agents had known they would be arriving this night, but it didn't really matter. He'd planned to hunt down a few after he settled in, and now he wouldn't have to. Now he could simply begin the negotiations. After he caught Macy, that is.

A few times she actually slammed into the thick trunks. She'd *humph*, shake her head, and jump back into motion. Once he clasped her jacket; rather than slowing her down, his grip merely ripped the torn material farther, revealing a shirt that was equally torn, as well as the planes and hollows of *his* back.

The second time he grabbed her, he encountered only hair. Hating himself, he yanked. She screamed, but continued to surge forward, leaving several strands in his fist.

"Stop," he commanded, moving the knife he'd confiscated from her to his boot. When he caught her, and he would, he did not want her having access to it.

"Do you really have to think about my answer?"

"You're not going to escape me. You might as well give up before I'm forced to hurt you."

"Says the man who's losing." She maneuvered around another tree.

Several vehicles loomed ahead. Was anyone inside them? If so, and they hustled away with Macy, he could lose her for good. He knew it, didn't like it, and wouldn't allow it to happen. He was tiring from the day's excess of speed, but he ground his teeth and forced his arms and legs to work faster.

Air beat against him, chilled and biting. His blood ran hot, though, hotter than ever before. He could hear the woman's hoarse pants and imagined her breath floating over his naked chest, then dipping lower, until her mouth encircled his cock in damp heat. Oh, yes.

Arousal spread and gave him strength. Again he quickened his steps, his gaze raking over her body. Or rather, *his* body. Which was weird, but didn't cool his ardor. As if sensing the fervor of his stare, Macy flicked a wild glance behind her. Whatever she saw in his expression panicked her and in less than a blink, she was average height with short red hair and dark brown eyes. Aged skin, a little too tanned.

She slowed abruptly, as if losing her ability to sustain the swift pace right along with her grip of his image, and lost her balance. Down, she tumbled. Breean was on top of her in the next instant, flipping her over and pinning her to a bed of leaves. Allowing his weight to settle atop her, he locked her arms over her head.

"You should have stopped," he panted.

"Calm down, calm down," she chanted, squeezing her eyes tightly shut. She dragged in a deep breath, released it, and was golden, muscled, and tall in seconds.

He scowled down at her. "Change back."

"No." Her eyelids popped open, and his own golden eyes glared up at him.

"Change!" No way would he kiss himself. And oh, yes, he was going to kiss her. Nothing could prevent him from doing so, not even the voice in his head demanding he be gentle with this woman.

"No!"

He ran his tongue over his teeth. If she possessed his appearance and his abilities, surely she possessed his vulnerabilities as well. Once, during a battle with a crowd of infected Rakan females, he'd been bitten in the side. The area had never healed properly and was a liability, for any type of contact would send him to his knees. Even now, there was a twinge beneath the scarred skin.

Knowing exactly where to touch, he reached under the torn shirt she wore and pinched. She screamed in pain.

"Change."

"No," she said, but it was a whimper this time.

He could not back down. He increased the strength of his grip. "The agony will stop the moment you change."

"Fine, okay, yes, but I have to calm down first. Okay? Calm, calm." While she chanted, her eyelids closed again, and she pushed out a shaky breath. Her body slackened. Slowly, so slowly, her face began to rearrange itself, the length of her nose shortening, her lashes becoming longer, paler, her cheeks rounding. Her hair altered from golden to pale.

Disappointed, he shook his head. "I want to see the black-haired wench."

She blinked up at him in horror. "W-what?"

"The black-haired wench with the green eyes. I want to see her."

"How do you— No. Never mind," she snarled, suddenly struggling to gain her freedom. One of her arms succeeded, and she drilled three quick jabs into his nose before he could stop her.

He howled as he snagged her wrist. The little witch. This was going to end. Now. "The time for pain is over, Macy. Now you're going to kiss me and make me better."

THREE

CALM DOWN, CALM DOWN, CALM DOWN, ALEAHA SANG IN HER MIND. Hard thing to do, though. Nearly impossible. A man was on top of her, pinning her down, and he somehow knew what *she* looked like. Not Macy. Not another identity. But Aleaha. How did he know which face truly belonged to her when she hadn't shown it to him? How?

And how could she like this position so much? *I am your master,* he had said, as if he owned her. Rather than enjoying his weight, she should be clawing his eyes out and feeding them to him, then later allowing herself a case of wine and a good cry.

A cry with dry heaves and a runny nose, because the fact that she enjoyed this man in any way scared her. Even the first time she'd accidentally become someone else—when an overweight, balding man had jerked little Aleaha into an abandoned warehouse, touching her in ways no man should touch a child, and she'd felt herself expand, lengthen, and transform, she hadn't been this scared.

That man had let her go; this man wouldn't release her until she'd given him what he wanted. She sensed it with everything inside her.

That's just how warriors were, and he was every inch the warrior. She should know—she'd inhabited that hard body. But she couldn't relent. He was a killer and her enemy, and he wasn't frightened of AIR. Maybe because he'd defeated the agents so easily.

Guaranteed he wouldn't defeat Mia, who was probably on her way right now. Something she'd assured herself a thousand times already. So where the hell was the commander?

Didn't matter, really, she told herself now. In the end, AIR would catch him. They always caught their targets. And when they caught this one, he would tell them what he'd seen her do, tell them what she truly looked like.

Oh. God. She would be ruined. Why wait until after scratching Breean's eyes to have her cry? AIR would then turn their sights on her. She would be on the run, hunted like an animal, just as she feared. And what if they found a way to prevent her from changing faces? She would never again be able to hide.

Would that be so bad? her mind suddenly piped up. *You can't take over yet another person's life.*

She'd found a sense of contentment as Macy, yes, but the guilt she'd denied, well, it was easier to deny than to admit. In truth, she battled guilt every damn day. Hell, she lost more and more of *herself* every day, causing despair to blend with that guilt. She hated that she was living a life that had been cut short for someone else. Hated that she'd done nothing to earn the blessings bestowed upon her. Hated that her friend Bride, if she still lived, couldn't find her because she didn't have the courage to live as Aleaha.

Don't think about that now. Escape!

She bucked and strained under her captor's hold, unintentionally meshing their bodies and fusing heat, breasts against chest, thigh against thigh. Sweet heaven, it felt good, which increased her need for freedom. If he could make her crave him, despite her fear *and* dislike of him, he would destroy her life.

"Get off me!"

His eyes closed and his lips curled in a slow, satisfied smile.

"You're trying to push me off, yet you're also gripping my shoulders, holding on. Which do you really want, female? For me to get off? Or for me to get *you* off?"

Damn it, she *was* holding on. How long since she'd allowed herself such close contact? Such warm, delicious contact? *There you go again, becoming distracted, wanting what you can't have.* Scowling, she pried her fingers from him, all the while continuing to flail. "Off. I want you off."

"Keep moving. Don't stop fighting." His penis was hard and thick and every time she arched, it pressed deep between her legs. "I'll get off, I promise."

If they'd been naked, he would have been inside her. And she would have liked it.

Okay. She was only making things worse—for both of them. She stilled, panting, and he moaned in disappointment. That strange honey fragrance wafted all around them, as if they lounged in a summer meadow of wild honeysuckle rather than a gloomy forest of ice.

She inhaled deeply to catch her breath, and her mind fuzzed just a bit. So good. Smelled so good. Why fight him when she could kiss him, as she'd craved earlier? She could delight in those muscles, enjoy every naughty inch of him.

Argh! "Just . . . let me go." Clearly, she couldn't win physically. "Please. I've let you go. Do the same for me."

His eyelids opened, revealing the golden glow of his irises. They were bright with hungry desire. A reflection of hers? "You should not have run." His voice was husky, rich. "The warrior in me liked it."

Liked was growled, layered with challenge and savagery.

For several seconds, her heart ceased beating. And when it finally kicked back into gear, her flailing and bucking renewed with more force, but did little to dislodge him. She didn't care that her actions rubbed them together. Didn't care that they aroused her as much as they did him. She had to escape before he tried to take things further—and she was tempted to let him.

Tempted? Ha! Willing to beg, more like.

Already her blood sang and her body ached from the delicious friction. When his erection stabbed at her clitoris, she had to clench her jaw to keep from moaning in ecstasy. "Let me go!"

"Your fate was sealed the moment I spotted you." Droplets of sweat beaded on his forehead, making the skin appear like liquid gold. "Actually, it was sealed the moment you stepped into this forest."

Damn him. What would Macy do in this situation? What would a real AIR agent do?

An AIR agent would already have cut off his balls, used them as earrings, and danced around his lifeless form. She could do no less. Maybe. Fine, she wouldn't be going near his balls, but she could definitely fight harder.

"I guess your fate was sealed, too." Aleaha lifted her head and bit him, using the only weapon she had at the moment: her teeth. They sank into his chin. The taste of sugar teased her tongue just as she remembered she feared contamination. Sugar? Mmm, as good as his scent. Heady, like aged wine. Clearly addictive, because she already craved another helping. Who cared about possible contamination, really? After all, Jaxon didn't think the Rakans were infected. So . . . Dinner, come to mama.

Breean ripped free with a howl. Golden blood trickled from the tiny punctures and onto her collarbone as he glared down at her. Angry as he was, the moonlight paid him nothing but tribute, washing over him with loving strokes. Had she truly just tried to eat him? Did that mean she was a cannibal like . . . no, no. Absolutely not. She didn't want to feast on anyone else.

"You bit me," he snarled. "Are you infected?"

"With what?"

"A disease. Any disease."

"No. Are you?" *Please say no.*

That soothed him, but only somewhat. "No. But what if you are, and you don't know it?"

"I'm telling you I'm healthy."

"Still. You should not have bitten me. Bloodshed is forbidden."

Forbidden? "But you made the agents bleed."

"Not me."

"If those responsible were under your charge, it might as well have been you."

A muscle ticked below his left eye.

"Just let me go, okay," she said, doing her best to sound strong and assured this time rather than frantic. She (might have) sounded breathless. "Otherwise, I *will* bite you again." A lie, but he couldn't know that. No way did she want to lose herself to that chomping urge again.

"Do not ever, *ever* draw my blood. Do you understand? You'll not like the consequences, I swear it."

Don't apologize. Don't weaken. "Well, get off me and save us both. I can't breathe."

He rolled his eyes. "Now you are just being silly. You're talking. Therefore, you can breathe."

Smart bastard. "You have no right to hold me like this."

"As the victor of this battle, I have every right." Another of those slow, wicked grins tugged at the corners of his beautiful golden lips, and her heart skipped another beat. "Oh, the things I'm going to do to you. And I know what you're thinking. Is he open to suggestions? The answer is yes."

Gorgeous and a mind reader. But she said, "Liar. I've suggested you get off me about a thousand times." How she'd love to cut that grin off him. And maybe his clothes. *Stop thinking like that, you slut!*

"No. You commanded." He anchored her wrists to the ground with one hand and sifted the length of her still-pale hair through his fingers with the other. "I think I will like the dark strands better. Why do you hide them?"

No way she'd answer that and incriminate herself further. *Think, Aleaha.* To escape him, she needed a weapon. Besides her teeth. She'd tried to sheathe her pyre-guns at her waist while running through the trees, but the unusual velocity of her motions had made her clumsy, and she'd dropped them. But she'd also had a knife, a knife Breean had taken and secured to his back . . .

Her eyes widened. Yes. Yes! Keeping it had been very stupid of him because now she could steal it back.

"My guess?" he continued, oblivious to her plans. "You don't want anyone to know your true identity."

"Wow, detective. I'm so glad you're on the case." She hoped her sarcasm hid both her chagrin that he'd already figured her out and her excitement that this battle between them could very well be over in minutes. All she had to do was convince him to free her hands. "For the record, *this* is my identity."

"Once again, you lie. *Alien*."

"I'm human, damn it!" Macy was human, so Aleaha was, too. That's how it had to be.

"You want to be, are trying to act like it, but you're not. AIR had to know."

A fear she harbored, no matter how much she relaxed. "Go to hell."

"Perhaps I'm already there." His gaze lowered to her mouth. "Soft," he said. "What's your real name, alien? Something that fits your real face, I'm sure."

"I *am* human. And I already told you my name." Shivering, trying to ignore the white-hot pulses hammering at every point of contact, she said, "Release my hands. Please."

"So you can hit me again? I think not."

"So I can *feeeel* you." She didn't have to force the words out; they wisped out of her mouth of their own accord.

He didn't pause to ask what had changed her mind; she was instantly freed. Her hands slid to his back, as if she meant to grab him and pull him closer. His nostrils flared at that first tentative, seemingly willing touch, and he braced himself on his elbows, pressing deeper into her body.

Automatically her knees fell open, welcoming him. She couldn't stop them. That honey scent . . . His hips surged forward, his erection sliding over her clothed but already moist folds. She gasped, unable to stifle the satisfied sound. And in that suspended moment, she almost forgot her true purpose.

"That's the way, Macy."

"Don't call me that. Call me—" The moment the words hit her ears, she sucked in a breath. Why would she want him to call her by her real name, especially when she'd refused to tell him what it was? She was Macy now, and she had to remain Macy, even with lovers. Not that she would become this guy's lover.

"Call you what, then?"

"Ale— Macy." Damn it! She'd almost told him. Again. What kind of moron was she?

A perverted moron at that, since she found the man responsible for the fall of her friends so damned sensual, erotic, and wholly masculine. A drug that overshadowed any hint of inhibition. Just looking at him, she wanted to drown in sensation. *For the sake of the others, don't lose focus.*

"Do you like it soft or do you like it rough, Ale— Macy?" he purred.

Why not both? *Knife. Get the knife.* "I—I don't know. Why don't you find out?" Inch by inch, she trekked her trembling fingers down his sides, not stopping until she reached the coarse material of the holster. Almost there . . . almost . . . Her palm found smooth material and hard muscle, but no weaponlike bulge.

"What's your real name? Tell me. Please."

Would he never give up?

"I promise not to tell," he murmured. "You have my word. But how can I kiss you properly if I don't know what to call you? Please."

She didn't want him to leave her yet. Not until she had the knife. And she feared he would indeed walk away if she refused yet again. That was the only reason she was giving in, damn it! "Aleaha," she found herself saying. She didn't trust him, but part of her did want him to know, which was why she didn't simply lie. "Happy now?" Where the hell was the knife?

"Aleaha." He closed his eyes for a moment, as though he savored the reverberation. "Much better. And now that we've got that settled ... are you looking for this, Aleaha?" In a movement so swift she saw only the remnants of his spirit, he palmed a blade from his boot and waved the gleaming silver tip over her nose. "I moved it during our chase. Just in case. Over the past two years, I have learned to plan ahead."

With a yelp, she shrank deeper into the cold ground. Ice-covered rocks stabbed into her bared back where her jacket and T-shirt were torn. "If you cut me, I'll ..." She'd what? Bleed all over him and ruin his clean clothes. Like he didn't know that already. She was screwed.

"I told you, there will be no bloodletting. Besides, I like the passion and concern you've shown for your friends," he said, tossing the blade out of reach. Then he baffled her by bending and sniffing her neck, his nose brushing the sensitive skin there, the thundering pulse. "I won't punish you for that."

Another shiver rushed her. *Concentrate.* Without the knife, there was no reason to remain in this position. No *intelligent* reason. "Let me up and I'll negotiate for the agents' freedom," she said, recalling his earlier attempt at bartering. "Just like you wanted."

"The time for that is over." The inflection in his voice was dark, carnal, and animalistic. His gaze lowered to her lips. "Now I believe I promised you a kiss."

"Don't you dare kiss me." The words were automatic, but there was no heat behind them. Passion, like fear, was not a good thing for her. Yet a part of her wanted him to take her mouth anyway. Take everything she had to give and demand more, forcing her to feel, to need, to crave. Finally. As she'd dreamed of for so long.

"Don't cut you, don't kiss you. Anything else I shouldn't do?" She started to tick off an entire list, but he added, "Never mind. I'm through with this conversation." And then his lips were meshed with hers, his hot tongue probing for entrance.

She flattened her palms against his chest and shoved. He didn't budge. In fact, he grabbed hold of her wrists and repinned them over her head, smashing her breasts into his chest—mmm, good, so good—at the same time cupping her nape and forcing her jaw up, preventing her lips from moving away.

"Open," he commanded against her mouth.

She shook her head, even though denying him was one of the most difficult things she'd ever done.

"Open." He applied a hard pressure with his chin, creating the smallest of gaps.

Still she resisted. She'd lose control, and he'd find himself kissing a stranger, maybe even another man. He'd become enraged, disgusted, and she wouldn't be able to blame him.

Determined, he changed tactics. The pressure gentled, and he pulled back slightly. Soft, so softly, he traced his tongue over the seam of her lips. "Open. Please. You'll like what I do. I swear."

Don't give in, her mind beseeched, even as she recalled all the nights she'd lain in bed, aching so badly she'd wanted to die, wishing intimacy weren't so dangerous for her. Wishing a lover could please her without discovering her secrets. She'd been down that road a few times, and she couldn't allow herself to take it ever again.

The first time, she'd been regarded as a freak. The second attempt had ended in a fight for her life. The third—and final—attempt had started rocky but had ended successfully. Or so she'd thought, until she was chased down and nearly locked up.

Breean has seen you in action, so he already knows what you can do.

But he's a monster.

So are you.

I am not!

The internal debate ended with an, *Mmm, he smells better with every second that passes, like cinnamon and honey, wildflowers and sex.* Down-and-dirty, nothing-held-back sex. The kind she'd always fantasized about having while she touched herself, alone, always alone, finger dancing over her clitoris.

She must have unintentionally obeyed him and opened her mouth because suddenly his tongue was pushing past her teeth, stroking, thrusting, twining. Every nerve ending in her body leapt to instant life. Liquid heat flooded the apex of her thighs, and she trembled.

"Sweet," he praised. "So sweet."

Make him stop, she thought, dazed, even as she wound her legs around his waist and locked her ankles, arching her back. His erection rubbed the new center of her world, and she gasped, lost to sensation. As feared, she felt her appearance change, expanding from average height to a bit taller, a little more rounded.

Shockingly, he didn't seem to mind. Seemed to like it, actually, as he hissed in a breath. "Again."

She did, unable to help herself. She arched, appearance changing to someone shorter, rounder. They moaned simultaneously, then his tongue was back inside her mouth, hotter now, harder, and he was sucking her the way he might suck on a woman's clit, laving and savoring every drop of moisture. Their teeth banged together as he drew her closer. Her still-hard nipples pressed into his chest, abrading deliciously.

"M-my shirt." She wanted to tell him to rip it the rest of the way off her, but was having trouble forming the words. She ached, oh, she ached, and that ache demanded all of her attention. A touch, a glide. *Something*. Except, she felt the hair on her head shorten, her legs lengthen, and something harden between her legs—and it wasn't Breean.

There wasn't time even to gasp in horror. Because of her sudden spike of fear, the male form was quickly replaced. This time her hair grew and the color of her skin went from tanned to pale, her body from lean to lush. In a snap, however, she changed yet again. Female, still, but longer, slimmer. She clutched at Breean, relieved, needy. He hadn't erupted when she'd sprouted a penis. He hadn't even stopped kissing her.

"I knew I'd like the dark hair." His tight clamp eased on her nape and his fingers slid to the front, stopping at her voice box, fanning over her pulse, then dipping to her breast. He kneaded the soft curve.

With his acceptance came a flood of uncontrollable, undiluted desire. And holy hell, did she have pent-up desire. That touch, so tender, so innocent, wasn't enough.

More, she thought. "I need . . . I need . . ."

"Me." He jerked the material up, revealing her navel, her bra—which he moved, too—and then her breasts. Her stomach quivered as he studied her. Cold air beat around them, but she felt only heat. Only need. "Pretty," he said, sounding as if he were in some sort of trance. "Like berries. Pink, ripe. Mine."

He palmed her, skin to skin this time. Yes! When he thumbed a nipple, plucked it, she lost hold on reality, arching, writhing, ready to beg. There was only amazement, wonder, pleasure. So hot, blistering, singeing all the way to the bone. "Yes, yes!"

"I could touch you forever, I think."

"Lick," she commanded. Something was flowing through her veins, so potent she was almost drunk with it. That desire, yes, but also . . . what? His scent? It was strong, heady, dizzying, but could it have caused this sweet urgency? This sizzling desperation? No longer did she care where she was, who she was with, or how many times she shifted. Satisfaction was the only thing that mattered.

Her body was not her own. In that moment, it was his. Breean's. His to do with whatever he pleased. She had no shame, truly no goal save climax.

"Give me," she said, only then realizing he hadn't obeyed her. He was still staring down at her, tension bracketing his eyes. "Lick."

"I don't think I'll ever tire of looking at you."

"That's great. But look and touch at the same time," she said.

He chuckled.

Finally his lips settled over one of her nipples, tongue flicking against it.

Raspy gasps escaped her, and she rode his cock up and down, sliding, sliding, still desperate, so desperate. He sucked, hard. She cried out, closer to heaven in that moment than she'd been in her entire life. Happily, willingly swimming in pleasure, the need for release a constant ache between her legs.

"More," she demanded. "Harder."

This time he obeyed quickly, giving her what she wanted. She chewed on her bottom lip, tasting blood, wishing it were *his* lip she nibbled. His mouth, his tongue. Perhaps his cock, thrusting in and out, filling her, stretching her jaw. Her tongue would lave the thick head, sucking, sucking, until he was wrung dry, until—

Who are you? drifted through her mind. *Who is this sensual creature you've become?*

His fingers abandoned her breast, only to slip lower to the waist of her pants. In a few seconds, he was going to delve past her panties and sink straight to the heart of her. He'd feel her wetness. He'd work those naughty fingers into her one by one. He'd pump them in and out, driving her to the brink.

Yes, yes. That's what she wanted; there was no fighting this desire. This fog. Yes, fog. That's what it was. That's what was swimming through her veins, clouding her judgment and lighting her on fire. Blazing, delicious. And wrong.

Wrong?

"S-stop," she managed to gasp out. The madness had to stop. And if she just paused a moment, she could figure out *why* this was wrong.

Instantly, he stilled. He was panting as their gazes clashed. "You want it," he growled low in his throat. "You want me."

"No," she said, then more loudly, "No!" It wasn't her writhing, but someone else. Someone he'd created.

Nailed it again, she thought. Somehow he was changing her, making pleasure her only concern. And okay, yeah. Some part of her suspected this was her fault. That she simply wanted him more than she had ever wanted another. But that was wrong for different reasons, so she *would* still stop him.

"I can feel the desire inside you. You need a man."

"Not you." *You, only you.* Damn it. *Stay strong.*

"*I* need a woman."

Pick me! Strong, remember? "Not me."

Desire was blended with irritation and anger, all three fiercely directed at her. He looked frightening just then, reminding her of the warrior who'd attacked and defeated AIR's best in a matter of minutes.

Now she felt shame. Now she felt guilt she would never be able to deny. What kind of woman tongued her enemy, no matter the reason, while her teammates languished?

"You deny us both, Aleaha."

Her stomach clenched, but she forced herself to say, "I don't know you, I don't like you. Of course I deny us both."

"Very well." He popped to his feet, dragging her with him. He was scowling. "In time you will learn about me, and you will like me. That's a command."

"I haven't obeyed you once." Or maybe she had. The details were as foggy as her mind. "What makes you think I'll start now?"

He peered down at her, one golden brow arched. "I'm halfway there already. Your nipples are still hard."

"So?" Cheeks flushing, she fought the urge to cover herself. "It's still cold out here."

"You begged for me."

That was not something she needed to be reminded of; she remembered, both hating and loving herself for it. Hating because of all the baggage that came with the pleasure, and loving because, well, it had felt so damn good. But just as soon as she'd spent a few minutes alone, she'd love herself to earth-shattering completion and could hate him without this pesky need being in the way.

"Temporary insanity. I also told you to stop."

Clearly frustrated, he tangled a hand through his hair. "Do you have an answer for everything?"

"Yes."

His tongue swiped over his teeth. She'd tasted that tongue, almost bitten that tongue.

Never again, she told herself. Enough stalling. It was time to act. She pictured Macy in her mind and felt her body respond accordingly. Her hair shortened, as did her legs. Her boobs grew—a lot. Much better. This was her shield. Her armor against the world. And now against Breean.

He scowled at her but didn't comment. "Come. There is much to do and I've wasted enough time chasing you."

Yes, she'd made sure of that. But still the backup agents hadn't shown. Aleaha prayed nothing had happened to them. With the bleak turn this night had already taken, however, she doubted the prayer would be heeded.

FOUR

BREEAN'S WARRIORS HAD GATHERED THE AIR AGENTS, as ordered, and started for the underground holding cell they'd hurriedly constructed on one of their trips here. It had taken him fifteen minutes to catch up with them and their human cargo, Aleaha tossed over his shoulder, and then another five to reach the dilapidated house they'd confiscated on the outskirts of the city; it was the perfect hideout, since the area was seemingly forgotten by Earth's inhabitants. Maybe because there was no vegetation or animals, the air drier than dirt, stinging the nostrils as though acid were being inhaled. It was still cold here, but there was none of that beautiful white snow.

Breean left Aleaha locked up in one of the bedrooms, comfortable and fed, yet separated from her people, for an entire Earth week. She tried to escape at least twice a day, but he caught her each time, attuned to her in a way he didn't understand.

He'd hoped to develop a resistance to her while he saw to the defenses of his true home in the city. He'd hoped to develop a resistance to her while the days passed.

Despite his best efforts, Aleaha never left his mind. His only hope now was that time had softened her dislike of him, that she craved another of his kisses. The first had nearly burned him alive. No woman had ever tasted so sweet or felt so perfect against him. And, yes, others had clutched him with utter abandon, moaning their pleasure, desperate for more, but none had ever affected him like this. Why, he didn't know.

No longer could he delude himself, even slightly, into thinking that any other woman would have done. It was her he wanted. Her specifically. Aleaha. The fierce glow in her eyes, the sharpness of her wit. The challenge of winning so strong a prize. What would she look like when she smiled? How carefree would her laughter sound?

He had to know.

Finally, it was time to move everyone into the permanent home. It had better security and was in a livable location. Yes, they would be more easily spotted by AIR, which had, thank the blessed sea, failed to find his hideaway on the outskirts, but it was worth the risk. He planned to contact them soon anyway, and start the bargaining process at last.

By the time the prisoners were taken care of, night had fallen. Breean returned to the wasteland with half of his forces. He couldn't contain his eagerness as he entered the house and walked down the crumbling hallway to gather Aleaha. What would he find? The blond goddess or the dark-haired vixen? Eagerness to match his own or anger?

He was actually shaking with anticipation as he unlocked Aleaha's door. *I won't bed her until she begs for it,* he vowed. After what she'd already given him, nothing else would be acceptable. The hinges creaked open, and he stepped inside. She stood in front of the bed, watching him warily, pale hair dancing around her shoulders.

His heart thundered in his chest. In arousal, yes, but also in disappointment. He'd wanted the vixen.

She wore the T-shirt and jeans he'd brought her, and the material hugged her body nicely.

"Nothing to say?" he asked, feeling tongue-tied himself. Never had he wanted something so badly. Never had he had to tread so carefully.

She arched a brow, as stubborn as ever. "What about, and stop me if you've heard this one, let me go. Let my friends go."

So. She still meant to resist him. He revealed no hint of his frustration. "You will stay with me. Your friends . . . maybe."

"Why keep us? You're going to destroy us anyway. That's why you're here, right?"

He frowned. "What do you mean, I plan to destroy you?"

"Why else would you be here?" Every word was layered with disgust. "I've been thinking about it, since that's the only thing to do here, and I've decided you're here to prepare the way for that stupid queen."

"What are you talking about? I have no queen." Not anymore. Apparently, the Rakan queen had been one of the first females to succumb to the disease. She had killed her own husband. Her own children.

Aleaha studied him, her expression pensive. "I know you're not ill since I bit you and haven't exhibited any symptoms, and I know you're Rakan rather than Schön, but why else would you have come to Earth if not to help the Schön queen? An alien was interrogated recently and revealed that warriors would be arriving that night in the forest with the sole desire of clearing a path for the Schön queen. Then boom, you arrive. You take out AIR. What's that if not clearing a path?"

Everything inside him locked down. First in panic—not again, he couldn't put his men through that again—and then in rage. "Schön? You expected those vile Schön?"

"Yes. We'd already killed a few of them, and you and yours won't be any different."

"We would *never* help them. We hate them." Mouth suddenly dry, he pivoted on his heel, exited the room, and locked the door behind him. He was trembling again, but this time it had nothing to do with desire.

"Hey," he heard her call. "If we were mistaken about your race, it's possible we were mistaken about you following the Schön queen. Come back! I'm not saying I believe you, I'm just saying we can talk about this."

Breean quickly called together all of the men who had accompanied him. They filled the living room, spilling out into the hallway. As he told them what he had just learned, they reacted first with panic, as he had. And then the rage set in.

"Bastards."

"Murderers!"

A couple jumped up to pace, bumping into everyone around them.

"I will leave the decision up to you," he said. "If you want to leave, we will leave. If you want to stay, we will stay." Either way, Breean wasn't letting Aleaha go. He wouldn't leave her here to face the deadly Schön on her own. Because she was female, she would be one of the first to fall. But knowing her as he thought he did, she would not go easily.

The debate began.

"We've worked so hard, finally found a home. We can't just abandon it now."

"Yes, we can. We deserve peace."

"Will we ever truly know peace? We are outsiders wherever we go. Here, at least, otherworlders aren't killed on sight."

"I can't watch another home be destroyed."

"And what happens when the Schön ruin this planet?" Talon, his second in command, scrubbed a hand down his tired face. "They will move on to another, perhaps the next one we have chosen. We need to destroy them. Now. Finally."

Breean agreed. "At least here we know there are medications and technology to combat such a loathsome enemy. That's why we chose it. Besides, my female told me that AIR defeated the first diseased warriors who came here."

"Think of it. We can kill the Schön, as we've dreamed for so long," Talon added. "For what they did to us. For what they did to our loved ones."

"How are we to kill them? They can make themselves invisible. As we well know, it's impossible to fight an unseen enemy."

That cast a gloomy shadow over the men, memories consuming them.

"AIR obviously knows how to fight them, and there are ways to get the information from them. So tell me." Breean eyed them one by one. "Leave? Or stay?"

In the end, it was unanimous. They would stay. They would fight. Or try to. If they died in the process, at least they would die as the soldiers they'd become.

"I am proud of you," he told them. "Surrender is unacceptable. Once we are established in our new home, we will figure out a plan of action. As for tonight, we have much to do. Go about your duties. I will meet you outside."

As they strode off, Breean returned to Aleaha's room. This time, she was seated at the edge of the bed. Still blond. But, damn, if she didn't make his heart stop. "Come." He waved her over.

"Don't you want to talk?"

"No."

She stood on shaky legs. "Well. Are you sure you're not going to take off again, leaving me here?"

"I'm sure."

"Why did you rush off like that?"

"You mentioned my greatest enemy." He saw no reason to lie. Not when he might gain information. "My men needed to know what they will soon be up against."

"Oh. So you really do hate the Schön?"

"Yes." Guess they would talk, after all. "Does AIR have any idea what those bastards can do? I know you told me some were killed, but I just want to make sure you understand the danger."

"Yes. They are infected with a disease that turns people into cannibals."

"That disease destroyed my planet. That disease is the reason we are here."

"Oh," she said again. "I'm—I'm sorry. You aren't . . . infected, are you? I mean, I know we've had this conversation and I know I bit you and tasted your blood and I haven't experienced any unusual symptoms, but you've got me worried."

"No, I'm not infected. You would be able to tell if I were. The skin turns gray, the eyes sink into the skull. *I* would have been the one to bite *you* that night in the forest."

She gulped, but that was her only response.

"How did your people defeat them?" he asked.

"I don't know. I wasn't working for them at the time."

He was glad. Though he wanted the information, badly, he didn't like the thought of Aleaha engaging such fierce creatures. At least there was hope, a way to win. He would like to work with AIR and increase the chance for victory, but he didn't think they'd welcome him.

"All I know," she continued, "is what I've already told you. Several warriors came here. They were crushed, and now their queen, the most powerful of them, is on her way."

Oh, yes. The queen was indeed the most powerful. She was also heartless, selfish, determined, and irresistible.

"Come," he said again. For the moment, there was nothing else to say on the subject.

"Are you taking me to my friends?"

Rather than start a debate—because no, he wasn't taking her to her friends—he remained silent as he escorted her out of the home and into the backyard, keeping her beside him with an arm draped around the feminine dip of her waist. She didn't try to escape. Perhaps she'd realized there was no place to go, nothing around them. Perhaps, as concerned as she was about her fellow agents, she didn't want to leave without them.

Or perhaps he wasn't giving her enough credit. Maybe she meant to bide her time and kill him while he slept. If he was lucky, she stayed because she wanted another kiss. Had she thought of him at all while inside that room? Dreamed of him the way he'd dreamed of her?

"The air," she said, nose wrinkling in distaste as her eyes scanned the darkness.

"Cold?" He removed his jacket and placed it around her shoulders.

"Yes, but also pungent."

"You become used to it." He peered down at her, hungry. "Change for me. Please. No one will see." There were no trees offering solace, but there was a tall iron fence surrounding the barren yard. Plus, there were no other homes nearby. They'd all collapsed.

She didn't pretend to misunderstand. "I will if you'll tell me where the agents are. I never heard them, and I'm trying not to go crazy, imagining them d-dead." There at the end, her voice shook.

"They were underground, in a cell not far from where we are standing." Truth. He didn't mind telling her since they had already been moved to the new home. "I swear to you, they are alive and well and will remain so. They are also angry as hell that you are not with them."

"I-I believe you. That sounds like them. Thank you." Her relief was palpable. "And now for my part of the bargain." Again, she glanced around. When she saw that they were alone, she began to grow several inches, becoming leaner. Her long dark hair fell over his wrist, and he basked in the silkiness of it. Her eyes were so deep a green he would have sworn he was standing in a lush, dewy meadow every time he peered into them. Her skin was translucent, smooth, and, as easily as she'd responded to him, probably sensitive. She might be able to come with only a caress.

A man could hope, anyway.

Actually, a man could hope for a lot more. Even now, he could taste her in his mouth, rainstorms and passion. So much passion he'd nearly drowned in it. Had *wanted* to drown in it. No matter which guise she'd worn, even as the male—surprising, but something he wasn't going to question—she'd tasted the same. And he'd loved it.

She could have eaten him alive with those sharp little teeth, and he would have died with a smile on his face.

"Beautiful," he said. The clothes were a bit too short for her now, though they bagged over her smaller chest and leaner waist, but, oh, did the sight of her like this please him.

A tremor slid the length of her spine, brushing her shoulder against his chest. "Thank you."

Renewed desire pounded through him, hot, readying his body for her. If he wasn't careful, his resolve to wait until she begged would snap and he'd try to seduce her. Here and now. No matter who watched. Even now that honey scent was wafting from him. . . .

"What are you going to do to me?" she asked, her voice raspy. Did she smell it? Yearn for him? "What are you going to do to the other agents?"

The doorway to the underground tunnel was thrown open, Talon climbing the makeshift steps, a metal box in his hands, barking orders in the Rakan language to the others, who were carrying large boxes of their own.

Aleaha gasped at the wide, dark pit now revealed. "Is the cell down there?" she asked, her previous questions forgotten. Then, she must have realized that someone else was seeing her true form, because the black locks began to lighten.

"Don't change. Please. I did not expect him to appear so soon, but hiding now will do no good. Besides, he will not betray you."

A moment passed, but then her hair returned to its full, dark glory. He offered her a grateful smile and was rewarded with a hesitant twitch of her lips. One day he would make her laugh. One day he would—

Forget his purpose if he didn't look away. "Do you need more men?" he asked Talon in Rakan. There was no reason for Aleaha to have this information, and every reason for her *not* to have it. "I want us out of here as quickly as possible."

Talon's golden braids slapped his temples as he faced Breean. "No," he said. "Cain and Syler just arrived. Said they couldn't listen to the AIR agents any longer. I've got them carrying the last of the weapons."

"Were the agents still demanding their release?"

"Yes. But they also want to know what we did with their dead." Disgust dripped from Talon's voice when he uttered the word *dead*.

"When Cain and Syler return, they may explain that we buried them." It was the truth. But Breean was as disgusted as his friend that humans had died. Killing the agents so viciously and so violently had been unnecessary. They'd had things under control—a few of their own men had been stunned, yes, but no one had been injured—so there'd been no need to resort to bloodshed.

Because of that bloodshed, he'd had to command everyone to burn their clothes and bathe the moment they'd reached this dilapidated, forgotten house. No exceptions. Not even for the prisoners.

"Speaking of AIR," Talon said, "neither Cain nor Syler saw any sign of them, here or there, during their journey. You were right. There is no better time to finish our switch."

"Good."

"What shall I do with Marleon? Leave him," which meant, *kill him here*, "or take him with me?" Which meant, *kill him there*. "I didn't know what to do with him, so I kept him locked up here."

Marleon was the warrior, the traitor, who'd whisked inside several of the agents, taking over their bodies and forcing them to shoot themselves. He'd been sequestered this entire week while Breean considered his punishment. A punishment he didn't want to deliver, for he loved Marleon like a brother. But there was no way around this. He'd merely been putting off the inevitable.

"Take him. It's past time I made an example of him."

"Consider it done." Talon's gaze shifted momentarily to Aleaha. "I know that you wanted no reminder of her while she was locked away, so I didn't ask what I've been dying to ask. Now that you have her . . . did you learn how she was able to become you?"

He sighed. "Not yet, but I will find out."

"The change was amazing. You are keeping her for yourself, I gather." Talon switched to the Earth language on the last sentence, a hungry gleam in his golden eyes.

"Yes," Breean answered, a little stiff.

"No sharing?"

His hands clenched at the thought, dark possessiveness clamoring through him. Aleaha stiffened as well. "No."

"She—"

"Is mine."

A nod and a grin from Talon; a growl from Aleaha.

"I thought as much. Very well," Talon said. "We have been monitoring the headsets from the agents as you told us to do, but the female voice has stopped talking in them. And this morning, Torrence found and destroyed the cameras they used to watch."

"Oh, God." Aleaha groaned, paling. "The cameras. I had forgotten about them. They must have seen me . . . what I . . . oh, God."

"Excellent," he told his second, ignoring her outburst for the moment. Otherwise he would have drawn her into his embrace and forgotten his purpose yet again. "How much do you lack before the tunnel is empty?"

"We're down to the last."

"Finish up, then. I'll stop bothering you."

Talon returned to directing the men, and Breean's attention returned to the woman as if pulled by an unbreakable cord. Finally. Her lips were puffy, as if she'd been chewing them, and a bright, vivid red. Like blood. He should have been repulsed.

He wasn't.

Moonlight bathed her, and he would have sworn stars twinkled around her, as drawn to her loveliness as he was. Her eyes sparkled like emeralds, and strands of dark hair whipped around her face.

Obviously, her agent's mind had flipped on. She was studying the surrounding area with sharp precision, taking in every detail. He could not wait to have all that concentration directed at him.

As if sensing his perusal, she faced him. His desire must have been evident because she shivered, gulped, even inched backward, sinking deeper into night's shadows. But when she realized what she'd done, she straightened and reclaimed her position in the moon's amber rays. A true warrior, she was.

"What's inside the chests?" she asked, only the slightest catch in her voice.

He liked that voice, layered as it was with equal measures of fear, courage, and sexuality. "Weapons."

Her attention whipped back to the boxes, as if she could burn a hole through the metal with her gaze. "What kind?"

"Does it matter? They all do the same thing." Kill.

"We've got everything," Talon called.

Good. Breean didn't remove his focus from Aleaha. "Close the pit and head out." He wanted the girl to himself for a while longer. "We'll be along shortly."

"As you wish."

He couldn't stay long; in a few hours, the sun would rise. Only once had he made the mistake of coming to Earth during daybreak. The sun was simply too hot for a Rakan's golden skin, too blistering, something they weren't used to since Raka had three alternating moons and a small, sun-like orb that produced only the barest hint of light.

From the corner of his eye, he saw Talon and a few others secure the tunnel doorway, then gather their supplies and stride away. He should be helping them—he never asked his men to do something he wouldn't do himself—but again, he couldn't force himself to walk away from this moment with Aleaha.

"I thought the agents were in there. Where are you moving them?" she demanded. "*When* are you moving them? What if they're injured and need medical attention. And why did you leave me in that room so long?"

He didn't have to answer, but he found that he wanted to alleviate her concerns. "They've already been moved to a house in the city. I moved them for safety reasons. They are uninjured."

"Take me there."

Soon. "Kiss me first."

For a moment, only a moment, stark desire played over her delicate features. But it quickly disappeared, obliterated by fear. He sighed. Why did she continue to fear him? He had not hurt her, even though he'd had every opportunity.

Then that same intense look of concentration darkened her features, the one he'd seen that first night. She meant either to run or to challenge him. Sadly, there was no time to indulge her. "I would not do that, were I you. It . . . excites me." Truth. "And I will catch you, you know I will."

She scowled. But slowly, bit by bit, her body slackened. "What I know is that you're a bastard."

"How so? I did not force you to my bed. Did not starve you. Kept the others away from you."

"Just . . . shut up. You're so annoying."

His lips twitched in amusement and his scrutiny intensified, as if he could discern everything about her simply by looking. What did she like, what did she dislike? What foods did she favor? How many men had she had?

The last had him ready to commit murder. Didn't take much these days.

Relax. She's with you. That's all that matters. Up close like this, he could see a scattering of freckles across her nose. Pretty. Unlike Rakan freckles, which were clear and sparkling like diamonds, these were tiny and brown, adorable. He reached out, intending to sift her hair through his fingers and trace the strands over those freckles.

She grabbed hold of his wrist to stop him. Where their skin met, he sizzled.

"No touching," she rasped.

"Silly girl." He increased the pressure, her strength no match for his, and tunneled his fingers to her scalp as he'd wished. The strands were thick and possessed a bit of curl. They were silky, like polished ebony. He reveled in the beauty, the luxury. "I can do anything I want."

"If that's your mind-set, I feel sorry for the women in your life."

"No reason for you to do so. They are all dead. And, no, I didn't kill them. Not with pleasure or menace. As I told you, they died of the Schön disease."

"Oh. I'm sorry," she said softly. Her expression turned pensive. "Your mother, too?"

He nodded. "And sisters."

"I'm sorry," she said again. "I wouldn't wish that kind of pain on anyone. Even you."

A sweet proclamation. One that disarmed him. For it proved that she was more than a soldier, more than a captive. She cared. She felt. Even for a man she deemed her enemy. While every part of his body already seemed to recognize her on a level he didn't understand, craving her, needing her, his mind now followed suit.

"You have lost someone yourself, I take it?"

She nodded sadly. "My friend, Bride. She was like my mother and sister rolled into one."

"How did she die?"

"I don't know." She chewed her bottom lip. "She could still be alive. *Is* alive. She has to be. I've been searching for her for years, but haven't found a trace of her."

"She could have traveled to another planet."

"No. She wouldn't have left me. Not willingly."

Perhaps he would find this Bride for her. Give her the woman as a present. As for now, he just wanted to continue basking in her. "Hiding your true hair should be a crime," he said. Soon that hair of hers would be splayed over his pillow. Her body would be draped over his bed, open and eager, spread completely. For him. Only him. She'd be wet, soaking him.

He might even watch her touch herself before he joined her. Might watch her sink her fingers between her legs, slipping inside that tight little sheath, arching into every glide, moaning, begging him to finish it. He nearly moaned himself. *Stop thinking like that.*

"People do whatever they have to do to survive." There was a trace of guilt in her words.

One of the clues to the mystery of her slipped into place. "And you would have been killed if your true identity was known? Sweet, to do whatever is needed to protect yourself is admirable, not shameful."

Her eyes narrowed, and he wasn't sure who her anger was directed at. Him. Or her. "You don't know what you're talking about. I'm—"

"No more lies, Aleaha. Please."

Her jaw clenched, the grind of her teeth loud in the surrounding silence. "You're not going to get away with this. AIR will catch you. They always do. And you'll be executed on sight as a predatory alien."

"Clearly your AIR team couldn't find their asses if I handed them over in paper bags."

A mix of fury and affront claimed her features, lending them a fiery edge. This time he had no trouble telling who had earned the bulk of her emotion. "You had the advantage that night. Somehow you knew we were there waiting."

"Not true. We knew nothing of the sort. You, however, knew we were coming. Therefore, you had the advantage. Yet I still consider that a fair fight."

"I doubt you know the meaning of *fair*."

"Of course I know the meaning. I just prefer to fight dirty. Fairness is an idea most often touted by the defeated. I'll use any advantage I have, on anyone, at any time. That's how battles are won."

"Oh, you mean like this?" Her knee jerked up and she nailed him in the balls.

He hunched over, wishing he could vomit his intestines. Anything to stop the excruciating pain. At this point, he might even have been willing to cut off his cock. The burn was agonizing, like someone had set fire to his pants. Worse, she would have darted off if he hadn't grabbed her wrist and held on tight.

"Well?" There was satisfaction in her tone, even though there would be no escaping.

"Yes," he gasped out. "Like that." After an endless, strangled minute, he was able to drag air into his lungs, cooling that searing fire. Finally, he straightened and released her—but he was still pant-ing. He couldn't fault her, however. She'd certainly fought dirty.

"Before you say anything," she said in that smug tone, "I refuse to kiss you there and make you feel better."

That had been an option? Hold everything. He might endure the pain again for such a kiss. "Shall I fight dirty with you now?"

Her lips twitched in amusement. "You can if you want, but I don't think a knee to my groin would have the same effect."

"I didn't say I'd knee you there, now, did I?"

At last her smugness drained away. He hated to see that grow-ing smile disappear, though, and cursed himself. Should have stayed silent. For her smile, he could endure anything.

"Why did you do that?" he asked, hoping to remind her of the reasons and thereby witness the return of her enjoyment.

Her chin lifted stubbornly. "Talking about the fight between AIR and your men reminded me of the agents who died. You didn't have to kill them."

Plan failed, he thought. And really, how many times would she chastise him for that? "Once again, *I* didn't kill them. But do you, as an agent, not kill aliens for a living?"

"I've never killed any . . . Well, I've never killed anyone who didn't deserve it."

Another lie? Her outrage seemed real. "How long have you worked for AIR?"

She licked her lips nervously, seeming to realize she'd admitted to something she shouldn't have. "A little over a month."

A month? She was a lethal baby, practically an innocent. "You are an alien in an organization that usually hires only humans. Are you an informant for your race, then?" That made sense.

"No! I'm not an informant."

There was enough disgust dripping from her high-pitched tone to legitimize her denial. The more she spoke, however, the more of a mystery she became, the single puzzle piece he'd slid into place seemingly insignificant.

What race was she? He still couldn't place her. Why did she work for AIR, hunting those like herself?

"A predator is a predator," she said, as though reading his mind. "They need to be put down."

Like him?

A muted ray of light suddenly broke free of the sky and glowed around them. He glanced up, saw the purples and pinks forming, and realized he'd been standing out here far longer than he'd meant to. He needed to escort her to her new home, like, now, but found he still wasn't ready to interrupt their conversation. No matter the risk to his skin.

"How do you and your men know English?" she asked, drawing his attention back to her. "And before you ignore me, remember that I've answered plenty of your questions. It's only fair that you answer one of mine."

Her curiosity pleased him, even if it wasn't for him specifically. "We've studied the people, their words, their *everything*. Plus, we've been here before. Many times."

"That's impossible. We would have known."

He shrugged. "Even if I lied, languages are easy for my people. We have only to hear one to know its nuances." As he spoke, he traced a finger down the curve of her cheek. So smooth, so warm. So sensitive. Goose bumps broke out over her flesh.

Frowning, she stepped away from him, and he bit the inside of his cheek as his finger trembled for more. "AIR doesn't know where to find us," he added. "So if you are resisting me because you hope to be rescued . . ." She'd seemed scared of them, now that she knew they'd most likely seen her change forms.

"They'll learn your location soon enough," she said, looking anywhere but at him. "They've probably been scouring the area, closing in minute by minute."

"They can search, but it doesn't mean they'll succeed." Besides, his men had seen no sign of them.

"Maybe they're hiding, watching for the perfect opportunity, even now."

He frowned, scanning the area with a sharper eye. Those thick iron bars surrounded them, the gaps closed with boards. Pyre-fire could quickly and easily burn wood, allowing agents to slip inside undetected in seconds. "We had best go. We have a thirty-mile hike ahead of us. Now, do you prefer to walk or be carried like before?"

"Wa—" She stopped and pressed her lips together. "Carried," she said, and there was enough satisfaction in her tone to make him suspicious.

Did she hope to tire him so that AIR would more easily catch him? He *was* tired, for he hadn't yet fully recovered from the first night's fighting. Moving at such a speed always did that. Plus, the pain in his side still bothered him—and now the pain in his balls. But outshining the fatigue and the pain, was exhilaration. He'd finally crossed the galaxies, finally made a home for his men . . . finally had a woman to warm his bed. Kind of. Soon. He'd die before he allowed himself to be captured now.

"Carried it shall be," he said, bending down and pressing his shoulder into her stomach.

"Wait. What are you doing?" she gasped out.

"I'm doing as you suggested." He hefted her up, her body curling over his shoulder. He locked her legs against his chest with one hand and splayed his fingers over her ass with the other. Perfection. She hissed out a breath. He wanted that breath on his bare skin, not his shirt, heating, teasing, taunting. A wave of longing crashed through him with such potency, his muscles tightened their grip on his bones.

"Put me down, Breean! I was joking, okay? I didn't mean for you to carry me like this."

His name on her lips was paradise. "How did you mean for me to carry you, then?" On alert, he crossed the yard and pushed through the gate. Mile after mile of dirt stretched ahead. That didn't comfort him as it should have. The more he thought about it, the more he realized she was right. Fierce soldiers that they were, AIR's agents should have caught his scent by now.

Why hadn't they attacked?

"Carry me in your arms, idiot!" Her arms and legs flailed. "Don't carry me like a sack of potatoes. You'll hurt me. And we're almost friends now. Right? You should treat me better."

Friends. He wished. He also wished he could go slowly, be gentle with her, but he needed to reach the new house as quickly as possible. He'd waited too long to head out, enjoying her a little too much. Cursed ballsy woman. He could have stayed here another day, he supposed, and that way, he would have been able to take his time when night next fell. But the weapons were gone, his men were gone, and he wouldn't be able to enjoy *and* protect her.

"This didn't hurt you last time. I'll be just as careful with you this time. Any injury I can take upon myself, rather than inflict upon you, I will, I swear it."

She stopped wiggling. Her hands even settled on his back. "That's . . . sweet. Damn it! You shouldn't be so sweet. I don't like it."

Or perhaps she liked it too much. "I plan to win a kiss from you. Get used to it."

Starting forward, smiling, he said, "I had a guard at your door, and he told me that when the lights flickered out each night, you spent the time talking to yourself." Breean had been furious that he hadn't been notified until this morning. He would have gone to her, comforted her as he was learning to do. "Are you afraid of the dark, Aleaha?"

"No. I was afraid of someone sneaking up on me."

Far worse. That was not a fear she would let him cuddle all better. "I would have kept you safe."

"Hardly. To me, *you* were the monster in the closet."

Monster indeed. But at least she'd said *were*. Maybe they were indeed almost friends. With every mile he traveled, he increased his speed, the world streaking past him. He knew he left a glow behind, but no one would know what that glow was. Well, no one except AIR's agents, but as he'd already proven, they wouldn't be able to catch him.

Finally they reached the city. That lovely snow. Cars, homes, and shops, people carrying bags whizzed past him, wind rustling his hair. He stepped carefully, precisely, keeping his motions as smooth as possible for Aleaha's sake.

The shop windows, he noticed, were lit with multihued bulbs— red and green were the most prevalent colors—and there were fake trees in every corner, decorated with bows, ribbons, and dangling ornaments. Those things had not been present the other times he'd visited. He'd often wondered why they were here now.

MERRY CHRISTMAS, a sign said. "What is Christmas?" he asked.

"God's birthday. We celebrate by giving each other gifts. And do you know what I want most of all? For you to put me the hell down!"

A celebration of birth. They had done something similar on Raka. Some of his best memories were of the nights he'd spent in front of his mother's fireplace, his four sisters all around him, passing out the trinkets he'd purchased for them. That would have been his father's right, except that his father had died at sea soon after his birth.

A pang of homesickness pierced him. How he missed them. If only he'd come home sooner on that last trip out, he might have been able to save his mother and sisters. They might be with him now. But then, he would not have met Aleaha and he found that he could not regret that, which filled him with guilt. In a perfect world, he would have them all.

"No holiday spirit, I see," Aleaha grumbled.

"Do you have a man waiting for you to return home?" A man waiting to win her heart with the perfect Christmas gift.

"Does it matter?" she snapped, giving him the same words he'd given her about the weapons.

"Answer me." He wanted to kill any man who might be waiting for her, wanting to strip her and taste her and fill her. This faceless man would do all of that as his "gift," he was sure. Well, that was Breean's gift to give!

"No. I won't answer."

He'd begun to relax—no, she'd said—only to tense again. "Woman, I am not someone to taunt."

"Neither am I. So if you want the info that badly, you'll bargain for it."

And he'd thought her smart before. She was a genius. His lips curled into a smile as he dodged a building, his shoulder catching on a jagged stone and snow cascading onto his chest and her legs. She yelped; his grin widened.

"Very well," he said. "What would you like from me? A gift? Say yes, and I'll even unwrap it for you."

"If you dare tell me your penis is the gift, I'll scream."

"In pleasure?"

"Have I told you yet that you're annoying? I want the agents released."

He snorted. "Nothing you have is worth that."

He could hear her teeth grinding. He'd lied, though. He thought he might give anything and everything to have her writhing in his arms again. Willingly and without reservation.

Stupid cock. Perhaps one day he would be commander of it rather than the other way around. He just, well, he liked her spirit, her courage, her tenacity . . . and, yes, her body. He wasn't going to lie to himself and claim that the attraction was completely mental.

"Let *one* of them go, at least."

"No. That one could lead your precious AIR army to my door-step." Those he'd captured and moved, he'd blindfolded, so that wasn't truly a risk, but she didn't need to know that, because really, his bargain, the trade-off, was the only viable option.

"What *will* you do for the information, then?" she asked, clearly frustrated.

"I'll give you a vow that they will not be killed by my hand. Or by anyone in my army," he added before she could mention Marleon again. Of course, he would see to it anyway, but still he would not tell her that.

"And how do I know you'll keep your word? You've already admitted that you fight dirty."

"As do you." He patted her bottom, strangely proud of her wit and the fact that she remembered what he'd told her. As if it meant something. Sure, he was undoubtedly deluding himself, and she'd remembered what he'd said simply because she'd smashed his balls into his throat immediately after, but that was neither here nor there. "You'll just have to trust me."

"Oh, really?" She sank her teeth into his back, past his clothing and straight into skin. He winced. Damn, but her teeth were sharp. Rather than scold her as he should have, however, he said, "I'll take this to mean you refuse to trust me."

"That's right." The words were moaned as if he were thrusting between her legs. She licked him through his shirt, sucked, murmured, "God, you taste good," then groaned in embarrassment and stopped. "There'll be no trusting," she choked out. She began kicking and slamming her fists into his back. "I won't stand for this kind of treatment. Do you hear me?"

"I believe everyone can hear you, Aleaha."

She bit him again, but her teeth quickly gentled and she released another of those moans.

His grin widened as he picked up speed.

FIVE

THE DIABOLICAL BASTARD CARRIED HER INTO A DREAM.

From her perch on his shoulder, she scribbled mental notes, trying to memorize the path they raced and the surrounding neighborhood. But he moved in that superspeed of his, one snow-covered building blending into another, so she had trouble garnering more than a few tidbits.

The neighborhood itself was meant for New Chicago's elite. That much she knew without looking. The air just smelled cleaner, wealthier, as if everyone scrubbed their windows with pine-scented hundred-dollar bills rather than cloth.

She remembered how Bride used to drag her to neighborhoods like this. They had stared at the homes, pretending they belonged inside. Once she'd even assumed the features of someone's little boy and entered. It had been dinnertime, and a mouthwatering spread of ham and dressing had been laid out before her.

Bride was a vampire and only drank blood, so she'd waited outside. Aleaha had barely begun to eat—and to stuff morsels into her pockets for later—when she'd lost her hold on the boy's image, the ecstasy of the food too much. The parents had screamed at her, cornered her, and demanded to know what she'd done with their son. Thank God Bride had rushed in, gathered her up, voice-voodooed the couple into forgetting them, and helped her escape.

After that harrowing experience, she'd stopped visiting neighborhoods like this one. The desire to belong, however, had never faded. Even though she'd known how impossible such a dream was.

How could Breean, a Rakan and new Earth resident, afford something in an area like this? Didn't matter, she supposed. However he'd done it, he was now the kind of guy she'd wanted to date as a teen.

We're going to marry rich husbands, Bride had told her one day. *We'll never have to worry about anything ever again.*

They'll be handsome, she'd replied.

Of course. We're gorgeous, so we deserve gorgeous men. And they'll be so in love with us they'll drool every time they look at us.

They'll think we're the smartest girls ever.

And they won't care about our origins, Bride had added. *They'll just keep giving us money.*

That had been Aleaha's main concern. Not the money but her origins. Breean met that demand. Breean met *all* the demands. He was rich, handsome and ready to drool. Not that she was thinking of him in terms of a husband. But wow, he was rich. She just couldn't get over that fact. Did she like him more because of it? Um, yeah. How shallow was she?

When he reached the wraparound porch of a house on the far end of a perfectly paved street, he slowed. As if sensing his presence, one of his men opened the door and Breean sailed inside.

She gasped at her first glimpse of marble floors veined in gold. From somewhere, water trickled into several bathing pools, and mist circled through the damp air. Satin pillows in every shade of gold, from the palest yellow to the darkest amber, lined the walls. The windows were stained black, allowing no light inside. Her gaze lifted to the ceiling, and she saw crystal chandeliers flickering with hazy luminosity.

This totally wasn't the den of iniquity she'd expected. As run-down as the other home had been, she'd placed Breean in the poor and desperate category.

Breean stopped and spoke to one of the warriors, keeping her draped over his shoulder. She didn't mind—the better to eavesdrop. But what was he saying, damn it? She thought she heard the word *tree* but she couldn't be sure.

She drew in a frustrated breath, catching more of that honey-suckle scent. And smoke. Ugh. She coughed, inhaling the odor of burning material. The warriors she'd fought only a week ago bustled in every direction, bare except for underwear, and not quite meeting her gaze.

All that golden skin . . . She tried not to stare, but they were huge. Everywhere. *Merry Christmas to me.*

Idiot.

"Do you like?" Breean asked, squeezing her legs to let her know the question was directed at her.

Did she like the men? The mansion? "No," she lied. "How did you get so much water in here?" After the human-alien war, its use for bathing and swimming had been restricted, the supply scarce and expensive. In fact, the water had probably cost more than the house. Most people were forced to clean themselves with a dry enzyme spray.

"We brought it with us, bucket by bucket. Water abounds on Raka," he explained. "There is nothing better than hearing the rush and feeling the warmth, the decadence."

"So why do you want to make a new home for yourself *here*? There's not a lot of water left."

"As I told you, our planet was in ruins. We needed a fresh start in a place where the female population thrives."

So he hadn't just lost the women he loved. He'd lost everything and everyone. She felt a wave of pity for him, but quickly tamped it down. *Don't feel sorry for him. He's the enemy—and obviously prowl-ing for sex!*

Still. His people had died of the Schön disease. AIR would find that interesting. Might even want to question him to find out how he'd survived, as well as what he knew about the race and their queen. Perhaps that information would save his life. Although, AIR wasn't known for its forgiving spirit. His people had killed several agents, and someone would have to pay for that.

"You can put me down now," she said. The position was uncomfortable, but it was being so close to him that disturbed her most.

"Not yet."

"Why? Payback?" She would deserve it. She'd given his dangly bits hell, after all. *All's fair to him when fighting, remember?*

"I told you how I would return that . . . favor," he said, and she couldn't tell if he was fighting amusement or anger.

Actually, no, he hadn't told her anything. He'd alluded to touching her, but nothing else. Diabolical bastard. It would have been so much easier to hate him—as well she should have, damn it!—if he'd flat out threatened her with violence. Instead, he'd practically threatened to kiss her better.

He rounded a corner, the hallways wide and spacious and leading to a multitude of rooms. There was even a staircase that wound to the second floor. He didn't take it, though he paused and stared up it for a long while. Finally, he sighed, then meandered down another hall before carting her *down*stairs, into a cold, dank basement.

Not a basement, she realized a moment later, but a dungeon. "Another prison?" In a home like this, she would not have expected a torture chamber to be a purchase option.

"Yes. You'll stay here only long enough for me to prepare your room."

That was a lie, she knew it was. He'd had all week to prepare a room for her. What was his purpose, then?

"Besides," he added, "the other agents are here, and I know you've been wanting to see them."

The other agents were here? Happy but panicked, Aleaha quickly pictured Macy. The blond hair, the shorter body, the bigger boobs.

Her appearance changed in a blink, and she expelled a sigh of relief.

There were multiple cells, each with a barred front and dirt sides, and inside each of those cells was an agent. Finally. Her eyes collided with Devyn's; he was now wearing a loose black shirt and pants. He didn't speak, but his grip tightened around the metal, his already pale knuckles bleaching of color.

Despite his stressed expression, he blew her a kiss.

She spied Dallas next, and he winked. Then she saw Hector Dean, tattooed and muscular, who always left a room when she entered. The guys he joked and laughed with, but he'd never warmed toward her. Today, he nodded in acknowledgment. Where was Jaxon?

"I'm fine," she told them all. "Nothing's been done to me."

Each of them relaxed.

"We're fine, too," Hector said in that deep voice of his.

"Enough," Breean said.

"Suck it," she told him, and several of the agents laughed.

He didn't set her down until he reached a small, empty cell. Inside, he slid her down his body, the action igniting heat between them. Heat she couldn't afford. The moment her feet touched solid ground, she scampered backward, unsure what he meant to do— and unsure of her reaction. Would she have the strength to stop him again if he kissed her?

To her relief, he didn't comment about the change in her appearance. That, too, would have weakened her. And destroyed her.

Please don't let him call me Aleaha. Please, God, don't let him call me Aleaha. She should never have told him her real name.

Eyes on her, he shouted something in his own language. She wished she knew what he was saying. A few seconds later, a Rakan warrior stalked into the cell. He was holding a bundle of clothing, and he didn't look at her. Breean took the garments and said something else. The man nodded before racing out.

One heartbeat passed in silence, two.

Breean met her glare. He seemed taller and more like total, in-your-face carnality than ever before. What would he say to her next, now that they were seemingly alone and she was at his mercy? What would he demand of her? *Take my cock into your mouth*, she could almost hear him say. *You're welcome. Merry Christmas.*

Her heart galloped—but not in abhorrence and oh, she was disgusted with herself. She'd failed to escape, to get help, to free the agents. She'd failed to resist Breean when he'd kissed her, and had even begged for more.

In that one night, hell, one hour, one minute, he'd stripped her of all common sense and inhibitions. Would have stripped her of her clothing, too, if she hadn't fought her way out of that crazy lust-fog. The week had not dulled her desires. And here she was, still freaking desiring him, *after* he'd set her inside a cage next to her coworkers. It was insanity.

Remember how it was with the other three men you allowed in your life. How, after she'd spontaneously changed during sex, one had slapped her. How two had called her names. How one had thought to use her ability to his advantage. What would she do if superstrong Breean hit her? Hit him back, of course. What would she do if he called her vile names? Cry like a dumb baby, most likely. What would she do if he tried to use her? To hurt AIR, even? Curse at him, surely, before crying some more.

Did she seriously *want* him to like her?

Yep, insanity.

"They aren't the best of quarters," he finally said to her, guilt in the undertones of his voice, "but as I told you, they'll do for now."

The warrior who'd brought the clothing returned with blankets, a pillow, and some type of bag. He placed the items in the corner and left. The sweet scent of fruit and chicken wafted through the air, causing her mouth to water.

Dinner, she thought, her stomach growling. The tastes she'd had earlier of Breean's sugar-laced blood had left her hungry, for each drop had been better than, like, anything she'd ever prepared.

She was a decent cook, but Macy had apparently been a genius in the kitchen. First night her "mom" and "stepdad" had come over, they'd expected four-star treatment. As rich as they were and as superior as their expectations had been, the mac-and-cheese she'd thrown together hadn't pleased them. They hadn't liked the changes in her personality, either. Where the old Macy had been a champagne kind of girl, the new Macy's beer-loving ways had not been acceptable.

They'd accused her of being on drugs again, then yelled at her for throwing away her life as a cop when she could have gone back to modeling. And Aleaha had had to listen, try to answer. But the truth was, she didn't know why Macy had chosen such a life for herself.

At least dealing with the parents had been easier than the boyfriend. He'd had a key to her apartment—she'd since changed the locks—and had let himself in one night. He'd been high on Onadyn, the drug of choice for the wealthy, and ready for a game of "ride the pony."

On his way to the bedroom, he'd knocked down several of her—well, Macy's—things, breaking them. Thinking he was an intruder, she'd first tried to stun him, then, when that hadn't worked, to kill him. But just before pulling the trigger, she'd seen his face. She'd already studied the pictures hanging on the walls and those in Macy's holobook, so she'd recognized him.

He hadn't been happy with her refusal to play. As with Breean, she'd had to introduce him to her knee. Funny that Breean, who was supposed to hate her, had treated her better afterward.

"You must change," Breean said, drowning her musings of the past. Now his voice was husky with want.

"Uh, not just no, but hell, no." She would *not* reveal her true self while being this close to the AIR agents. But what a sweet man, not uttering the words "your appearance" while agents could hear.

He gave her a pointed glance. Aw. He meant her clothing.

"Why?" she asked.

"There's blood on your shirt."

Yeah, but it was his blood, from when she'd bitten him. "There's just a speck." A golden speck, at that, tasty and soul-shattering and maybe she could lick it off . . . *Stop, you idiot.* She'd actually been reaching for the hem of her shirt to bring it to her mouth.

Okay, time to regroup. He wouldn't rest until she'd changed out of her dirty clothes. He'd made her change that first night, too, she recalled, after she'd bitten him. She'd been happy to do so—when he'd left her alone. But why the anal need for spotless garments? She almost snickered. Anal.

He crossed his arms over his chest. "Are you going to be stubborn about this?"

"No. As before, I'll change when you leave."

"I need to take your clothes with me, so that they can be burned. We walked through the city, and I'm unsure what we came into contact with. More than that, I believe I mentioned that the sight of the blood offends me."

She'd been scanning for blood on *his* clothing; now her gaze snapped back up to him and she tried to read his expression. Surely he was joking. "You're a warrior."

"Yes. You know that I am."

"You *deal* in blood. How can the mere sight of it offend you?"

"Blood carries disease and death, diseases that are more painful than a knife through the gut. Now, I need the clothes you are wearing so that I may dispose of them."

The Schön disease, she realized. He feared it, and that made sense. But strangely, she didn't like that so strong a man, even her enemy, had been brought to such a point. "Sure you don't just want to watch me strip?" She'd meant the words as a taunt, hoping to soften the tenseness of the situation; they emerged as an invitation.

He gulped, every muscle in his body hardening. "To protect your modesty, I will wait outside. Toss your old clothing through the bars when you are done." He turned on his heel, his posture stiff.

She liked him better when he was trying to charm her.

And he wanted to charm her, right? To win another kiss, right? So, why was he leaving her? Why wasn't he forcing her to do what he wished? Did he no longer desire her?

Unacceptable. *Make him want you again. He'll relax his guard. You can free the agents.* Yep, that's the only reason she was filled with such a need. "Wait," she called just as he was opening the cell door. Oh, God. Was she really going to do this?

Slowly he faced her, the most beautiful creature she'd ever seen. A man who'd had plenty of opportunity, yet hadn't hurt her. A man who'd taken pretty good care of her, all things considered.

Yes, she was going to do this. "You can watch."

"No," he said, though the word was soft, as if he didn't actually want to say it.

"Don't you want me to be happy?"

His brow furrowed, but there was hope in his eyes. "Why would my presence make you happy?"

"Just because."

"Then you know what you must first do," Breean croaked out.

Show her true appearance. He'd demanded this time and time again, yet it still managed to shock her. How could he prefer the real her? In no way did she compare to Macy. She was flatter, leaner, with more patrician features. She was way less . . . stirring.

Still, she shifted back to her own image and nervously fidgeted with the ends of her hair.

"Better?"

"Much. Begin."

That had sounded like a plea, and spurred her on. Hands shaky, she bent and unhooked her scuffed boots. She kicked them off, launching them at Breean one at a time. A girl had to preserve hints of her this-isn't-what-I-*really*-want facade. To his credit, he didn't cringe or move out of the way. He let them slam into him without a word. Because he was entranced? She hoped so.

This is for his benefit, remember?

She reached behind her head and pulled her shirt up and off. The shirt, too, she tossed at him. The material swooshed into his chest and floated to the cold, hard ground. Her too-large bra was next—it had been made for Macy's ample chest and was one of two things she'd kept when she'd handed over her AIR bodysuit—which left her small breasts bared. Her nipples immediately puckered against the cold. Or maybe from the heat of his stare.

Breean sucked in a—reverent?—breath. He even reached out, then caught himself and dropped his arm to his side. All the while, his gaze bored into her, white lightning slamming against all of her pulse points.

Why had he stopped himself?

"The rest," he said, his voice deep and husky with arousal.

Her trembling intensifying, she jerked her too-loose pants and underwear down her legs. Underwear—the second thing she'd kept. Her other prison had had an enzyme shower stall, so she and the garments had managed to remain clean.

When she stepped out of them, she stilled the urge to cover herself. She just stood there, daring him to say something about her concave stomach or the thickly puckered scars on her inner thighs.

He tore his gaze from her breasts, from her quivering navel, lingering for a few seconds on the fine tuft of hair between her legs before staring at the scars. He frowned. "What type of injury rendered those?"

Silent, she raised her chin. That was information she'd *never* offer, not even under torture.

"Ale— Macy," he said, catching himself. Thank God. There was a warning in his tone.

"I'm cold," she said, chattering her teeth for effect. "I'm going to dress now?" A question when it should have been a statement. "And please don't ever . . . you know." *Call me by that name in front of others.* "Okay?" It was a gamble, asking him such a thing. He could threaten to do so if she didn't obey him in all things. That would be fighting dirty, after all. But as hesitant as she'd been about revealing the truth, he had to know already that it was important to her.

For a long while, he didn't reply. Then he sighed and tossed the clothes at her. "You have my word. Now get dressed. Sleep. Eat. Tomorrow we will have a long talk." He turned and exited the cell, locking her inside.

As he stood outside Aleaha's chamber, Breean's blood was on fire.

Before, he'd thought he wanted her. Now that he'd seen her naked, stubborn determination in her eyes, he knew better. He *needed* her. She was exquisite, breathtaking, a fighter to her core, and it had taken all of his self-control not to launch himself at her, nipping and kissing all that white flesh. Sucking those ripe little nipples into his mouth and feasting for days. Fingering the moist heat between her legs, then licking away every drop.

He tried to calm the riotous beat of his heart and the raging inferno blooming with his every breath. No luck. *Push her from your mind. For now, at least. Until you are stronger than your desire for her, for a prisoner, an AIR agent, you can't have her.*

That's why he'd placed her in the cell, after all, when that had never been his intent. He'd meant to keep her in his room. Where she was concerned, however, he still didn't have any defenses. And he needed defenses or she would always have the upper hand.

"Breean," Talon called.

His attention veered to the right. He found Talon standing beside Marleon at the far end of the tunnel. Fury flooded him, and he welcomed it. The warrior's actions had nearly ruined him in Aleaha's eyes.

"Marleon," he snarled.

The soldier paled, the fine swell of veins under his golden skin visible. He was dirty from his time in the dungeon, and clearly worried. "My lord?" The words trembled.

He closed the distance between them with a purposeful stride. "As you know, you are charged with causing bloodshed without permission." He deliberately spoke in the Earth language, knowing Aleaha would be listening.

"Yes, but—"

"I have spent the last week pondering your case." Not a sound did any of the agents make. "There are not many of us left, and I did not wish to destroy another of us. But you know the punishment for your crime, do you not?"

Blanching, Marleon backed into the wall. "My lord, they ambushed us. They meant to torture us."

Talon gripped his shoulder, keeping him from bolting.

"There is no excuse great enough for what you did, for you have endangered all of us. What if they had been disease carriers?"

"I . . . I . . . didn't think. I'm sorry. So sorry."

"No. You will die. As is our law. I have waited long enough to render your sentence. Know that I hate to do this, but it is necessary. Were I to be lenient, others would think such actions acceptable." Without another word, Breean walked straight into Marleon's body, melding them into one being. He could have eased into the man so there would be no pain, but didn't. He allowed his subject to feel every ounce of his possession.

Marleon screamed.

In control of the man's every movement, every breath, Breean forced his organs to shut down one by one. Marleon jerked and spasmed, still screaming, still begging, until finally growing quiet and collapsing to the ground.

Dead. Just like that. Quick, but not easy.

This would weigh Breean down for months to come.

He exited with only a thought, once more standing in front of Talon, the body at his feet. "He knew better," Breean said with disgust. Disgust for himself as much as for the dead soldier. But as leader, it was up to him to mete out justice. He had not lied; if he'd shown Marleon mercy, others would not have thought twice about spilling blood during the next battle.

"He knew," Talon agreed. "You did what you had to do."

Would Aleaha think so, or view this as more proof of his black nature? "Burn him." As was their custom. They'd only buried the AIR agents because that's what they knew earthlings preferred.

Handling the dead was abhorrent to them, but they'd done it to show their respect.

Talon nodded. "Everyone has disposed of their clothing and most are in the pools, even as we speak."

"Good." His gaze swung over his shoulder, zeroing in on Aleaha's door. Switching to Rakan, he said, "The two men she slapped in the forest, do you know which ones they are?" It was past time Breean spoke to them. Now that he was done readying this place, traveling back and forth between it and the other home, he had the time.

Again Talon nodded.

"Bring them to my office within the hour."

After bathing and changing into clean clothes, his tainted ones burning with the others', Breean left his room and sat at the desk, outlining the best defense against the Schön. He'd only seen a handful of the vile race before they'd disappeared and all but the queen had been male.

She had been . . . strange. Dainty, deceptively innocent, with a lilting voice he and the others had found themselves obeying without question. Her followers had managed to capture him and the others, and they'd been forced to watch as she seduced one after another. But Breean and those with him now, she'd sent away with a disgusted snarl. He'd never understood why. He would have welcomed her into his bed—and not just because he'd been without sex for so long. Whatever she'd spoken, he had wanted to do.

He'd thought her powers over men similar to a Rakan male's power over a Rakan female, his lust-scent like a drug. Only, they used their power for pleasure. She used hers to hurt. And hurt they had. Almost immediately the disease struck them, ravaging their bodies.

Once she'd mated with the men, they had then been given prisoners of their own. And once they'd mated with someone previously uninfected, the grayish tint had left their skin. Their hollowed cheeks had rounded out.

He'd wondered, why hadn't they worsened, weakened as the women had done? Why hadn't they become cannibals? Why had they gotten better?

The only answer he'd been able to come up with was that sex healed them. Would the women have remained strong if they, in turn, had had sex with their men rather than eating them?

If not, would those that were infected heal the moment the queen was killed?

Perhaps he could capture and destroy the queen, as AIR had done to her brethren. Locked up, she would not be able to have sex—*if* he could do something about that magical voice of hers. Wouldn't be very productive if she ordered him to release her and he obeyed. This way, he could learn if she weakened without sex. And if so, he could leave her in there to rot to death, all without having to spill a single drop of blood.

So easy, he thought dryly, pinching the bridge of his nose. She kept guards around her at all times, and those guards could vanish and kill you before you had time to blink. But somehow, someway, there had to be a way to catch a warrior you couldn't see. AIR had done it.

He could always steal AIR's weapons, he supposed. Then they'd be even less inclined to trade with him, however. What to do, what to do. He sighed.

When he next glanced up, the two agents Aleaha had tried to awaken were stomping into the room, Talon behind them, keeping them docile by pressing their own pyre-guns into the bases of their necks.

He studied them. Both males were tall and muscled, one with the tanned skin the humans seemed to love so much, the other with pale, glittery skin. Breean preferred Aleaha's, a white rose flushed with pink. Lovely. And irrelevant. Both men had dark hair, and both could be considered handsome, he supposed, hands fisting on his notes and crinkling the precious paper.

Were they the girl's family? he wondered, jealousy easing. He did not want Aleaha seeking aid from a lover. A brother, however, was allowed.

Breean searched for similarities. One had eyes the color of an ocean. One had eyes the color of a sunset. They weren't related to each other, and they weren't related to Aleaha. Her eyes were piercing green, her features more aristocratic. Unless they could change their appearances as she did? But no. There was no mask under either man's face. More than that, she wouldn't have minded if they saw her true self.

Breean's teeth ground together as he leaned back in his seat and scrubbed two fingers over his jaw.

"Are you human?" he asked them. Both pulsed with a strange sort of energy not inherent to the human race.

Blue Eyes nodded, features strained as if he were in deep concentration. "Yes. Now what's your plan for the girl? You will tell me. You want to tell me."

"No, I don't." Strangely, Breean felt a sudden urge to tell the agent anything and everything he wanted to know.

"Your plan," Blue Eyes insisted. "You were just about to tell me."

Yes, he thought, dazed. He wanted to tell, but he only allowed himself to say, "What is any man's plan?"

"Indeed," Glitter said with an appreciative laugh.

How odd. Amusement was not the reaction Breean would have expected.

Blue Eyes tensed to launch himself at Breean. Now, there was the reaction he'd expected. Fury. Talon cocked one of the guns and pushed the cool barrel into the agent's skull, and the man froze.

"Will she remain alive?" Blue Eyes gritted out. "Tell me."

That voice . . . nearly irresistible. Utterly powerful. He *had* to answer. And yet, as quickly as the feeling had hit him, it abandoned him. "Of course she will remain alive." What was going on? Mind control? Some races exhibited such a power, but he hadn't thought earthlings among their number. "I am not a monster."

Glitter popped his jaw, all traces of humor suddenly gone. "Have you hurt her? Forced her?"

"Believe me, I have forced her to do nothing."

Both men relaxed, but only slightly. "Let her stay with us," Blue Eyes said in that persuasive voice. "In one of our cells."

The thrum of jealousy returned but the urge to obey did not. Either the agent was not very good or Breean was building an immunity. "Are you related to her?"

"Do you want us to be?" Glitter asked.

Breean ran his tongue over his teeth. "Is she your woman?" The question burst from him before he could stop it.

A pause, heavy, tight.

"What if she is?" Blue Eyes flashed an evil smile.

Breean could have entered the bastard's body right then and punished him. Something, *anything* to hurt him. But he recalled the disgust on Aleaha's face when she'd spoken of Marleon doing it—and his own disgust at the punishment he'd carried out only an hour earlier.

"Are. You. Her. Man? That is a simple question."

"Hurt her, and I'll fucking murder you while you sleep," Glitter said without any inflection of anger. He would enjoy it, too. That much was obvious. "How's that for an answer?"

"She's innocent. She's not like us. Let her go."

The thought of releasing her without knowing the full depth of her passion was abhorrent to him, and he shook his head. "She stays," he said, then arched a brow in curiosity. "Have you no care about my plans for *you*?"

"Not really."

"Nope. Can't say that I do."

"Is this conversation over? Because I like the view from my cell better."

Obviously, the irreverent men weren't going to tell him what he wanted to know. He wasn't going to beg, nor was he going to torture them. That would smack of desperation.

"No. This conversation is not over." He did, however, switch topics. "We have a common enemy, it seems. The Schön."

That got their attention. They straightened, glanced at each other, frowned.

"The Schön destroyed my home, my family. My planet. That is why we are here. We'd hoped for peace. We'd hoped to live among people who knew how to combat such an enemy. Yet we arrive only to learn that our enemy beat us here and they even plan to send their queen."

No response.

"We have decided to stay and fight them. Fierce as they are, we could use your help."

Again, no response.

Damn them, making him work for every scrap. "*You* could use *our* help. Unless, of course, you want to see your own planet destroyed, your women eyeing you like a tasty meal just before trying to gut you with their teeth."

Nothing.

"I've seen their queen. I've dealt with her."

Blue Eyes gulped.

Nearly imperceptible, but a show of interest. Finally.

"She came after the males had taken out our royal family and their guard. She's one of the most beautiful women I've ever seen, with a powerful voice very much like yours." He motioned to Blue Eyes with a tilt of his chin. "She kept a harem. They all did. But they only slept with each of their victims once. After that, the ones who weren't warriors were discarded out on the streets to fend for themselves, even as the disease began to consume them."

"How did you survive?" Glitter asked. There was no hint of mockery in his tone. Not any longer.

Sweet progress. "We aren't sure. None of us were chosen by the queen. Nearly all of us were bitten at some point as we were forced to fight our own people and loved ones, but we never sickened."

Blue Eyes and Glitter shared another of those dark looks.

"I'm willing to aid AIR against them in exchange for our freedom to roam this planet."

"To be honest, I don't think anyone will trust you," Blue Eyes said. No hesitation. Which meant, he didn't have to think about it.

He simply knew. "You came on the night the Schön were due. You killed several of our men."

That damn Marleon.

"And, let's face it, this could be a trap," Glitter said.

Blue Eyes spread his arms, an I'm-here-to-help gesture. "Let us go, and we might, *might*, be able to convince our captain that your intentions are good."

Rather than answer, he said to Talon, "Take them away." He needed to think some more, weigh the pros and cons of each avenue. Then, in his own language, he added, "I want at least one spirit walker in town at all hours of the night. Everyone else is to take shifts. Guards are to be posted here, of course, enough for every exit, but others can head into town and find females." How could he deny his men while he luxuriated in Aleaha? "Those who spirit-walk are to find out what they can about AIR and the Schön. They probably won't hear anything, but it's worth a try."

Spirit walking. Propelling your conscious mind from your body, roaming without being seen or heard or sensed in any way. It was how he had learned so much about Earth before anyone had discovered his presence.

The only problem was, when your mind left your body, your body was completely vulnerable. If someone attacked, you couldn't defend yourself. In fact, you wouldn't know you were being attacked until it was too late. Until you were dead.

Not all Rakans possessed the ability, unfortunately. Both Breean and Talon did, along with five others.

"Consider it done," Talon said with a nod.

"Those who are hunting sex know they are to hide their skin as best as they are able and be careful, I'm sure."

"Of course, but I will remind them anyway."

"Thank you."

Neither agent said a word during the exchange or even as they were led from the room.

Alone again, Breean ran a hand down his face, trying to scrub away his questions, his dark emotions, even his desires. He wanted Aleaha here, wanted to discuss all of this with her. But if he had her brought here, they wouldn't talk. She might deny it, but she wanted him. She'd stripped for him, after all. But the simple fact was, his desire for her was wild, fierce, while she seemed to have no trouble resisting him.

Perhaps he should join his men in New Chicago and find a woman to warm his bed. A woman who was meek and docile, who would delight in his every gesture. A woman who would fill the aching void that had grown each time one of his people had died. Once he'd had sex, he could do what he was supposed to do: plan.

But he could not work up a single shred of passion for anyone save Aleaha.

His body wanted *her*. Only she, with that dark hair, those piercing green eyes, that lean body, would do.

Just picturing her caused him to harden, to ready.

Damn this. He needed some relief so that he could better deal with her and his problems.

To prevent himself from changing his mind and going to her tonight, Breean pushed to his feet and stalked to his bedroom. When he was shut inside, he stripped and stepped into the waterfall he'd erected in place of the enzyme shower stall. Scowling, he slapped a hand against the cool title to brace himself. With his other, he gripped his cock. He used the moisture beaded at the tip as lubricant and began slow, measured strokes.

He imagined Aleaha's mouth in place of his hand, her hot tongue swirling, her teeth lightly scraping. His testicles drew up tight; his strokes quickened. She'd kiss those testicles, of course, making them feel better after her earlier mistreatment of them. Her hands would grip his ass, perhaps delving where none had been before, her nails scoring deep. She might suck one of his balls into her mouth, might then lick her way up the shaft before sucking the head again. Sucking until he was dry. Until he couldn't take any more.

Breean's entire body jerked in ecstasy. With a roar, he came, hot seed spurting from him. "Aleaha," he shouted. Sweet, challenging Aleaha.

He stood there for a long while, panting, hand still circling his cock, Aleaha still in his mind. Jacking off, as the humans said, had helped, but it hadn't alleviated his need completely. He *still* wanted her with a hunger that surprised him. Still couldn't think of anything but being with her.

Damn this! he thought again. And damn her. He strode to the bed and fell onto the cold, empty sheets. He wished Aleaha were here. He yearned to hold her, to smell her delightful scent, feel her soft skin.

There had to be some way to win her. Some way to tear down her defenses against him. She wanted him; more than stripping a little while ago, the way she'd kissed him that first night was proof. She was just stubborn and probably scared.

What could he do? What could—

His eyes widened as an idea began to take root in his mind, growing. He grinned slowly. Oh, yes. He'd never done such a thing before, but he had fantasized. Now, he would experience.

Tomorrow, he would summon her. He would do that which he'd never allowed himself to do to another. And he would show her no mercy.

Six

"COME WITH ME."

Ignoring the unfamiliar Rakan's command, Aleaha remained seated at the far end of the cell. She wasn't sure exactly how long she'd been inside it. At least eight hours. Probably twelve. Maybe an eternity. She'd heard the other "guests" clanging against their bars, heard the whisper of their conversations, but when she'd called out in Macy's voice—where's backup, these warriors hate the Schön as much as we do, tell me what you want me to do—no one had answered her.

"Come," the warrior said again.

He wasn't *her* warrior, Breean, so she didn't feel any urge to comply. "I'm not going anywhere with you." Surely Breean hadn't tired of her already. Surely he wasn't palming her off on one of his men. *Oh, God.* What if he was? She hadn't exactly been the nicest of captives.

Captives aren't supposed to be nice, idiot. He'd seen her naked. Maybe he'd disliked what he'd seen. *Oh, God,* she thought again.

The warrior looked like him: golden skin, golden hair, big, lovely features better suited for a woman yet somehow completely masculine. But his golden eyes didn't mesmerize her. He didn't smell of honey and cinnamon, and she had no desire to try to seduce him to kindness. She had no idea how to deal with him, actually.

"Are those . . ." His eyes widened as he spotted the trail of blood she'd accidentally created along the floor.

"Diamonds?" she finished for him, pretending to misunderstand. "Fat stacks of cash?"

Panic consumed his expression when that gaze reached the blood dried on her wrists. He backed away, probably not even aware that he did so. These men hadn't blinked at facing down the lethal members of AIR, but show them a little blood and they wanted to hide.

"Did you cut yourself?"

She saw no reason to lie. "Yes."

"What did you use? You're wearing our clothing, which means Breean checked you for weapons when you changed. And," he gazed around, "there is nothing sharp inside this cell."

She just shrugged.

"Tell me how—" He jumped away from her as if she were poison.

Jeez. She was just stretching out her legs to get more comfortable. She was all for precaution, but really, these men took their hatred and fear a little too far. What would he do if she bit her arm and dripped on his shoe?

Hey. That might actually be a good escape plan. She'd hold out her bloody arm, and the guys would beat feet, too afraid to grab her. She could walk right out of the house. But what about the rest of the agents? She could come back with help—*if* she could find it.

So much time had passed without an AIR assault, part of her now thought something nefarious had happened to Mia and her backup squad. They were good at their jobs, after all, and knew how to track and find the unfindable. The other part of her wondered whether Mia and her squad had stayed away on purpose. But why would they do that?

"Doesn't matter, I guess," the warrior before her said, reclaiming her attention. "You are not mine to deal with." Trying to hide his disgust but not quite managing it, he motioned her over with a wave of his fingers. "Come. Breean has requested your presence. But, please, maintain your distance from me."

The magic word: *Breean.* Aleaha popped to her feet, anticipation slithering through her. He hadn't tired of her, then. She ignored a sudden, intense rush of relief working through her. *Him,* she could deal with. Kind of.

Before, in the forest, Breean had craved her desire. If she hinted that she would ultimately fall into his bed, she could buy time. Time to "get to know each other" without being kissed, touched, or caressed—which she shouldn't want but couldn't stop thinking about. Time to figure this out.

"I was told not to hurt you or even to grab you. If you run, I am to alert Breean. He wants you to know that if he is forced to chase you, he will catch you. And he won't stop what was begun last week." The warrior's head tilted to the side. "What was begun last week? Sex?"

Her cheeks heated, and she told herself it was in embarrassment. *Not* arousal. "Just lead the way. I'm not going to run."

With a disappointed nod, the warrior ushered her past the other cells. As she walked, her gaze clashed with that of Dallas, whose hard expression and fierce blue eyes told her nothing. Beside him, Devyn grinned at her, eyebrows wagging. They remained silent, just as they had last night.

Upstairs, down a long hall, and around two corners, the Rakan stopped. "Here we are." He placed his palm over the ID box on the door. Azure lights scanned between his fingers and all the way to his wrist. A moment later, the entrance slid open.

She sailed past, changing her appearance as she walked. Gone were the blond hair and blue eyes. Gone were those magnificent breasts. She was herself again, just as Breean seemed to like.

The guard, who was gaping at her now, didn't enter behind her. He merely said something in that language she didn't understand

and shut the door between them, locking her inside. Her heart began to hammer wildly as the scent of honey filled her nose.

Breean was here.

She gulped, trying to concentrate on something *unexciting*. The room was spacious, lovely and . . . her brow wrinkled in confusion— looked like Christmas had exploded inside it. There was a tree in the corner. A fir. A real fir. She could smell the dew on the lush green bristles.

Cutting down a tree was illegal, for every species belonged to the government. Since he was already known as a murdering outlaw, Breean probably didn't care. Red and green bows were tied to the branches. White lights dripped from the ceiling like stars.

There was no sign of Breean, but there *was* a large bed draped in soft-looking white sheets, rumpled from a night of tossing and turning. Or hard-core, sweaty sex. Her stomach quivered. *Don't think like that.* There was a lounge, a marble vanity that boasted a decanter of whiskey and a plastic mini-tree. There was a faux-bearskin rug on the floor with a green bow tied around one of its ears.

What drew her eye most, however, was the sunken tub in the center, filled with hot, steamy water. At least it was clear and not emerald or ruby.

"B-Breean?"

"I'm here." He stepped from the closet, and he was as beautiful and mesmerizing as she remembered: tall, thickly muscled, with golden angel-features and an innate animalism that couldn't be denied. Her heart picked up speed, slamming against her ribs with so much force she thought they might crack.

He wasn't wearing a shirt. His nipples glistened as if they'd been dipped in glitter and were beaded into hard little points. Rope after rope of muscle tapered to his navel . . . then deliciously lower. Black pants hung low on his waist and hugged his thighs.

"I knew it!" she said, doing her best to sound outraged. "This room is a mock Christmas party and your cock is supposed to be a present, isn't it?" Okay, yeah, maybe she preferred that to any of the presents Macy's family would have given her. That didn't mean she could accept it. "Or am *I* supposed to be *your* present?"

His gaze raked over her, his nostrils flaring in anger. "Were you hurt?" His eyes went black, opaque completely overshadowing amber. In that moment, he looked like the cold-blooded murderer she'd accused him of being. "Did someone touch you?"

"No, not at all. I'm fine. Swear. But back to the present thing . . ."

Gradually, the dark haze abandoned his eyes and he met her stare. "How, then, did you get blood on your new clothes? And under your nails?" he added, frowning. "Syler thinks you cut yourself. Did you?"

Or not. She swallowed the sudden lump in her throat. Convincing him to give her time to get to know him and grow to like him wasn't going to be as simple as she'd hoped. Obviously, the thought of her being hurt upset him, and that affected *her*, deeply and inexorably. Only Bride had cared enough about her to kiss her boo-boos and make them better. That someone else now seemed to want to do so was irresistible.

"Why would anyone in her right mind cut herself?" she asked. That way, she wasn't lying to him but wasn't admitting to the truth, either.

Of course, he didn't allow the subject to drop. "That does not answer my question."

"Well, it's all the answer you're going to get from me."

"You scratched or bit your wrists until they bled. *After* I told you of the dangers of contamination. Why? Why would you place my men at risk?"

"One, I'm not infected with anything, so they're safe. And two, why I cut myself is none of your damn business." There. She'd given him a partial answer. Yes, she'd done this to herself. But tell him why? Not going to happen. She would not say the words aloud. They could be used against her in the most painful, horrifying way.

"Did you hope I would command you to strip if your clothing was tainted?" He ran his tongue over his teeth, his anger seeming to swell despite his sensual suspicions. "Well, guess what? You get your wish. Take off the clothes. They offend me."

She'd half expected the demand, but that didn't lessen its impact. Her stomach tightened and her hands quivered. "No." Naked, she would lose all control of the situation. There would be no getting to know him, no buying time.

"We went over this yesterday, Aleaha. Take them off or I'll do it for you. You *are* going to wash."

She squared her shoulders. She wouldn't be cowed, not in this. She'd fight him if she had to, but she was staying dressed—and staying sane.

But if you fight him to stay dressed, he'll put his hands on you. And if he puts his hands on you, you'll cave. Damn it. Either way, they would have sex. She just couldn't win. Still she said, "You stay on that side of the room, and I'll stay on this side, and we'll chat." Curse his good looks. And his money. And his concern. And his smell. *Okay, you can stop now.*

He surprised her by grinning. "As you are fond of saying, no. We will not chat."

That smile . . . She lost every whiff of breath in her lungs. Maybe that was a good thing. Her every inhalation was filled with him, branding her every cell. "I don't want you," she said, more for her benefit than his.

"We shall see." Still grinning, he tugged at the waist of his pants. They immediately loosened and floated to the ground in a pool at his feet. Leaving him completely bare.

His penis was golden and hard, long and thick, and seeing it caused the moisture in her mouth to dry. Her hand fluttered over her lips to hold back her gasp of need. "I'm telling you now," she croaked, "I want this." Wait. What? "I mean, I want to talk to you, to get to know you."

Pleasure infused his eyes, but he shook his head. "That will come after," he said huskily. "But don't worry. *I'm* not going to take you. Yet."

He was in front of her in the next instant, moving so quickly she barely had time to register the fact that nothing was going as planned. He was supposed to bow to her desire to chat. He was supposed to give her time to accept him—so that she could then betray him.

The smell of honey wrapped around her, filled her, more intense than before, instantly clouding her thoughts. Sex with him wouldn't be so bad. It *did* take time, and time was all she wanted. Right? Seriously, screwing him blind should have been her plan all along.

"Don't move," he said. "I don't want to hurt you."

She forced out a sigh, even as a tremor of pleasure slid the length of her spine. "I thought men liked for women to move, but whatever. I'm your captive and you're in charge, so if you want to do this, we'll do this. For the record, I'm completely unwilling."

His smile fell away.

She almost cursed. Had she overplayed her hand? "What I meant to say was that, uh, I'm willing. But only because you're—"

"I believe I mentioned that chatting was for later." And then he was stepping inside her—oh, God, oh, God—just as she'd seen that soldier do in the forest.

Her skin tingled and burned, but it wasn't unpleasant. "Breean?" His name trembled from her. Her bones gave a sharp ache, but quickly settled into a pleasurable hum.

Shhh, she heard in her mind. *Almost done.*

Her body seemed to expand to accommodate him, but as she stared down at her hands, she couldn't see an outline of him. Couldn't see any hint of him, for that matter. Yet *he was inside her.* They were joined.

"Get out of me," she demanded. Another tremor hit her, and this time it had nothing to do with pleasure. Did he plan to kill her? Make her put a gun to her head?

Take off your clothes.

Her arms obeyed without hesitation. And there was nothing she could do to stop them, no matter how hard she tried. She watched, wide-eyed, as her hands pulled and jerked at her clothing until she was completely naked.

"How did you do that?"

I control your actions. Not your thoughts, not the sensations you feel, but your actions.

"Get out of me," she repeated, harsher this time. "If I spontaneously change shapes, you could—" What? Become trapped inside the new body? She didn't know. Nothing like this had ever happened to her before.

You won't change. I'm in control. Now, I know you wanted my cock as your Christmas present—

"I did not!"

He continued as if she hadn't interrupted him. *—since you mentioned it more than once, but I'm giving you something else.*

"What?" And was that . . . disappointment slithering through her?

You'll see. Walk to the tub.

Her feet were moving in the next instant, and she yelped in frustration and fury because she couldn't stop them. "Damn you! You can't know for sure what will happen if— Ah!" She stepped into the water and sat on the bench, the wet heat lapping and licking at her bare skin. She moaned in ecstasy as the water rippled, laving and caressing.

"Why are you doing this?" Her gaze locked on the scabs on her inner thighs, and she heard Breean give a soft sigh.

Tell me why you did that to yourself and perhaps I will answer your question.

"Unequal exchange. No deal."

Another sigh. *No more pain, sweet. Not for you. Only pleasure. Now, take the soap and cleanse yourself from head to toe. Be careful not to rub the sores.*

She didn't see the soap, but her hand somehow knew where it was and reached. Her fingers curled around the honey-scented bar and brought it to her body, where she massaged herself from head to toe as ordered. She even dunked under the water and came up sputtering.

"That's enough." *I want more.* The contradiction belonged to her, not him. "I'm clean." *Dirty.* "Let me out of the tub." *In an hour.*

Could he hear her naughty thoughts?

Not just yet. Nope. He couldn't. Otherwise he would have said something. *I want to make you come.*

Make her— Oh no. No, no, no. It was one thing to enjoy him. One thing to sleep with him. Maybe. One thing to come together. Again, maybe. But it was quite another to allow her enemy to give her an orgasm, while *he* felt nothing. No maybe about it.

"And I want you to. Get. *Out.*"

Let's see if I can change your mind. Knead your breasts.

A heartbeat later, she was cupping her own breasts, plumping them up and moaning at the scandalous decadence. "Stop. Don't . . . stop."

Do not worry. Stopping isn't an option. Now thumb your nipples.

She didn't even try to resist this time. It was futile, her body obeying before she even realized what he'd said. Her thumbs slid over her wet nipples as commanded, stroking and circling. Felt . . . so . . . good . . . Her mind was darkening, concentrating only on the pleasure.

"Oh, God, Breean."

I like when you say my name. I can't wait to hear you shout it.

"I won't." He forced her to pinch, then caress away the sting. "Won't, won't, wont." *Breean, Breean, Breean.*

You will. Because it's good. So, so good. Too good.

Yes, too good. Her skin was burning, tingling, her stomach quivering. The ache between her legs was growing, spreading. As he'd promised, however, she remained Aleaha, slave to Breean, not once changing into another person.

Pretend it's my tongue flicking over those pretty peaks.

That was not a command he could enforce because it wasn't physical but she found herself obeying anyway. As her fingers played with those hard, sensitive tips, she pictured him in her mind, golden head bent over her, hot tongue flicking.

Another moan slipped from her. "Breean. I don't . . . I don't understand how this is possible." Her hips were writhing in sync with her efforts, and water was pumping over the sides of the tub.

Are you aroused?

"You know I am." As if she could really deny it.

Do you want to touch yourself between your legs?

And finally assuage the ache? She could have sobbed, the anticipation was so consuming. Her knees were already open and spreading, waiting for that first heated touch.

Do you?

"Yes," she whispered. Just then she was beyond caring about the circumstances, what she'd come here for, what she'd hoped to avoid. About the shame she'd probably feel afterward. *I'm so weak,* she thought, but she *needed* to touch herself. Would die if she didn't. Since the moment their eyes had first met, they'd been building to this point. Her body had been ready, desperate, and she'd resisted. That had only made it worse. She realized that now.

There could be no more resisting.

She tried to slip one of her hands down her stomach, but it wouldn't move away from her breast. "Breean. Please."

Please what?

"Let me touch myself there."

What will you give me in return?

"Presents are—presents . . ." She was panting, having trouble getting the words out. "You aren't supposed . . . to expect anything . . . in return. Now please."

What will you give me in return? he insisted. *I can give you pleasure, and I can prevent you from changing. Isn't that what you want?*

Argh! "Yes. Fine. Fine, but what do you want in return?"

You. As my lover. My lover in truth.

"Okay. Yes. Deal. Whatever you want?" She'd meant it as a statement, but it emerged as a question. God, she was about to explode. The more she fondled her breasts, the more the ache between her legs increased with dizzying frenzy. If she didn't do something soon, her heart really was going to burst from her chest.

I want you now and, your god knows, maybe forever.

"No," she said automatically. "Not that." Her head fell against the rim of the tub, dark hair floating around her shoulders. Steam curled through the air, a sensual haze. A dream. "Breean. I'm dying. Please."

A growl. *Why won't you have me?*

"Lover, yes. Forever, no. We're enemies."

We don't have to be.

"Breean!"

We will discuss this again. Understand?

"Yes, you sadistic bastard." Anything for relief. "Yes."

Touch your clitoris.

Her hips arched upward to meet her hand, and she cried out as her finger circled the drenched bud once, twice. "Yes. Yes!"

That's enough. Touch your breast again.

"Motherfucker!" She was once again massaging her breasts, her nipples so hard they abraded her palms. "Tell me to touch between my legs again."

So you want more?

"Yes, damn you. Yes!"

Am I a sadistic bastard?

"No. You're a sweetie pie. Honest!"

Good, that's good. Because this sweetie pie wants you over and over. Hard the first time, slow the second. Who knows what will happen the third time.

"Oh, God." In her mind, she could see his naked body straining for release on top of hers, pumping, gliding, sliding. His weight would be delicious. His eyes would blaze down at her with passion. He'd shout her name the way he wanted her to shout his, her real name, not someone else's, as his shaft delved deep.

I want it to be my cock inside you, not your fingers. I want you to come because of me.

She wanted that, too. "Breean," she panted. She was still massaging her breasts, and her clitoris was still throbbing. "One more touch between my legs. Let me touch myself one more time. Then you can have me. Then you can take me."

Pump your fingers inside yourself.

She braced her feet on the sides of the tub, spreading herself wider. She sank a finger deep inside, cried out again, pumped. Pumped. So good. She was hurtling toward release. So close. Just one more and she'd—

Stop.

Her finger froze. She screamed in frustration.

Do you have a man? The question was barked. *Give me that much, at least.*

"No. No man. And I'm not going to have you if you do this to me again, you sick fu— sweetie pie."

The two agents in the forest, the ones you slapped?

"Friends only. Swear."

He gave a satisfied purr. *I'm glad.*

She couldn't imagine doing this with Devyn or Dallas. She liked them, she did, and she even admired them, but she'd never felt as if she'd been set on fire in their presence. She'd never wanted to rip off their clothes and attack, licking and biting her way down until she'd tasted every inch.

"Command me to come, Breean. I'm begging you."

Finger yourself. Use two, then three.

Moaning as she obeyed, she filled herself with two fingers and pumped them in and out. When that wasn't enough, she added the third, stretching herself for a fuller sensation. Oh, oh. Yes. Yes! Just like that.

Next time, you'll feel my tongue there.

"Yes." She pictured Breean licking her clit, and she blessedly hurtled over the edge of completion, flying out of control, spinning toward the sky, a scream ripping from her throat.

Gradually, the sensations faded, her body relaxed, and she came back to her senses. She slumped over the side of the tub, panting. "I didn't change," she managed to get out. "I didn't change."

And you won't. I'm in control, remember? A second later, he added, *But, darling. I'm not sure why you stopped. You're not done. Come again.*

"W-what?" Even as she spoke, her fingers started working between her legs again, her core immediately readying itself for round two. So long she'd denied herself, she was unprepared for another onslaught. "No. No more."

You'll take it all.

"Yes, okay," she found herself groaning. Oh, God. The pleasure truly was building again. Steadily. Mercilessly. Her legs were falling farther and farther apart, giving her fingers more room to work.

Soon you'll take me.

"Yes." She couldn't deny that, either. She wanted him in a way she'd never wanted anything else. Even a life of her own. A life as Aleaha, without being hunted, without being different. And clearly, her body was already addicted to the pleasure he could give.

So lovely, he purred.

As her hips pumped, water sloshed back and forth, stroking her like a lover. Aleaha was very close to asking Breean to join her, to step out of her and assume control like he'd promised, like she'd told him she would accept. How much more powerful would the sensations be then? But somehow she held the words back, not yet ready to make that leap anywhere but in her mind. Soon, though. If she wasn't careful, soon.

Come.

Release hit her in the next instant. She bowed her back, pushing her fingers as deep as they would go, shuddering, rocking, shouting because this was more than an orgasm; this was a possession that lasted for eternity.

Finally she sagged, completely sated—and still shuddering. "Dear God."

I could feel it, Breean said, awed. *The vibrations were so strong I could feel them.* There was unabashed arousal in his tone. *Come for me. One more time. I want to feel it again.*

"I can't." Her limbs were like rocks.

Yes.

"Breean, I really can't."

You can.

"Too much," she panted. "It's too much."

Never enough.

"Let me . . . let me . . . catch my breath."

Come, sweet. Please, come for me.

The newest orgasm hadn't yet dissipated before another one sneaked up on her. Her clit was swollen, the water making her skin all the more sensitive, so every sensation was intensified. With one hand still at her breasts, she pinched her nipples and rode the waves of the third orgasm, shaking and quaking all over again.

Inside her head, she could hear Breean roaring, as if he, too, were coming. Somehow, that only increased her pleasure. "I . . . I . . ."

Breean was shouting her name, just as she'd craved, and then, suddenly, she was shivering, experiencing a fourth eruption—*his* pleasure becoming hers as well. Her blood sizzled and blistered through her veins, just like in the forest, and the scent of honey drifted from *her*, filling the entire room, branding her soul-deep.

Utterly replete, Aleaha slumped over the rim of the tub once more. She might never be able to move again, was more exhausted than she'd ever been in her life. She was breathless, her heartbeat racing, her bones like jelly. Yet she'd never felt better.

She hadn't slept in the cell, too keyed up, wondering what the future held. Now her eyelids closed of their own accord and stayed closed as if they'd been glued.

"I guess you liked your gift," she managed to say.

He chuckled. *I did indeed. Sleep now.*

And she did.

Breean had never, in all his years, experienced anything like that.

He exited Aleaha's body, reforming into a solid mass, then carried her to the bed and gently splayed her over the mattress. The ends of her dark hair were wet, dripping. Moisture danced along every inch of her flushed skin, her nipples were still hard, and her limbs were boneless.

She was the most erotic sight he'd ever beheld.

Naked, he crawled in beside her and pulled her into his side. He'd come inside her. His spirit had somehow experienced absolute release while inhabiting her. He'd never heard of such a thing happening, much less being possible, but it *had* happened. They'd been fused, one being.

Several times, he'd felt her body try to change images. Felt the bones trying to lengthen or shorten, even felt the pigment in her skin trying to lighten or darken. But he'd maintained a firm grip on her, on Aleaha, and she'd remained the same, just as he'd promised her. Just as she'd hoped. Surely that was a sign they were meant to be together.

Together. Yes. He wasn't going to let her go, he decided. Not ever. She was his, from this moment on. She didn't have a man, and she desired him. She might still be fighting it, but she did desire him.

His next mission: making her admit it.

SEVEN

IN THE WEE HOURS OF THE MORNING, Breean left Aleaha in bed. With her cozied up to him, he'd been too keyed up and hadn't been able to sleep, and now he needed to meet with Talon. Though he desperately wanted to take her with him, she was still lost in slumber, at peace, and he was loath to wake her. He really had worn her out, he thought, grinning. He'd satisfied his woman into a stupor.

Even as grateful as she would surely be—in his dreams—he didn't trust her, and made sure to lock the door. And smart boy that he was, he'd nailed the window permanently shut before ever inviting her into his bedroom.

He nodded to the men striding through the halls, keeping guard. Nodded to those cleaning and sharpening their weapons, getting ready to stand watch. Seeing them work so diligently, a wave of guilt hit him. He'd have to take a shift soon. His army worked hard; the men deserved a break, and god knew he'd already had his. But damn if he was ready to leave Aleaha for an extended period, now that he had her where he wanted her.

Finally he reached his office, where Talon was waiting for him.

As Breean claimed his chair at the desk, his friend, seated in front of him, glanced up from the book he'd been perusing.

"Who spirit-walked?" he asked, jumping right into business.

"I took the first shift," Talon said, "and Cain the second."

Breean studied the warrior. The tension that had shadowed his face for the past two years was gone. "After your shift, you found a woman, I take it."

Talon grinned slowly, revealing perfect white teeth. "Two, actually."

"And you kept your skin covered?"

"Completely. My scent drew them in, and after that I had only to unfasten my pants. They couldn't get to my cock fast enough. You know," Talon added thoughtfully, "I really like this planet. I'm glad we decided to stay."

If only Aleaha were as easy as Talon's females. Her resistance was her biggest flaw. Silly him for ever thinking the harder he had to work for a victory, the more he'd appreciate it. He would have given anything to have all of her *now*. "Did either of you learn anything?"

"I admit my attention wasn't where it should have been, and I was easily distracted. But Cain, well, you know he is a force to be reckoned with, more determined than most. He found AIR headquarters."

"How?" In all their visits here, they'd failed to locate the building that housed AIR's elite. Apparently, they'd been overrun by reporters one night and had since moved their headquarters to somewhere secret.

"He watched as an otherworlder was arrested, then slid unnoticed into the car that drove the blindfolded creature in."

Of course. So simple, so easy. Breean leaned forward, eager. This was better than he had hoped. "What did he learn?"

"AIR is run by a woman named Mia Snow. Her man is an Arcadian, a king, and he can move as swiftly as we can. He was with her that night, the night we arrived. They were waiting a mile or so away, ready to swoop in if a second line of defense was needed. But we weren't the Schön, as they'd expected."

Aleaha had told him that. Which meant, Aleaha had told him the truth. Darling girl. He should reward her with another orgasm.

"Still, they were coming after us when another solar flare erupted around them, as if it had purposefully been directed at them, and they disappeared."

Breean had learned that every planet had a way of utilizing those solar flares. Some used stones as a guide—if they carried a stone from a certain planet, that was the planet the solar flare would take them to. Some, like him, used visualization. Breean had imagined a planet with a thriving metropolis, and this was one of the places he'd ended up. Some simply knew the celestial gate those flares opened and which doors to enter.

Could some actually control the flares?

"Have the agents returned? Where did they go?"

"They have returned, yes, so Cain said. Where they went . . . I'm not sure this can be true. They claim to have traveled into the past. Into another plane or dimension, they weren't sure. A state called New Orleans, where females with pointed ears and unnatural strength reside alongside men who suck the blood from your body. The females called themselves the Nïxies. Nïxies house of pain. Nïxies house of pleasure, Nïxies house of crazy—something like that. Cain was confused, and could have gotten some of the details wrong."

How . . . odd.

Talon continued, "They didn't stay long. Just long enough for us to have left the forest."

Again, had someone controlled the flare, keeping them away? If so, that being would have been aiding Breean. But who would want to aid him?

The Schön queen? Most likely. After all, a group of her men had been destroyed by AIR. Perhaps she had thought Breean would take care of the problem for her. How had she known Breean was coming here, though? Since leaving Raka, he'd had no contact with her.

"Anything else?" he asked on a sigh.

"Yes, but you will not like it." Shifting in his seat, Talon massaged the back of his neck. "One of the agents escaped during the move here. Syler chased him but lost him."

Breean's hands fisted. "Why did no one tell me?"

"Syler told no one."

First Marleon's betrayal, and now this. He was losing control of his army! "By keeping this a secret, he has placed us all in danger."

"Yes."

"I will not kill him for the offense, but he must be punished. Ten lashes should teach him to use his tongue when necessary."

Talon nodded. "Fortunately, the agent doesn't seem to know where we are now located."

One small favor, at least. "Was nothing learned about the Schön?"

"No. AIR still has no idea when the queen will arrive. The one Schön they have in lockup refuses to speak about her."

He straightened. "They have a Schön in lockup?"

"Yes."

A killing rage sprang to life inside of him. That bastard might very well be the one who had seduced his mother and sisters. And if not, that bastard still needed to die, for surely he had seduced someone else's mother and sisters.

"Cain did well," he said, forcing himself to calm. "Give him the day off and tell him to do as he pleases."

"He will be overjoyed."

"I will take his shift tonight, so he does not have to worry about that, either."

Talon's eyes widened, and there was a spark of delight. Breean knew the two men had spent time together throughout the years, even a few lonely nights. What they'd done, he didn't know but could guess. They might both crave females, as Talon had proven with his excess, but they must have enjoyed each other. Now that women were in plentiful supply, he'd expected their association to end. Looked like he'd been wrong.

He pushed to his feet. "As for now, I have something to attend to." Or rather, someone.

Aleaha came awake instantly, deeply asleep one moment, fully cognizant the next. Her entire body ached—and not in pleasure this time. Her blood was rushing too quickly, and there was too much of it, filling her veins at an unnatural rate.

She moaned, trying to fight the pain. Trying to stop the unfolding of events that always followed this sensation. Not now. Not after everything she'd just experienced with Breean.

Oh, God. Breean. Was he still here? *Please let him be somewhere else.*

She searched the bed with swollen eyes. She was splayed on the mattress, still naked and covered by soft white sheets. Breean was beside her—and he was awake, watching her every move. No. No! She'd fought so hard to keep this part of her life to herself. To be forced to reveal her secret now . . .

More than anyone, she didn't want *him* to witness what she was about to do. What she *had* to do. He'd no longer be caring or kind. He'd no longer seek pleasure from her.

She chewed on her bottom lip to cut off a groan. This shouldn't be happening, not for another few days.

"Are you hurt?" he asked, frowning. "Did I hurt you?"

"I need some time alone, okay?" she told him, voice a ragged mix of faux light-heartedness, pain, and desperation.

"What's going on, Aleaha? You're swelling."

"Leave. Please." Only the desperation emerged this time.

"I'm not going anywhere."

She could see the determination in his golden eyes. *"Please."*

"No. You will tell me what's happening to you and I will help you. That's your only option."

Seeing no other choice, the agony intensifying, she said, "I—I need a knife."

He snorted, losing all hint of concern. "There are only two things I'll give you right now, and a knife isn't one of them."

"Please. A knife." Wildly she glanced around the chamber, looking for something, anything with a sharp tip. If she had to crawl to it, she would. Last night she'd used her nails, but that hadn't released enough blood. Obviously.

Her line of vision was shrinking, and she saw nothing she could use. No. Wait. In the corner by the door was a bowl filled with fruit. She could dump the food and break the bowl. Surely one of the pieces would be jagged enough to slice through skin and veins.

"I'm not letting you out of this bed," he told her, "so don't even think about getting up."

Ignoring him, she threw her leg over the side. The action nearly felled her. Sharp torment exploded through her every curve and hollow, and she whimpered. *Don't cry. Don't you dare cry.*

"Aleaha?" he said, concern returning. "Is this a game?"

"No game. Please. A knife."

"But why? Help me understand what's happening."

"I have to cut myself." Soon. Oh, God. Soon.

His eyes narrowed. "Bloodshed is forbidden, Aleaha. You know that. I will not let you spill mine."

"I don't want to spill yours," she admitted weakly. "I want to spill *mine*."

He blinked in surprise. "Again, why?"

"I just need a fucking knife! I won't use it on you, I swear." The last word left her mouth on a groan. She tried to sit up, to slap him, to force him to understand, but couldn't. Hurt. So badly. She'd waited too long.

"Aleaha?" His voice was devoid of emotion, his eyes flat.

"Breean. *Please.* I must."

"You're in pain, I can see that, but I can't aid you until you've told me what's wrong."

She wasn't given a chance to respond. He hissed in a breath and jerked away from her, as if he finally understood. "Are you sick? You told me you weren't infected. Did you lie? Did biting me—"

"No. Not sick. Breean, the knife." A tear slid down her cheek, followed quickly by another, until there was an unstoppable flood of them. With every second that passed, her pain and swelling increased.

"Tell me why you wish to do something so barbaric as cut yourself. Now!"

The words exploded from her on a desperate breath. If the truth was what he needed to propel him into aiding her, God help them both, she'd give him the truth. "I produce too much blood. I think it has something to do with the way I change forms. And I've changed a lot these past few days. Every week or so, I have to cut myself to drain the excess. I tried to drain some last night, but when we . . . in the tub . . ."

"You didn't change in the tub. I made sure of it."

"The pleasure, maybe . . . I don't know. Help me. Please, just help me." She was babbling, but couldn't stop. She expected him to leap away from her with revulsion. He continued to stare down at her, something hard in his eyes.

"What happens if you fail to cut yourself?" he asked raggedly.

"I swell. My organs will burst. Knife," she cried, doubling over. She must have squeezed her eyes shut because the next thing she knew, Breean was hovering over her, teeth bared.

Finally, though, he held a knife, hilt out. "I am giving you this because I would rather deal with the possibility of contaminated blood than watch you suffer. If you are lying . . ."

There would be hell to pay. "Not . . . lying." She tried to reach out, but her elbow locked in place, too swollen to move. Even her fingers had become unbendable. No. *No!* "Can't move. You . . . must do it."

His eyes widened, and there was the revulsion she'd expected.

That didn't stop her from continuing; it couldn't, not if she wanted to survive. "St-stab me. In the thigh. Biggest artery, will drain the most."

He shook his head violently. "Surely you are jesting. I have killed men for shedding blood, and you want me to stab *you*?"

"If you don't, I'll die." The more the blood built up, the faster she would destruct. "Hurry. Cut and leave the knife inside. Otherwise, heal too quickly."

"No."

"Bree-an. Need to bleed," she whispered. Then her eyes swelled completely shut, blocking his image. Maybe that was for the best. Now she wouldn't have to see that revulsion intensify in his golden eyes when he did what was necessary. Or watch when he finally abandoned her.

"There has to be another way."

If there were another way, she would have found it by now. "No, there's—" Her jaw clamped and her throat closed, jamming up her airway, her words. Her lungs began to burn and burn and she jerked, every muscle she possessed clenching on bone. Her stomach knotted, rolled. Her nose stung, desperate for air, and the stinging only increased when warm blood began to pour from her nostrils.

"Damn this!" In the next instant, the sheet was whipped away from her, a cool breeze was drifting over her, and a sharp, agonizing pain ripping through her thigh.

Almost immediately her jaw eased and her throat opened and a scream pushed its way free. Breean dug the knife in deep and twisted. He left the tip inside as she'd asked, allowing more and more blood to flow out. With that flow came sweet relief as the pressure inside her lessened, the swelling faded.

Suddenly she could move. Could see Breean hovering over her, his hand curled over the knife hilt. His gaze was fastened on her face, his expression unreadable. Much as he hated blood, she was kind of surprised he hadn't killed her outright. Instead, he truly had aided her.

As if he sensed her thoughts, he said, "Is this all you need?" No hint of his emotions in his voice, either.

"Yes," she rasped.

For a long while, he didn't speak, just watched that crimson liquid trickle onto the sheet. Then he nodded, as if he'd just made a very important decision. She was too afraid to ask what that decision was.

"How long do I bleed you?" he asked.

"Until I pass out." Even as she spoke, she could feel the darkness slinking into her mind. Sweet oblivion, she thought with relief and then knew nothing else.

Breean pulled the blade from Aleaha's leg and watched as the wound slowly healed itself, muscle and then flesh weaving back together. Why she still scarred when she healed so swiftly, he could only guess. The front runner: the number of times she'd been forced to do this. A close second: her curative process wasn't as thorough as it appeared. Either way, this precious female suffered.

Reeling, he cleaned up the blood then burned the rags and sheets before making the bed with Aleaha still in it. She slept through it all, a testament to the brutality of the entire ordeal.

The thought that this woman—or anyone—had to bleed to survive should have been abhorrent to Breean. *Was* abhorrent. Half of him feared causing another plague, killing the only survivors of his race, because of his actions this day. She could be a carrier for some disease he'd never heard of, never dealt with. But the other half of him didn't care about the consequences.

He would do whatever was needed to keep this woman alive.

She was his, connected to him on a level he still didn't understand. When he looked at her, he wanted only to please her. Well, and himself. Hurting her had ripped him up inside, but that had been better than watching her writhe in pain.

"My poor baby," he cooed, stroking her soft cheek. She hated what she was required to do to live. He'd realized it the moment she confessed, for there had been shame in her voice. She'd also expected him to be disgusted by her, for there had been grim acceptance in her eyes. But he hadn't been able and still couldn't work up a single spark of the emotion. Not when his actions had saved her.

From now on, he would help her. Be with her through it all. For there was no going back now. They would be together.

While she slept, he remained at her side. Even when Talon came to inform him that darkness would soon fall and his shift would begin.

"I need a few more minutes," he said.

"Very well." Rather than departing, the warrior transfered his weight from one foot to the other. "The others begged me to ask if they might have a turn in town."

"Of course," he replied. "They may go in pairs, each returning in an hour."

Talon was careful to keep his gaze away from Aleaha. "They will be very happy to hear this. Oh, and we have finally properly installed the security system around the property. If AIR invades, you'll know."

"Excellent." When Talon pivoted to leave, he called, "Tell the men to be careful when choosing their women. They might end up with a wildcat."

His second in command laughed before disappearing into the hall.

Breean stared down at Aleaha for the rest of his remaining minutes, then stood. Her features were relaxed, the swelling completely gone. He never wanted to see her like that again, hurting so badly. *You're mine. I'll take care of you now.*

Once again, he left her sleeping. Fortunately, his shift proved uneventful and he was able to check on Aleaha multiple times. She never moved from that supine position, and that began to worry him.

When he returned to the room once and for all, he found her sitting up in bed. His relief was palpable. And so was his sudden desire. Her breasts were bare, the sheet around her waist, and her hair tumbled down her back, dark ribbons he wanted to wrap around his fists. Yawning, she rubbed the sleep from her eyes. Had she only now awakened?

"Feeling better?"

"Breean," she said on a trembling breath. "Yes. Much. Thank you."

"I'm glad and you're welcome," he told her, rushing to her side, dropping his weapons along the way. Much as he wanted her, he would be a fool to give her such easy access to his knives and guns while near—and intoxicated by—her. He also removed his shirt before caressing her arm, marveling at the smoothness. See? Intoxicated. "Now, there's something we need to finish."

Her gaze flicked to him, widened, then moved to her legs. "The blood—"

"Is gone," he assured her.

Shock curtained her entire face. "Why did you clean me instead of kill me?"

"I do not want to kill you." He crawled in beside her, then rolled on top of her. She gasped but didn't try to push him away. "I want to make love to you."

Eight

The feel of Breean's muscled weight pinning her into the mattress was amazing, Aleaha thought, dazed. More amazing? He still desired her. After everything he'd witnessed, after everything he'd had to do, he *still desired her*. She could feel the length of his erection, thick and hot against her thigh.

"But I'm an abomination to you," she whispered, afraid to place her hope in this enemy who wasn't really an enemy. "Aren't you disgusted by me?"

"You make me feel many things, sweetie pie, but disgust isn't one of them."

She felt herself melting, falling under his spell. Already he'd satisfied her in ways she'd never thought possible. But she couldn't let herself forget that AIR agents were locked in his dungeon. How selfish would she be to luxuriate in his arms while they merely endured? Well, to luxuriate *again*.

She'd been a little too selfish lately, taking Macy's identity, living a life she hadn't been meant to live. Yes, Macy had died before she'd taken over, and probably wouldn't care about the changes she'd made—or perhaps Macy was even now looking down (up?) at her and wishing her to everlasting hell—but those agents *had* become her friends.

"Breean," she said, pushing at his chest. She could have cried at the distance she gained.

"Aleaha," he said, not allowing the distance to last. He grabbed her wrists and pinned them over her head. A favorite position of his, obviously. Her back immediately arched, mashing her breasts into his chest. Her nipples were already hard and rubbed against him.

"This is wrong," she breathed. "We have to stop."

"You cannot stop a fire once it has been ignited." He rotated his pelvis, and she hissed in a breath when his cock slid across her clit, then anchored her legs to the mattress with his own.

Her hiss blended with his. "Actually, you can. With water."

"Then we'll stay away from the water. Now, do you want to talk or finish this?"

As she looked up at him, desire swirled in his golden eyes, almost a living entity, beckoning her to give in. *Just one time.* But one time wouldn't be enough, not for an addict like her. And, oh, was she an addict. She'd had a taste and now craved more.

"T-talk," she forced herself to say.

"Liar. But that's all right." His tongue swiped over his lips. Was he imagining tasting her? "I will talk with you, too."

"From opposite sides of the room."

He shook his head. "Just like this."

Thank God for stubborn men. If he'd left her, she might have stabbed him. "What about the agents?"

"I won't release them," he said darkly. "I told you. That would put my own men at risk."

"Well, you can't keep them locked away forever."

"I can, however, use them as bargaining tools. A life for a life."

They must do things differently on Raka, because she doubted "bargaining" would work out for him. Not favorably, at least. "You might want to rethink that. You'll go to trade and receive a death sentence."

"Maybe," he said. "Maybe not. Until something can be arranged, however, I want you to know that I will not hurt them. That was never my intention."

"*Until something can be arranged* could take forever. They should be home with their families."

"And they will be. Soon."

"Now."

"First, I must ensure AIR will keep its end of the bargain." He didn't give her time to respond, but quickly changed the subject. "No matter what happens in this room, no matter what we say or do to each other, I want you to know that you will never have to cut yourself again. I will take care of you from now on, and I will tell no one your secrets."

She opened her mouth to return them to the agents, but his words sank in and he won a little piece of her heart. No more hiding? No more being afraid someone would find out who and what she was? Amazing. And that this man would be the one responsible for her liberation . . . "I can't ask that of you."

"You aren't asking. I'm simply doing." One of his hands moved from her wrists and curled around her nape, forcing her head to lift slightly. He bowed his back, placing her gaze on his chest, just above his nipple, all the while pulling her mouth closer. "And now we have talked," he said, voice husky, rich. "Ready for the loving to begin?"

He planned to release the agents "soon," which meant she had two choices. She could wait until he did so to be with him. Or she could be with him now, knowing she could lose him during the exchange if AIR decided not to work with him.

Actually, as she'd warned, that seemed most likely. They could very well agree to his demands, then start firing the moment the agents were free. Honor was for those who wanted to lose their loved ones, she'd heard Mia Snow say more than once.

Should she do everything in her power to convince Breean of the truth of her claim? No, she thought next. If she did, he might decide to keep the agents forever, and that she couldn't allow.

"Aleaha," he said, claiming her attention. He was watching her expectantly, desire still swirling in those golden eyes. "Decide."

He was a good man. An honorable man despite his assurances to the contrary, and his plans, if successful, would provide a happily-ever-after for everyone. Aleaha was not like Mia Snow. She respected honor. *I want to be with him now,* she thought. She would be selfish one more time. Otherwise, she might not ever know what it was like to be his woman, truly be his woman, and she *had* to know.

"I don't know." She flicked out her tongue, meeting his skin and trailing it over his thundering heartbeat. "What if I change? You're not inside me this time." Wait. That hadn't sounded right. "I mean, you're not—"

"I know what you meant. I won't mind if you change."

"Even if I become a man? Or you? I know it didn't bother you in the forest, but that was only for a second and it could surprise you, feeling dangly bits, and you could toss me—"

"Aleaha." Dark desperation rang from his tone. He rolled them over, placing her on top. "Give me a chance to prove myself before you condemn me." He smiled slowly, sheepishly as she settled against him. "Right now, I need you. You, no matter who you are or what you look like."

There went another little piece of her heart. His words were a mix of soothing balm and white-hot embers of arousal. Being with him was no longer a need. It was a necessity. "I've decided," she said.

"And?"

"And I don't know why you're still talking." Trembling, she inched down his chest, not stopping until his navel came into view. She licked again, and his muscles clenched.

"Thank you. Yes. More." He was babbling. She liked that.

Lower . . . lower . . . she continued to move. His cock strained high and proud, drawing her full attention. *Mine.* His golden balls were drawn up tight. She tilted her head and allowed her teeth to graze his inner thigh. The cool press of his skin was an electrifying contradiction to her hot tongue.

"Shall I kiss you here?"

"Anywhere," he croaked.

"Free rein. I like that." Unable to stop herself, she curled her hand around his testicles and sank her mouth on his shaft, taking him deep, all the way to the back of her throat. Her jaw stretched wide, burned.

"Yes," Breean roared. "Yes."

She moaned, somehow feeling as if he were sinking his fingers deep inside her. Then her eyes widened as she realized that yes, she was feeling his fingers, phantom fingers, pumping in and out of her. Closing her eyes at the bliss, she sucked him up and down, writhing her hips all the while. *Don't switch bodies, don't switch bodies.*

"Don't stop." He grabbed her and swiveled her around, keeping her mouth on his dick while placing her moist clit right over his face. With barely a pause, he licked her, first the outer shell, then inside, probing.

"Breean!" The sensations were too much, not enough, and her physical form began to lengthen. She forced herself to still, forced her mind to blank. Breath singed her lungs. "I'm changing. I—"

"Just let yourself go, sweet. You taste so good, and I know the woman underneath. I told you. I don't care who you are or what form you have."

As she gave him yet another piece of her heart, something broke inside her. Tension, guilt, fear. She simply allowed herself to fly, relaxing into whatever form her body happened to take. At first, she changed into one person after another, never maintaining a certain image for more than a few seconds. Through it all, Breean continued to kiss and caress her, not once pulling away in disgust.

Then, panting and sweating, she realized the changing had stopped. For several minutes, she simply lay there, Aleaha, only Aleaha. Perhaps she'd run out of identities, or perhaps Breean had left pieces of himself inside her, maintaining a grip on her image.

Breean... inside her... the first tremors of an approaching orgasm rocked her. Either way, she was truly free, her fear vanquished, leaving amazement, gratitude, and awe, each adding to her enjoyment.

"Yes, yes," she cried.

Breean gave one more lick and another tremor crashed through her, propelling her closer to the edge. Just a bit more and she'd—he spun her around until they were eye to eye. He grabbed her wrists and locked them behind her back with one of his hands, the action arching her forward, reading her. But he didn't enter her.

"More," she said, willing to beg. He'd given her so much already, but she had to have more.

"Remember how you felt in the tub, touching yourself, pumping yourself to orgasm? Do you want that again or do you want me?"

Her heart sped up, hammering at her ribs. "You."

"Perfect answer," he said, gently rubbing his cock against her.

Moaning, she closed her eyes again. "But I . . . we have to . . . I want to make you feel good, too."

"You do. More than any other, you do. And do you know what will make me feel as if I've reached the gates of heaven? Caressing you. Starting with your breasts, rolling the nipples between my fingers this time, making you writhe. Then I want to dip lower, sink my fingers between your legs. I want you to feel *me*. Only me, not a spirit version of me."

Her breathing became erratic, uneven. "Yes. I want that, too."

"You'll be hotter and wetter than you are now. I know you will be. Just like I know you'll be tight. Tighter than a fist."

She bit her bottom lip, drawing a single bead of blood. "I'm ready. Do it."

But he didn't. He didn't move. "And when you've drenched my hand, when you're practically screaming for release, I'll replace my fingers with my mouth. I'll lick, taste, and suck you again."

"Yes. Please, yes." She gasped in need, the sound of it like a little catch of wonder. Her hips moved toward him, seeking deeper contact, but, damn him, he twisted out of reach.

"I won't be able to help myself," he said. "I'll bite you, as you did me in the forest. Just a little sting, though, then I'll lick it away."

She moaned. Caught herself. Pressed her lips together. He was holding back, so she would, too. Only, her hips were moving consistently now and she wasn't able to hide the action. The scent of his arousal was so thick, it was almost a honey cloud enveloping her.

"You're all talk," she gritted out.

"No, I'm so hard for you." He released her hands to cup her cheeks. "I've never wanted a woman the way I want you."

"Then take me." *Take me in a way that they'll be no holding back for either of us.*

An animalistic sound escaped him, and he tangled his hands in her hair, jerking her head toward him for a bruising kiss. His tongue thrust inside her mouth, feverish, desperate. Finally. Sweetly. He was putting his mouth where his money was. Wait. That wasn't how the expression went. Oh, who cared. Delectable!

"You make me so crazy."

Brain fogging, she arched into him. "More," she breathed.

More? "All," Breean said, and deepened the kiss. They were both so wild, their teeth scraped together. Didn't help that her flavor was pure decadence. Not the honey he'd once been used to, but better. Sweeter. A rose blooming amid a tempest, he would have said if he were a poet. Caveman that his brain currently was, all he could think was *mine.*

He licked his way down her neck as his fingers explored her body. There was a fine, silky tuft of hair between her legs where he dabbled, tickling, exciting, before sinking his fingers into her already soaking folds.

She nearly shot off the bed. "That . . . that . . . right there. Yes!"

Her clitoris was swollen, eager. He circled it, and her hips followed the motion. *Beautiful.*

"Breean," she groaned.

"So wet," he praised.

"Hurt."

He'd already vowed to take care of all her hurts. This one would be his pleasure. "I'll kiss it and make it better." And he did. He pinned her to her back and inched down her body, licking along the way. She was delicious curves and sweet angles, and he hadn't gotten nearly enough of her. Would he ever?

He wanted her to come with his cock buried deep, but he had to have another sampling. Was already addicted to her feminine flavor. Besides, what kind of lover would he be if he couldn't make her come more than once?

She arched into him, writhing, head thrashing from side to side. Her hands found her breasts, and she squeezed. The sight was erotic, as foreign as she was. He hadn't seen her in the tub, but he'd wanted to. Oh, he'd wanted to. He liked that Aleaha was pushed so close to the edge right now that she was willing to do anything to find release.

"Want my tongue on you again?" he asked.

"Yes."

"Licking you?"

"Yes."

"Sucking you off?"

"Yes. God, yes."

His tongue was flicking out in the next instant. She was still hot and wet and she still tasted of passion. He thought he might fight a thousand wars if it meant being with this woman. He thought he might kill violently and without mercy for the privilege.

"I can't get enough." He moved his tongue back and forth, then tunneled it inside her, mimicking sex.

"Breean, Breean," she chanted.

His cock was so hard it could explode at any moment. Already he could feel the hot glide of seed on the tip. "Spread yourself for me."

Instantly she obeyed, reaching between her legs and opening herself for him. Pink, wet. His. He gently clamped her center between his teeth, sucking as he'd promised.

Didn't take long. In seconds, she was screaming her release. Still he didn't stop. He reached up and palmed one of her breasts just as she had done. Trembling, she arched into his touch, riding the waves of bliss. Then, as she calmed, she grabbed his wrist and brought his fingers into her mouth, sucking two inside, deep, so deep.

At that, his blood reached the searing point, burning through his veins, blistering his organs. He pumped his free hand up and down his cock, thinking to find a little ease. That only made it worse.

"Ready?" he asked her. He was too desperate, couldn't wait any longer.

"Give me."

"Everything?"

"And more."

Beautiful female. He climbed up her body, nipping along the way. She was simply irresistible. When he was in position, just about to sink home, she gave a strong shove to his shoulders. Taken by surprise, he fell to his back, and for a moment, he thought she meant to leave him. He wanted to curse . . . until she straddled him.

Grinning, she curled her fingers around his swollen length. "Hard," she praised. "Big."

"Like?"

Her head fell back, all that dark hair tickling his chest, and she breathed a sweet, "Oh, yes."

Aleaha more than liked. She loved. Temporary insanity, she was sure, because right now she was drowning in bliss, on fire, achy, so much more so than in the tub—something she wouldn't have thought possible.

She was fascinated by Breean's body, by the grunts of delight he'd emitted as he tasted between her legs. Actually, everything about him fascinated her. Maybe because he'd done nothing she'd expected. They were captor and prisoner. Master and slave, he'd once said, and she was everything he should hate. Yet he'd freely given of himself, ensuring she found satisfaction, all the while acting as if she were important to him, as if her needs mattered.

The knowledge was as heady and intoxicating as his honey scent.

When she'd lain in bed at home alone, touching herself, this was what she'd dreamed of. Craved. And now, finally, she was getting it.

With her enemy. As doomed as they surely were, this might be her only chance to enjoy him and that saddened her.

"You look ready to cry," Breean said with more tension than she'd ever heard him use before. "Do you plan to stop?"

"Not even if your home is invaded."

"Then let me have you. Please."

Hearing him beg sent a shiver down her spine. Yes, oh, yes. She rose on her knees, placing her wet core over his cock. He gripped her hips, squeezed, and the round head pressed for entrance, stretching her, tantalizing her.

"Deeper," he rasped.

Another inch.

It had been so long for her, she felt a slight burn, but the rapture exploding through her soon made her forget any discomfort.

"More," he urged, the vessels in his neck bulging.

"Yes." Another inch.

"That's the way. Take it all, sweet. Take it all."

Yet another inch, and another, though he still wasn't all the way seated. The few other men she'd been with had not been as large as Breean. Was anyone? Well, she had been, she thought with a small smile. That amusement relaxed her and she fell another inch. The stretch was more noticeable now, shoving through that rapturous haze.

"Big," she told him again.

"You can take me."

Yes, she could. Aleaha Love, wanton sex goddess, could do anything. She stopped resisting and slammed all the way down. Breean roared in approval, the sound blending with her own needy moan.

"Move for me, sweet." The words were barely audible.

Slowly, she rose; slowly, she lowered. Her head fell back, and she gazed up at the ceiling, lost, flying. A powerful warrior was under her, hers to do with as she pleased. He was enjoying her, delighted by her. Dream come true.

"Faster," he beseeched.

Yes, faster. She moved again, increasing her pace. Up, down. Perfect. So perfect.

"Faster," he repeated. His fingers, wrapped as they were around her waist, dug into muscle. There'd be a bruise, but it would be worth it. "It's been so long for me, and you feel so good. I don't know how long I can last for you."

She wouldn't last, either, was already hurtling through the stars. Faster and faster she allowed herself to go.

"That's the way," he praised.

"Give me everything," she said. "I want it. Want you."

He cupped her ass, spreading her even wider, making her take him all the deeper. Faster still they slammed together. She could actually see the outline of his spirit, glowing as if it wanted to burst free of his body and into hers.

"Aleaha," he growled.

Something was thrumming through her. Tenderness and caring, perhaps, making the climax she'd experienced before seem like a pale imitation. It consumed her with honey and cinnamon and glimmered as it washed through her. This was her man; his ecstasy was hers.

"Breean, Breean," she chanted. Just then, his name was the only word she knew.

He rolled her over, drilling into her, and her entire body erupted in a cascade of sparks and light, spasming, arching. *Must have another taste.* Lost again, forever, she gripped his hair and jerked him down for another kiss.

As his tongue plundered her mouth, he, too, erupted, spurting hot seed inside her and sending her on another tailspin.

He shuddered over and over before finally collapsing on top of her. She closed her eyes, basking, more alive than she'd ever been before because, in that moment, she was a woman. Not an agent. Not an alien. But a woman. She was Aleaha.

Nine

THE NEXT SEVERAL DAYS PASSED IN A WONDROUS DAZE for Aleaha, dulled only by her arguments with Breean about the AIR agents. Her thought to be selfish just one more time? Completely obliterated. Breean kept her with him and they rarely left his room. The few times they had, he'd taken her to his office where he'd spoken with his second in command, Talon.

The two had used their own language, which Breean had yet to teach her and she hadn't yet figured out, so she had no idea what was said. Afterward, they would return to the bedroom and she would pester him for information—which would in turn lead to another argument. Somehow, someway, he always managed to distract her. Maybe it was the way he savored her body, praising her wit, her sweetness, even her determination to save her friends.

He made her feel special, cherished, something she'd never experienced before. But, damn it. She would have to do a better job of resisting him to get the kind of results she wanted. Like, her friends' happiness. Like, Breean's happiness. And continued good health. Surely there was a way to meet all three objectives.

Right now, she was naked (again) and snuggled into Breean's side (again), his fingers tracing her arm. And she let him gentle her. Luxuriated in him, actually. *You are in so much trouble, girl.* From enemy to lover. From hated to adored. *What are you going to do now?* She'd wondered a million times.

Macy probably wouldn't have gotten herself into this situation. Aleaha frowned at the thought. *I'm not Macy; I never was.* Still, she was a friend to those agents locked below—if she needed to remind herself a thousand times, she would—and she couldn't leave them helpless. *More than you already have,* her mind supplied.

"Can we talk about the agents now?"

"We discuss them every day," he said, fingers stilling. "Just because they are prisoners doesn't mean they are miserable. They are well fed, given blankets. They aren't tortured."

"What if I said I wouldn't sleep with you again until they were free?"

"I'd call you a liar and kiss my way to your sweet spot."

She gritted her teeth. Clearly, resisting him wasn't going to get the job done. She was going to have to start fighting him. Truly fighting him. She might even have to hurt him. "Why haven't you tried to bargain with AIR?"

"They aren't yet ready to deal with me."

"How do you know?"

"I just do."

Frustrating! "Let me talk to them. I'll explain that you're willing to help them fight the Schön queen. Because of your skills and their desperation to defeat that woman, they might overlook your past behavior."

"No. I don't want you leaving."

"I'll call them, then."

"Calls can be traced. You know that."

Argh! "You can't hide out forever."

"I know."

Not just frustrating, but stubborn. He was making her rehash, and she hated to rehash. "If I had your men locked away, I suspect you wouldn't care how they were being treated. You would want them freed."

"You're right, but I can't simply let the agents go. I can't place my people in even more danger. And let me respond to the other objections I'm sure you're about to raise. They were blindfolded when brought here, yes, so I could blindfold them again and drop them off somewhere and they would not be able to find me. If I do that, however, I'll be without my backup plan if AIR decides not to risk working with me."

"Breean—"

"It has to be this way. I'm sorry. I wish it were otherwise, but . . ."

He felt guilty, she could tell from the tattered emotion in his tone, but she also realized there really would be no convincing him to rethink his strategy, no matter what she did or how hard she tried. His determination was as solid as hers.

That depressed and angered her, because it meant their time together was over.

Still. If she'd learned anything about him these last few days, it was that he truly wanted to make a home here and would never purposely hurt the innocent. So she tried one more time to make him see the light. "You want to destroy the Schön, yes? Well, if they were to appear today, AIR would be divided, trying to find you *and* fight the Schön. What if this planet falls because you are too stubborn to try to make something work? Please, just let the men go and—"

"Enough. I've spent the last two years fighting, searching for a new home, and making preparations for that home. Finally I'm here. Finally I have a moment's respite with a beautiful woman I—a beautiful woman I like. Why can I not enjoy that for a bit?"

"Because time is our enemy. AIR will find you. And knowing them as I do, I know that if you have failed to initiate a gesture of goodwill, they will show you no mercy."

He sighed. "I'm monitoring things, Aleaha. I promise you that. I'll know when the Schön queen arrives. I'll know when AIR has softened toward me."

She laughed bitterly. How many times had she told him that AIR was not known for softening? *You have to act now. No more stalling, waiting, hoping.*

Despite her resolve, she knew it was only a matter of time before he attempted to seduce her again and she caved. His scent was in her nose, his touch branded on her cells, and she would soon find herself begging for more. She always did.

"I hate to disappoint you, Aleaha. I do. But this is for the best, I promise you."

"Of course." Hating herself—and him—she rolled from his side, facing away from him. She would free the agents, no matter what needed to be done, and then she would . . . what? Come back for Breean? Would he even want her after that?

Probably not, but it was worth the risk. To save his life, to save her friends, it was worth the risk.

His fingers traced the line of her spine. She shivered, even as her blood heated. How could she still desire him? How could she still crave him so potently, knowing what was about to happen?

"Where are you going?" he asked.

"I'm hungry," she said, rising and walking to the bowl of fruit he had refilled every morning. Her legs shook. *Stop,* her heart shouted. Or rather, what remained of it. *Don't do this.*

This is the only way, her mind replied. As if clumsy, she knocked the bowl from the vanity, and it shattered on the floor. Pieces of fruit spilled in every direction. "I'm sorry," she said, trembling as she bent to pick them up.

Don't. Stupid heart. First, she palmed the longest, sharpest, shard. *No other way.*

Breean was by her side in the next instant, helping her.

Do you really want to do this?

No, she didn't. But she would.

"Go lie down," he said, clearly concerned for her. "I don't want you to cut yourself." Yep. Concerned.

If you do this, you are the monster you always considered yourself.

Not true. And damn it, why couldn't her heart and mind play nice? Keeping the shard hidden, she did as Breean had requested. For Devyn and Dallas and even Macy, for *Breean,* she *would* do this. She gulped back the lump forming in her throat. When the smoke cleared—and by *smoke cleared* she meant *blood dried*—she would speak to Mia and tell her what Breean had not. His purpose, how his planet had fallen, what he wanted, what he needed, how wonderful he was, and how she herself planned to aid him.

And if that got her fired, fine. If that got her imprisoned for aiding an alien, fine again. She'd find a way to escape. She'd find another way to save Breean and his people.

After he'd cleaned up the mess, Breean settled beside her, an orange in hand. He tossed it in the air, caught it. "Still hungry, sweet?" By the sensual bent of his tone, she knew he was thinking about her licking the juice off him.

Now or never. Do it, just do it. It's for his own good, after all. Aleaha rolled into him. Before he could figure out her intent, she pressed the shard into his jugular, deep enough to draw blood but not deep enough to kill. Blood trickled down his neck, thick and gold. Her hand was wobbling.

He stiffened, and the orange hit the mattress. "What are you doing?" The words were strained.

She shifted as close to him as possible, making it tougher for him to shove her away. "I'm doing what I have to do." Yet she couldn't deny a sense of wrongness. *Damn it! He didn't give me any other choice.*

"Threatening me is a *have to*?"

Her gaze swung guiltily away and landed on the Christmas tree. Only a few more days until Christmas Eve. Maybe she should have waited to do this. They could have exchanged gifts—not that she had one for him—and then—

No. No! With the holiday approaching, the agents needed to be home with their families more than ever. She'd made the right decision. "Apparently it is," she said.

Breean's tongue traced his teeth. "I thought we were past this."

"You thought wrong. As long as you're in danger, as long as my friends are captives, we will never be past it."

A pause. A slight transfer of his weight. "You do realize I could move to the door in the blink of an eye, do you not, taking the weapon with me, leaving you helpless against my fury? All you've done is proven I cannot trust you."

"You can trust me more than any other. And just so you know, I could sever your head before you moved an inch. I can move quickly, too. Don't forget."

Eyes slitting, he pushed out a shuddering breath. "It doesn't have to be this way."

"If you won't see to your future, I will do so. Afterward, I want to be with you. I want to make this thing work between us."

"You plan to make it work by cutting my throat? Funny. To Rakans, that's the fastest way to end something." The fragrance of honey began to thicken the air. "Put the shard down." Even his voice was like honey now. "I want you to be with me, too. You must trust me in this."

She hissed as her nipples hardened and her mind fogged with desire. "Stop that!" She pressed the shard deeper, and more of that golden blood trickled. Knowing how it tasted, like sugarplums plucked from a freaking rainbow, caused her mouth to water. Was no part of her safe from his appeal?

"Remove your breasts from my side if the smell offends you."

Offends? Had the situation been any different, she would have snorted. "I'm not moving." Yet. She had to make him understand why she was seemingly choosing AIR over him. "Someone has to make you *and* AIR see reason. Working together will benefit you both."

He reached up and grabbed her wrist, though he didn't try to shove her away. "I do see reason. I want to work with them, but your boss wants my head. Which you now seem perfectly willing to give her."

That touch . . . Her skin flushed, her blood pumping wildly for him. Only him. Aleaha held her breath and tried to figure out what to do next. She'd hoped he wouldn't force her to take this all the way.

"Drop your weapon and we'll pretend this never happened," he coaxed. There was a dark glint in his eye, and she knew there would be no forgetting. Not for a long while.

Still she surged ahead. "Promise to release the agents. Today."

"You would believe me?"

Would she? More than anything, she wanted to. Then she could curl back into his arms and give him time to heal from the wound in his neck, and they could make love again. "Yes."

"Even knowing I always fight dirty."

"Even knowing." With her, he'd always been honorable.

"Damn you, Aleaha. As I've told you multiple times, I would be putting everyone in this house at risk."

"As I've told *you* multiple times, they're already at risk."

His expression hardened. Had he expected her to say something else? "Either kill me or drop it." Obviously, he'd reached the end of his patience. He squeezed her wrist, and it was enough to make her bones ache, but not enough to make her release the shard.

You know what you have to do. There wasn't going to be another opportunity like this, he would make sure of it.

His grip tightened, his anger clearly overriding his promise never to hurt her. "I'm done waiting, Aleaha." Tighter . . . tighter . . .

Do it. Now! "If there'd been any other way . . ." she whispered with a sob. "I'm sorry. So sorry." Then she slashed. Hard.

He jerked in shock, and instantly blood poured, thick like syrup. His eyes were wide and accusing as they stared at her, but he was unable to speak. His hands flew to the injury, knocking her to the side.

Tears filling and burning her eyes, she next cut her own wrist. She had to push his hands away to hold it over his wound, dripping her blood into the center, mixing red with gold. "You'll heal faster this way. I know because I've done this before. Not slit someone's throat, but shared my blood. You won't die. I won't let you die." Babble, babble. "And I promise you, you will not catch a disease because of this." But he *would* be too weak to come after her. "I'm sorry."

All he could do was gurgle. He'd bled her that day to save her, as well as a few times afterward, all of which he'd considered dangerous. Her actions now were a thousand times more so, and they were *against* him. He might not be able to get past them.

Wiping at her eyes with the back of her hand, she shoved to her feet. As fast as her feet would carry her, she rushed around the room, grabbing his garments. She quickly dressed, unable to stop her shaking. Constantly her gaze roved back to Breean. He, too, was shaking.

I really am a monster. How could I have done that to him? "I'm so sorry," she choked out. He'd only given her joy, and this was how she'd repaid him. *You had to do it. There was no other way.* Except . . .

What if she freed the agents and they really did bring AIR to his doorstep as he feared, her recommendation to make peace disregarded? What if he was killed or imprisoned? What if he was tortured for information? She'd never seen an interrogation firsthand, but she'd heard the screams.

Maybe she could blindfold the agents, as he'd suggested, and lead them out. Maybe— She snorted bitterly. Yeah, right. Like they'd really wear blindfolds. *Free them, talk to Mia, and if she won't cooperate, help Breean hide.*

If he'd let her. Stomach rolling, she bent and pressed a soft kiss on his lips. They were still warm, yet stiff from the pain. "I'll come back for you. I'll help keep you and your people safe."

He glared up at her. He'd probably rather kill her than spend another moment in her presence.

A sob congealed in her throat. "Good-bye for now, Breean."

She strode to the door, forcing her body to grow, to develop muscles. Her skin became that lovely shade of gold, the power inside her humming. When the switch was complete, she pictured the house, mentally navigating her way toward the cells. Now all she had to do was walk there. Without incident.

Twice she was stopped and questioned in the Rakan language; both times she merely nodded and shooed the men away with a wave of her fingers, as if she couldn't be bothered. They regarded her strangely, but allowed her to pass. God knows what she would have done if they hadn't. She couldn't get her heartbeat under control and was sweating profusely.

Finally she reached her destination. The air was stuffier here, laden with dust, and she could hear an urgent murmur of voices. Poor guys, stuck in this dank, ugly place while she'd enjoyed the royal treatment.

In the corner were two Rakan guards. They straightened when they spotted her.

"I'm taking over tonight," she told them, praying they found nothing odd about her use of English. "You're free to do whatever you wish."

Grins split both their faces. "Even go into town?" one asked.

"Absolutely. Tell everyone else they've got permission to go as well."

Waiting only until they rushed off, she kicked back into gear. Just before she reached Devyn's cell, she summoned Macy's image. Her body shortened, the bones shrinking, and her facial features rounded. She didn't have to see herself to know her skin was now tanned and her hair pale.

I'm not this person, she wanted to scream.

The clothes might be hard to explain, since they suddenly bagged on her, but oh, well. Curling her fingers around the bars, she saw that Devyn was seated against the far wall, his knees upraised and his head in his hands. "Devyn," she said, her voice no longer her own, either. She'd just gotten used to being herself, damn it.

His head whipped up, and when he saw her, he grinned and stood. In no way did he look like a man who'd spent several weeks in captivity. He looked ready for a party.

"Lolli, darling." His eyes were like amber fire in the murky darkness, raking over her. Other agents had been moved to his cell; a couple tried to approach the bars, but he waved them back and they obeyed. "How'd you escape the big guy?"

Nausea churned in her stomach. *Oh, I slit his throat and left him bleeding in his own bed.* "I made myself look like him and walked out." It was the truth.

"Cool." He didn't sound surprised.

Her knuckles squeezed the bars, losing their color. "You know what I can do?" Had he seen her that night in the forest? He'd been unconscious, and she'd thought she had been so careful.

Slowly he approached her. "I'm not a trained AIR agent, just their hired help, but I know drug addicts, and Macy was an Onadyn user. AIR hired her only to use her to find out who was dealing to her. I got to be the one to seduce her for info, not that she told me much. Which is why I planned to continue seeing her. But even though she and I had already had sex, you didn't recognize me the first time we met, and I didn't recognize your smell."

All this time . . . she'd lived in fear, but they'd known. They'd already freaking known.

"Anyway, AIR figured out you were different, though no one knew how or why you were there. So we all observed you instead, trying to discover if you were someone's plant." He shrugged. "But you never saw anyone outside of work and never told anyone the false stories we fed you. And then, not too long after your arrival, someone found Macy's body. We interviewed a few witnesses and figured out that her dealer went loco and killed her, that you saw an opp and took it."

"There was never a story in the news about her death." Aleaha knew. She had watched and waited for the day, knowing she'd have to switch identities yet again.

"AIR made sure of that."

Warmth drained from her, leaving only a cold shell. She'd had no idea. She'd been in danger, constantly scrutinized, and had been utterly clueless. "W-why didn't they kill me?" She wanted to release Macy's image, but didn't. Even though these agents knew what she could do, she didn't want them seeing the real her. That was for Breean. Only Breean.

"As far as I know, you're the only one of your kind. Human or alien, they still don't know. You'll be a great asset."

An asset. That's all she was good for, which wasn't comforting. But even more upsetting? They didn't know what she was either. She'd hoped *someone* had that information. Even her parents hadn't known.

Stay hidden, Aleaha love, her mom had said the last time Aleaha had seen her. She couldn't see the woman's face, for shadows surrounded them. *If anyone finds out what you are, they'll hurt you.*

We'll come back for you, her dad had said, taking her mother's hand.

But they never had. The two had walked off while she sobbed. They hadn't run as if they were being chased. They'd walked. They hadn't looked back.

She supposed they could have been killed, and that's why they'd failed to return for her, but deep down she suspected they were still out there, glad to be without the stigma of her origins. Whatever they were.

She would have died had it not been for Bride McKells, vampire extraordinaire, who had found her and taken over her care. Bride hadn't cared what she was. Bride had loved her.

What would Bride think of Breean? She would approve, surely.

Breean. Oh, God. Breean. Was he okay? *You gave him your blood. He's fine.*

"—listening to me?" Devyn asked with a chuckle. "I was saying how it's better to keep your enemies closer than your friends, so AIR kept you close. Just in case. Besides, I wanted a go at you so I cast my vote to keep you around."

He'd wanted her?

He must have read the question in her eyes, because he added, "I collect women. You know that. And I've never had a woman who can change personas. So if you're interested . . ."

"No," she said quickly.

He shrugged as if it was of no consequence. "As I said, AIR planned to use you if you proved trustworthy. The things you'll be able to do, the places you'll be able to get them, the information you'll be able to glean, will be invaluable."

"Why are you telling me this? Why now, of all times?"

His fingers curled around hers, warm, comforting. "I like you. I can't have you. Not right now," he added with an amused tilt of his chin, "but I do like you and I didn't want you to fear anyone's reaction to the truth, since you've clearly gone to a lot of trouble to help us escape."

Hello, reminder. Escape, the reason she was here. The chitchat needed to end. She leaned down and studied the ID box. "I don't know how to open your cell," she said. "I've never rewired anything."

"I'll tell you what to do just as soon as you tell me where the Rakan is."

"And *I'll* tell *you* just as soon as you tell me that you won't hurt him."

"Done. I vow it."

That easily? Why? And could she trust him? She would have to, she supposed.

"Breean is in bed, unable to move." She squeezed her eyelids closed, trying to block that last, heartbreaking image of him. "I didn't see a lot of his men on my way down here, and I hopefully sent the remaining ones on their way. Whoever stayed, I'll convince I'm Breean and lead you guys outside." She hoped.

"Macy?" she heard Dallas call from down the hall. Had they played musical cells?

"You're next," she told him. "Hold tight."

"So you escaped Stud Muffin."

Stud Muffin? "Looks like it." *And all I had to do was shred his neck.* "Now, how do I get through the ID box?"

Dallas laughed that razor-sharp laugh of his. "We shoulda known she'd do it," he said to Devyn. To Aleaha, he added, "You shouldn't be down here. If you're caught, I'm sure you'll be punished."

"I won't be caught. Now how do I open this?"

"Don't look at me," Devyn said, splaying his arms. "I don't know how to disable them."

"But you said—" She gritted her teeth. Bastard. He'd manipulated her for information.

There was a pause, then a sigh from Dallas. Why so reluctant? Were the situation reversed, she would be shouting orders until the bars were out of the way. Finally, he said, "Remove the lid." He reached a dark arm through the bars and pointed at the black case.

She had to pound at it to loosen it, but ultimately it slipped free, revealing a multitude of wires. "Which do I cut?"

"Only the red one."

"You sure?" Devyn asked. "I'd go with blue myself."

"They're all red!" she snapped. "There's not a single blue one."

With another sigh, Dallas rested his forehead against the bars. "I hoped they had the cheaper model. All right. Sort through them and try to find the thread that's woven through all of them."

Thread? She began sifting through the sea of red. "You guys ignored me that first night of captivity. Why?"

"There was a guard pacing the halls," Devyn said. "We couldn't risk him overhearing."

Wasn't like she'd asked for detailed escape plans. "You guys know Mia better than I do." She didn't remove her attention from the wires. All of them seemed to be connected to the rest, no common thread holding them together. "If Breean agrees to help her fight the Schön, will she let him do so?"

Dallas laughed.

Devyn snorted.

"What?" she demanded, finally glancing up. The wires had begun to blur together, anyway. Dallas, she noticed, was peering off to his left and mouthing something. Who was he talking to? She followed the direction of his gaze but didn't see anyone. Perhaps captivity had driven him insane.

He must have sensed her gaze, because he faced her and grinned. "Mia forgives no one, and the Rakans killed several of her men. Men she was charged with protecting."

"He's not exaggerating. Even I wouldn't bed her, and believe me," Devyn said, "I've slept with some real bad-asses."

"Hey, man," Dallas interrupted with a laugh. "She's like my sister. No talk of bedding her."

Aleaha suddenly felt like she was back in the forest, the night the Rakans had come. For the most part, Dallas and Devyn hadn't taken that seriously either, overflowing with jokes. "Well, Mia will lose even more men if she refuses this golden opportunity. And, yes, pun intended. Breean can help us defeat the Schön queen. You saw how quickly he can move. You saw how his men can step into bodies and force them to do what they want." She turned back to the box. Ugh. Red was now her least favorite color. "But what you probably didn't notice was the scent these men produce. It . . . lures women. Fogs their minds. What if a Rakan could lure the queen into a trap? AIR could be there to pounce, and her blood would never have to be spilled."

Devyn regarded her intently; she could feel his amber gaze probing the depths of her soul. "Was this Breean's idea? You coming here and talking to us?"

"No. It's mine," she said, hoping Breean would agree to such a plan. Not that she wanted him to be the one doing the luring. One of his warriors could do it. That Talon guy, maybe. He was kind of cute in a boy scout slash psycho killer way.

"I don't know, Mace. That would involve trusting the Rakans, and well—"

"AIR trusts no one," she finished for him. Exasperated, she shook her head. "One of his men killed the agents, and that was against Breean's rules. Breean punished him. You remember the guy we heard him castigating that night in the cell, right?" She paused, bit her lip. "I don't want him hurt. He's not predatory. Tell the commander to leave him alone, okay? Please. All Breean wants is a peaceful life for his men, and he *is* willing to aid AIR to find that peace."

"Tell the commander yourself," Dallas said.

"I . . . can't." Right then and there, Aleaha realized she loved Breean. She hadn't just given him pieces of her heart; she'd given him the whole thing. And temporary insanity couldn't be blamed this time. She wasn't lost in a passion-haze. She did. She loved him. He was gentle and kind, attentive and hard, passionate and determined. He was wild and savage and tender and protective. He was . . . everything.

She didn't want to live Macy's life anymore. She wanted to live her own. Now, always. She would free these agents as planned, but she wouldn't leave and come back. She'd simply stay here and do whatever it took to win Breean's forgiveness. And his heart. She would follow him to the ends of the Earth, whether he wanted her or not.

They *would* be together.

"I'm not going with you," she said. "And, damn it, I can't find a thread. Should I just start jerking wires out?"

Dallas sputtered, and her gaze lifted. He'd disappeared into his cell.

Devyn, she noticed, was frowning at her. "Little girl, that's not a decision you get to make."

What? Jerking the wires? "What does that mean?" As she spoke, something brushed her shoulder, and a honey-scented breeze quickly followed. Her blood heated—then chilled. No. Not possible. Not freaking possible.

Heart once again slamming against her ribs, she backed away from the cell.

"What are you doing?" Devyn demanded.

"He's here."

"The leader?" His gaze slid the length of the hallway. "I don't see anyone."

"He's—" Her entire mind went black as Breean's essence slipped into her body, utterly consuming her.

TEN

How could she have done that to him? Breean wondered. How could she have cut his throat like that? Not a paltry wound, either, but a death wound. Delivered mere hours after he'd sated her.

Fury seethed through him. When he'd realized his body was indeed healing as swiftly as hers had the times he'd sliced into her thigh, he'd decided to spirit-walk, even though he'd left his physical being without a personal guard, something he hated to do. Anyone could stroll into his room right now and cut him—as Aleaha had done—and he would not be able to defend himself. But he had to stop her from escaping, and had been too weak to go after her physically.

So he'd allowed his spirit to rise from his body, detaching one from the other, and had stalked the home, unseen, unsensed, searching for her. Of course, he'd found her with the prisoners.

He shouldn't have been surprised that she'd chosen to injure him and save them. They were her friends, her coworkers, and he probably would have done the same. To anyone but her. He'd thought . . . what? That she'd come to like *him*? That she wanted a future with him? Damn this!

"Macy," the agent in front of her said. Glitter. He was reaching through the bars, trying to grasp her arm and hold her in place.

In control of her movements, Breean made her step farther away. Unlike when he'd entered her for the bath, she was not aware of him or her surroundings. That time, he'd wanted her responsive. This time, he wanted only her obedience, so he'd overtaken her completely. Her actions were his. Her thoughts were his. Even her voice was his.

"Macy?" Glitter said again.

"Do not worry for her. I will not hurt her," Breean said. A lie? He wasn't sure. Never had he been in such a murderous mood.

Without another word, he walked her up the stairs and back to his bedroom. The agents called for Macy's return, not understanding what was happening, but he paid them no heed.

She'd chosen the perfect time to escape, for many of his warriors were once again in the city. No one would have known of her—or the agents—release until morning. By then, the agents would have been safely ensconced in AIR headquarters, he was sure, and the hunt for him and his people would have begun.

What made it worse was that she'd used her ability against him, an ability she had feared but one he had accepted. Not once had he condemned her for what she could do. Yet she'd used it against him, *becoming* him. The remaining warriors would have let her do whatever she wanted, no questions asked.

Was she at all sorry? She'd claimed to be but . . . He released his hold on her thoughts and her voice filled their head. *What are you doing? Breean, stop this! Let me explain.*

No, not sorry for her actions. Only sorry she'd been caught.

Still inside her, he gathered four ties and anchored them to the bedposts. His physical self was still lying on the mattress, a slight rise and fall of his chest the only sign that he lived. Amber blood was dried to his throat, but the wound was weaving itself together and had healed considerably. He thought perhaps he would be completely normal in a few hours.

That didn't lessen his rage.

He had Aleaha strip before encasing her own ankles in the ties, spreading her naked thighs and anchoring them in place before making her lie on her stomach beside him.

Breean, let's talk about this. I wasn't going to leave. I had decided—

"Silence." He had her bind one of her wrists to a post, then had to use her teeth to secure the other.

Finally, she was tethered to the bed.

Breean.

He ignored her, tendrils of satisfaction blending with the heat of his anger.

Breean, please. I—I love you.

She—no! How dare she say that now. Now, when he couldn't be sure whether she meant it or merely wanted to soothe him. Love. It was what he'd come to want from her. To go to bed with her every night and awaken with her snuggled in his arms every morning. To talk with her, learn all that he could about her, to simply enjoy all that she was. But really. How could she love him after what she'd done?

Don't soften, he told himself. *You gave her more than you've ever given another and she tried to kill you.*

Well, she did *heal you.*

Silence. He didn't want to converse with himself either.

Sleep, he commanded Aleaha's mind, and she did, fading to quiet, to black.

Grim, Breean pushed his spirit from her, rising like a wave in the ocean, once against detaching from a solid form, before falling back into his own. Conscious mind and body connected, weaving back together like the wound in his neck until he once again had control over his own self.

Then, he waited.

As Aleaha drifted slowly into awareness, she realized four things at once. One, her face was smashed into a white silk pillow. Two, she couldn't move her arms or her legs, and cool air was stroking the wet heat of her core. Three and four, the most significant, she was naked and Breean was straddled over her hips, his knees at her sides.

How had she gotten here? She recalled being in the dungeon, trying to disable the ID box, then nothing. No, wait. That wasn't true. Breean had taken control of her and forced her to walk to his bedroom. He'd forced her to tie herself up.

The ties . . . that's why she couldn't move. Her stomach rolled and twisted, dread filling her veins. She tried to raise her head, tried to turn and face him, but each action was limited and gained her nothing. "Breean, let me explain. Let me—"

"Silence." There was no emotion in his tone.

"I did what I had to do. I didn't want to hurt you. I swear I didn't. Let me go and we'll—"

"I said, silence!" This time, his voice boomed through the room, echoing menacingly from the walls.

He was angry and hurt, and he had every right to be. But she didn't hold her tongue. "Let the agents go, and I'll run with you. Anywhere you want to go."

"I'm not running, Aleaha. *This* is my home. One home of mine was already destroyed. I will not allow the same to happen to this one."

"But—"

He moved so quickly she had no time even to blink before he was leaning down, in her face. "Not another word from you. What you did to me—" He banged a fist into the mattress beside her head.

She gulped. She didn't like this side of him, not when she knew how tender he could be. But she *was* aroused by his nearness. She couldn't deny it. "Breean," she said, then pressed her lips together.

His chest meshed into her back, hot, always a brand. "You tried to kill me, Aleaha. You have no defense."

"God, you're so unforgiving! I made sure you survived, didn't I? And hello, you would have done the same thing in my situation, and you know it." Struggling, she arched her back so that her ass was in the air. His cock glided between the two mounds, a stroke as sure as the ones from his hand. "Free me."

As furious as he was with her, he was still hard. "You don't get to make demands. I do. Do that again."

She stilled, panting. She'd liked it, yes. But... "No. I want it to be like before." When his every touch had been like a prayer.

"Too late." He ran his finger over the path his swollen cock had just taken, and she sucked in a breath. "I like you like this, helpless to anything but the passion. Mine to do with as I please."

"You won't hurt me." The words trembled from her.

"So sure of that, are you?" Breean asked, and, damn, she was right.

"Physically, yes, but I know you could tear me apart emotionally," she whispered, and that nearly broke his already shredded heart.

He moved his hands over her spine, riding the ridges. "Such soft skin. Perfect and pale." Even after what she'd done, he still desired her more than he'd ever desired another. It was shameful.

"Hate me if you want, but look at what you've done to free your people from disease. How can you blame me for trying to save my own?"

Don't soften. Don't you dare soften. "I would not have tried to kill you to do it. *That* is the difference."

"How many ways do I have to say it? If I'd wanted to kill you, I wouldn't have given you my blood," she gritted out.

"Blood that was forbidden for me to accept. Your actions could have damned us all."

"You've dealt with my blood before."

"That was different. That was to save you." His gaze slid over her curves, the elegant slope of her shoulders, the dip of her back, the flare of her hips. His mouth watered.

"No, it wasn't different. You're just being stubborn."

Flicking her hair out of the way, he bent and licked the base of her neck. She gasped, shivered. His hands tunneled their way to the mattress directly under her. He let one dabble with a ripe little nipple and the other drift down. He should hurt her in some way, but he couldn't seem to make himself do it. As she'd said, she trusted him with her physical well-being.

He strummed her hot center once, twice, never ceasing his play with her nipple. All the while she gasped. But when she began writhing for more, he severed contact, and her gasps became moans.

"Don't worry. I'm not done." He licked and nipped his way down her back before gripping her ass and giving it the same attention he'd given her breasts. Soon she was arching into his touch, again seeking more. Seeking something deeper.

Again, he severed the contact. "Are you wet for me?"

"Yes," she breathed, not even trying to pretend disinterest.

"Going to change bodies?"

"N-no. I've got that under control."

He knew that. The more they'd made love, the more control she'd gained, until she'd stopped changing unintentionally altogether. "Lift your hips, and I'll kiss you right"—he sank a finger inside her wet sheath—"there." But he wouldn't let her come. Would he? This had started as revenge. To get her worked up so that he could walk away as she had done, proving to them both that he could. That she meant nothing to him. The more he touched her, however, the more he needed her.

Moaning, she did as commanded.

He didn't move. Not yet, not yet. "Ask me nicely." *Want me the way I want you.*

"Breean," she groaned, waving that perfect little ass in front of his face. "Kiss."

"Ask."

A pause, a suspended heartbeat. "Will you please kiss me? *Please.*"

He'd expected her to protest. Then he could have walked away as planned, leaving her like this. That she hadn't . . . With such a sweet surrender ringing in his ears, he licked his way right into the heart of her, savoring her decadent flavor. Two of his fingers joined the play, sliding in and out of her, just as his cock yearned to do.

"Stop. I need to touch you, too," she breathed. "Let me suck you."

His blood heated another degree. Already she was close to coming, her sex swelling under his tongue. He *had* to stop. He lifted his head, delighting in her aroused flesh. She groaned in frustration and began pumping against the sheets, trying to find release without him.

"Oh, no, you don't." He crawled up and settled beside her head. He didn't have to say a word. She turned and fitted her mouth over his straining erection. "Don't you dare bite me."

"Only want you to feel good."

He gripped the back of her neck, fisting her hair. Just in case. Up and down she glided, her hot, wet tongue nearly undoing him. Those silky strands of hair pulled, and, fearing he was hurting her, he released them, reaching up, gripping the headboard and surging as deep into her throat as he could go. She took him, took all of him, and was still greedy for more, her tongue circling the head of his penis with every upward thrust.

She worked him mercilessly. Within minutes, his muscles were so strained and bunched, so desperate for release that he was transported to a torturous heaven-hell. Too much pleasure, yet not enough. And when he could take it no more, she sucked as hard as she could and he exploded into her mouth, hot seed shuddering from him.

How long passed before he fell back to Earth, he didn't know. Aleaha was still on the bed, still tied, still licking at him. Her hips were moving swiftly against the sheets, seeking the same release he'd just experienced.

Now was the time to walk away, leaving her in pain, needy. But he found that he couldn't do it.

"Breean," she practically sobbed.

He moved behind her again. Instantly she raised herself in the air.

"Take me," she said. "Please. I'll beg if you want."

"No begging," he said, the words choked. He didn't want her humbled, he realized. He just wanted her to crave him more than she craved air to breathe. He wanted to brand himself on her every cell, make her live only for him. See nothing but him, the agents forgotten the way he sometimes shamefully forgot his own people.

"Tell me. I'll do anything you want. Just please, love me."

Love her. He feared that he would, now and always. He sank two fingers into her, and she screamed. Not with release, he knew, but with the sheer relief of having something buried inside her heat.

"Like that," she panted. "More. More."

"Are you ever going to leave me again?" The question slipped from him before he could stop them.

"No. No!"

He skimmed his thumb over her slickness. Again, she screamed, and the sound of her desire brought him back to full life, his penis filling and swelling, hardening. "Spread your knees as far as they'll go."

The ties offered enough slack to allow her to bend her knees and widen them several more inches. She was completely helpless like that, completely at his mercy. He plundered inside without preamble. But then, she was so ready she didn't need more preparation. She arched her hips to meet him, coming the moment he was in to the hilt. She spasmed and spasmed and spasmed, her climax going on forever.

He pounded in and out of her, lost in the pleasure. She was as hot and tight as he remembered, a perfect fit, he thought as he leaned down to kiss her. She turned her head, eager for it, as lost as he was, and their tongues clashed. Kittenish purrs sprang from her throat, her orgasm still rocking her. Their teeth banged, and he tasted the sweetness of her flavor. Like rain and magic, slightly different than usual, but then, her taste and scent were always changing, becoming more central to *her*.

"Mine," he said, repeating the word he'd uttered the first time he'd seen her. Last time, it had been a mark, a warning for all others to stay away from her. This time he meant it as a promise. He hated himself for it, but there it was. He loved her, had to have her in his life.

"Yours," she replied. "Good. So good."

He reached in front of her and circled a fingertip over her clitoris. She came again—or rather, her climax reached another degree of satisfaction. She cried out, and he circled again.

"Breean!"

When he heard his name on her lips, *he* came. Loud, long, the most intense orgasm of his life. As he spurted inside her, they rocked together, locked in a bliss so intense they should have died from it.

For a long while afterward, he didn't move. He just remained in place, inside her, sated, not wanting to ponder what had happened and what he was feeling. Eventually, though, he did have to move. He was probably crushing her.

He unlaced the ties. As she rolled to her back, her hand fluttered over his throat, tracing the still-healing scab. He wanted to lean into her touch, but didn't allow himself the luxury. Already he'd done too much this night.

"I'm sorry," she said. "For what I did."

"Perhaps you are merely sorry you were caught." He hadn't meant to voice his fear; it slipped free of its own volition.

Her gaze clashed with his. "No, that's—"

"Stop. Please." He couldn't deal with this. Not now. Not after what they'd just done. He needed time. When had he become such a needy female? "I am not going to hold you tonight." He had on every other night, and it had only made him fall harder for her. Yes. Definitely female. Which was fitting. Aleaha could grow a penis, after all.

For a split second, he saw true hurt in her emerald eyes. But she nodded and inched to the other side of the bed, away from him. His chest ached, seeing her like that. *Don't soften any more.* How many times would he have to issue the command? He gripped the sheet and tossed it over her lower body.

"Breean—" she began again.

"Go to sleep," he told her, more harshly than he'd intended. At the very least, he should lock her up with the other agents, but he couldn't force himself to part with her, even now. He wanted her in the room with him, in his sight every moment. To prevent her from causing any more trouble, he rationalized.

So why did he want to apologize for taking her like he had, facing away from him as if she meant nothing? Why did he want to beg for forgiveness for not tucking her in beside him, warm and safe?

He stared up at the vaulted ceiling, trying to block her image. That didn't help. From the corner of his eye, he saw her curl into a ball. Another sharp lance shot through his chest.

"I don't know what to do with you," he said, more for his benefit than hers.

"You could forgive me," she said softly. "I had decided to stay, you know."

Oh, but she was killing him. "Just . . . go to sleep," he repeated. They'd finish this in the morning, when they had regained their strength.

"And if I don't?" she said, some of her bravado returning. "The big, bad alien will kill me?"

No. The big bad alien might do whatever she wished. She had the courage and audacity of a warrior. She would never stand behind him, but would always fight beside him.

A man could ask for nothing more.

"Your men," she said with a sigh. She rolled to her back and, like him, stared up at the ceiling. Trying to block *his* image? "I noticed that a lot of them are gone, and I maybe kinda sorta sent the others into town."

He didn't tell her to be quiet this time; he couldn't summon the will. "The house is wired to an alarm, so their absence won't cause too much of a problem."

"Well, you should know that there are microphones throughout the entire city. They record constantly and somehow only pick up alien voices. It's the frequency or something, which is different from that of humans. Anyway, when aliens are taken in for questioning, AIR records their voices and plugs them into the system. From that point on, those aliens can be found the moment they speak."

"Were there microphones in the forest?"

"I honestly don't know. But most likely, yes. That's not public domain, but government, as most forest areas are. Trees are precious because they were nearly wiped out during the human-alien war. Anyway, I'm thinking your voices were recorded that night in the forest. I'm thinking your men can be traced if they talk while in the city."

Would he ever understand all of the nuances of this world?

Breean sighed. He could go into the city, hunt down his men, and tell them to be quiet, but they'd been making this trip for days now. AIR hadn't found them yet. That he knew of. Damn.

"Why are you telling me this?" Now, of all times.

"Because I just now thought of it. I haven't been an agent for long, you know. Just . . . tell them to be careful."

Trying to save him now. Would he ever understand *her*? He didn't think so. "Go to sleep, Aleaha. As I said, we'll talk later."

ELEVEN

A LOUD, PIERCING SCREECH WOKE HER.

Aleaha jolted upright, her muscles protesting at the abruptness of the movement. She grimaced. Breean sat up, too.

"What is that?" she asked.

Scowling, he burst from the bed in a lightning bolt of speed. "Get dressed," he demanded, moving through the room so quickly she couldn't see him. Not even the glowing outline of his spirit.

"What should I—" A bundle of clothing was tossed at her so abruptly she wasn't able to catch them, and they floated to the mattress around her. Heart pounding, she gathered them up and jackknifed to her feet. Her hands shook as she dressed. "Thank you. Now what's going on?" she asked over the alarm.

"What do you think?" was the grim reply.

Either agents were escaping, or AIR had finally arrived. Fear poured straight into her bloodstream. Fear for Breean. She didn't want him hurt or captured.

"Wait here," he said, his eyes fierce and golden. He'd already dressed, and even held a pyre-gun. His swiftness amazed her anew.

He'd gotten that gun right in front of her, yet she hadn't seen a thing. "Do not even *think* about disobeying me."

"I can help you."

"Me?" One brow arched. "Or the agents?"

Okay, fine. She'd deserved that. "You."

He scrubbed a hand down his face. "I'm going to find out what I'm up against," he said, then lifted the gun. "Is this set to stun?" The question was growled, as if he despised himself for having to ask.

She gave it a quick glance. "Yes, but stun doesn't work on humans. Only aliens."

"Then let's just hope some of the other agents are like you, hiding who and what they are." Tension crackled between them. "If you leave this room, Aleaha—"

Before he could finish the sentence, she rose on her tiptoes and pressed her lips to his. He immediately took over, plundering his tongue into her mouth. It was a hot, wild kiss, and it was over all too soon.

Without another word, he pivoted away from her and disappeared out the door.

That quickly, she felt cold and bereft, scared. What should she do, what the hell should she do? She hadn't felt this helpless, even in the forest. Then, at least, she hadn't really had anything to live for. Now . . . Racing through the room, she searched for a weapon. Anything to help her man.

Breean returned a short while later, and he was scowling. Bleeding. "There's a swarm of them. They must have been here awhile, because they're already spread out and your friends are free. What few of my men are here are already frozen."

Frozen was good; frozen was alive. But she heard his unspoken worry. He'd never be able to defeat AIR *and* save his people. Not on his own.

"Don't hurt the agents," she said, pulling Macy's image into her mind and forcing her body to realign, to change shape and color. "Please."

"I had no plans to do so."

"Good. Then I've got your back," she told him, raising her chin. "I need a pyre-gun of my own." As dedicated as he was to protecting his people from her, he'd clearly made sure the room was weapon-free before leaving her. She'd found nothing during her search.

He snorted, shook his head. "You, help me? Sure. Because I'm a fool. Now, I want you to hide under the bed. When the fight is over, you can come out. Until then, stay put. I don't want you caught in the crossfire."

He didn't believe her, yet he still sought to defend her. Was it any wonder she loved him? "I'd rather leave with you before they reach us, but I know you won't abandon your troops." Something else she admired about him. "Since it's too late for that anyway, I'll help. I won't harm them, but I'll do what I can to distract them so that *you* can escape. If you're free, you can spring your guys from prison. And just so you know, I realize I shouldn't have hurt you like I did, and I'm sorry for it. But I'm not sorry I was trying to take care of *my* people."

It was as if she hadn't spoken. His urgency was too great, she supposed. "You're hiding, and that's that." He grabbed hold of her and was dragging her to the bed before she could blink. "I can't risk losing you."

He couldn't risk . . . did that mean . . . surely it did. "Breean," she said, struggling against him while melting inside. He had to love her. Had to—

The door burst open, black-clad agents flooding into the room. Breean immediately released her and kicked into superspeed. He was firing his weapon, blue beams jetting from it, while maneuvering through the agents and somehow knocking them unconscious.

Even though they must have recognized her, the agents began firing at her the moment they spied her. As she dodged, she swiftly morphed into Breean's image, using his superspeed to avoid being stunned herself. She was still awkward at it, but she managed to swipe a fallen gun and fire back.

The stun ray only affected one, leaving the others, the humans, free to battle.

As many as Breean was knocking out, more were running in, closing in on them. She couldn't allow him to be taken. Tossing the gun aside, she circled through the agents. Most were wearing black masks, so she didn't know whom she was combating. Didn't matter. She was on Breean's side.

She put her self-defense lessons to use, chop-blocking throats and sending gasping agents to their knees. She even kneed a few in the balls. Always, though, she was careful to hurt them only enough to stall them, not to incapacitate them completely.

"Woman," she heard Breean shout. Even then, he was careful not to reveal her true name. "Macy!"

"Not now." She whipped behind a man and kicked the back of his legs. He stumbled forward and she doubled her fists, slamming them into his temple as he went down. "I'm busy. You should be running."

"Duck," he said, and she did.

He zipped to her side and punched the agent who had been closing in behind her. The man toppled out of the room, along the hall, and down the stairs like a plane from the sky. "I want you to leave."

"No."

"Things are about to get bloody," he growled.

He was going to cause bloodshed? Or he was about to be pulverized?

"No!" she shouted, just as Devyn stepped into her path. She jammed to a halt, fist in midair. He wasn't wearing a mask, his amber eyes were pulsing eerily, and it felt as if he were reaching phantom hands inside her, holding her hostage.

Dallas was suddenly beside him, and both wore expressions of grim resolve.

Someone knocked into her back, and she stumbled forward, losing her hold on Breean's image. Dark hair tried to sprout, but she anchored on to Macy's appearance with all her strength, her body forming into the beautiful agent's.

"I don't want to fight you two," she said as she righted, "but I won't let him be taken."

"We don't always get what we want," Devyn replied. "Do we?"

She backed away, meaning to latch onto someone and use him as a shield. But neither Devyn nor Dallas fired a weapon. Devyn simply tilted his head, and the next thing she knew, those phantom hands were once again holding her hostage.

What the hell? He hadn't stunned her, but she couldn't freaking move. She was frozen in place, her mind still active but her body unable to obey the simplest command.

She had lost, she realized, and could have sobbed.

"Noooo," Breean shouted, *absolute panic* filling him as Blue Eyes and Glitter lifted an unmoving Aleaha and carried her from the room. A red haze blanketed his mind. All the rage he'd experienced throughout his life combined could not compare to what he felt just then. *Mine, she's mine.*

He would kill every one of these bastards. They would know nothing but pain and suffering. Agony that lasted . . . and lasted. And if Aleaha did not awaken unharmed from whatever had immobilized her, that agony would be the least of their worries.

She'd fought with him, choosing him over AIR, and he could do nothing less than get her to safety. If he had to take her and run, just as she'd wanted, he would. He couldn't be without her; he wasn't giving her up. Even in death.

"Ale— Macy," he growled, fighting his way to the door. He kicked and elbowed and tossed men out of his way. Blood splattered over him, but he didn't care. Any man in his path, he took down mercilessly.

Only one thing mattered.

The agents who had her were standing at the end of the hall. Clearly, they'd expected him to follow, for they were smiling, waiting for him. Glitter was on one side of her and Blue Eyes on the other. Both were leaning against the wall as if they hadn't a care, their arms crossed over their chests.

Breean was huffing for breath, each drag into his lungs like inhaling fire. He forced himself to grind to a halt. He didn't think they'd hurt her, one of their own, but he couldn't know for sure. They didn't love her as Breean did and might be willing to sacrifice her life to defeat him.

"She's mine," he spat.

"I don't think so," Glitter said.

Hands clenched, he stalked forward.

"Stay where you are," Blue Eyes commanded. "My fingers are feeling twitchy." He stepped behind the still frozen Aleaha and reached around, dangling a knife in front of her throat.

Breean stilled, his heart pounding like a war drum. "Damage her in any way, and I will kill you slowly." He was afraid to use his speed to close the distance between them. If he spooked the agent and Aleaha was cut, he would never forgive himself.

"You can't kill me if you're already dead."

"What do you want from me? My head? Fine. It's yours."

Glitter's eyes widened. "Really? It would look nice as a centerpiece for my kitchen table. But can I have your skin, too? I think a golden rug is just what my bedroom needs."

Bastard. "If you will set her free, unharmed, yes."

Blue Eyes remained in place, that knife poised precariously. "A few things you should know, Rakan. The agent who escaped you, Jaxon, came back today with all of AIR. There are hundreds of us here right now. We could have slain you and yours at any time today, but we didn't."

Glitter laughed. "We were almost busted, though. When Macy showed up in the dungeon to free us, I almost had a heart attack." Another laugh.

"She almost succeeded, and would have, if I'd actually told her which ID wires to cut," Blue Eyes added.

"Why didn't you attack right away?" The knowledge that he'd been surrounded all day burned. He'd had no idea, had been too lost in his fury with Aleaha. Fury he couldn't summon now. Her friends had been in danger, and she'd wanted to save them. Now that his men were in equal danger, he realized exactly how his refusal to discuss them must have torn her in half. .

Yet still she'd tried to save him this day.

"You offered to help us defeat the Schön queen," Blue Eyes said. "Right now, you're a link to her. A link we need. We've never seen her, you have. You know how she operates, and you even survived her plague."

"I've had men watching AIR, listening. Even last night, your boss threatened to decapitate me if she saw me. She wanted me and mine dead."

Blue Eyes shrugged. "Yes, and she calmed down when told you'd punished the guy who killed our men. That, and the moment she saw that we were all safe. Well, that *I* was safe. I'm all that really matters to the woman."

Glitter snorted. "That would be me, and everyone knows it."

Breean could barely believe this was happening. Everything he'd hoped for was being offered to him. "You would trust me help you?"

Now both men snorted. "No," Blue Eyes said. "But you could have tried to kill us, and didn't. You could have tortured us, and didn't. Agents have been watching your men in town, and they haven't caused any trouble. They've only been interested in the women they can bed. Or rather, they were. Now we've got them herded into *our* cells. But my point is, you're not as much of a risk as was assumed."

"So, if I'm not to be trusted, how am I to help?"

"You'll be monitored, of course."

Monitored, as in guarded. Controlled. His hands balled into fists.

"Listen, if you aren't with us, you're against us," Blue Eyes said flatly. "The world is changing, and things get more dangerous every day. More and more aliens are coming here, their abilities unknown. A predator is a predator, and if this is to be your new home, I'd think you'd be happy to protect it."

Breean's eyes narrowed at the blatant attempt at manipulation. "How do I know I won't be shot in the back for my efforts, once the queen is dead?"

"I guess you don't." A slow grin spread over Glitter's face. "You'll have to trust us."

The way they planned to "trust" him? "If I decide to help you, I want only two things in return. Freedom for my people"—it was what he'd planned to bargain for all along, and one bargain was as good as any other—"and possession of the girl."

"I'm afraid she isn't on the table," Blue Eyes said.

"Of course she isn't on the table," he said, confused. "She's right in front of you."

Glitter flicked Blue Eyes a strange glance. "Was I ever that clueless?" With a shake of his head, he turned back to Breean. "She's not up for grabs, Goldie. You don't get her unless she wants you. But who knows? Maybe she'll be assigned as your guard."

She'd fought for him, but did that mean she wanted him? he suddenly wondered. Now and always? After the way he'd treated her? He just didn't know. He needed to talk to her, he thought with a scowl. "You're not taking her out of this house."

"Like you can stop me. You want her, you're going to have to win her." Glitter grinned, pointed a gun Breean hadn't known he'd been holding, and fired. "Oh, and come out of stun."

Before Breean could sidestep, a blue beam hit him directly in the chest, and he found himself locked in a body that refused to obey him. Fury seethed through him as the AIR agents gathered Aleaha and their fallen, as well as him and his remaining men, whistling all the while.

He could have spirit-walked—he was already helpless, after all—but he didn't want to leave Aleaha's side. So he endured. And he waited. AIR he could deal with. They wanted to monitor him, fine. They could monitor him. He'd help them since they both wanted the same thing. But if they wanted to post a guard at his side, they had damn well better chose Aleaha, as Glitter had suggested. Otherwise, they wouldn't have to worry about the Schön queen.

Breean would tear their planet apart.

When Aleaha was next able to move, she was inside AIR headquarters. She hadn't been incarcerated for aiding Breean, as she'd feared. She'd simply been placed in an empty office. Alone. To think. To agonize. To fume. Her legs were shaky, as if they'd fallen asleep, and didn't want to hold her weight, but she forced herself to lumber into the hall.

She had to reach Breean. Where had they placed him? What were they doing to him? To his men?

They'd stunned him, that much she knew. She'd heard his conversation with Devyn and Dallas, understood they now wanted his help, but had watched Devyn raise that gun and fire. Never had she felt so afraid. Or guilty. If she hadn't injured Breean earlier, he would have been at top strength and might have been able to win. Now, he was trapped.

She couldn't go back and change the past, but she could do something about the present. And the future.

Following the sound of chatter, she skirted a corner and entered the pit, where desks and agents abounded. It seemed like she'd been away forever, but the room was just as she remembered it. People meandered in every direction, while others sat in front of computer consoles, poking at their keyboards. Christmas was only a day away, so decorations were still up. A few agents had small plastic trees on their desks. Someone had even placed mistletoe over *her* desk.

"Where are they?" she demanded of the first agent she reached.

Hector Dean looked up from a file and eyed her with curiosity. Though he'd been among those imprisoned in Breean's house, he appeared no worse for wear. Well rested, well fed. "Who?"

As if he didn't know. "Devyn and Dallas. Where are they?"

He pointed to the break room before returning to his file, and she stomped forward, strength returning with every second that passed. Maybe because her determination was growing.

The door was closed, but she shouldered her way in. And there they were: Mia, Dallas, Devyn, and even Jaxon. The boys were discussing someone's boob size and Mia was sipping coffee, her black hair hanging down her back the same way Aleaha's did—when she was herself. God, she already missed being herself.

"Where is he?"

"Well, well, well." Dallas's brows rose and he grinned. "Look who Devyn freed from body-lock."

"'Cause I told him to." Mia waved her over, a sharp glint in her eyes. "There's some things we need to discuss, little girl."

Ignoring her boss, Aleaha walked right up to Devyn, morphing into Breean's image for added strength as she did so, and slammed her fist into his nose. As his head whipped to the side, she turned to Dallas and did the same before reshaping into Macy.

Though they were bleeding, both men laughed.

Mia clapped her hands, a smile of her own twitching at the corners of her lips. "Knew she had spirit."

"I need popcorn," Jaxon said.

"I told you not to hurt him," Aleaha growled to the agents.

"We didn't. We stunned him." Devyn rubbed his bleeding nose. "That doesn't even sting."

"You stunned him *after* you'd hired him! Why couldn't you have told me that Jaxon had already sneaked inside and you guys were going to take Breean up on his offer to help? Why did you leave me in the dark? I sliced his goddamn throat to set you free."

"What?" everyone asked in unison.

Mia's mouth fell open in shock. "Yeah. What? He didn't mention you had done anything to him."

So they'd tried to talk to him. Had they interrogated him the usual way? She'd heard agents liked to stick pins under the suspect's nails, dunk their heads in water, and break their bones.

Breean was now their ace, and they had to realize that, Aleaha thought, calming slightly. Surely they wouldn't have done anything like that to him.

"You heard me. To escape, I sliced his throat." Her cheeks burned bright with shame. She might never forgive herself for that.

"Lolli doesn't fit as a nickname anymore," Devyn said. "Maybe now we should call you Slash."

Her hands fisted. "I did it for you, each of you, but you didn't need me."

"If you wanted in on the plan," Mia said, crossing her arms over her chest, "you should have trusted us with the truth about yourself and not picked your boyfriend over your coworkers."

"And I still pick him over my coworkers! Like you did your boyfriend, as I hear it. But you know why I kept silent about my own abilities? You're the freaking AIR. Lethal enemies of all things different. I did what I had to—"

"Macy!" a hard voice shouted from the pit.

Her breath caught in her throat. He was here. Breean was here! And he didn't sound as if he were in pain.

Dallas grinned slowly. "I guess Stud Muffin heard you're up and around. Before you go, though, you should know we had a chat with him, put him through a lie detector, had him show us some of the things he can do. He's not a bad guy, as far as interloping other-worlders go."

"Hey," Devyn said. "I resent that."

"Macy!"

Aleaha shifted impatiently from one foot to the other, but she stayed where she was. "So you have no plans to hurt him?"

Mia shrugged. "As long as he proves useful . . ."

"What the darling girl is trying to say," Devyn added, "is that Breean is far more useful than even she realized. In the forest that night, someone threw her and a few others into another dimension. Breean had some interesting ideas about that and offered to help discover the truth. Mia needs him like she needs Kyrin to screw her blind. And we all know she needs that desperately."

This was better than she had hoped. "I'll be his guard. I'll give you daily reports on his actions, if you want. But I'm telling you, he means us no harm."

"We know that. Now." The words grumbled out of Mia. "Still. You're not objective, so, no. You can't be his guard."

"Then I'll give the reports." Dallas tossed up his arms, the picture of exasperated male. "Not like I've got anything better to do with my free time."

Aleaha could have kissed him.

Silence filled the room, an eternity passing. Then Mia sighed. "Breean's already been warned, but I'll tell you as well." Her eyes narrowed. "If he does one thing wrong, one damn thing, I'll have him strung up without thought or hesitation. Whether I need him or not. Got me?"

Aleaha nodded. "What about his men?"

"They're being questioned one by one, but will be released once that's completed. As things stand now, they've all agreed to work for us. We'll pair them with other agents so that they're monitored, too, but it looks like we've got an army of eager new hires."

"Macy!"

Could things have turned out any better?

"Get out of here." Grinning, Mia waved her away. "Go to him. His voice is giving me a headache."

Grinning herself, she sprang from the room. Breean was still in the pit, looking left and right and ready to toss a few desks over his head. The agents must have been told to leave him alone, because they kept their distance, even backing away from him. A few had pyre-guns trained on him, though.

"Macy!"

"I'm here."

His gaze latched onto her. He settled in place, chest rising and falling rapidly. "I'm sorry," he choked out. "I'm sorry. I should have let your friends go. You were right. I would have done exactly as you did. I—"

Audience forgotten, she ran to him and threw herself into his arms, wrapping her legs around his waist and dropping kisses all over his face. "Don't ever refuse to snuggle me again."

That earned her a strained chuckle. "Never," he vowed. "I want to be your man, your protector."

"I don't need a protector, but I do need a man," she said, tangling her hands in his hair. "I'm sorry for what I did. I wish—"

"Speak of it no more. We both hurt each other, but we will start over. I wanted to die when they took you from me. You've become my entire reason for living, woman. I am nothing without you."

She melted into him. "Talk about the best Christmas present ever. I finally got what *I* wanted."

He grinned and squeezed her tight. "My cock?" he whispered into her ear. "I know how much you wanted me to give it to you. You hinted enough."

"That, too. God, Breean. I love you so much."

"Thank you," he said, expression softening, tenderness gleaming from him. "I love you, too. So much I ache." Never looking away from her, he called, "I'm taking her home."

"I expect you both back by eight tomorrow morning," Mia replied.

"I guess that means I'm leaving, too," Dallas said, and it was clear he was trying not to laugh. "I have to monitor the man's every move, after all. God, I hate my job sometimes."

"This sounds like a flat-out dirty mission. You'll need backup," Devyn told him with a pat on the back. "I'm going with."

They must have followed her from the break room, the perverts. "Stay where you are."

Amid cheers, Breean carried her out of the building into the twilight. "I'll lose them," he said, and then he ran, just ran, as fast as he could go. They were ensconced in his house in minutes, where he quickly undressed her, threw her on the bed, and dove on top of her. She cast Macy's image aside and donned her own.

"I meant what I said. I love you." He kissed the dark strands of her hair, then smoothed them from her brow. "I think I loved you from the first moment I saw you."

"Same here." She cupped his face and peered up at him. "We're in this together. You and me."

Slowly, he grinned. "Always. Just . . . next time you try to kill me, make sure it's with pleasure."

She returned the grin, glad that he'd truly forgiven her. That they'd made this thing work between them and even with AIR. "Kill you with pleasure, huh? Give me half an hour," she said, rolling him over and kissing her way down his body.

"Love, I think you'll only need five."

That made her laugh. "Merry Christmas, Breean."

"The sound of your laughter is the best present *I* have ever gotten. So yes. Merry Christmas, Aleaha."

Aleaha. Yes, she was. Now and always. With him.

EPILOGUE

Two weeks later . . .

OKAY. So. Aleaha'd had the best Christmas ever. She'd rung in the New Year properly, meaning she'd had an orgasm last the entire countdown. Dallas treated Breean more like a friend than someone to watch closely, Mia treated him like a pet, his men were happy with their situation, and now she was snuggled in her man's arms, naked—a common occurrence—and completely sated.

The Schön queen hadn't arrived yet, and no one knew when she would finally make her way here. But AIR was prepared, and so was Aleaha and Breean. Meanwhile, when they were off the clock, he was helping her look for Bride.

Being Aleaha Love, soon to be Aleaha Nu, was pretty damn awesome.

"I've been thinking," Breean said, grip tightening around her waist.

She grinned. "You know I love it when you do that." Always ended the same way. In bed. Oh, wait. They were already here. Maybe they'd end up on the kitchen floor this time.

"I know it bothers you, not knowing if you are human or alien, and I do not like when you are bothered. As your warrior, it is my duty, no, my privilege, to give you everything that you want, meet all of your needs, and—"

"Be my slave," she finished for him.

His lips twitched with his amusement. "Yes. So I have been thinking long and hard, and I do not think you are alien, after all. I think you are human."

"Why do you think that?" she asked, brow furrowing.

"Aliens have been here for many years, yes?"

"Yes." According to Bride, aliens had been visible for around eighty years but had snuck onto the planet long before that.

"Well, I think humans are evolving, developing abilities to help protect them from this new, possible threat."

Now that made a lot of sense. Except— "I can be stunned," she told him. "Stun never works on humans, yet it works on me."

"Stun doesn't work on the average human, no, but you aren't average. Far from it."

She rose on her elbow and peered down at him. The sight of him never failed to delight her. All that golden skin, those bedroom eyes, those plush lips. "Thank you."

"You're welcome." He reached up and traced a fingertip along the curve of her jaw. "Either way, though, I love you."

"As I love you."

He jolted up, tossing her under him and pinning her to the mattress. She laughed, and his expression softened as it always did when she laughed. "Now, time to do what we always do when I am done thinking."

"Insatiable," she *tsk*ed as if such a thing were a curse.

"I know you are. I can barely keep up."

Another laugh escaped her, and she wound her arms around his neck. "Try."

"With pleasure."